"You got any sisters?"

No. Why?" Cole turned curious blue eyes my way, his bronzed face and surfer's 'fro making me long for a pristine beach and a bottle of SPF 80. Anything that would put thousands of miles between me and my dad while preventing skin cancer had to be a good thing.

I shrugged. "I thought your folks might like a daughter. As in me. I'm in the market for a new set." When his glance wandered below my neck I punched him in the arm. "Of parents, you nimrod."

"Then we'd be siblings," he said. "Which would make what I want to do with you illegal."

Praise for the Jaz Parks series:

"This latest Jaz Parks adventure is the most jam-packed yet!"
— scifichick.com on *Biting the Bullet*

"A wonderful light read with engaging characters and an interesting storyline."
— Dragonpage Radio on *Once Bitten, Twice Shy*

ONE MORE BITE

A JAZ PARKS NOVEL

Jennifer Rardin

www.orbitbooks.net

NEW YORK • LONDON

Orbit
Hachette Book Group
237 Park Avenue, New York, NY 10017
Visit our Web site at www.HachetteBookGroup.com

First Edition: January 2009

Orbit is an imprint of Hachette Book Group. The Orbit name and logo are trademarks of Little, Brown Book Group Limited.

The characters and events in this book are fictitious. Any similarity to real persons, living or dead, is coincidental and not intended by the author.

Library of Congress Cataloging-in-Publication Data
Rardin, Jennifer
One more bite : a Jaz Parks novel / Jennifer Rardin. — 1st ed.
    p. cm.
ISBN 978-0-316-02209-5
1. Parks, Jaz (Fictitious character) — Fiction.   2. Assassins —
Fiction.   3. Vampires — Fiction.   4. Murder for hire — Fiction.
I. Title.
PS3618.A74O64 2009
813'.6—dc22   2008024780

10 9 8 7 6 5 4 3 2 1

RRD-IN

Printed in the United States of America

For my mother, Carol Ryan Pringle, who never once said, Would you drop this impossible writing dream and get a real job already? *Thanks, Mom.*
And for my sister, Erin Pringle, whose love has made me a better person.

One More Bite

Chapter One

asmine, do not pull that gun."

Vayl spoke in a voice so low even I could barely hear him, which meant the people in the blue and white seats next to the bathroom door where I stood still had no idea what I meant to do.

"I'm gonna kill him," I growled. My fingers tightened on the grip of Grief, the Walther PPK I kept stashed in the shoulder holster under my black leather jacket. I couldn't see my intended victim at the moment. Vayl had set his hands on the edges of the doorframe, spreading his black calf-length duster like a curtain, blocking my view. But I could hear the son of a bitch, sitting near the front, chatting up the flight attendant like she was the daughter of one of his war buddies.

"You do understand what a bad idea this is, do you not?" Vayl insisted. "Even poking fun at murder on an airplane could bring the passengers down on you like a mob of after-Christmas sale shoppers."

"Who says I'm joking?"

He fixed me with warm hazel eyes. "I would hate to see you beaten to death with that woman's boot."

He jerked his head sideways, directing my attention to an

exhausted traveler who must've made her armrests squeak when she'd squeezed into her seat. I glanced her way, and as people will when they feel eyes on them, she looked back at me. For a second her saggy pink cheeks and black-framed glasses swam out of focus. A lean, dark-eyed face sneered at me from beneath her shoulder-length perm. It said, "Are you certain you know my name?" I squeezed my eyes shut.

You're dead, Edward Samos. I saw your smoke fade into the night. I ground the bits of ash and bone you left behind into the dirt of the Grecian countryside. So stop haunting me!

I turned my head so that when I opened my eyes they fell on Vayl's short black curls, which always tempted me to run my fingers through them. And his face, carved with the bold hand of an artist whose work I'd never toss aside.

"Are you all right?" he asked.

Yeah, sure. For some bizarre reason I'm seeing the last vamp I assassinated on innocent people's mugs. I can't stop thinking about my boss in a totally unprofessional and yet toe-curling way. And, at age twenty-five, I still haven't escaped the man who made my childhood pretty much a misery. I'm cruising, thanks for asking!

I picked the part that bothered me most and ripped. "You're the one who let my father tag along. I told you it wouldn't work. I warned you blood could be shed. But did you listen?"

"It is partially my fault," he allowed. "If I had taken time to fly home between my trip to Romania and this mission, I do not believe this would have happened. But meeting you in London seemed more efficient. And without our Seer along to warn me otherwise, how was I to know your father would rendezvous with you there as well?"

I said, "I miss Cassandra." Especially on days like today. Not just because her psychic abilities could've detoured this steamroller. But because she always seemed to know what to say to keep me from ruining my so-called life.

Vayl's eyes traveled to my hand, still stuck inside my pocket. Or was he checking out my boobs? And if not, should I be even more pissed? His half smile showed he knew exactly what I was thinking. He said, "Perhaps we should consider bringing Cassandra with us more regularly. As for the bloodshed, I supposed you would wait until we had reached Inverness."

"Who brings baby pictures with them on a trip?" I griped. "If I'd wanted my bare ass paraded in front of all the premium ticket holders I'd have mooned everyone before we took off!"

Vayl knew better than to tell me the photos were adorable. Then I'd have had to kill him too. If that had been the real issue. Problem was, when my dad had cracked that old album, he'd done it upside down first. So the picture that had caught my attention was a copy of the one I'd locked in my safe nearly eighteen months ago. A shot of Matt and me just after he'd slipped his ring on my finger. I wondered if two people had ever been so sure they were headed for eternal happiness. Or had their mistake shoved so violently in their faces two weeks later.

"Look into my eyes," Vayl said.

"What, so you can hypnotize me? No thanks."

He shook his head. "We both know my powers have a minimal effect on you. Come now, my *pretera*. Humor me."

"What's a *pretera*?"

"It is a Vampere word, meaning wildcat."

"Oh. In that case . . ." I locked stares with the guy who'd started out as my supervisor, upgraded to *sverhamin,* and ended up . . . well, sometimes the possibilities practically made my skin steam. Other times I still felt like Matt's traitor. *Can* you betray a dead man? Since I didn't know the answer to that one, I forced my mind to pettier subjects. "I can't believe my father's here. This is like my first date times ten."

"How do you say? Money talks."

So true. In this case, the bucks had come from Albert himself.

"What are we, the Russian Space Agency?" I demanded. "Selling seats on our trips to the highest bidder?"

Vayl said, "I realize the shock is only now wearing off. Once again, I want to assure you that I would have warned you. But Pete did not inform me Albert would be joining us until he called just before I met you in London. Apparently your father felt you would strenuously object to his presence—"

"Ya think?"

"Thus the secrecy surrounding his joining us at Gatwick."

"He must've known I'd have thrown him off the plane in Cleveland," I muttered. I realized I'd taken my hand out of my jacket and Vayl had used the chance to curl his fingers around mine. No romance in that touch. He was probably just trying to keep me from reaching again.

I sighed. "Okay, I won't kill him yet. But you get those pictures out of his claws, and keep him away from me, and—"

Vayl slid his fingers up my arm, sending trickles of awareness shooting through me. Suddenly I couldn't think of anything but his touch. A deliberate move on his part—underhanded and mean. I kinda loved it. "I never thought I would say this," he murmured, leaning in so his lips nearly brushed my ear. "But I would suggest you spend the rest of this flight concentrating on Cole."

Who? Oh. Damn, Jaz, would you kick your brain into gear? Remember Cole? Your third for this piece-o'-crap job? The one Pete has decided to fund using your dad's 401(k)?

Jerking my arm from Vayl's hand so I could *think, dammit,* I began plotting a revenge so intricate and satisfying I barely heard him say, "I will deal with your father."

"Fine." *Wait, maybe not.* "Um, Vayl? Do me a favor?"

"Anything."

"Be discreet, will ya? He doesn't know about . . . us . . . yet. And I think I should probably be the one to tell him I'm involved with a vampire."

CHAPTER TWO

When I retire I'm going to write a book. Not about the CIA. I know too many secrets that could get me killed. Or worse, elected. Nope, this one's going to be called *My Dad Is an Asshole: The True Story of a Shithead's Daughter.*

As I stared out the window, using Cole as a buffer between the butt-flap and me, I knew I should be trying to figure out his game. Mostly retired consultants to the Agency don't just pop into the field whenever they feel the urge for some exercise. Especially ones who've just recovered from a major vehicular collision. But I was still too pissed to follow any logical train of thought for long.

I heard Vayl say, "Perhaps we should stow your album under the seat for now, Albert. I understand we are about to land. And we have had so little time to discuss football. I understand you are a Bears fan?" At which point I decided I owed my *sverhamin* an elaborate dinner that would not include any of the gross dishes I'd heard some native Scots preferred. Haggis? Who eats something that sounds like an eighty-year-old husband-beater who sees Jesus's face in her porridge every morning but devours it anyway?

"When do you think they'll let me get my cell out?" Cole asked. "I promised Mom I'd text her as soon as we land. I'm going to stick my phone up some guy's kilt, flash a picture, and then challenge her to guess what she's seeing."

"That is so disgusting."

"What? I'll get his permission first."

"Sending dirty pictures to your mom?"

"She'll laugh so hard her teeth will probably fly across the dinner table. She lost them in a car accident, you know."

"Really?"

"She was drag racing. Oh, I'm supposed to tell you she won. She made me promise to always say that when I mention her dentures."

I shook my head. Not just because Cole probably needed psychiatric help. But because he liked his mom. And she reciprocated. Weird concept, that. Mine had suffered a fatal heart attack. Currently the unburiable part of her resided alongside the other skeptics and unrepentants in a version of hell I never wanted to see (or smell) again. Oddly, that reminded me of Matt. One of our last conversations had been about my parents. I'd been bitching about my dad.

"He's all right, you know," Matt had said between bites of the burgers we'd just grilled on the little deck outside our cozy country-themed duplex. "Once you get past all the bark there's a quality human in there. Your mom's the one to watch out for."

I'd violently disagreed with him about Albert. After all, he hadn't grown up listening to the man's lazy-ass lectures. "Get your lazy ass off the couch and do your damn chores!" But he'd had a valid point when it came to my mother. What a depressing duo.

"Your mom can bake too, right?" I asked Cole.

He nodded. "Like a pastry chef. She said Grandma Thea made her try a bunch of girly hobbies after the car crash, and baking was the only one that stuck. She and my dad run a little coffee shop in Miami that's famous for its homemade desserts. In fact, she likes to say her cinnamon rolls put all four of her boys through college."

"You got any sisters?"

"No. Why?" Cole turned curious blue eyes my way, his bronzed face and surfer's 'fro making me long for a pristine beach and a bottle of SPF 80. Anything that would put thousands of miles between me and my dad while preventing skin cancer had to be a good thing.

I shrugged. "I thought your folks might like a daughter. As in me. I'm in the market for a new set." When his glance wandered below my neck I punched him in the arm. "Of parents, you nimrod."

"Then we'd be siblings," he said. "Which would make what I want to do with you illegal."

I sighed. "Dude, you can't still want to marry me. Now that you know I'm with—" I jerked my thumb toward Vayl.

"Why won't you say his name out loud if you two are such a pair?"

I yanked my tray out of its upright position and depocketed the poker chips that had become a balm to my troubled spirit ever since I'd had to give up my playing cards. As I divided and re-combined them, the familiar clack of clay against plastic eased the kinks out of my knot-infested muscles. "My dad doesn't know."

When I felt Cole's shoulder shaking against mine I glanced over. He was laughing so hard he couldn't make a sound. As soon as he paused for a breath, the plane's cabin would be filled with the echoes of his mirth. And I'd have to kill him too.

I whispered, "You make a sound and I'll tell Pete you compromised this mission and should be reassigned to a desk. Forever."

The giggles blasted out of him in a single shocked whoof. "You wouldn't!"

"Okay, not forever. Two weeks, max. But, believe me, it feels like eternity."

Cole's eyes narrowed. "Remind me never to break my collarbone. Apparently all the forced rest causes you to peel the skin off your face and reveal your inner monster."

"It was more of a crack than a break. And I've been perfectly reasonable—"

"Save it. I didn't want to believe the rumors, but now I have to think they were true. You really did come off sick leave three weeks early to answer the phones at the office, didn't you?"

"Martha hadn't had a vacation in years. So I just thought—"

"Is it true that you repainted the whole floor? One-handed?"

"The walls were turquoise. Who can concentrate with that color looming over them all day long?"

"Did you, or did you not, reorganize all of Pete's files so now he can't find anything?"

I bit my lip. "I don't see what the big deal is. Most of it's just backup for what's on his computer. But that was when he sent me to Florida, which, in my own defense, I'm pretty sure he was planning to do anyway—"

Cole shook his head direly. "Not so fast. I saw you plowing toward the back of the plane just now like you meant to tear off the tail and stuff it down Albert's throat. No, don't get that dreamy look on your face. I want some straight talk from you, dammit!"

I gulped. Cole didn't swear much, and never at me. In fact, he'd been nothing but charming, funny, and pretty much perfect since we'd met in a women's bathroom when he was still a PI specializing in supernatural cases. "Okay," I said. "What do you want to know?"

Cole turned fully toward me, bracing his hand against the seat in front of him. He lowered his voice to intimate. "To me this is just another aspect of your recently upgraded weirdocity."

"That's not a word."

"Shut up."

Since the alternative was kicking a huge dent in his face, which he really didn't deserve, I pressed my lips together and listened. He said, "Why do you keep holding back with Vayl if it's the real thing? You won't tell your dad. Nobody in the department knows. Isn't true love something you want to shout about from the nearest rooftop?"

I murmured, "Dude, every time I step onto a roof somebody tries to throw me off. Plus that's so . . ." I rolled my eyes and made an ick-I-swallowed-a-gnat sound.

"That's not an answer," he insisted.

I took one of the chips off the pile I'd made and turned it between my fingers. "It's Matt." I didn't need to remind him that my fiancé had been murdered, along with my sister-in-law and the rest of our vamp-killing crew. It was one of the first personal stories I'd ever told him. Which said a lot about the kind of guy he was.

For an answer he draped his arm across my shoulder.

Once I would've blown off this conversation. Too hard. Major chance of a marshmallowy aftertaste. Now I stuck with it. Although I did entertain the fleeting thought that personal growth sucks. "Every time I think I'm ready to move on, something happens to remind me of him. That's one part of it. But it's not the hardest."

"What's the rest?"

"I guess I'm more superstitious than I realized. One corner of my brain is convinced that if I make some big announcement, that'll be the same as a challenge."

"To who?"

"I don't know. God? Fate? Whoever thought it was okay to wipe out everybody I really cared about in the first place."

"First of all, that chapter of your life was written by Aidyn Strait. He was the vampire who killed your people, and nobody else should get the credit. Also, don't you think you're exaggerating? Just a little?"

Where did Cole get off with the superior attitude? "I have no idea what you mean," I snapped.

"Your brother survived that massacre."

"Only because he was already in the hospital."

"What about your sister? Don't you love her?"

"You're missing my point."

"I don't think so. Look, I'm not trying to undercut your loss. It was huge. I'm just saying, maybe you're not seeing it clearly because it was so horrific to start with."

"Did you want me to answer your question or not?" I growled.

"Well, yeah."

"That's all I'm doing. I'm telling you that I'm not anxious to make anything official between me and Vayl. Because I think that if I do he'll die."

Cole smiled. "By that logic, you should date me, then."

"What?"

"Think about it. Why would Fate want to turn Vayl into vapor if It thought you and I were getting busy?"

"That's nuts."

He leaned over and kissed me, *smack,* on the cheek. His breath, smelling faintly of grape bubble gum, blew across my lips as he murmured, "You said it, not me."

When he sank back into his seat nothing was left to block my view of Albert. In the time since Vayl had settled beside him, my dad had managed to extort another bag of peanuts from the flight attendant. I watched him pop them into his mouth one by one and chew them without once closing his lips, so that the sound of his masticating between complaints about his favorite team's lame-ass secondary bounced off the curved walls of the Embraer like the wet plopping of a knife slicing through layers of bloated animal skin.

Ugh!

I stuck my fingers in my ears and glued my eyes to the window. The landscape should've cheered me. The green fields and thick trees that surrounded Dalcross Airport had always lifted my spirits. They were the part of the landscape that reminded me most of home. But the deep blue of the Moray Firth flowing off into the North Sea let me know I'd come a long way from Ohio. As did the knowledge that if we turned this plane just a touch to the west and kept flying we'd be sweeping into the Highlands, where peaks with names like Liathac and Ben Dearg made you think of the old gods. The ones who probably still lolled among the mountains, gouging out grooves with their elbows and asses, joking about how the mountaineers would have a fine old time ascending their dirty new cracks. Yeah, my sense was that they had the humor of thirteen-year-old boys. Except for the goddesses, who had none.

Since Vayl was with me on this trip, the fact that I could see anything besides runway lights and the sparkle of a growing city should've seemed miraculous. But I was too disturbed to get all slobbery about the reason he'd begun to wake early, which had everything to do with his way-cool ability to suck another vampire's powers into his permanent arsenal. During our last mission, his former nestling had tried to make their arrangement eternal. She'd literally shoved Vampere magic through him, forcing him to stay awake through an entire day. The process had left him changed. Now he woke at least three hours before dark and stayed up about that long after the sun had risen.

This can be a problem for a guy who sizzles in the sun.

Enter Bergman, our tech consultant, whose genius had saved our asses so many times I'd considered tattooing his name on mine. He'd come up with a lotion that temporarily blocked the sun's rays so Vayl could at least walk from building to building without frying. Unfortunately it darkened his skin so radically he looked like he'd fallen asleep inside a tanning bed.

I looked over at him now, wondering how the hell we were going to pull off this mission with so many variables to control. Then his eyes met mine. And when they lightened to amber I knew that as long as we stuck together, nothing could stop us.

Chapter Three

Driving is my thing. Not only do I kick ass behind the wheel, but I love controlling thousands of pounds of road-eating people-hauler with little more than a twitch of the pinky. I had planned on playing chauffeur out of Dalcross, since the route to Tearlach—Floraidh Halsey's bed-and-breakfast—mapped "tricky" when you typed in the address. But Jack turned out to be a fearful flyer and needed major comfort. As soon as I transferred him from pet carrier to leash he ducked between my legs, which meant I practically rode him to the urine-yellow Alhambra we'd rented. Actually, I could've hopped on and he wouldn't have noticed. He weighs twenty more pounds than I do. And eats twice as much. We won't even discuss the pooping. Gawd.

Yeah, I know, I'd said I was gonna adopt him out to a good home after I killed his master on my last mission. Samos had loved the malamute more than anything or anyone else he'd ever known. And why not? He was a fabulous dog. Good humored. Obedient. Smart and sensitive. I could go on, but I'm pretty sure I'd start sounding like one of those batty old ladies who eventually gets devoured by her forty-two cats. In the end, I couldn't let him go. But Jack had come with a few issues, which meant I couldn't leave matters in their original state either.

"Tell me you're joking!" Cole demanded as we sat in the second row of seats with my dog lying between us. Vayl, at the wheel, wearing dark glasses and a black fedora, glanced in the rearview. Albert sat next to him, immersed in the map he held, trying to make sense of directions that, while written in English, still needed a translator.

"I'm dead serious," I insisted. "I got him fixed."

Cole threw his arms up and hunched into the corner of the ivory seat. He rolled his eyes at the canine, who'd undergone a dye job for this mission since we figured he'd mixed with the coven while he was still Samos's pet, and we didn't need his seamy past coming back to bite us in the ass. The vet said he'd been cheerful about the shampooing that would leave him coal black for the next three weeks. But that was Jack, always willing to play along, especially if you offered him something to nibble as part of the deal.

Now he regarded Cole curiously, as if trying to divine whether or not somebody who smelled like bubble gum could be a source of doggy treats. "Sorry, Jack," said his disgusted buddy. "If I'd known about this, I'd have done more to protect your manhood."

"He was humping everything in sight!" I fumed. "I had to throw out my ottoman!"

"That's no reason to snip a guy's nuts!"

"He's not a *guy;* he's a *dog.* Who won't be making puppies. Or screwing my shoes anymore! Yeehaw!"

Cole shoved his hands into the crooks of his elbows. "Well, this mission sucks."

"It's barely started! And *I* should be the one bitching!"

"Turn left here," Albert told Vayl calmly, as if the two of us yelling didn't even exist. Suddenly I could hardly keep myself from kicking the back of his seat.

"What are *you* doing here anyway?" I demanded.

and said, "Our cover can take another member, easy. We're going in as ghost hunters attending a big shindig called GhostCon. Good timing for a hit with all the strangers coming into town, which is probably why the assassin chose this week. Anyway, the lectures and whatnot are taking place at Castle Hoppringhill, which is pretty close to Floraidh's B and B. One or two of us will have to poke our faces into GhostCon every few hours just to make sure our cover sticks. Having you along to do that will give the rest of us an even better chance to identify the assassin."

"You don't know what she looks like?" Albert asked. The disbelief in his voice reminded me of a disgruntled restaurant patron. *What do you mean you're out of roast beef?*

"She's new," I snapped. "All we got from our guy is that her contact name is Bea. She first surfaced about six months ago, but she's gained impressive credentials since. She's credited with the assassination of the president of Southern Kordofan as well as General Imran Salim, Ambassador Baldric Smythe, and the women's rights activist Safia Mian."

Albert shrugged. "You'll get her."

Despite the fact that I still wanted to punt him out the door and watch him roll down the hill, his confidence warmed me. "That's the plan. However, Safia, besides traveling with two superbly trained bodyguards, also kept a Seer on her payroll. The fact that the Seer never had a clue about the origin or identity of Safia's killer means we're going against superior skill and atypical power."

I put a lot of no-big-deal into my tone, but underneath I was shaking hard enough for my organs to sprint for the nearest sturdy doorway. Because I wasn't convinced we were going to survive this mission. The third we'd originally requested might've been able to understand and combat the kind of power I'd described. A warlock with impressive skills and a helluva record, he'd have come in handy both in sniffing out our assassin and in warding off any surprises Floraidh and her coven might throw at us. The fact that Vayl, who'd been denied nothing in his eighty years with the department, had been assigned Cole instead did not bode well for support on the home front should this mission start to stink. And I'd already begun to smell sulfur.

Albert, still mulling Safia's fate, said, "Well, there had to at least be a fight, right? I mean, with that kind of firepower at hand, the activist bimbo didn't die quietly, did she?"

How has no woman ever yet clonked you over the head with a purse full of quarters? I shook my head, wishing I could be the first, but knowing it wouldn't be likely. Since I didn't carry a purse. I said, "No, Dad. Our understanding is that the neighbors heard the *bimbo* and her staff screaming for several minutes before the house they were renting burned down around them."

Albert didn't wince. He'd taken too much of my crap and seen too much other shit in his time for either sarcasm or arson to part the stones that held his expression in its regular, harsh lines. "So Bea's a firebug?" was all he asked.

"We thought so at first," I replied. "Nearly all of the bodies had been thoroughly charred. But now we think she was trying to disguise the real cause of death."

"Which was?"

"Snakebite."

Albert shifted in his seat so he could see me better. "Why would that make any difference?"

"Not sure. But the sprinkler system preserved one of the bodies well enough that we can surmise it was covered in bites, almost like somebody had dumped a barrel of snakes on it. And these were ones from a particular species. The most venomous land snake in the world. It's called the Inland Taipan, a shy mouse eater that's only found in Australia. Strange deal, because Safia and her people were living in Lebanon at the time."

The longer I talked about the Taipan the tighter Vayl clutched the wheel, until it began to creak under the pressure. He loathed snakes. Even worse than I disliked tight spaces. I wanted to reach out, give my boss a comforting pat. I lifted my hand, looked at it, ran it through my curls.

Meantime Albert had not digested my news well. The bushy eyebrows inched upward as his green eyes pierced right through me. Ten years ago I'd have given up every secret I thought he hadn't already discovered under that glare. Now I just waited silently for his verdict. "Son of a bitch," he said. "Inland Taipans as an assassin's tool? That's pretty sick. Did you bring antivenom?"

"Yeah. But I gotta tell you, it's not a hundred percent effective. Something about the venom can sometimes sneak past the cure. Obviously we believe she's a Medusa, so we're hoping to kill her before she makes her move."

As Albert imagined the horror I'd just described, a woman who wound her pets around her hair like a turban only to set them loose on her unsuspecting victims when the killing mood struck her, he produced that sucking-on-teeth noise that made my ribs ache. It meant he was about to say something important. I waited for him to tell me he was impressed that the CIA trusted such a tricky assignment to his own daughter.

"You should've brought a warlock," he said before turning back to his map.

I leaned over to Cole. "I *should've* killed him on the plane."

Chapter Four

Albert surprised me by navigating us straight from the A9 to a winding country road to the long tarmac lane that led to Tearlach. As we drove toward the house, I realized it may have been our first trip together where he didn't decide on a last-minute detour to some obsolete hole like the Museum of Big Gray Rocks or the Littlest Loch in the Nairn Valley.

"Would you take a look at this place?" Albert said as he folded the map.

"Reminds me of the Hansel and Gretel story," Cole replied.

Much like the woman herself, Floraidh's place exuded warmth and hospitality. From a distance we could glimpse orderly gardens just beginning to blossom in the promising warmth of mid-May. They surrounded a four-story confection whose designer must've had a wife who adored jewelry. So why not throw a bunch of doodads on the house as well? Six gables that I could see made the roof a reshingler's nightmare. The front porch, which ran around three-quarters of the house, had been enclosed to begin with, along with the two sunporches that jutted above the main entrances, which were at its east and west ends.

"What the hell kind of monstrosity is that?" wondered Albert as he eyed the four smoking chimneys and the gingerbread molding edging the roofline.

"I believe that is called a Queen Anne Victorian," said Vayl.

"No wonder they have to take in guests," he replied. "It must cost a fortune to heat. And it probably never gets warm inside. Not even in the summer."

Yeah, go ahead, Pops. Enjoy the show. Even the trees marching down the edge of this smooth, straight lane want you to believe the sham. But wait'll you hear Floraidh's secret.

She and her coven worshipped Scidair, a sorceress whose legends told how she'd become Satan's concubine in the afterlife. When you kept that in mind, you could see the reality behind the advertising: a looming old construction laced with manipulative magic, guarded by green, bushy lumps with hidden thorns poised to reach out and grab the unsuspecting guest. Backing up my observations were tall thin rocks that jutted from the earth at random points in the yard, as if Mother Nature herself was giving us the middle finger. She'd shaded most of them gray, but at just the right angle they glittered so brightly that if you looked at them wrong you saw dots for the next two minutes.

Jack jumped down to get a better look out the window. Something on my side of the lane had caught his attention. He began to scratch at the glass.

I ran my hand down his back. "I don't see anything, dude. What—"

Movement. I caught a blur out of the corner of my eye just as Albert yelled, "Watch out!" and threw up his hands.

I leaped forward, putting myself between my dad and whatever had startled him, practically sitting on his lap as Vayl jerked the wheel to the left. The van spun sideways, giving me half a breath to realize that a man had stepped into the vehicle's path. He didn't even look up as the tires squealed, signaling imminent impact. I got the impression of shaggy brown hair with a matching beard. A suit coat and pants in the same color that sagged so badly the man must've bought them when he was forty pounds heavier. And a gold chain running from pants to vest pocket.

Then our window swung sideways. I braced myself against the dashboard. Craned my neck, trying to see whether the man had jumped out of the way in time, tensing against the thud that would signal the beginning of a dreadful few days. It never came.

As soon as the Alhambra screeched to a stop we jumped out and ran to the spot where the man's body should be lying. Nothing.

"You all did see him?" Vayl asked as he yanked off his sunglasses and shoved them into his pocket.

We agreed somebody had walked in front of the van. "Even Jack noticed him," I said. But now the dog, who should've been straining at his leash to explore new scents, stood right next to me, his shoulder leaning against my knee as if to push me back into the vehicle.

"He cannot have gone far." Vayl strode toward the trees on the west side of the lane. I followed him, pulling a reluctant pup behind. Beyond the nice, neat outer row of Scots pines grew a thick copse of spruce, larch, and fir that pressed so close to one another we couldn't find any easy way to step among them. At least not without taking cuts and scratches that our pedestrian would surely have avoided.

"Where'd he go?" I whispered as we turned back to the road. Cole had knelt to look under the vehicle while Albert leaned against the hood and worked on lighting a fat cigar.

"I cannot—" I lost the rest of Vayl's sentence in a furious red haze as I raced back to the van, Jack galloping gleefully by my side.

"Are you out of your *mind?*" I demanded. I yanked the cigar from between Albert's teeth and threw it on the ground, grinding out the barely smoking tip with the heel of my boot. "What, you're free of your nurse's care for a few days and suddenly you think you're cured? Shelby must've wanted to shove his resignation down your throat when he saw you'd started smoking again!"

"He didn't quit," Albert growled. "He got married. And I haven't started anything. I just thought it would be a treat."

"Diabetics don't smoke for a reason, Dad! For chrissake, the last thing I need in the middle of an important assignment is to haul your ass to the hospital!"

"Aw, would you look at that? Now your mutt's eaten my cigar!"

I glanced down. Sure enough, Jack had chewed up and swallowed the best part of it. *Goddammit!* "When he pukes it up, I'm going to make sure he's standing over your suitcase," I informed him. Unfortunately Jack had an immediate reaction, which left the remains of Albert's treat all over the lane. "There you go," I snapped. "Smoke that!"

"I don't see why you're getting all bent out of shape," Albert grumbled. "It was just an old stogie." He shuffled back to the van, his ruined knees making him much more the candidate to carry Vayl's cane than the vamp who swung it thoughtfully between the fingers of his left hand as he, too, made his way back to the vehicle.

I gestured for it. Inside the tiger-carved sheath was a sword I could use right now.

Vayl shook his head. *Behave yourself,* his eyes told me.

Huh.

I followed Albert around to the passenger door. At least I knew why he'd come now. Without his nurse to take care of him, he'd had to resort to one of us kids. Dave had taken his Special Ops unit deep into North Korea for some major hush-hush mission, so he was off the hook. Albert had just spent the past couple of weeks with Evie. So now it was my turn.

And how exactly did I feel about an extended visit with dear old Pops?

When he turned his back on me to open the door I performed several head kicks and one sweeping skull punch that just missed him every time. *My Dad Is an Asshole*. I'm telling you, it's going to be a bestseller.

CHAPTER FIVE

By the time we pulled into Tearlach's drive, all the inhabitants had piled out of the house to greet us.

"Are you all right?" gasped the leader of the pack as we emerged from the Alhambra. "I heard tires squeal and then, when I looked out the window, your van was parked sideways on the lane!" Floraidh Halsey's picture didn't do her justice. She looked even sweeter in person. A plump, shiny-haired forty-something who gave the impression that she was about to run off to volunteer at the nearest nursing home.

"We're fine," I assured her, keeping a firm grip on Jack so he wouldn't jerk us both back into the van. As Vayl went around back to grab some luggage, I let Floraidh see my alter ego's smile. Lucille Robinson could bullshit with rapists and serial killers without losing any wattage off it. *I* wanted to snap at her to cut the crap. I knew exactly what crawled under that thick layer of L'Oréal.

"We nearly hit a guy, though," said Cole as he joined me. He gave Floraidh the once-over and, having seen what he expected, moved his gaze to the crowd. Someone there caught his interest, because I felt him go watchfully still.

If he's found another stray from the department's hit list I'm going to bang my head against the van. Strike that. I'm going to bang his head against the van. No, that's not hard enough. Maybe the side of the house.

"That's awful!" said a woman from the group, the six of whom looked us over with varying degrees of curiosity. She plowed through the rose-covered arch that marked the end of the walk, her sensible heels clunking against the bricks like tiny jack-hammers. "What did he look like? Maybe we know him," she announced in a precise British accent that let you know she came from money, knew how to spend it, and didn't intend to give you a dime. She motioned for her companions to join her.

Before Cole could describe our near-victim Floraidh said, "I'm sure it was that Sean McGill from down the road. He'll get himself killed walking so close to traffic one of these days." She turned to the crowd, beckoning for the backmarker to push her way forward. As the woman rumbled to the front Floraidh said, "This is Dormal, my right hand. If you have any questions or needs during your stay and you can't find me, please feel free to ask her."

I looked up. And then up some more at the coven's Gatherer. No, I wasn't referring to new recruits. Or spell ingredients. This one brought in the sacrifices. Her size had evidently gained her the position. She towered over Vayl by a good three inches and must've weighed in at three hundred pounds, most of that muscle.

"Nice to meet you," I said, making a mental note keep any confrontations with her short and sweet. No talking. No wrestling. Just point and shoot.

Floraidh went on. "And this is Humphrey Haigh and his wife, Lesley, also here for the convention."

"We won tickets!" Lesley gushed, her gray-brown pageboy bobbing as she spoke in an accent so thick it took me a second to understand.

"Oh? That's great," I replied. "Where are you from?"

"Just Inverness," she said. "But it's been so long since we had a vacation from the store, this feels like a hundred miles from home!"

Her husband nodded and beamed happily.

"Your business sounds demanding," said Vayl.

"We started with just one small shop selling wedding rings and gold necklaces and the like," Humphrey told him. "And now we have a whole chain of them right across the country. Still, we keep our headquarters in the same building. Remember your origins, I say. Don't I always say that, Lesley?" He glanced at his wife.

"That he does!" she agreed.

He's as tight as a factory-wound bolt, I thought as I took in the frayed cuffs of his faded brown trousers and the tiny stone in his wife's engagement ring. *Or maybe it's her.* But I didn't think so. In another time and place she'd have probably been feeding him grapes and kissing his feet, because that's just what women in her position did. *Yeah, she's pretty deferential in public. But maybe she's had it up to her eyeballs with playing poor when her bank account must be fat and sassy. Maybe she's got no access either. Which would give her good reason to find a steady source of income elsewhere. But is she the type who could kill in cold blood?*

Hard to say from first impressions. *Dammit, when we couldn't get the warlock, we should've insisted on Cassandra.* But that might've put her in serious danger.

Albert's descent from the van distracted me, since a couple of grunts and some pops that sounded like fireworks accompanied it. Turned out the explosives were just his knees deciding to hold him up a while longer. I supposed the Marines wouldn't be using him as a poster boy anytime soon. But he still gave off that proud military air as he inspected the three women who'd lined up beside the Haighs. "Are you from around here?" he asked.

The eldest of them, the one Floraidh had interrupted earlier, had dark, puffy bags under her eyes and the sallow skin of a lady who proclaims that her work is her exercise. She'd pulled her bottled brunette hair back tight enough to give herself a temporary face-lift. The resulting bun sat on top of her head like a tank turret. I wouldn't be surprised if she used it to shoot bobby pins at uncooperative cabbies and grocery clerks.

She said, "We're up from London for GhostCon. I am Rhona Jepson. This is my daughter, Vivian, though she prefers to be called Viv. She's deaf." Rhona announced this last bit of information in such an aggressive tone it sounded like she expected us to laugh at the news. As she spoke she gestured to a petite, dishwater blonde wearing a gray skirt and brown blouse, who gave the girl beside her a rescue-me look before stepping forward.

At first glance, Viv Jepson looked like a runner. And not the type who did it for health. I imagined she ducked anyone she didn't know or care to converse with. In fact, I'd bet money she had no friends beyond the two women she'd traveled to Scotland with. Which made her just the kind of loner that tended to snap and kill multiple numbers of people. But not usually on a contractual basis. She didn't emit enough gumption to saw into a tough steak, much less an annoying neighbor. In fact, the only items that gave me hope for her personality were the gauzy pink scarf wrapped around her neck and her shoes—bright pink heels with swooshes of red and purple flying down each pointed toe. She waved weakly and stepped back.

Rhona went on. "This is Viv's translator, Iona Clough."

Beside me Cole's stillness became so predatory, if I hadn't known better I'd have wondered what he was after. One look at Iona made it obvious. Her generous curves were emphasized by a tight black sweater, wide-legged jeans, and a giant steel belt buckle in the shape of a mirrored teardrop. Her smile appeared easily, giving her long face a mischievous appeal, though as soon as it faded she seemed distant, almost distracted. Her hair, parted in the middle, hung straight down her back. And though she'd obviously dyed it auburn, I still envied her the perfect lines of her do, which didn't stray or muss no matter how many times she turned her head or nodded.

Mine, on the other hand, perhaps sensing the nearness of the River Nairn, had decided to do its Carrot Top impression. I wanted a hat. And some gel. And a Sharpie, because no amount of hair coloring would turn that one white strand that bobbed next to my face back to red again.

"Hi," said Cole. His smile encompassed both Iona and Viv, who looked to be in their early twenties. Not much younger than me, really, but I knew if we staged a girl's night out, it would only take about five minutes for me to feel ancient.

He stepped forward, moving his fingers in elegant accompaniment to his words as he spoke. "I'm Del Taylor," he said aloud and silently. I guess I shouldn't have been surprised that Cole knew how to sign. Languages were one of his specialties, along with sharpshooting and driving me crazy. If I'd asked how he'd gained this particular ability, he'd probably tell me he'd dated a hearing-impaired honey during college.

"Why'd you dump her?" I'd inquire, because that's how it always went down.

His reply would be something off-the-wall like, "She talked too much. At the end of the day my hands were so tired I didn't even have enough juice left in them to play video games."

Viv's face lit up like a Broadway marquee. She focused on Cole as if he'd just told her she'd be quizzed on this conversation at a later point and every wrong answer would cost her money. Iona, noting her reaction, began to sign as she spoke. "You can sign! And you're American! How amazing!"

The girls traded impressed smiles. Cole gave them his aw-shucks grin that still assured them he outranked every stud they'd met before by a factor of ten. "My little brother lost his hearing really young, so, you know, it was either learn this or beat the crap of him without explaining why he should never touch my G.I. Joe action figures."

Iona laughed. But because she knew it was expected of her, as if she'd given Cole all the attention she could spare and now her mind must swing back to whatever had been occupying it before he showed. Viv, on the other hand, practically glowed. She had to nudge Iona to remind her to translate her half of the conversation for the rest of us. "Uh, why have you decided to come to the Con this year?" Iona asked

Cole chuckled as his fingers flew. "We have plenty of ghosts to choose from on our side of the Atlantic. But we're sure you have a lot *more* over here. Which means steady work for us. I've got some great ghost stories I could tell you. Are you ladies going to the opening ceremonies tonight? We could ride together. Our van holds, like, ten people. Twenty if we sit on laps," he added with a smile that said he knew they weren't the type, but he was.

Viv nodded, but her mom jumped in. "We drove here for the express purpose of having the freedom to come and go as we pleased. I'm sure we'll see you around the place." The pinch in her lips assured him she was just being polite and if these were more savage times she'd have built a fence around her daughter, chopped his head off, and left it on a pike outside to warn off the other undesirables.

When he gave me his this-doesn't-happen-to-me head tilt, I sent him a reassuring smile. *She's probably the assassin anyway,* I told him silently, hoping he'd get my signal.

But maybe not. All the women we'd just been introduced to scented human to me. Not as in, *Sniff, sniff, geez you poured the Chanel on kinda strong tonight, didn't you, Gloria?* My Sensitivity runs deeper than nasal cavities, back into my brain where it developed after I died. Yeah. As in, *Should we give her last rites?*

Nope, never mind. Raoul the WunderSpirit has brought her back to life, because some people are just meant to fight the extra scaries. Besides, she's not Catholic.

She is, however, almost as suspicious of people and circumstances as her former roommate and present tech guru. Bergman would've taken one look at Rhona and Viv, leaned into my ear, and asked, "Why isn't the mother translating? Don't family members usually learn sign language the second their relatives go deaf? Cole did."

Huh, good point. Maybe she has arthritis? I glanced at her hands. Nope, they looked nimble to me. *Okay, then. Something simpler. As long as she doesn't learn to sign she doesn't have to admit her daughter has a permanent disability?* But Rhona didn't seem the type to bury herself in denial. Suddenly I missed Bergman. Though his paranoia generally made me want to pinch his little head off, at the moment he was just too far away for my own good. I'd have loved to get his take on all these women.

As Vayl came around the side of the van toting half our luggage, Rhona pointed her long nose at my dad and said, "So you people are professionals?"

"Uh—" Before Albert could say something stupid and screw us over for good, Vayl put down his suitcase, released my trunk's handle, and stepped forward.

"Indeed, we are." I felt his powers lift, a slight cooling of the air that made Rhona adjust her stone-gray blazer. Most of the women smiled, as did Humphrey, charmed by the big man with the antique cane. Only Floraidh and Dormal seemed unaffected. Vayl said, "I am Jeremy Bhane and this is my associate, Lucille Robinson." He gestured to me, so I nodded and smiled as he went on. "Our company, Rest Easy, specializes in locating and releasing ghosts." He reached into his coat pocket for business cards, which he distributed with the flare of a magician who's just pulled a quarter from his volunteer's ear.

"Oh, how wonderful!" enthused Rhona as she read her card.

"I'm giving a talk on the entrapment and exploitation of ghosts by certain members of the tourism industry. I wish you would sit on the panel."

"Certainly, if I have time. But Lucille and I must do a great deal of networking in the next few days if we are to continue to grow our business."

"Of course."

I said, "Before we go in we should really apologize to the guy we nearly splatted just now. Floraidh, maybe you can put us in touch with this Sean McGill. Or if it wasn't him, would one of you others have seen a brown-bearded man in his thirties wearing a coffee-colored suit at least three sizes too large for him?"

I kept Lucille's sweet smile on my face, but my inner eye narrowed when nobody responded, allowing me to ask the question I really wanted answered. *Which one of you bitches is going to die this week?* Humphrey jerked.

"Are you all right?" asked Floraidh. She went over to the man, patting him on the shoulder as she hovered.

"I think something just stung me," he said. He grabbed at the back of his arm, began rubbing it. "Lucky thing I'm not allergic to bees." The whole time he spoke, Iona signed to Viv, who did a remarkable job of catching the gist of her conversation while also taking in the view, since her eyes often wandered off course. She signed something to Cole, whose brows rose into his unruly bangs before they dropped back to base.

He said, "Viv wonders if it was an Africanized bee. They like to swarm, you know."

"We have no Africanized bees here," Floraidh responded instantly.

"How do you know?" asked Rhona.

"I simply wouldn't allow it." She went to the back of the van, grabbed a couple of cases that contained our ghost hunting supplies, and said, "Shall we go inside? I believe the opening ceremonies start in just under an hour, which will give you time to unpack and freshen up before we must be off."

"Oh, you're going too?" I asked. We'd figured whoever was tailing Floraidh on any given shift would be spending craploads of time hanging around Tearlach. Now it looked like our plans were changing.

Floraidh's laugh trickled out her bow of a mouth like a bright meadow stream. "Of course. I haven't missed a GhostCon in ten years! I always bring a tableful of goodies to sell. Homemade cookies, puddings, and shortbreads to tempt people to stay at Tearlach next year. But my biggest sellers are the protection amulets and charms I bring for ghost hunters who fear to meet angry souls during their journeys." She put her hand beside her mouth, as if she was sharing a state secret. "I get them from a Wiccan in Edinburgh."

"Ah."

She led the way through the trellis, past garden beds lined with gray rocks bigger than my head. I didn't recognize all the flowers, but I knew a lily when I saw one. And damned if she didn't have some poisonous bloomers growing among the innocents, including foxglove and a couple of different kinds of nightshade. Though it was a beautiful evening and most hosts might've suggested we enjoy the gardens, she towed us right inside. Which meant the subject of our mysterious stranger fell flat on the walk, half chewed and regurgitated, just like the cigar Jack had eaten.

Next to it lay my Spirit Eye, snoozing. Oh sure, I'd sensed the Scidairans the second they'd walked out of the B and B. Big whoop, I'd expected that dark tweak to my Sensitivity. The fact that nothing else had stirred it, though I'd met every other guest, had left me thoroughly disappointed. Surely a Medusa scented at least as gross as your typical vamp. But everybody who was a suspect seemed . . . normal. And that should've been my first clue that most of them weren't.

CHAPTER SIX

Tearlach tried to reach out and embrace us. The second we entered the arched double doorway of the bed-and-breakfast's wide central hall where we temporarily stowed our luggage, we found ourselves surrounded by homey details designed to remind us of Granny's house. If Granny had been rich.

To our left a floor-to-ceiling pocket door had been opened to reveal a room that could be closed off at its far end by a similar door. But Floraidh had also slid that aside to reveal the room's twin. Just what a B and B needs. Double lounges with fireplaces at each end and comfy chairs upholstered in pink and blue, as if to give the boys and girls a clue where to sit. At our end of the house the chairs grouped around a TV; I figured Floraidh's for the comfy one beside which sat a basket full of multicolored balls of yarn.

The second lounge had been arranged for games. A chess set had been erected at a table for two by the window, while a bigger table in the middle of the room was reserved for your choice of the boxed funsies stacked on the shelves at its left. On the clean white walls hung old family portraits whose oval frames were probably more valuable than the glassware and rose-patterned china sitting in the cabinet in the corner opposite the TV.

Doilies on the arm cushions, fluffy pillows, and flowered curtains at the windows all conveyed a sense of femininity that I questioned. Could a guy really get comfortable in a twenty-foot-long gossip pit that smelled of potpourri and sprouted figurines like weeds? Hell, could I?

Looking around for an answer to that question, I spied a fancy staircase to my right. According to the B and B's Web site, this led to the guest rooms. Ours should be on the second floor, which meant the other guests took up the third level, with Floraidh and Dormal staying on the fourth. I wandered past the stairs to scope out the dining room, which held a twelve-person table and matching oak sideboard. Over the table hung a candelier that held dozens of red pillars of varying heights. The table, already set for breakfast, glittered with polished silver. Neatly folded red napkins rested in gold-rimmed bowls, which sat on matching plates. It should've pleased the eye. Except mine had evolved. Unfortunately the same couldn't be said for the rest of my family.

Albert came up beside me, nudged my arm, and said in as low a voice as he could muster, "This setup is better advertising than a McDonald's commercial. All of a sudden I'm starving."

"We just ate," I reminded him as I turned, putting the yellow pine woodwork that framed the dining room's entrance to my back.

"It didn't stick with me." He looked at Vayl, who'd quickly moved to join us. Could he sense trouble brewing? Well, he wasn't completely dead. "You're hungry too, right?" Albert asked him. "Big guy like you?"

Vayl dropped me an amused glance. "Always," he replied.

"See that? Your boss is famished. Get us some food."

I uncrossed my arms so hard one of my fists connected with the trim behind me. I didn't tell him I'd been looking for an excuse to check out the kitchen. It stood at the back of the house behind a pass-through to the dining room and a sturdy oak door, both of which were closed. I didn't say a word. Just glared and wished I'd been switched at birth.

Albert misread my look. He said, "Oh, yeah, Floraidh." He dropped his voice another notch. "Don't worry. I'll watch her while you make me a sandwich. Lunch meat is fine. Go heavy on the mustard, wouldja?" Without even a pause to give me time to decide whether I wanted to wring his neck or test my theory that holy water would turn him into steaming glop just like a vampire, he stumped back into the front lounge. "Hey, there, Floraidh. This is quite a place you've got here. Would a lovely young thing like you have time to give an old man the grand tour?"

That's never going to work, I thought as I followed him back. *She and Dormal obviously have something brewing. Look at them— oh for—well, hell, who thought the old fart could make a Scidairan giggle? Especially a grizzly like Dormal? Holy crap, they're all going off together! It's like a scene out of* Shrek: Uncensored and Uncut. *I'd really like to know where he draws the line. Because at this point, I think there's nothing he won't do for a snack.*

As Cole and the girls carried on a private, unspoken conversation at the back part of the twin room, Rhona stomped up to Vayl and me, the Haighs following her like a couple of acolytes.

She cleared her throat, though we'd already turned toward her. "I would like to know if your employee, Albert, is eligible." Behind her Lesley's hand flew up to her mouth to capture her shocked gasp. And then I could see the reasoning wind behind her eyes like a stock exchange ticker tape. *Oh, well, they're American. This is probably how they operate.*

I stole a look at Vayl, whose eyes had crinkled at the corners. Oh goody, at least one of us found this situation amusing. "Uh—"

"The reason I ask"—Rhona charged on—"is that I am a widow

with a great deal to handle. For instance, the ghostly community is far too disorganized for its own good. As I note in my presentation, disreputable hoteliers and GhostWalk guides routinely take advantage of their unfortunate situation, forcing them to linger when they have the means to find the peace they so desperately crave. My goal is to help ghosts form a sort of union, which will at least afford them certain rights and privileges until such time as they are ready and willing to take the next step. And, even in that plane, the innocents must find a way to protect themselves against the evil souls who have not been rounded up to be punished. But I find it so difficult to pursue the task alone. Especially with Viv requiring so much care."

"Oh." Sounded like a load of horseshit to me. Especially after I glanced at Viv, who seemed pretty healthy, her focus glued to Cole like every word that dripped from his lips to his fingertips should be commemorated in the Library of Congress.

"So . . . about Albert?" Rhona asked, her black button eyes bright with anticipation.

"He's divorced. And she's dead."

"Is she a ghost?" asked Rhona.

"No." *Should we be thankful for that small favor? Can I get a hell yeah?*

"Is there anyone he's interested in?" Rhona persisted. "If I am to compete with any women besides Floraidh and Dormal I should like to know."

I could've lied. Easily. But the asshole had just demanded food. From me! I didn't even make *myself* snacks. And I enjoyed *my* company. "No, he's not dating anyone right now," I said. Looking straight into her eyes I added, "Go for it."

Rhona nodded happily. "If you'll excuse me, then, I believe I have some freshening up to do." She turned to Viv and Iona. And clapped. Like they were her little slaves. "Girls? Time to get ready for the opening ceremonies."

Oh, I hope she's Bea. Did I bring explosive ammo? That would be sweet—take the whole back of her head off. No, even better— Lesley Haigh's sweet, round face beamed up into mine as she shook my hand. "So nice to meet you. I believe we're going up too, but we'll see you at the castle?"

Humphrey cleared his throat. "Actually, if you still have room in your van, we wouldn't mind taking the girls' place." He nodded to Viv and Iona, his raised eyebrows reminding me that they'd recently refused Cole's offer of a ride. "Seems silly for us all to drive since we're going to the same place."

And it'll save you a couple of pounds worth of petrol, won't it, Humphrey? I knew I was right when Lesley's smile turned mannequin and her sharp little elbow dug into her hubby's side.

"We would be glad to have you," Vayl said warmly. He meant it. If Lesley was Bea, better to keep her close. In which case she wouldn't be happy with the traveling arrangements either. She tried hard to hide her irritation, but it seeped out in the way she dug her heels into the stairs as they went up to their room, and the dirty looks she thought no one saw her give her hubby. Of course, she might just be pissed at him for being a major-league cheapskate. Still too soon to tell.

Cole wandered over, wearing the look of a man who's just discovered his pay-per-view porn channels are showing freebies for the weekend. "You make friends fast," I said as he joined us.

"Yeah," he breathed. "They're rooming together, you know."

"No." I gave him a second to explain why that was a big deal. "And?"

"Who knows what they with each other do up there?"

"Oh, for—"

His eyes began to shine. "It could happen! It probably does happen!" He sighed. "If only it would happen with me there to watch."

"You're a perv."

"You're jealous." He began nodding before I could even deny it, his hair bouncing against his head like a kid on a trampoline. I looked into those bright blue eyes and tried not to echo his dawning grin.

"Nuh-uh."

"Are too. And just wait. Before I'm done with you, you're going to be on the floor, writhing with envy, begging me to fantasize about you and some other random girl." He thought a second. "Or maybe you and Viv and Iona. And you know what I'm gonna do then?"

"What?"

"Make you a happy woman!"

"Del—," Vayl began, the growl in his tone a clear territorial warning.

"Fine," Cole told him. "You can be in the fantasy too. But fully dressed. Blindfolded. And playing the accordion while a monkey sits on your head like a little monkey hat."

I rubbed my temples and said, "What were you and the girls talking about?"

"What presentations they're going to sit in on at GhostCon."

"Oh."

"Why do you sound so disappointed?"

"I just figured you'd be trying to dig into their backgrounds." I gave him a significant look. "You know, because it's always nice to get to know the people you're staying with."

"We'll have the chance in a few minutes. They've invited us up to their room. They said they wanted to ask us something privately."

"Us?"

He nodded. "Hey, maybe if we go in without knocking we'll catch them kissing!"

"Would you *stop*?"

He put both hands on his hips and stuck out his bottom lip. In his best imitation of a whiny teenage girl he said, "How dare you crush my dreams!"

I glanced up at Vayl, who shrugged. "It is a common male fantasy. You are aware of that, yes?"

"Do you have it?"

He stuck his hands in his pockets. "Not anymore." The expression on his face said he didn't need to. Because he'd fulfilled it.

As Cole said, "Whew, Jeremy!" and gave my boss a standing O, I experienced a flash of hatred for all the women who'd ever given Vayl pleasure. And in nearly three hundred years how many could that have been? Especially if they'd doubled up. And how could I ever stack up against that long line of lovelies? The bitches! Suddenly the yarn in the sewing basket began to smoke.

"Shit!" I took a deep breath to calm myself as Cole grabbed the basket and ran it outside to the van, where we'd stowed a fire extinguisher for just such incidents.

Those kinds of solutions were necessary because ever since I'd donated blood to a dying werewolf named Trayton, things tended to catch fire when I got überpissed. I'd been advised to avoid this at all costs, since the burning also took place inside me. And it takes a long time to grow back bits of your soul. I took a deep breath.

Maybe it'll be spectacular when Vayl and I finally get together, I told myself. *Okay, so I'm sadly out of practice and I've only ever been with one other guy. I might still perform so amazingly it'll put Vayl in a semi coma. If he's already been shot in the head first. Goddammit!*

Before I realized what was happening, Vayl had wrapped his arms around me. "Our first moment alone since I returned from Romania," he whispered. "And you are angry. How do we fix that?"

"We could always kill somebody," I suggested. "Are any of your old girlfriends still alive?"

"How about this?" He pulled me closer, until my face pressed against the soft gray turtleneck he wore under his coat. I could hear the slow thump of his heart, the creak of leather as his arms tightened around my waist. His thighs, warm and firm against mine, his breath in my hair as he kissed the top of my head, the brush of his fingertips against my back. One more moment, to inhale the scent of pine that assured me he still held to the philosophy that had led him, and *others* like him, to blend with society rather than exist apart from it. I pulled back.

"I like hugs," I said.

"You sound surprised."

"I just can't believe I'd forgotten how great they feel." I clenched my fists. "How great you make me feel." *Why is stuff like that always so hard to say? There must be some way to—I know! Bergman owes me an invention. I'm going to make him build me a Jaz doll with all those phrases preprogrammed into her. So all I have to do is wait for the appropriate moment, break out plastic me, and pull the string. Genius!*

Vayl searched my face, his smile growing as time passed. "Do you know what I just realized?"

"No."

"This is going to be quite enjoyable."

"This what?" But Vayl didn't have time to answer. Cole had blown back inside, his hair standing on end from his firefighting experience.

Vayl released me before our third could figure out what we'd done during his brave act. A pretty good call, I thought, especially when Cole shoved his fingers through his locks and said proudly, "It burst into flame just as I opened the door to the van. You should've seen the smoke! I killed the fire and hid the evidence. But I think we're going to have to bury it somewhere before we leave." He sent me a shame-on-you look. "I believe you killed a half-knitted scarf and a pair of baby booties."

Jack's nose in my hand reminded me that I shouldn't even

be fantasizing about slapping that smart-ass grin off Cole's face without locating the nearest fire department first. I crouched and gave the dog a good rubdown. "You know why you're here, you panting, pooping mink coat, you? So we can practice biting bad guys in the nuts, right? Because that's your new trick, isn't it?" I smiled at Cole from between Jack's ears, which perked with interest as I asked, "Who do you think we should practice on next?" When Jack looked over his shoulder at Cole and ran his massive pink tongue across his lips and nose, Cole's face dropped so suddenly it looked like a fast-motion clip of a guy aging twelve years in three seconds.

"Watch out there, Lucille, you may lay an egg you're cackling so hard," he said as I laughed into Jack's neck. He grabbed his suitcase and strolled past me. "I'm going to the girls' room. If you're not too jealous, why don't you join me?"

"Gladly," I said as I strode to where Vayl had left my trunk. "By the way, did you happen to pack a cup in your luggage? Jack could really use some dry runs."

As Cole walked ahead of me I noticed his stride tighten. His knees didn't quite meet in the middle, but if he could've managed it, I think he would've. "Didn't your brother ever tell you not to joke about stuff like that?" he asked over his shoulder.

"Are you kidding? He's worse than I am! One time—"

"No! I don't want to hear it!"

"Oh. Okay." Vayl walked beside me, his lips quirking in his typical smile. I asked him, "Do we even have time for this Viv/Iona deal?"

"I believe so. Your father has seen to that, at least."

That's my dad, always going out of his way to be helpful. Which was why I'd just set him up with Rhona. Like my granny May always said, "Do for yourself—and others will make sure you get yours in the end."

Chapter Seven

After we'd dumped our bags in our rooms, we met outside the girls' white-painted door.

I didn't love the setup. It would've been more efficient for Cole to deal with them while Vayl and I checked our cover chores off our to-do list. But I was pretty sure my boss wanted to accompany us because he didn't savor Cole and me spending much alone time together. And I knew my presence was required because I could clear a room. The easy method would've been to pull any number of lethal weapons from the worn black bag on my shoulder and make all the inhabitants run screaming. But before we'd taken this mission I'd also learned how to block Scidairan magic.

It had meant a trip to Miami to train with Cassandra. Usually I'd have bitched nonstop about the exile from work—and Vayl. But, as noted earlier, events in Cleveland had escalated to the point where Pete couldn't wait to boot my ass out of the office. And since Vayl had flown straight from our last assignment to his old stomping grounds near Mogosoaia, Romania, I was happy to go.

So I'd spent a week living above Cassandra's health food store. We reminisced about the times she'd spent with Vayl and me working as our Seer, and gossiped about what the future might hold for her and my brother, Dave. In between I read old books that made my nose itch and cross-referenced stories that various members of her guild had stored in the mobile library she called the Enkyklios. The last two days went by the fastest, because one of her fellow guild members, a Sister of the Second Sight named Tolly Mendez, showed up to, as she put it, "take this *chica* to school."

She talked like the Bronx and moved with a rhythm that said, *Only Latinas can samba like girls oughtta.* Though I hadn't thought it humanly possible, she wore more jewelry than Cassandra. Rings on her fingers and toes. Bracelets, anklets, biceplets—is that even a word? And in what she liked to call her "punkass hair," dozens of silver clips from which dangled tiny chains holding miniature charms.

Her bright yellow shorts would've passed uniform inspection at a bike race, and her aqua-blue tank scooped low enough that when she leaned forward the top edge of her black lace bra showed. *So how,* I wondered, *does she skim past skank on first impression?*

Attitude, I decided. *Something in that quick smile and those steady eyes that tells you she's traveled enough to realize nothing's worth the price of her soul.*

I'd been chilling in Cassandra's living room, drinking iced tea and reading up on Scidair. I'd just learned her following dated back three thousand years when Tolly clomped up the stairs in her open-toed platform slides and called out, "Let's have ourselves an entrance, shall we?" The wooden rocker beside the royal-blue couch I sat on began to move on its own. Immediately afterward the candles Cassandra had arranged in the fireplace all flamed at once.

"Nice," I said as she sashayed through the door. I tried hard not to wish Cassandra was beside me. Psychics pick right up on that crap, and she had nobody else to mind the store today. Plus, what harm could there be in a little magic lesson from one of her buds?

I tried a laugh and just managed a weak cough as Tolly introduced herself and in the same breath said, "Cassandra tells me you're a Sensitive."

"Yeah." I told myself if she didn't touch me she couldn't See how wide my powers had stretched since I'd shared my blood with *others*—Vayl and Trayton included—not to mention accepting the tears of an Iranian power named Asha Vasta. She might not like knowing that now I'd scented her psychically, I could pick her out of a rioting crowd and follow her through a sandstorm.

She closed the space between us, holding out her free hand for a shake, her other weighted down by an enormous bag covered with quarter-sized metal plates that jingled softly when she moved.

Putting off the inevitable, I said, "Wow. Your fingernails are really—"

"Spew green," she informed me. "It's my own brew," she went on, like we were discussing a great piece of cake. Her eyes sparkled. "Don't worry, my Sight isn't based on touch."

I shook her hand. "Sorry. I'm just—trained to be cautious."

"And private?" When I didn't answer she nodded. "Okay, we don't have to go into the event that birthed your Sensitivity. Nobody likes to remember that kind of violence anyway. Just tell me. What did you feel when I lit the candles?"

"I never feel anything. It's what I see in my mind. Like a new color mixed with the memory of a dream." I shook my head. "I don't know how to describe it any better."

"And?"

"Yours is fresh. Like silver rain on a mountain lake."

She nodded. "That's Wicca. True witchcraft will always show the same shade to you now. What Cassandra tells me you're about to face is not real witchery. They only call themselves that because they know it hurts the rest of us, and they love spreading pain."

"How do you know so much about Floraidh and her coven?" Despite Tolly's connections to Cassandra, I found myself mentally reviewing the weapons I currently carried. Just in case. She dropped her bag on the floor, where it landed with a metallic *clunk*. Sinking into the rocker, she clasped her hands in her lap and asked, "How old do you think I am?"

What the hell? Weren't we just talking about witches? "I don't see—"

"Humor me."

I shrugged. "Twenty-seven."

"I'm fifty-three."

I stared at her for a full thirty seconds, looking hard for the plastic surgery scars. But that still shouldn't have been able to hide the *youthfulness*.

"Bullshit."

She shook her head. "I was one of them once. I worshipped Scidair right alongside them. If I told you the things our coven did to cheat death you'd puke all over Cassandra's furry white rug here. As you can see"—she gestured to her face—"they've learned how to put the brakes on. But they still haven't succeeded completely. Floraidh's group is the most powerful both because they descend from the first priestesses who buried Scidair, and because they still guard her cairn to this day. We think Floraidh is nearly a hundred and fifty years old."

This was all news to me. Her birth records put her age at just over forty, and nobody knew what her coven wanted beyond the power its alliance with Samos had given it. "Did Scidair live a long time?"

Tolly nodded. "Legend says she died at the age of one hundred and fourteen, when the villagers finally got up the nerve to burn her for still looking thirty-five."

Damn. "What kinds of acts did you perform?" I asked.

"Even if I wanted to, I couldn't get detailed. As a Scidairan, when you swear yourself to secrecy and then start blabbing, the people you give up have ways of shutting you down."

"Can you tell me anything?"

"All I can say is that Scidairan magic is wound around death. And it will read to you like a sky full of stinking black pollution."

"So how am I supposed to counteract it?" I asked. "Isn't it going to be laced all through that bed-and-breakfast?" I recalled the last stronghold we'd visited, a Vampere villa so packed with power even the knickknacks seethed with it. The scale didn't exist that could measure how badly I wanted to avoid a situation like that again.

She said, "My guess is that the coven will have set permanent shields around the house, like runes carved into the hardscape. Ghosts naturally interrupt their spells, so if you need to run, go to a cemetery or any other place that's likely to be haunted. But for privacy while you're in the house, or for a temporary shield, I'll teach you a quick spell that'll work just fine."

As she pulled a funky-looking lantern out of her bag I said, "Won't they be able to tell I'm messing with their goodies?"

"I don't think so. You'll read as an amateur, so they'll think it's a natural occurrence. A talent one of their guests was born with and never learned to manipulate."

"Until they look into me?"

She pulled a fat, tortoiseshell bracelet off her wrist and handed it over. "Cassandra asked me to make this for you. It'll repel any spells designed to invade your aura. I don't imagine they'll go to the trouble though. The Scidair focus intensely on their goal.

Which is why most of them are single and childless. Also, rumor has it Floraidh's taken up an expensive hobby. Nobody knows what it is exactly, but she's been so obsessed with raising funds lately that as long as your credit's good, I don't think anybody in the coven will bother with you."

We'd spent the rest of the time practicing clearing rooms.

Of course, they hadn't been teeming with Floraidh's special brand of *sizzit*. Not that I could feel it. Unlike the last place where we'd set up shop, this one's artifacts didn't exude their own special *snap, crackle, pop* of power. They were just innocent landscapes hung from pink ribbons in the third-floor hallway. Half-moon tables covered with yet more doilies that held a collection of antique teakettles. And a half-shaded window hung with white eyelet before which dangled a fabulously healthy ivy whose tendrils had almost reached the blue and red woven floor runner.

"No, Jack," I said as he sniffed at the plant before deciding it was edible. He closed his massive jaws without snipping off a leaf and turned to give me his pathetic face. It involved lots of blinking and—I kid you not—a sort of frown. "Are you hungry too?"

He trotted back to me, eyes bright with anticipation, his tongue practically lapping his neatly trimmed toenails. "Okay, we'll get you something afterward. I brought you a whole suitcase full of goodies that Floraidh said you could eat in the kitchen."

"You're nicer to that dog than you are to me. You know that, right?" asked Cole.

"Sorry," I said, with real regret. "But you have to admit, he's a lot less demanding."

Vayl slipped his hands into the pockets of his black jeans. "Would it make you feel better to know she does not sleep with Jack either?"

Cole glared at him before turning to rap several times in succession on the girls' door. "Why did I ever agree to do this job?"

"Because you wouldn't get paid if you didn't?" I guessed.

He made his temper-fraying, breath-blowing sound and said, "You do remember everything that Rolly woman taught you, right?"

"Her name's Tolly," I said. "And I'm fairly certain I didn't contract Alzheimer's between Miami and Inverness."

I leaned against the wall, its pale blue coloring reminding me vaguely of drowning victims, and crossed my arms as Jack sat beside me.

Vayl leaned over to whisper, "I really was trying to improve his mood with that observation."

"Probably the less said between you and him right now, the better," I suggested.

The door flew open. Viv took one look at us, burst into tears, and slammed it shut.

I said, "Obviously your incredible good looks overwhelm her, Cole. Should I try?"

Wearing an expression of utter confusion, he bowed me into his spot. I opened the door and walked in.

"Hey, Viv. Hello there, Iona," I said. "Sorry our entrance bummed you out so much. Is it because we didn't bring nachos and beer?"

Viv, her face buried in fistfuls of tissues, couldn't have seen Iona's flying fingers. Still she shook her head. She wiped her eyes, blew her nose, and attempted a soggy smile.

Cole leaned into my ear and whispered, "This is totally ruining my fantasy, you know. There they are, sitting beside each other *on the bed.* Viv would look so great wearing that little scarf around her neck and nothing else. Plus, if Iona scooted over two inches their hips would be touching. This would be ideal—if Viv wasn't blowing snot like a whale with bronchitis."

"Are you sure whales get bronchitis?" I murmured.

He nodded wisely. "They're mammals, aren't they? I'll bet when they sneeze, the only liquid that comes out of their blow-pipes is drippy green mucus."

"Eww!"

"I'm saying! It's such a turnoff!"

"Do you know what women find attractive?" Vayl asked him.

"You mean ladies like our lovely Lucille, here?" he replied, draping his arm across my shoulders while he ignored the spike in my boss's powers that sent a shiver through the girls.

"I mean all of them," Vayl replied darkly.

"What's that?"

"Men who comfort them when they are feeling blue."

Cole dropped his arm. "Can we at least wait to see *why* she's sniffling? Maybe *she's* got bronchitis!"

Viv dropped her tissues in the trash, but it was only to pull out a fresh batch. Iona said, "Thank you so much for coming. And I know Viv feels really badly about this scene. She's just so relieved you came. And truly hoping you can help her. Because, as you can see, she's desperate."

"Of course, you know we'll do what we can," said Cole in the voice he brings out for single moms at the zoo whose kids have just spilled their slushies on him. He went to the bed, knelt at Viv's knees, and began asking her questions that seemed designed to soothe her. But they should also help us figure out if she was who she said she was, or just a terrific actress who spent her spare time offing public figures for wild sums of money.

He wasn't nearly as good at comforting as Vayl. But my boss had decided to stay clear of the youngsters. Instead he'd gone to the window and flipped aside the curtain to glance at the countryside, glowing with the soft light of evening. After spending his first thirty-eight years as your average Roma family man, he'd turned. Which meant it had been over two and a half centuries since he'd seen daylight. Now that he didn't have to concentrate fully on the job, he could relax and just enjoy. His face settled into a new sort of immobility. One I equated with Buddha statues and transfixed lovers.

I could've watched him reacquaint himself with twilight for hours. If the room had been quiet. How could he just stand there while Sniffette honked her way through an entire box of tissues? I looked at the watch Bergman had made for me. At this rate it might continue for hours. I was voting with Cole on this one. *Geesh! She's like a damn sob machine!*

Trayton would've peered at me through his curtain of fine black hair and said, "You really need to work on your people skills, woman. Where did you learn sensitivity anyway?"

To which I'd reply, "The Marines." End of conversation. At least until I was sure I wouldn't have to kill the girl hiccuping into her hand.

Vayl tossed his handkerchief to Cole, who gently dried her tears with it before wrapping her fingers around it.

She wiped her nose and dropped the handkerchief on her lap so she could sign as she spoke. "I'm sorry," she said, through Iona, her lips forming the words along with her hands. "I've just been overwrought lately."

"Hold that thought," I said, raising my palm toward her. Some signs must be universal, because she stopped talking and stared at me as I began to clear the room. Starting at the corner nearest the door, I pulled the incense holder out of my bag and fired up the sage already packed inside with the lighter Tolly had given me before she left.

"This is how *you* light fires," she'd told me sternly. "Any other way is gonna lead to you staring out the barred window of a high-security psych ward. Guaranteed."

The incense holder Tolly had lent me, a cast-iron goddess

image with hollow eyes and a gaping mouth, swung from my hand as I moved clockwise around the perimeter of the room. I whispered words she'd made me memorize, remembering that I must genuinely want to push Scidair and her trollops from this room for the spell to work. After a single lap I stopped and rang the bell that doubled as the holder's handle. The shield closed with a psychic *whoosh* that made my scalp tingle. If I'd taken two more circuits it would've lasted as long as I stayed in the house. But that felt too extreme, at least until I knew Viv and Iona were innocent. So it would only work until I left the room.

"Why did you do that?" asked Iona as I sat the goddess by the door and sank down beside it, mainly to keep Jack from knocking it over. I'd discovered quickly that anything within reach of his nose either got sniffed, poked, flipped, or sneezed on.

"We didn't want the ghosts to eavesdrop," I said. "You wouldn't believe how snoopy they are. We have this one that follows us everywhere we go. I think we picked it up in Pamplona when we were putting the shade of a murdered chef to rest."

I waited for the girls to call my bluff. Okay, Viv might be too upset to catch the lie. But if Iona had really spent any time around Viv and her crusading mom she'd know that—

"Ghosts don't travel," she said flatly.

I smiled. "You got me there. I'm kidding, of course. The sage ceremony is just something I do to cleanse a room before important conversations. Helps everybody relax and also ensures that the conversations remain honest." I shook my head regretfully. "You'd be surprised how many people try to lie to us about their haunt problems. And we can't be effective when we begin with false information. You can see that, can't you?"

The girls nodded as if they completely understood our predicament.

"So how can we help you?" asked Cole.

Iona said, "Viv would like to hire you to eradicate a ghost. Not lay it to rest," she emphasized, "but get rid of it forever."

As Vayl and I competed to see whose eyebrows could rise the highest, Cole sat back on his heels, moving so fast he nearly fell over. He finally managed to say, "That's a tall order. Why us?"

Viv began some mad signing. Iona said, "She agreed to accompany her mother here because she knew that every year a few groups like yours also come to GhostCon trying to drum up business. We looked you up on the Web and phoned your references. You come highly recommended."

Thanks a lot, Pete. You know, you could've told the operators to tell callers we sucked!

"Viv can pay you well," Iona added. "And it's for a good cause. The best, in fact."

"And that is?" asked Vayl as he dropped the curtain and turned to listen to Viv's explanation.

"Finally ridding the world of a murderer."

Chapter Eight

To give the girl credit, Viv didn't burst into tears again, though it looked for a minute like we were going to have to break out the sponge mop. Then she gave a full-body shudder and went on signing, with Iona launching into first person, probably hoping to affect our decision by speaking as if her words were Viv's.

"Last year, when I was at university, my roommates and I were attacked by a man. He raped them and cut their throats. But when it came to me he had to hurry. My mum had been calling all that night, and when no one answered she and my dad had shown up at the door. So he stabbed the knife into my throat, severing my vocal chords. He had a gun too, which he used to shoot through the door. He killed my dad. While my mum was on the floor, trying to stop the bleeding, he ran out of the apartment. She told the police she didn't get a good look at him. And she made me agree that I hadn't either."

Viv had begun to lose so much color I considered shoving her head between her legs to make sure she didn't pass out. Her fingers were also shaking so bad Iona couldn't have been able to tell what she was saying, but she must've heard the story before, because she went on without a break. "Mum tells strangers I was born deaf and mute so she doesn't have to explain the real reason

I need to sign. To friends and relatives, she said I'd been injured in a car accident and, because she knows a lot of highly connected people, my part in the tragedy was left out. The newspapers related that I'd gone home for a few days because I was sick and needed tending. And I *was* ill, too weak and distraught to do much more than cry. It wasn't just what had happened to me and my friends. He'd killed my dad too. Leaving me with a mum who'd never really understood or connected with me. But she loved me. How much I came to understand months later. When I saw the ghost of my dad's murderer at the bus stop."

I held up my hand. "Hang on. Are you sure it was him? And that you weren't, you know, having a little bit of a breakdown?" Especially since I knew they could reattach vocal chords. Which meant if she couldn't talk now, the reason might not be totally physical.

"I'm positive. Because Mum saw him too. She gave a little scream and said, 'Viv, that's him, isn't it?' as she pointed beyond the waiting crowd. How could I mistake that thin brown hair and those long yellow teeth?" Viv shook her head. "She was so furious! 'He's died!' she said. 'I've been paying private investigators to find him for months, and he's gone and snuffed it! What do you think of that?'

"I said that I thought it was the best news I'd heard in forever. But she couldn't be consoled. 'It's not enough for him to be gone,' she said. 'I've got to chase him into the afterlife and make his existence there a misery as well!' And ever since then she's been obsessed. She only sleeps two or three hours a night. She won't entertain any other topic of conversation. She keeps me close to protect me, but it's making me feel *wrong* now just being around her. I can't get shed of my past because she won't let it go. So I want you to do it for her. Kill that ghost. Make it so she can never lay eyes on him again. Can you do that?"

Oh, shit.

Cole looked back at me with such hope that I felt doubly guilty for agreeing to a cover that desperate people would flock to. Vayl walked over to Viv and held out his hand for hers. He rubbed the small, nail-bitten fingers between his as he said, "Let me explain what is happening so that you understand what you ask of us."

She nodded, as if she believed Vayl really needed permission for anything he decided to do. He said, "Ghosts are not typical spirits, most of whom find absolute release when they die and can only be reached through mediums. Even then contact is limited and communications often confused. They are so far away, you see. Ghosts, on the other hand, exist in a place we call the Thin, because the wall between their plane and ours is so often breached. You do not have to possess special abilities to see or even interact with a ghost, though the latter is highly inadvisable."

"Why?" asked Iona. "You do it all the time."

After a pause Vayl replied. "We understand the dangers involved. Why do you suppose you have heard so many ghost stories since you were old enough to sit with a flashlight shining into your face?"

"Because it's fun?" suggested Cole.

Since I sat too far away to kick him I shot him a shut-*up!* look instead. He zipped it. Vayl continued. "Most cultures understand how important it is to instill the fear of ghosts into their children. Because they truly are the shades of their former souls. The dark and hungry remainder of what was abandoned when the rest was either saved or condemned."

"I don't understand," Viv signed. "Why are you telling me this?"

"Because these creatures exist in torment. Think of it. When a soul is offered paradise, it sheds all that was evil and despicable within it. But that part does not always dissipate. In the same way, when a soul is ravaged unto hell, a section is sometimes left behind. Like a lobotomy, the soul's rebellious tendencies are ripped away, so that the tortures Lucifer designs for his victims are endured rather than revolted against."

"But it doesn't happen in every case?" asked Iona.

"Only in extremes," he said. "But this causes the Thin to be a savage world from which ghosts constantly seek escape. When they find a way to rip through, into our plane, sometimes they find a moment of tranquillity. A time when they remember who they were. What you are asking us to do by releasing this man from the Thin, the man who raped and murdered your friends, who killed your father and tried to kill you, is to give him peace."

Vayl paused, searching Viv's eyes. "Are you ready to do that?"

Viv had begun to shake. Just a fine tremor throughout her body that hardly even moved her unless you looked closely. And then you could see it everywhere, as if we'd connected her to a low-voltage current while Vayl talked. And he wouldn't stop. He said, "You must also understand that even if we lay his ghost to rest, your mother would still be obsessed. Her fury at your father's death and your injuries is so immense that it terrifies her. So she pushes it outward."

"Still," said Iona, not even looking to Viv for confirmation, "maybe this would help her."

Vayl nodded. "Perhaps. I simply want you to understand all the parameters of this solution before you make the choice."

Viv sighed and dropped her hands to her lap, her eyes studying the painting of a bright red poppy that hung over the bed on which she sat. She signed something and when Iona nodded without speaking I asked Cole, "What did she say?"

He looked up at her sadly. "She said she just wants it to be over."

I would've suggested that she talk to her mom about how she

felt, but I also had a bullheaded parent who wouldn't listen to reason. Eventually Viv would have to figure out that she was a grown-up, and it was time for her to do what she needed to make herself whole again. Even if that meant she left Rhona alone, ranting about organizing ghost town so she could somehow achieve revenge on the shade of her husband's killer.

Cole stood up slowly and rubbed the kinks out of his legs. Without consulting either one of us he said, "We'll do whatever you need, Viv. Just let us know your decision, okay?"

She nodded, tugging at the scarf around her neck like it was a noose. As I stood to leave, hefting the goddess lamp and scratching Jack on the head when he leaped to his feet, Vayl said, "I wonder if you would mind answering one last question for us. Floraidh seemed anxious to avoid discussing the man we nearly ran over in her lane. Are you sure you have not seen him walking in that area?"

Iona said, "Actually I did, just as we turned in. I hated to mention anything earlier; Floraidh seemed so disturbed by the idea. But he was standing on the corner with his hands behind his back, watching us rather mournfully. I pointed him out to Viv, but when she tried to get a glimpse, he'd gone. He seemed an old-fashioned dresser to me. Almost like an actor in a costume, wouldn't you say?" she asked.

Vayl nodded. "Indeed. The longer I think on it, the more I believe his suit was from a different era. Perhaps the late 1800s."

Cole asked, "How could you tell?"

"I recalled his suit coat was buttoned only at the top. And his vest was cut straight across at the waist."

"So you're into period clothing?" asked Iona.

"We run into a lot of ghosts from that age," I said. "Don't know why. Just plenty of remnants from the 1880s."

"So we saw a ghost?" Cole asked.

"Certainly this discussion has made me wonder," said Vayl. "I suppose there is only one way for us to find out. We will simply have to set up our equipment. With Floraidh's permission, of course." He turned to Viv. "As for your issue, it is as Del, here, suggested. We will await your decision and act accordingly."

She nodded, the contemplation on her face transforming it into a beautifully fragile portrait. But I realized that behind that delicate picture lurked the soul of an Amazon. Those funky shoes proved it. And if she could just get through this terrible time, I had a feeling Viv would finally discover it for herself.

Chapter Nine

We left Iona and Viv with the agreement that we'd sit with them at GhostCon's opening ceremonies, and split up in the hallway outside their door. Vayl and Cole went to track down Floraidh. Their plan: charm her into saying anything-you-like to setting up our cameras and various other phantom detectors, which, of course, detected no such thing. We'd already manufactured an excuse to flood the house with our Bergman-made goodies, all of them meant to help us track an *assassin's* movements. But our experience on the lane had provided us with a better story, one Floraidh might buy. Especially when Vayl waved a few hundred-pound notes under her upturned nose.

Since the guys had deserted us, I grabbed Jack's supplies from my trunk and we trotted downstairs to the kitchen. Like the other rooms in the house, this one tried its hand at cozy. A farmer's table holding a blue bowl brimming with fruit and surrounded by six tall chairs dominated the south side of the pea-green room. On the north side, a work island and white cabinets whose doors had been stenciled with red flowers connected by leafy vines gave it balance. Though when I began to imagine what all the coven members chopped on the hard maple surface of that island, the kitchen stopped seeming so quaint.

The fake wooden countertops held your typical assortment of canisters, cookbooks, and small appliances. A refrigerator took up space by the door we'd just entered, and an oven stood by the second exit, the window above it overlooking the backyard.

After supplying the dog with his supper, I checked the fridge and found it packed with leftovers and bottled drinks. As I helped myself to a couple of waters, I noticed Jack had deserted his Iams to sniff at the spotless white stove.

"Whatcha got there, pal? Something fall out of a casserole dish that you need to sample?" I opened the door only enough to get a look, since I could imagine him shoving his whole face in and licking charred grossness off its floor. He didn't even try. Just looked up at me as I tried to decide why Floraidh would store a bowl full of ashes on its bottom shelf.

It's probably just burned hickory. Maybe she flavors roasts that way, I told myself as Jack trotted back to his dinner. If it had been any other B and B I'd have left the bowl alone. Since it was Tearlach I pulled it out and set it on the counter.

Time to check for unscheduled interruptions. All I could see out the window was an herb garden leading to a stretch of deep green lawn and a stone barn with red doors and matching roof, all of it backed by a thick, spooky forest called Culloden Wood. So I tiptoed to the lounge. Yup, the Scidairans stood out front with Vayl and Cole, who seemed to be deep into their sales pitch. Albert had decided that meant he was dismissed and turned to come inside.

I rushed back to the kitchen, put a finger to my lips when Jack looked up at me in surprise. As he shoved his nose back in his food I returned to the ash bowl. *Okay, I'll play archaeologist. But only for a minute.* I found the silverware drawer on the third try. Used a spoon to sift through. Because not everything burns when . . . yup. There it was. A human tooth.

Fuck!

The thoughts hit me simultaneously. *I'm scooping through human remains like they're freaking Raisin Bran!* And. *I have to put them back where I found them.* I hated the idea of not rescuing them, giving them a proper burial, or at least scattering them somewhere so the coven couldn't use them for their obscene little rituals. But that would so blow my cover.

I found a Baggie in another drawer, deposited the tooth, some ashes, and the spoon, stuffed it in my jacket pocket and returned the bowl to the stove. Albert had stumped upstairs by now. And since Jack had nearly finished his grub, I grabbed a banana and an apple out of the fruit bowl.

"We need to go," I said, reaching for the leash. I didn't have a lot of free minutes. Cole and Vayl would convince Floraidh to allow them to set up the equipment, and one of them would keep an eye on her while the other worked. That just gave me time to call a courier for my gruesome find and run the names of the guests through the Agency's database. Then it'd be my turn to shadow her.

This sucks! There's human ashes in the oven. I'm fetching food for my dad like the Tearlach bellboy. And I have to play bodyguard to the bitch who recently advised Edward Samos to burn me alive.

I tried to console myself with the memory of how my brother had come up with the idea of escaping Samos's trap. How we'd turned his magic against him and ultimately watched him die. *He is dead. And you'll only have to protect his former ally until you find Bea. Or maybe till you figure out who's in the bowl. It wouldn't be the first time Pete changed his orders midmission.*

My mood lifted suddenly, and as he often did, Jack took note with a curious look and a pricking of his ears. "Come on, dog. Let's go feed the gorilla."

We ran upstairs. Our doors stood in a row, Vayl's at the head of the steps, mine next, and Cole's last, with a sauna-sized shared bathroom across the hall. Cole had agreed to room with Albert, so I strode to the door with the little basket of fake daisies nailed to it and the numbers 203 painted in bright red underneath.

"How pissed is he gonna be when he finds out we got him something nutritious?" I asked Jack as we stopped. I paused with my hand on the knob when I heard a voice from inside that didn't belong to Albert. Though I couldn't make out the words, they sounded threatening.

"Go to hell!" he yelled.

I threw the door open as a second voice murmured, "I'm already there."

Albert stood between twin beds covered with blue flowered spreads, holding a long black remote control in his shaking hand. As Jack stuck his nose in the back of my leg and I reached for Grief, I looked sharply to my left and right. "Who were you talking to?" I asked, striding toward the wardrobe. I threw open the door. Nothing there but some shirts and a stack of underwear. Geez, how long was he planning on staying?

"It was the TV," he said, clenching his teeth so hard I could hear his molars rub. I turned to look at where it sat on a corner entertainment center stacked with videos and games. BBC was showing one of my favorite cop movies.

"You're yelling at Simon Pegg?"

"He's . . . such an ass."

"What?"

"Just—he just pisses me off is all!"

"How is that possible? He's playing this unbelievable policeman—"

"Did you bring me anything to eat?"

I looked at the food in my left hand, feeling off balance and slightly bewildered. As if I'd come in to find my father dancing around in ballet slippers and a tutu. He grabbed the fruit and, without a single complaint as to its lack of chocolate content or sugar glazing, bit into the apple.

"What's wrong with you?" I asked. "Are you dizzy? Do you need to do a test? Did you shrink your sweatshirt again?"

"I'm fine," Albert growled. "Quit hovering. You remind me of one of those goddamn blimps." That sounded more like him. "Don't you have somewhere you need to be?" he asked.

"Yeah." I turned to leave.

"Hey."

"What?"

"You taking the mutt with you tonight?"

I looked down at Jack, who blinked at me soulfully. "I figured I would."

"Why don't you leave him with me?"

"Huh?" The offer caught me so far off guard I was sure I looked like a total cave brain, with my mouth hanging open to give all my loose gray matter a straight shot to the floor.

"He could keep me company while I watch TV."

"Are you going to yell at him?"

"Why would I do that?"

"You mean like you're yelling at me right now?"

"I'm not yelling!"

"Promise to talk nice or he leaves with me."

Albert shook his head and stared at Jack. "Do you want to stay with me for a while, Jackster? I may have a few treats for you in my suitcase to help pass the time." Albert hobbled to the dresser and threw open the lid to his luggage. Right on top lay a box of doggy snacks.

"You didn't."

For answer, Albert dug one out and offered it to Jack, who immediately deserted me to make friends with the man who had informed me, at the age of eight, that if I couldn't figure out how to manage all by myself I might as well skip my independence and check right into Greenfields Assisted Living.

I left my dad and my dog bonding over Milk-Bones and *Hot Fuzz,* thinking, *The way this day is going, things are only gonna get weirder.*

Chapter Ten

As I walked through my room, repeating the clearing ceremony I'd performed for the girls as well as for Vayl, Cole, and Albert, I tried to talk myself into liking the place. The wallpaper, which only ran up to the white chair rail, was covered in a ripe plum design. I should be tempted to pluck them right off the wall. Except I kept thinking they looked like frozen testicles, and I was feeling sorry for the model. The part above the rail, painted lavender, just depressed me.

I did appreciate that I had my own bathroom, so I wouldn't have to share with the guys. It was situated right across from the entry. Around the corner stood the bed, its frame consisting of long wooden spindles that reminded me of my niece's crib. And the table beside it was so tiny the lamp looked like it was going to topple off in the night, possibly electrocuting me in my sleep.

Floraidh had also furnished the room with an interesting piece that was part dresser, part makeup table. Half the thing had drawers, which I'd left empty because this wasn't a place I wanted to get cozy in. The other half had a flat desk under which Floraidh had pushed a richly cushioned stool. A square mirror framed in lightly stained pine had been hung on the wall above it. Since I wore the bare minimum cosmetics-wise, I'd probably use it five minutes a day. Okay, maybe ten. Fifteen if my damn curls wouldn't start cooperating.

As soon as the shields snapped shut I set Tolly's incense burner on the floor by the door and opened my trunk. Out came the laptop and all its components, which only took a couple of minutes to set up. While I waited for the computer to connect, I changed for GhostCon. This included adding a few weapons I hadn't worn on the flight. My black bag provided wrist sheaths for both arms. The one on the right held holy water, my first line of defense against vampires. It wouldn't kill Bea, but it might poison or paralyze her, taking her down long enough for me to use Grief or the blade my seamstress had expertly hidden in my right pocket. Since I wore Tolly's bracelet on the same arm, the logistics of using the syringe that held the water might become a little tricky. So I strapped it on, hoping I wouldn't need to use it.

I'd given up the throwing knives I'd once carried on my left wrist. Hadn't wanted to use them since that mission to Iran, when I'd been forced to slit my brother's throat with one in order to free him from a necromancer's spell. Despite the fact that he'd survived, the knives had become a nightmare reminder of those long minutes when I'd thought he wouldn't come back from zombieland. So I'd finally ditched them for good. Instead I'd loaded a new sheath with a piece of technology Bergman had sold the Agency under the name of Mongoose.

A mini cannon that shot some sort of foam, the Mongoose looked about as effective as a movie prop. But it felt as heavy as a tank of grill gas. I didn't know what Bergman had loaded the sucker with, but when he assured me it would stop anything like a Medusa I had to trust him. The guy knew his science and, increasingly, his magic as well as doctors know the Hippocratic oath.

The ghost hunters I'd researched (all quacks from what I

could tell) favored black, so I dressed with that color scheme in mind. I pulled on a fresh pair of jeans to which I transferred the contents of my pockets, and a peasant blouse that I'd just started to button when the laptop made its final connection.

Within five minutes I'd arranged for the pickup and found out everything the CIA and Interpol knew about the guests in Floraidh's house.

Rhona Jepson was the widow of a banker named Currie, whose murder had, indeed, been related to those of Viv's roommates. It remained unsolved.

Humphrey and Lesley Haigh could've carpeted their home with the money they'd made and used the spare change to repave their garden paths. But they still lived in the same tiny two-bedroom cottage they'd rented when they were newlyweds. The only difference was that now they owned it. They had one child, a boy named Nesbit who ran their London store.

Iona seemed clean, but we had too little information on her for me to come up with a firm conclusion either way.

When Viv Jepson's file came up, I shoved the stool back from the dressing table and strode over to the window. Mum might've convinced the press to lie, but Interpol had a complete report. With pictures. Staring out at the towering Douglas firs and Scots pines of Culloden Wood, I tried to gear myself back to neutral. To swallow the lump in my throat and clutch the curtains hard enough that they'd soak up the sweat pouring from my palms.

Even caught in another woman's tragedy and my own struggle not to drown in it, I sensed him coming to me. I was surprised enough to turn and look when he didn't knock, but opened the door and walked in, shutting it softly behind him.

"So you don't need an invitation to cross my threshold anymore?" I asked.

Vayl's gaze went to my left hand. "When you accepted Cirilai, you made a great many things possible for me that could not have happened before."

I glanced at the ring he'd given me. A gold and ruby masterpiece his grandfather had crafted, it had been imbued with all the powers his family could summon to protect him from the horrible fate his mother had envisioned for him before she died. It connected us in ways I still didn't quite understand. Though I was beginning to wonder if it, more than anything else, was the catalyst that had matched us in the first place.

"Where's Floraidh?" I asked.

"Cole is demonstrating our equipment to her. He has, how do you say, ramped up the charm, so she is quite fascinated." His eyes wandered down my body, and when they returned to mine, brilliantly green in a face taut with desire, I remembered I hadn't quite finished dressing.

"Why—" I cleared my throat. Husky wasn't where I wanted my voice to be right now. "Did you need something?"

Oops. Loaded question, and one Vayl seemed only too willing to answer with action as he closed the distance between us. But he didn't touch me. Just stood near as a whisper as he said, "I know you hate it when I eavesdrop. But I felt your anguish from outside. What has upset you?"

I wanted to turn back to the window. Climb out and run into the trees, maybe do a little Scottish version of *Tarzan*. Only I couldn't blame my need to escape on my wild upbringing. Just a sense that I might never be free of horror. That in twenty years I could be skipping through life, thinking I'd somehow "made it," and I could read a story in the newspaper or see someone on the train who reminded me of that day in Virginia when my own nightmare had begun, and I'd *know* it had never let me go. It never would.

I took a deep breath, started with the least of my worries. That sad bowl of ashes and the samples I'd be handing off to some stranger during the opening ceremonies tonight. Vayl accepted the whole story with nothing more than a lowering of the brows, his substitute for any of a number of the four-letter words that relieved the worst of my stresses.

I moved on to the part that had burned holes into my guts. "Viv's on the level with her story. Whether that makes her our killer or not . . ." I shrugged, unable to go on. Those pictures. *Jesus.* You could distance yourself from the victims. But not from Viv's stoned and tragic face. Especially when you put it next to the before shot of an outgoing debate team member with a promising political career ahead of her.

"Viv's had it pretty rough since. She dropped out of college. Doesn't see any of her friends. Works at the library in her home-town and lives with her mom and Iona."

"So do you believe she has simply come because her mother will not let her stay home alone?" Vayl asked. "That she is, indeed, Bea? Or that she truly intended to find someone like us all along?"

"I prefer choice number three."

Vayl's brows lowered. "Disturbing, is it not, that the living allow the dead to exert so much power over them?"

We stared at each other for a second and then shook our heads, trading sheepish grins. "We're a couple of hypocrites, Boss."

He inched closer. "I wish you would not call me that."

I lifted my chin so I could look into his eyes, glittering like gems in his immobile face. "*Sverhamin,* then?"

"Ahh." His breath blew across my lips. "When you agreed to accept me as such, did you ever think you would find yourself here?"

"In Scotland?"

He gave me that semi smile that made my knees want to buckle. "Why is it that you love to tangle with my patience?"

"Well, having spent some time in the Vampere world, I can now say that being your *avhar* has taught me to entertain myself at your expense whenever possible. Because who knows when I'll have to turn around and smoke your ex-wife or kick your old girlfriend's ass?"

"Disa was never my girlfriend."

"She wanted to be."

Vayl slipped his hand around my waist. "What about you?" He ran the fingers of his other hand along my collarbone, which had mended during his trip to Romania. His touch sent such tremors through my body that my tongue flew to the roof of my mouth and stuck there.

"I did as you asked," he said. "I revisited the site of my worst memories. My sons' tombstones still stand where I set them over two hundred and fifty years ago. You cannot read their names anymore. I considered recarving them, and then I decided to let it be."

As they always did, his eyes had darkened while he talked about Hanzi and Badu. I was beginning to understand that their murders felt as fresh to him as my own losses did to me. He said, "You asked me to let them rest. To accept that I lost them so I could move forward. With you. All I can tell you is that I have begun."

I raised my hand to his cheek, slightly rough with evening stubble. I slid my fingers into his hair. "You are *so* brave."

Our lips came together so quick and hard that our teeth clicked and I felt blood on my lip, though I wasn't sure if it was mine or his. Didn't matter. The world had narrowed to breath, hot and quick. Fingertips leaving fiery trails across skin. His tongue tracing a path down my torso to my abdomen and, amidst my gasps of pleasure, his delighted whisper. "You wore it!"

I looked down as he brushed his finger against the belly ring he'd sent to me while we were apart. The interlocked golden hearts with their ruby centers swung gently from side to side as I smiled at him. "It's my favorite," I told him.

He pressed his lips against it and I clutched his shoulders, letting my head fall back against the window. Forget the Highlands. This was the escape I needed.

"Yo, Lucille!" Rapid knocking at the door and Cole's insistent voice calling, "You about ready to go?"

Shit, fuck, dammit! When Vayl rose he looked even more pissed than I felt. As he buttoned my shirt he murmured, "We are not finished with this."

"You'd better *not* be that big of a tease."

He wrapped his arms around me, lifting me until our eyes were on the same level. "Kiss me, woman."

CHAPTER ELEVEN

W hat took you so long?" Cole demanded when I opened the door.

"Where's Floraidh?" I asked.

"In her room getting ready. It's the one on the right across from the linen closet. I have a camera set up in her hallway and Albert's watching the feed, so you're free until she comes out. You have maybe five minutes before you're on." He stepped in and looked around suspiciously. "What's *he* doing here?"

"Research on your girlfriend," I said as I shut the door and went to look over Vayl's shoulder. He'd pulled the stool up to the makeup dresser and keyed Iona Clough into our database.

"She's not my girlfriend," Cole said, distracted from the door-knocking delay as I'd hoped he'd be. "What are you finding out?" He searched for a chair, found a cushy purple number in the corner, and pulled it up to the computer.

"Yeah, I'm kinda curious myself," I said. "I've already done the check on her."

"Nothing," Vayl told Cole.

"What do you mean, nothing?" he asked.

Vayl typed, entered, typed some more. "I mean Iona Clough seems normal enough." He dropped his hands to his lap.

"So you think she's Bea?" said Cole sarcastically.

"Perhaps. I do believe she is hiding something." He regarded Cole thoughtfully. "Ever since I have known you, women have consistently fallen at your feet. In all my life I have only met one other with such charm to turn feminine heads."

"Oh yeah?" Cole grinned. "What happened to him?"

"He died in an asylum. I think now he must have contracted syphilis, which was never diagnosed. Thus the dementia later in his life."

"Ew."

"My point is that the both of you truly appreciate women. You admire them, respect them, even love them for a time, and they sense that. They want to snuggle up to you as if you were living teddy bears. Except for Iona."

"Maybe she's a lesbian," I suggested.

Cole's eyes lit up and he practically clapped his hands. Vayl regarded me thoughtfully. "Do you suppose so?"

I shrugged. "She's obviously got somebody else she's really serious about."

"So serious she is not even warm to him? Jasmine, even you are Cole's friend."

I glanced at our third, acutely aware that I'd never given him an answer to his proposal. That I'd just hoped he'd figure out on his own we could never be more than friends, but we'd be idiots to let a stunted romance get in the way of that. I waited for the light to dawn. For Cole to look at me with a sense of letting go.

Didn't happen. He was too keyed on the mystery behind Iona.

"Maybe she's some heiress trying to escape the clutches of her overbearing parents."

I rolled my eyes at him. "Maybe you should write for Harlequin."

Vayl rose from the stool. "Try your charm on Rhona, Cole. Iona must have come with references. A woman like Viv's mother would never hire someone otherwise. Perhaps we can trace her through her last employers. We also need to capture a picture of her as soon as possible. I cannot believe the one in our database is so badly out of focus."

"That should be easy," said Cole. "Our cameras are set to shoot the second they detect movement."

"Are you sure Floraidh's convinced they're not just regular video monitors?" I asked.

Cole clapped a hand to his heart. "How could you think I'm such a bad actor? She believes we brought spectervids and electromagnetic field detectors and phantasonic probes for the 'job' we have lined up after this convention. And she couldn't wait for us to set them up when Vayl started counting out the notes. Albert's going to keep track of the feed while we're gone in case Bea decides to do some setup work when she thinks the place is deserted." Now it was his turn to frown. "You did clear my room? We wouldn't want Dormal charging in there and using your dad for a rug beater when he's turning out to be such a big help."

"They're all Scidair proof," I assured him, practically grinding my teeth that Albert had recruited himself another fan. "I should go," I said. "Floraidh could be leaving her room any minute."

"Me too," said Cole. "I want to make sure all the feeds are working before we take off."

"Jasmine, would you wait a moment? We need to discuss the assassin's most likely plan of attack." As Cole hesitated at the door, Vayl said, "Go on. We'll catch you up shortly."

His face pinching like he'd just swallowed one of his gum balls whole, Cole stomped out the door and slammed it shut.

"What's the deal?" I asked. "We've already decided Bea's probably going to hit Floraidh while she's asleep."

"This." Vayl grabbed me around the waist and backed me to the wall. Before I could take a decent breath his lips had covered mine. Fierce. Wild. Like taking a barrel over Niagara and stopping just short of the bottom. When he lifted his head I could hear myself panting.

"Again," I breathed.

"Soon."

Before I could truly see straight I found myself standing in the hallway, my hands braced against the wall because my legs still weren't teaming up, listening to my heart pound against my ribs as Vayl's door opened and closed just feet from my buzzing ears.

"Holy crap, I think I have just lassoed a comet."

Chapter Twelve

As I hiked upstairs I pulled a thin silver case out of my back pocket. It held the communications device that would allow me to talk to the guys from a distance of at least two miles. Cole had decided we needed a cool name for it, something catchy like walkie-talkie, only much less lame. After trying out and rejecting possibilities that included chattie-splattie and speak'n freak, he'd settled on the party line.

The microphones resembled beauty marks. Mine rested beside my lip. The receivers, just slivers of clear-coated wire that used a dangly gold earring as an anchor, wound around and into the ear. When we'd tried them in the airport, Cole had commented that his hoop made him resemble a pirate. If he'd have slid on an eye patch and blackened a few teeth I might have agreed. But Vayl pulled his off the best. Maybe it was his Rom ancestry or Bergman's sunscreen, but I thought he looked freaking *hot*. Kinda like Jake Gyllenhaal with fangs and a shudder-to-think-of-it past. Especially when he slapped on the transmitter, a barbed-wire tattoo that emphasized the bulge of his right bicep.

I grabbed the rail. *Holy crap, are my knees spazzing out under me? I thought that only happened in Victorian romance novels! Geez, the next thing you know I'll be having the vapors just when I need a steady aim!*

Resolutely redirecting my thoughts to matters more support-ive to my muscles—like whether I really believed Bergman's wrist-launched Mongoose-juice was gonna work against Bea's head fulla snakes—I made it to the fourth floor without once falling on my butt. When I reached the landing I noted the wall on my right, which led to Floraidh's room, had been covered with peach-tinted paper featuring tiny white flowers with yel-low centers.

Photos of the Scidairan and various women smiling as they posed in woodsy settings hung between the two doors to my left. I peeked in the first, surprised at how deep the linen closet ran. These old houses might not provide much storage space, but by damn when they built one, that sucker offered up some shelving. I didn't try the knob to the next room, my senses telling me a run-in with Dormal would be the result. And since I didn't have to play brave at the moment, I could freely admit she scared me a little. Walking close to her felt like sidling up to a pissed-off silverback.

With that in mind, I snapped the band of my way-cool watch, which had been storing up my kinetic energy for just such a mo-ment. As I sneaked past the doors it helped shield the sound of my movements. With that and Tolly's bracelet to protect me, I felt pretty confident that neither Scidairan could detect me.

As I passed Floraidh's room, I noticed a unique symbol inked on the upper-left-hand corner of the door. It resembled an upside-down Celtic cross. I didn't stop to study it, but it looked as if a real diamond had been set in its center. A glance at Dormal's door confirmed the same design.

Assuming Floraidh wouldn't allow a camera up here, Cole had only asked if he could set up an ectoplasm sensor at the far end of the hall. It perched on a round, cloth-covered table, nes-tled against a silk flower arrangement like an electronic tumor. It resembled a pair of mini binoculars held upright by a small tripod. On top of the binoculars sat a rectangular scanner whose marquee lights blinked red, green, and yellow in quick succession. Bergman had disguised all the equipment so beautifully it could've convinced an avid fan of the *Ghostbusters* movies. I stuck my tongue out at the double lenses as I returned to the stairs to wait.

I took a seat a couple of steps below the landing, just out of sight of the hallway. My noodly legs thanked me for the break, encouraging me to review the events that had led to their less-than-stellar function. And I'd like nothing better than to lose myself in the memory of the past few minutes. My whole body tingled, like I'd taken a bath in hot peppers. I had a wild urge to run back to Vayl's room, where I'd demand some sort of exotic striptease before shoving him onto his bed, after which—

Concentrate, Jaz. If Floraidh dies because you were fantasizing about the hunka-hunka-burning-love in the room next to yours, you will never, ever forgive yourself. Even if she is a certified scuz.

Within a couple of minutes I heard a door open. Then a knock. I eased to my feet. "Floraidh?" Dormal murmured.

Another click. "I'm ready."

"You look worried."

A pause. Small thump, as if Floraidh had let herself fall against the wall. "He came to me just now. Rose right out of Oengus's skull. Just a vision, of course, but Lucifer! I could have had a heart attack, it happened so sudden!"

Dormal sounded shaken herself when she said, "What did he want?"

"We have to do it sooner. He said tonight. Tomorrow at the latest."

"But . . . we're not ready! We need a thousand more—"

"We have to find a way! That young stud and his chic boss gave me five hundred just now to set up their useless equipment.

If we do well at the convention, we might make enough to force him to sell—"

"We can't press the spell that hard and you know it! Manipulations like these must be finessed, or they'll be discovered. Especially by a man with as tight a fist as that Haigh fellow. Scidair's wig, Floraidh, this scheme of yours is going to get us burned!"

"Or make us the most powerful coven ever to walk the earth! Think what we could accomplish if we succeed!"

"Are you sure this isn't personal?" *Huh, I'd have expected worry in her tone still. But that almost sounds like jealousy.*

"We've been *over* this!"

"Admit to me you don't miss—"

"This is about *us!* About our chance at eternity. Even Scidair finally had to leave the Path. If we succeed we will live *forever!*"

Low-voiced reply that I missed most of. The only words I caught were "I suppose" and "diamonds" before the women paused to think. Finally Flordaih said, "I might have an idea. Come on." Bustle of big women's thighs brushing quickly against one another as they rushed to the stairs. I sped down ahead of them.

"The Scidairans are on the move," I reported, glad that the party line picked up whispers.

"We will meet you downstairs," said Vayl.

"I'm getting the girls first," Cole said.

"Bring me back something to eat that isn't fruit," Albert demanded. *I knew we should've left him out of the loop!*

I preceded Floraidh and Dormal into the lounge. As soon as they saw me they stopped whispering like a couple of backbiting adolescents and gave me their version of a friendly smile. "Ready to go?" asked Floraidh sweetly.

"Just about," I said. "You know men. Always futzing with their clothes and makeup. I'm sure they'll be down soon."

She didn't even blink at my joke. Just turned to Dormal and said, "Would you be a dear and check the oven? I can't remember if I left it on or not." Her head swiveled back to me as if an invisible hand had cranked it. "You know, if I leave that blessed old cooker on long enough without something stewing inside it, the stench begins to be enough to raise the dead!" She howled, opening her mouth wide to let all the mirth escape in a gust that might have knocked over a less hardy broad. Since I'd left Lucille in charge, she joined in Floraidh's laughter, though she cut it off as soon as Dormal returned.

"All set," she said, wiping her fingers on a blue-and-white-checked towel. What had she done in the brief time she'd been gone? She was sweating like a shot-putter at the World Championships. And I was pretty sure that gray smudge in the middle of her forehead wasn't from bread mold.

What are you biddies up to? Before I could ask any probing questions, the rest of the guests trickled downstairs, first Vayl, then Cole, Viv, and Iona, followed by Rhona and the Haighs.

Iona had changed into a long denim skirt with a brown lace inset. It was held up by her teardrop belt, which she must've taken a buffer to since we'd last seen her, because it was now so shiny it almost glowed. Into it she'd tucked a gold short-sleeved sweater. Low-heeled boots completed the outfit.

Viv wore a boring beige knit dress that at least flattered her curves, and a pair of crimson heels with neat black bows at the toes. She and Cole were grinning at each other as they compared footwear, since his red high-tops matched her pumps. He'd opted for a pair of khakis with more pockets than a pool table and a black T-shirt with a Halloween ghost pictured on the front. The caption read, LOOK AFTER YOU LEAP CLUB: CHARTER MEMBER.

Rhona and Lesley Haigh hadn't changed, though they'd definitely refreshed their lipstick. Why did older ladies always go for cherry red? It made them look like corpses. And Humphrey had decided he needed extra cologne, which circled him like a life preserver as he came up to me.

I smiled as my nose hairs began to burn. Humphrey responded with equal kindness. "I couldn't help but notice that lovely ring on your finger," he said, motioning to Cirilai. "Curse of the trade, I suppose. Do you mind if I take a closer look?"

"Oh." *Shit yes! Get away from me, you reeking old penny-pincher!* I raised my hand. "Not at all."

He fished a jeweler's glass out of his pocket and squinched it into his left eye. "Oh, my, that is exquisite. Where, may I ask, did you get it?"

"From Vayl."

When Humphrey glanced his way, my *sverhamin* added, "It is a family piece."

"Ahh." He turned back to his inspection. "Would you mind taking it off? If I could just take a gander at the inside of the band—"

"Yes," I said flatly, leaving Lucille to be polite to some other stranger. This one didn't deserve her anymore. When he raised his eyebrows at me, as if he didn't take my meaning, I pulled my hand out of his paw and wiped it down my pants. Suddenly I wouldn't blame his wife if she had picked up a little hobby. This son of a bitch made me want to kill things, and I already had that outlet.

"Pardon me?" he said.

"I don't take it off." Okay, I had that one time. But it didn't count because I'd been under the influence of funky Vampere powers. Plus Vayl had been acting like an ass. For the same reason.

Lesley bustled to my rescue. "Leave the poor thing alone, Humphrey," she said, laying her hands on her husband's tweed-covered arm. "Engaged girls don't like to remove their rings."

"Well, it's damned hard on the stones and the settings," Humphrey declared. "Better get that cleaned and checked regularly," he said over his shoulder as his wife dragged him toward the front door, past Rhona and Floraidh, who were talking transportation.

"We were thinking of following you, if that's all right," Rhona said. "But is Castle Hoppringhill hard to find? And will you leave Tearlach open? We may want to return earlier than you'd planned to."

Floraidh tapped her fingernail to her chin. "The castle is straight down the road, about three kilometers from here. And your room key will open the front door." She dropped her arms as if coming to a decision. "Do let me know if you decide to leave GhostCon before me, won't you? I'll make sure Dormal goes back with you in case you find there's something you need before you go to sleep."

Yeah, you sound like a concerned innkeeper, but you just don't want them nosing around your goodies unsupervised, do you, Floraidh?

As if she'd read my mind, the Scidairan shot me a sharp look. "Where is your man, Albert?" she asked.

The lie slid off my lips ready-made, as if my subconscious had done the baking in advance. I said, "The trip exhausted him, but you know how it is when you're overtired. He felt too juiced to nap. So he took a sleeping pill. He'll be out till morning."

Her satisfied smile let me know I'd hit the mark on my earlier guess. Floraidh must have more nasty crap hidden around here than just her bowl-o'-death. The realization made me wish I had the time, and the backing, to spotlight *this* woman's ghosts. But since I had neither, I turned to ask Rhona a leading question about snakes.

A clatter from the kitchen startled me into silence. "What could that be?" wondered Dormal. She was such a bad actress she wouldn't even have made the cut for a high school play.

We all shuffled into the hallway and stared at the kitchen door, as if we thought it might sprout lips and explain the antics of its hidden inhabitants.

"Perhaps one of your cats?" Vayl suggested.

"I can't abide cats," Floraidh said. "Dogs are fine, which is why I allowed you to bring yours along. But cats are sly, sneaky creatures. We don't let them anywhere near the property."

Rhona's mouth dropped. I could see her prepping a protest. But Viv's hand on her wrist held her back. Both women jumped at least an inch off the ground when another series of metallic clangs shot through the door.

"Do you have a maid?" asked Cole. "Because it sounds like somebody's in there making milk shakes."

We crept to the kitchen door like the original group of characters you see in a horror movie. If I'd been forced to pick our first victims of the masked serial killer with the steak knife/hanging rope/sharpened high heel . . . Viv and Lesley. They looked about as scared as you can get without puking or peeing yourself. Since they seemed like responsible adults, I assumed they'd used the bathroom before coming downstairs. That left the upchuck. I slipped to the back of the group, giving them uninterrupted aim at Dormal's broad back just in case their cock-a-leekie soup came unglued.

Floraidh nodded at Cole and he opened the door, pushing it all the way into the room so the ten of us could squeeze into the doorway, as if a photographer on the other side had demanded a group shot of our heads peeking in from every which direction.

Viv hid her face in Cole's shoulder and Lesley screamed as the brown-suited man who'd nearly wrecked our van hours before yanked another cookie sheet out of the cabinet and let it bang to the floor. He straightened and turned to the women, scratching his short brown beard as he searched their faces, as if trying to place them in his memory. He'd pushed his hat back, revealing the wasted planes of his face, making me wonder if the rest of his body looked just as skeletal. Hard to tell beneath all that loose material, especially the way he stood, with his shoulders hunched over his lean chest, as if he'd been punched by too many bullies as a kid and still felt his midsection needed protecting.

"Who are you?" demanded Iona, her fingers pressed firmly against her belt buckle as if she thought it might snap if she breathed any harder.

He pointed his finger at her. Then he opened his hand to encompass all of us. "King Brude is the master of this territory. Defy him at your peril!"

Floraidh and Dormal exchanged satisfied little smiles. Expressions I'd have missed if I hadn't been watching for them.

"It's a ghost!" shrieked Humphrey. Despite the fact that I could've used hysteria as an excuse, I stifled an urge to slap him. There's always one dumbbell in the group who has to admit the obvious. As proven by his next statement. "He's gone!"

Yup, as soon as Humphrey'd put a title to him, our visitor had faded. We squeezed through the door, fighting for space since all of us wanted to be the first to touch those cookie sheets, determine they at least were real. I made it through first. Picked one up and put it on the counter, where it banged just like it had when he'd touched it. *Damn.*

Rhona began polling us. "Did you see it? You did? Are you certain?" When she was satisfied she announced, "We have all seen a collective apparition! Here, in Tearlach! History has just been made!" In an aside to Lesley she added, "Wait'll I tell the girls on the GAPT—Ghosts Are People Too—committee. They'll be so jealous!"

Viv had collapsed into a chair, pale, shocked past tears. Iona knelt beside her, rubbing her hands as if she'd just come in from a blizzard. "Did you get that recorded?" Floraidh asked Cole. "With your spectrum doohickey, I mean?"

He shrugged. "I might have. Let me check." He pulled out his Monise, a portable computer Bergman had designed. A multi-talented gadget, it talked to all the cameras as well as our laptop. "Un-freaking-believable," he murmured.

"What is it?" asked Vayl, who'd come to stand beside me next to the stove. I badly wanted to crack it open, see if the death bowl still rested inside.

"No video from the kitchen. At least, nothing until we came in." He glanced up at Floraidh. "I'm going to have to tinker with the settings. This shade is giving off much lower impulses than our equipment is built to record. But I think I can adjust it to pick up its energies if it comes back again."

As she nodded, Rhona strode up to her and grasped her arm. "You must let me help this ghost. The GAPT group was made for this very purpose! To protect innocent souls like the one we just witnessed from the foul specters in their own plane as well as the crass abuse of establishments who would use them as little better than zoo specimens!"

Floraidh narrowed her eyes until Rhona snapped her hand away, as if the Scidairan's skin had suddenly become too hot to handle. "We are a proper business. In my point of view, he was trespassing. If he returns, I can't be responsible for who sees him. And if it happens to be a group of tourists who have come calling just for that purpose, so much the better. I've got to make a living same as anyone else."

"WHAT!"

Viv leaped at her mother, with Iona following so closely the three of them resembled a huddling football team as Viv's fingers flew. Iona turned her back to Rhona as she interpreted. "Viv says maybe we should all get going. The convention organizers won't wait for us, even if her mum is presenting later in the week."

Rhona tried to shove through the shoulders of the younger girls so she could confront Floraidh as she spluttered, "You can't just put him on display like some sort of trophy! He's an innocent man!"

"No man is innocent, especially not that one." Floraidh made an I've-sucked-the-lemon-now face as she realized she might've let a little too much information slip. Then she rushed on, maybe hoping that none of us would stop to wonder how she knew the dead guy from the late nineteenth century. "I'll be welcoming tour groups through during the GhostCon if they wish to come. They won't be allowed to disturb your rest, of course. But if you prefer to find another place to stay, I completely understand."

"There *IS* no other place to stay! Every room within fifty miles has been sold out for the past six months!" Rhona declared.

"Well, then, I'll just have to do my best to see that your time here is as pleasant as I can possibly make it." Syrupy sweet, that voice, and so fake that if somebody could've given it shape and form, a plastic surgeon could've used it to round out some flat-assed woman's derriere.

"Oh! Oh!" said Rhona, her tank turret bouncing as she bobbed her head like she was trying to click off a few rounds and fuming because some blockhead had loaded all the guns with dummy shells. I looked into those bloodshot brown eyes of hers. Yup, if she could've, she'd have blown Floraidh to bits right there on the shiny wood floor. Which made her a more likely suspect. And me less inclined to stop her once she made her move.

I needed a conference.

Chapter Thirteen

While Viv's fingers flew and Iona murmured in a comforting tone, Floraidh moved to take a rectangular black silk shawl off of its spot on the coatrack by the front door. She flung it around her shoulders, covering the V-neck of her silky brown blouse, which complemented the teal in her stretchy slacks rather nicely. In contrast, Dormal's Alice in Wonderland ate-the-cake size probably made it tough for her to find socks that fit. Which might explain why she'd pulled on a white pantsuit whose jacket wouldn't button over her powder-blue polyester shirt and whose bottoms stopped an inch above her ankles. From the way she kept shifting they also looked to be giving her a permanent wedgie.

I dove into the uncomfortable silence like a first-timer off the cliffs of Hawaii. "Jeremy, if we're going to have a bunch of tourists cruising through here, maybe we should go outside and make sure our equipment is set up in more discreet locations," I said. Yup, that sounded just as awkward and loud as it had felt. Geez, why couldn't they grow grace in a test tube and then glue it to your personality like they do hair extensions?

Vayl said, "An excellent idea, Lucille. Do you suppose we have the time for that, Floraidh?"

"If you can accomplish it in ten minutes. We really must leave after that."

"Ten minutes it will be, then."

We slipped out the kitchen door, which took us into the garden I'd seen earlier, a grid of rock-lined plots containing masses of edibles that reached toward the last rays of the setting sun. We went to the first camera, which Cole had set up near the front corner of the house where the lane curved around to meet the barn. While Vayl moved it to the other side of the lane I told him about Dormal and Floraidh's discussion. "That makes this ghost's appearance quite convenient, does it not?" he asked.

"It's not a ghost."

"No?"

I shrugged. "I haven't had a chance to tell you about the time I spent with Tolly Mendez, but she's kind of an expert on Scidairans. And she told me ghosts disrupt their magic."

"Why is that?"

"Nobody's sure. The current theory is that because the Scidairans' main goal is to avoid death, and ghosts kind of personify that, the two mix about as well as geeks and gladiators."

Vayl said, "So, assuming we did not just see a ghost, what was it? I would not guess hologram. I do not believe they had the time to subvert our technology." I kinda thought he knew the answer and was just quizzing me. Good old Vayl. Why offer up your own vast store of knowledge when you have so much more fun eeking small nuggets out of others? Luckily I'd been paying attention in college.

I said, "I agree she wasn't playing camera tricks. But were you watching Dormal during that whole episode?"

"Not the entire time," he said.

"Me neither, but I did give her a glance or two, and she was working her ass off. Sweating, wordless chanting, and a couple of tugs at her hair. I couldn't tell for sure, but I think she's got something tied up under that shaggy do, because as soon as she touched it my senses went *zapola*. Considering that our visitor came with a message, I think what he was, what she raised, was a *loeden*."

Vayl's brows lifted. Okay, I admit, I'd reached with that one. *Loeden* weren't ghosts, but they weren't alive either. I wasn't sure where they fit into the nether hierarchy, except that as its postal system, they probably ranked near the bottom.

He said, "That is a powerful drawing spell. Especially for a single Scidairan."

"Well, who's to say she did it all by herself? They've got a whole coven going on. And even if the rest of them are lying low to keep the guests from bolting, they could've stored their powers somewhere for her to draw on. Kinda like the juice in all those masks the vamps had displayed on the wall back in your old Trust."

The tightening of Vayl's jaws told me he didn't appreciate the reminder of the time, not long ago, when his former mate had tried to suck him back into the community he'd barely escaped a century before.

I hesitated, reached out, and rested my hand on his where it gripped the camera's tripod. The other held just as tight to the blue jewel that topped his cane. I said, "Sorry. I shouldn't have—"

"No. You are my *avhar*. That gives you the right, no, the responsibility, to speak your mind."

"It doesn't mean I should dump on your feelings along the way."

His expression reminded me of a kid seeing an amazing new magician's trick. "Do you know how long it has been since anyone concerned themselves with my feelings?" He answered himself. "Such a stretch that I had begun to think my emotions were as damned as my soul." He looked down at our hands. Turned his so our fingers intertwined. The slide of his skin, warm against mine, made my breath come quicker. *Really? Is that all it takes? You are so easy.*

"Maybe there's hope for them both yet," I said.

His smile, so wide that it showed fangs, might've made me run once. Now I just responded to that fierce happiness with a couple of hard nods. No doubt anything else would've led to indecent exposure and my eventual humiliating arrest.

"Let's say Dormal did do a spell," I suggested, reminding him of why we'd left the house in the first place. "Maybe Floraidh even gave her a boost in there."

"It is possible," Vayl replied after taking a deep breath. "She was the one I watched the most, and I did note a few odd gestures that might be attributed to spell work."

I sighed. "It doesn't matter, does it? Because Bea is the one we're after."

Vayl nodded. "You are correct. But perhaps, once we know who the ashes belong to, we may take a new approach to this mission."

We shared a grim nod, understanding how remote that possibility stood right now. I said, "Remember, she was talking about somebody's bones earlier. What if she murdered the guy we just saw?"

"We turn her over to the authorities."

"Vayl, if you're right about his age, he's probably been dead over a hundred and twenty years. Which means she's done a helluva job ducking death. And I'm pretty sure it also means the statute of limitations on that crime expired a long time ago."

"Not as far as I am concerned."

"What, are you going all maverick on me now?" *And do you know how much that turns me on?*

"Not over this issue," he said seriously. "I simply mean there are courts other than those you humans run. Ones that would burn her to ash if we proved she had killed a man with magic."

I felt my eyes go oh-boy round. I'd never heard of such a thing before. Here again was part of that *avhar/sverhamin* deal Vayl had warned me about. One of the perks of our bond was info on the world of *others*. But he only leaked it when he thought I'd earned the right to hear it.

I said, "That sounds—interesting. And taking out Samos's strongest allies makes me feel a little bit like a kid again. But won't it upset the bad-guy balance the new Oversight Committee is trying to maintain?"

Vayl's eyes went black so suddenly I felt like all the air had been sucked from the room. I'd seen him mad. Just not this fast. And when he spoke, it was with the absolute lack of mercy he usually reserved for our targets. "You have not spoken with the senators, have you?"

"No."

"Avoid it. They are an even bigger group of fools than the last. All of them have agendas that lead me to believe they do not have our, or the department's, best interests at heart."

"O-kay . . ."

Vayl pinned his eyes to mine. I shivered and then stood still, thinking, *Wow, what did they do to piss him off?* He said, "While we will do our utmost to complete our assignments as charged, we are no longer concerning ourselves with what the Oversight Committee does or does not recommend, should extenuating circumstances force us to act independently."

"Did you get that from Pete?"

"No. He is too bound by their budget to dare oppose their harebrained suggestions."

"Vayl?" I licked my lips, trying to convince myself the fist squeezing my guts wasn't a scary premonition. "Are you going to get me fired?"

Those black-on-black eyes bored into my brain as his husky baritone echoed in my ears for several minutes after. "Maybe."

Chapter Fourteen

After that neither of us had much left to say. We joined every-body at the front door and led our group to the van while the rest went to their cars, which were parked in a small paved lot just off the circular drive our vehicle dominated. I kept my eye on Rhona, secretly hoping she'd stage a big catfight. That would be a nice distraction from my dark thoughts. Unfortunately Viv and Iona stuck to her like a couple of Secret Service agents, hustling her into a titan-gray Bentley Brooklands before she could do anything worse than shoot Floraidh a dirty look.

So I drove the three miles to Castle Hoppringhill, following Floraidh's blue Volkswagen Polo and Rhona's I'm-a-bitch, hear-me-roar car down black and winding roads. Our pace would or-dinarily make me scream at them to move the parade route off the main drag. But I was so distracted I only vaguely registered the fact that I'd reached down for a comforting Jack scratch and encountered an empty space where he usually sat. Because Vayl was going to get me fired. I just knew it. And my brain couldn't decide whether to shriek or explode.

No, I'm not doing this again. Flipping out about possibly losing this job while I try to kick ass at it. I can't function like that anymore. I won't. I took a deep breath. *I'm gonna help Vayl whip this mission.*

And if there's any bullshit to straighten out afterward, I'll deal with it then. Wait, can you straighten bullshit? Maybe "flatten" would be better?

Having made a game plan, I felt more focused than I had since Albert had shown up at Gatwick's Gate Three, toting his ratty brown overnight bag, his Bears jacket hooked over one arm. I didn't think I could've been more blown away if he'd shoved the barrel of his .45 against my forehead and shot my brains out the back of my skull. It was nice to finally regain some of that balance.

I glanced into the rearview. Lesley and Humphrey had taken the seat just behind mine, their silence making me wonder if they'd had a fight during my brief absence from the group. Maybe she'd finally told him to stop acting like such an ass.

Cole sat alone in the back while Vayl rode shotgun, keeping a sharp eye on the vehicles in front of us and the surrounding area. So far, nothing. Bea was still playing it conservative. *Good call. I wouldn't pull a hit while guests crowded Floraidh either. Better to wait until everybody was snoozing. Especially if you really are a Medusa.*

When the castle appeared, shooting above the surrounding trees like an enormous old war machine, my first reaction was relief that I wasn't a raider trying to take down the well-armed Scotsmen inside. Damn. That massive collection of towers and battlements seemed to stretch for a couple of miles in every direction. Not to mention the wall around it, which was only interrupted by a single electric gate. And once we got inside, we had to cross a stream using one of those plank bridges that made you feel if you put a tire wrong you'd end up replacing your entire exhaust system.

GhostCon workers, wearing orange vests and waving glowing yellow devices that looked so much like dildos I could hear Cole snickering behind me, directed us to a stretch of lawn beyond the castle's interior wall. Green as a golf course, it was big enough to hold eighteen holes, so the couple of hundred cars lined up in neat rows fit just fine.

Granny May, who spent a lot of time lounging around the forefront of my brain, had taken to hanging out the wash as she did her imaginary gabbing with me. She used the old-fashioned, no-spring clothespins, and her line kind of sagged in the middle because Gramps Lew tended to let home improvement chores go until he finally got fed up with her bitching. As I pulled into a space between a couple of vehicles that looked more like packing crates than automobiles, she said, *Take a look at this parking lot! These ghostlusters are crawling out of the damn woodwork!*

Some patience, Gran. A lot of them are here because they've lost somebody dear to them and they think the person's still floating around.

What would you do if you thought I was a ghost?

Force you into business. You'd be great entertainment at slumber parties.

We managed the hike to the ironbound front doors without losing anyone, though Dormal was panting slightly from carrying bags and boxes, and the Haighs complained the whole way that the Con organizers should've picked a more accessible spot for their gathering.

Cole rolled his eyes at Iona, who responded with an indifferent shrug. Despite her lack of interest in him, we'd still decided he should stick with the girls. Since Viv clearly dug him and Iona had to hang with her, he shouldn't have a problem keeping an eye on them. Plus Rhona should stay close to Viv, giving him charge of three suspect-Beas. But the matchup couldn't be too obvious. So we'd come up with a plan that would lump them together, leaving Vayl and me to shadow the Scidairans and the Haighs. Of course, the fluidity of events might require us to change partners and responsibilities, but at least we had a place to start.

Our plan began along with GhostCon, just inside the front door. In a hall where sky-high pillars held up the room's corners, and a parquet floor had been designed to portray the story of Morag emerging from Loch Morar to bite off some poor fisherman's head, convention organizers dressed in black polo shirts and beige slacks had set up two rows of tables on opposite sides of the entryway. Behind the tables to our left sat four groups of two women, each of them guarding a stack of papers, a three-by-five file holding preprinted name cards, and plastic badges on red lanyards. Signs taped to the front of the tables told us where to line up alphabetically if we were preregistered. Another sign directed walk-ins to the other side of the aisle.

People packed the room. Some of the overflow even straggled up the grand staircase, which intersected the walk-in tables like a superhighway. It, in itself, caught the imagination with its enormous stone balusters and a mile-long tapestry at the first landing depicting a coiled serpent with a dragon's head rearing to strike as a knight charged it with a burning lance. Pretty striking stuff. But even that didn't draw the eye like the paying customers.

When I say they dressed for the occasion, I'm talking costuming by Hollywood on its best day. I recognized Dickens's Christmas ghosts, as well as Casper, the Headless Horseman, and Harry Potter's poltergeist, Peeves. Others had chosen less identifiable characters. Guys in monks' robes with fake axes buried in their heads. Women in eighteenth-century frocks with nooses dangling from their necks. And one odd couple whose blue makeup and sewn-on kelp seemed to symbolize a double drowning. I got the feeling the getups were supposed to be cool, but I kept getting the oddest urge to whip out handfuls of candy for their tricks-or-treats.

All of us Tearlachers found our respective tables and took our places in line. Floraidh finished first, but decided to wait for Dormal, whose line wound around a metal pole with a red velvet rope connecting it to another pole standing in the center of the room. I guess that's how karma slaps you when you claim your last name is Smith.

When it was my turn I pasted on my best smile and said, "Lucille Robinson." The volunteer looked up at me. And just as I was thinking she should never sport a ponytail because it made her look like she needed a year's supply of Rogaine, her face did one of those stretchy numbers the TV camera sometimes pulls to simulate an acid trip.

I leaned forward, bracing my left hand on the table, moving my right into my jacket. As my fingers slid around the grip of my gun, another face swam into focus on top of hers. Edward Samos. Looking healthy and smug as a Grand Champion Fair pig. "Such power in a name," he said. "Can you really kill a man if you don't know his true identity?"

Since Cole's cover name started with a T, his was the hand that snaked out to pull me upright. "Lucille? Are you okay?"

No way was I looking away from that face again. "Are you feeling anything . . . unusual right now?" I asked Cole.

Samos's body clapped her hands. She said, "Oooh, are you channeling a Visitor? We usually get quite a few at the opening ceremonies." The longer she talked, the less she resembled my nemesis, as if his features melted into hers with each expression switch.

Cole said, "No. I've got nothing."

I grabbed the tag the woman held out for me and backed up a step. "Me neither. Not really." By now Samos had faded completely. *Son of a* bitch! *I can't really be seeing his ghost. Can I? But that would be better than the alternative. Which would be that I'm losing my marbles. Again.*

I mentally reviewed the moment of his death. It had seemed like every other vampire's passing. That horrified moment of realization. And then, poof. Vapor, wafting away on the wind while the few bits and pieces that remained of his physical self fell to the ground. But before that. Just prior to the big finale, he'd scraped up a small pile of grass and dirt, spit on it, and begun to chant over it in a language I now knew belonged to the followers of Scidair.

Did he manage to save some part of himself? And if so, how can I find out for sure?

I know one tall, buzz cut, and handsome bumming around in the stratus that you haven't talked to in a while, said Granny May as she bent over her brown wicker laundry basket. *He'd probably have an idea. Or at least give you some peace in the matter.*

He's not allowed to interfere. Besides.

What?

He doesn't like Vayl.

So?

I haven't figured out how I feel about that, okay? I thought we were all pretty much on the same team.

There's dissent in every rank.

But he's supposed to be above that. Literally. He's an Eldhayr, for crying out loud!

Granny May shoved back the edge of the sheet she'd just clipped to the clothesline. *From what I understand, so are you.*

Okay, we're not even going there. You got that?

She gave a whatever shrug. *Raoul is your Spirit Guide. Sooner or later you're going to have to work something out with him.*

You dropped a sock.

Where?

With my sensible side distracted, I ignored the problem a while longer while I assured Cole I was fine. I moved toward the murmuring crowd filling the back section of the front hall and heading toward the open doors of the great room, where most of the activities would take place. I took a program from a woman dressed in the Hoppringhill tartan and used it to fan myself as I leaned against a wall and eyed the rest of Tearlach's guests back at the registration tables. Cole sidled up beside me.

"I'll bet this place is a bitch to clean," I said as I motioned to the series of velvet banners hanging from the ceiling.

Cole didn't want to talk about dusting. At least not that kind. "Tell me you weren't going to pull on that nice woman," he murmured.

Vayl's voice filled my left ear. "Did the clerk threaten Floraidh?"

I didn't want to tell him the truth. But what kind of lie would make me sound less crazed? I said, "Her face morphed into somebody else's while I was looking at her, talked to me in his voice, and then changed back."

"Who?"

"Samos."

He didn't laugh. Not even that choking gasp that passed for his chuckle. "Has this happened before?"

"Yeah, once on the plane. And once at Gatwick, when I was standing at the counter, waiting to buy a muffin."

"We need to discuss this. But now Floraidh and Dormal are moving toward the great room. I overheard them discussing their table setup. Perhaps you two should take your places."

Cole and I allowed the Scidairans to pass and then moved into the crowd after them. As we ambled toward the arched openings leading to a vast, open-span room, Rhona came up from behind me and grasped my forearm, her grip bruising. "Come on, now, let me give you the grand tour," she said as she dragged me forward. "On the way we can talk about parliamentary reform. Did you know my MP has a degree in Occult Studies?"

Just as I was narrowing my choices of pressure points and taking advance pleasure in the look on Rhona's face when I knocked her out, Vayl reached my side. Rolling our plan into motion he said, "Rhona, I believe Iona is looking for you. They cannot seem to find Viv's identification tag or her name on the list. The woman is getting rude, which is upsetting her. She says she wants to go back to the B and B."

Rhona dropped her hand and swung around like she was about to pound through the doors of the nearest saloon and gun down the first hombre who crossed her. "These people are complete nitwits! *Now* do you see why I prefer dealing with the dead?" As she stalked off, Vayl slipped Cole the missing papers.

Palming them so neatly I wondered if he'd worked his way through college as a card shark, Cole said, "Hang on, Rhona. Maybe I can help. I once organized my Scout troop's father-son wiener roast." Flashing us a grin, he strode after her.

Chapter Fifteen

With the Jepson group about to fall into Cole's debt and his charm dialed to life-of-the-party, Vayl and I felt comfortable turning our backs on them for the time it took to lock on to the rest of Tearlach's boarders and assess the most likely means of Bea's attack, should it come during the opening ceremonies.

Lesley and Humphrey had hustled to the front row, where they'd scooped up the seats to the right of the aisle and, from the look of their campsite, didn't intend to release them for the duration of the Con. Floraidh and Dormal, weighed down with supplies for their booth, were working their way through a swelling crowd of avid ghost fans who'd only now begun to seat themselves. Most still stood in groups of anywhere from two to fifteen among the double rows of chairs set up in the east half of the red-carpeted room. They kept looking eagerly toward a temporary platform, on which the organizers had placed a podium with a microphone wired to two large black speakers that sat at the front corners of the stage. A pair of long, narrow tables set with pitchers of water and glasses, and slightly nicer chairs than the ones reserved for the audience, flanked the podium.

You reached the entire setup via a set of rickety stairs that made me hope all the speakers had sworn off donuts the month before. If they made it safely to their seats, they might be impressed by the roughly plastered wall, which soared to a peak behind them. It had been painted with a massive representation of the Hoppringhill's coat of arms, five scallops on a crossed scarlet ribbon.

A minute later Floraidh and Dormal popped out of the crowd onto the west side of the great room. This held a variety of booths, some built to resemble lemonade stands, some looking like mazes with their multiple lattice walls folding in odd directions. This portion of the room could be shut off by an electronically controlled curtain that moved up and down like a shade. At the moment only a couple of feet of it peeked out of its tubular metal ceiling-mounted casing.

The Scidairans found their booth right away. The haunted-house facade, complete with a ghostly figure staring out the tower window, was kinda hard to miss. A young woman dressed in white sat on the "front porch" behind a long wooden table. Dormal started unpacking while Floraidh chatted with the woman, who had to be a coven member. Even from across the room she scented *other* to me. But without my Sensitivity I think I'd still have guessed bad guy the second I laid eyes on her. She had Floraidh's steam-cleaned demeanor, her bouncy blond hair and rosy cheeks making her seem like the kind of girl who'd organize a food drive for the homeless. Until you spent some time on those snapping brown eyes that left her lips and teeth to smile without them. Plus, she let them linger on people a beat too long. Like a python who's sizing up her next meal. Floraidh said something to her and she bared those teeth again. Was it me, or did they seem a little sharper than your normal burger grinders?

"I wonder what they are talking about," said Vayl.

"Too bad we couldn't put a bug on them. I wonder if they really would've found it."

Vayl's shrug was less, *I don't know,* than, *Hey, you're the one who consulted the Wiccan.*

I opened the program as Floraidh and Dormal turned back toward us. While Vayl kept an eye on them I began to read. A couple of paragraphs later I said, "These Connies function like vampires."

"Excuse me—Connies?"

"Yeah, you know, people who spaz out over theme conventions? Like that dude over there who's dressed as Hamlet's father?"

"Ah, I see. Go on."

"They've got a whole night full of goodies planned. Panel discussions here in the great room. Smaller talks by different experts in the kitchen, dining room, library, and billiard room, not to mention several of the bigger bedrooms. GhostWalks every fifteen minutes starting right outside the front door. Those you have to pay extra for."

"How long do the opening ceremonies take?" Vayl asked.

"Half an hour. It looks like the lights are going out at the end, so be ready for that," I said. "They've hired a couple of the best Raisers in the biz, according to the program. Gerard Plontan and Francine Werry. Have you heard of them?"

Vayl shook his head. "Should we assume they know what they are doing?"

"Well, they're here. That's probably significant. This says they're going to try to summon the castle ghosts for the crowd." I held the booklet up for him to see. "They actually have a warning in here for people to keep their hands off the phantoms."

We looked at each other and together chimed, "Liability."

Vayl added, "Surely everyone here understands how angry a shade would become if he were to be touched by the warmth of humanity. The reminder would throw him right back into the Thin."

"It seems weird to me that a place like that should exist," I said.

"Why?"

I shrugged. "I just wouldn't think either side would tolerate such chaos."

Vayl shook his head. "You must always factor in freedom of choice, my *pretera*."

I thought of the deaths I'd witnessed since my Sensitivity kicked in. The multifaceted souls that had split apart like shards from a perfect stone, each of them taking off in a new direction.

"I'm trying to imagine why any bit of a soul would want to linger in a place as brutal as the Thin," I said.

"Come now," Vayl scoffed.

"No, really, I don't get it."

He leaned in, took a deep breath with his eyes closed, as if the smell of my shampoo made his digits tingle. "Life is sweet. Even when all you can hope for is to catch the scent of a human heart filling its body with vigor."

"Is that—"

"No. You know you mean infinitely more to me than that. Now, what else is in the program?"

I flipped through the pages. "Well, according to the program, the castle has at least seven ghosts ranging from a warrior who died at Culloden, to a young groom who was kicked in the head by a horse, to a nineteenth-century owner who either fell, jumped, or was pushed from an upper-story window, leaving his wife free to marry the guy she'd been boffing on the side. But in case you start feeling too bad for him, she died six months later and is rumored to haunt the bedroom where the cheating took place." I looked up at Vayl. "She did it right under his nose?"

"He must have been stupid *and* blind."

The lights dimmed, like in a theater setting, to let the crowd know the show was about to begin. People took their seats, led by the convention's star speakers. They crested the scary steps without incident (though the middle one creaked alarmingly beneath one guy who probably hadn't seen his toes since 1975).

Floraidh and Dormal found a spot left of the aisle, about halfway back. We worked our way toward them as Cole's voice rang on the party line. "No, really, it was nothing. I'm just good at finding things, that's all. When my mom misplaces her purse she still calls me."

Trickle of appreciative feminine laughter as he went on. "Hey, I see Lucille and Jeremy. Should we sit with them?"

At this point Rhona might've demanded that they all charge the stage, requesting group photos and autographs, but Viv and Iona would've clung to Cole like barnacles on a barge. He'd worked his magic again.

Vayl and I stopped, looking over the field of chairs as if to discuss where to sit to get the best view, but really to give the rest of the Tearlachers a chance to close in. Cole put his arms around both our shoulders as he and his groupies caught up to us. "Good news!" he said, grinning. "Viv is back in business!"

He stepped aside so we could see her, showing off her name badge as Rhona and Iona beamed beside her. *What a happy little group we make. And out of the six of us, at least three are assassins. No wonder people never truly get to know each other. So much happens under the surface that we never reveal. Even to ourselves.*

Which was when it struck me. *I think I know why none of the other guests have tweaked my Spirit Eye, despite the fact that Bea must wield some major powers if she can subvert a Seer and control the most venomous land snake in the world. She doesn't know about her violent side.*

My brother had also functioned for some time completely unaware of his actions. Only two months ago he'd been the puppet of a necromancer. Yeah, it takes badass power to kill a man, trap his soul, and enslave his body, but the Wizard had accomplished just that, using Dave as a mole within his own unit until we'd finally rescued him.

Another reason you should keep talking to Raoul, Granny May reminded me. *Dave would've died for good without his intervention.* Uh-oh. She was setting up the bridge table. That meant she was in it for the long haul.

Could we talk later? I asked. *I'm trying to figure out why Bea is out of touch with herself. So much so that I can't pick up even a pinch of her power.*

Do you think someone else is pulling her strings?

I considered the possibility. Nope. Our contact had specified that the Weres had hired Bea personally. Which meant she was in charge. Some of the time. But if she was a dual personality, shouldn't I still be able to read *other,* even when Bea was latent?

Talk to Raoul, Granny May urged.

All right, I will, I snapped. *But I won't be happy about it.*

Which was why I toted my alter ego around on every assignment. I might throw off disgruntled vibes so thick you wanted to bathe in peaches and cream after standing beside me for five minutes. But Lucille beamed at her new friends as we all found seats a couple of rows behind Floraidh and Dormal, and waved happily at Lesley Haigh when she made eye contact. She wiggled her fingers at me, made an aren't-these-great-seats? gesture, and then leaned over to whisper in Humphrey's ear. He shushed her as the first speaker walked up to the microphone.

The ceremonies began with the typical introductions and profuse thanks of organizers nobody knew or cared about. But we smiled and clapped. Anything to stroke the egos while we pined for the real fun to begin. I sat midrow, with Vayl to my left and Viv to my right. Cole and Iona filled the seats next to her, while

Rhona took the chair to Iona's right. Despite the number of laps between us, Rhona didn't hesitate to lean over our companions to tell me, "It should be very exciting this year. The keynote speaker is an author friend of mine who lives in a haunted house in Wales. Some of the most well-respected researchers on the planet have come to lecture, and the Raisers they've brought in are top-notch! Watch, just watch!" she demanded, jamming her finger toward the stage, as if to depress an imaginary button that was wired to the Instant Obedience section of my brain.

I nodded politely, gave her a thumbs-up, which I just barely kept from turning sideways and jamming into her eye sockets. *Not killing the annoying ones. Some days that's the hardest part of this gig.* From the look on her face, Viv might've felt close to the same. Only mothers can make us so crazy.

As I sat through the introductions of the most well-known guests and the keynote speech, I could hardly keep myself from heckling. Like most people who want something so badly they can taste it, this group had chosen to ignore some of the basic truths involving those who couldn't quite manage to depart this life. Among those, the fact that, despite resembling their human selves (when they managed to form at all), they'd become something else entirely. Balls of confused, obsessed, spirit-potential. Highly unpredictable. Prone to outbursts of rage that could cause small splits in the wall between worlds. And if you were standing too close to that wall, the impact hit you like a red-hot knife blade piercing your flesh. Which was why Raisers carried so many scars.

Despite the fact that a really irritated ghost could cut deep enough to sever an artery, these "experts" and their loyal fans saw them as victims. Poor, trapped souls who needed to be released, educated, or, in Rhona's case, protected by law so their rights would no longer be trampled by the living. At least Rhona wanted the most vicious among them punished.

She cheered the loudest when her hero, Dr. Oliver Bendelfield, stood up to give a brief overview of his upcoming lecture, which would detail how the living continued to exorcise ghosts, effectively destroying them, when what they needed was the attention of companies like his. (Profitable) enterprises that worked to either free them or direct them to hell, depending on the color value of their ectoplasm.

"That's why we have to organize!" said Rhona, tears in her eyes as she pounded her hands together after Dr. Bendelfield had gone back to his chair. "So ghost rights will be recognized and they won't be exterminated before groups like his, and yours, can be found that will give them the afterlife they deserve!"

As Viv dropped her head into her hands, clearly wishing she lived on another planet, the woman in front of Rhona nodded enthusiastically. But I noticed her twisting her wedding ring around and around her finger. Smiling down at it regretfully. To me she represented the other school of reality deniers. The grieving bereft who'd heard the house creak after midnight, seen a long-lost face in the mirror mist after a shower, and decided their loved one hadn't completely moved on after all.

Her view was the one I understood. Hell, right before I'd come on this assignment the phone had rung, and for a split second I'd thought, *Maybe it's Matt!* The yearning to turn around and see him, even as an indistinct figure lost in an ethereal haze, had overwhelmed me at the beginning. What pissed me off now was the number of amoral assholes who'd set up stations around the perimeter of the great hall solely designed to take advantage of that kind of longing.

Viv's feelings had intensified to such a degree that my Spirit Eye had begun to click like a Geiger counter. Though she worked to keep her face blank, I knew that Rhona's behavior humiliated and worried her at the same time. She kept an eye on Cole's hands, since he'd taken over the translating for now. She clapped at the appropriate moments. Laughed in the right places. Followed her program by keeping her finger on the spot and moving it down a tick every time a new speaker came up to the stand. But her mom wasn't making it any easier for her to survive tragedy. It was starting to tear her up all over again.

As Gerard Plontan and Francine Werry came to the front of the platform to do their ghost-raising routine, Vayl, Cole, and I shared a nod. My eyes went to Iona. One last glance before the lights dimmed. She looked, not at the stage, but around the room. Her eyes rested on an exit near the front, to the right of the stage. Bounced to two or three different people I'd have picked out as troublemakers. Twisted around to double-check the back exits: the main one we'd come through, its doors now closed, and a single door on the west side of the room. Then, stroking her belt buckle, she turned back toward the stage, ignoring Floraidh and Dormal completely.

Hmm, interesting moves there, Iona. Almost along the lines of what I'd choose. If I was some sort of cop. Or bodyguard? It made sense. Viv probably needed a little extra protection to make her feel safe nowadays. So you hire Iona to do translating you don't necessarily need to mask the fact that you're paying her to give Viv some peace of mind. But her skill set would be a rare combination in anybody. One I'd almost expect her to use a little voodoo to put together. Which I didn't sense in the least.

While my suspicions of Iona inched upward, I couldn't find one extra reason to wonder at any of the other women. Neither Rhona, Viv, nor Lesley Haigh had even glanced at Floraidh since they'd entered the great room. But should that surprise me? If my theory held true, whoever Bea was must have no idea she was half of a personality pair.

But just in case Bea decided tonight might be a fine night to introduce herself, I considered the weapons I'd brought in with me. I carried the Mongoose on my left wrist. I'd kept the holy water strapped to my right. For backup my bolo still rode in my hip pocket. Grief hid under my jacket, more a comfort than a go-to gun in this situation. Not that I expected anything now, surrounded by witnesses as we were. Then Viv excused herself.

Really? Now you decide to leave?

"But this is the best part!" Rhona fumed.

"I can't help it," Viv said through Cole. "I have to go to the ladies' room."

As Iona rose to accompany her, Viv waved her back to her seat, her impatient gesture one even I could interpret. *I can pee all by myself, dammit!*

Rhona moved her sensible black bag out of the path and Viv inched her way toward the center aisle. As soon as she reached the exit, Vayl stood. "Not you too!" Rhona exclaimed.

Vayl's hypnotic voice soothed her. "I will only be a moment. Do not fret. I shall not miss a thing." She sat back happily as he left in the opposite direction Viv had taken, moving past eight or ten eager Connies who were straining to see the Raisers better. If he was trying to annoy fewer people by taking a different route out, he failed. But he did make it to the western side of the room, where he left by the smaller door.

Gerard Plontan, standing at one corner of the stage, watched them go. A Jack Black clone, he wore a navy blue bowling shirt with green diamonds running down the front over a pair of baggy green corduroys. I wasn't sure why he didn't wear socks with his loafers, but it was better than Francine's choice. Yeah, somebody really should've told her pink bobby socks with beige sneakers, a red plaid skirt, and a SAVE THE WHALES! T-shirt spelled embarrassment-to-your-grandchildren. She held down the other corner of the stage while the two of them waited patiently for the background music to build. At the melody's climactic moment, beams of green, purple, red, and yellow lights flashed across the stage.

The Raisers held their hands out nearly perpendicular from their bodies. The choreography, simple and yet stunning, timed perfectly with the music as their hands inscribed runes into the air that the lights imitated. As they began to step toward each other, their movements so measured and precise that neither one wavered for an instant, I wondered why they did it. The danger of their profession was written clearly across Francine's forearms and both their faces. Scars, most white, a couple still pink and glaring, crisscrossed each other like tic-tac-toe boards.

Hypocrite, drawled my inner bitch. She'd moved from her regular bar stool to a booth, the better to ogle the half-dressed cowboy dancing on the stage in front of her. *It's not like you spend all day knitting afghans for the homeless.*

Yeah, but at least the risks I take make sense. I'm saving lives.

Sure. But I'll bet the Raisers make more money.

I tried on that perspective. So what was a little permanent disfigurement when you compared it to a hefty bank account?

Nope, it just wouldn't fit.

But Gerard and Francine, well fed and eager for more dough, thought it looked terrific on them. Moving in perfect unison, they tiptoed gracefully toward each other until they stood shoulder to shoulder.

I leaned toward Cole. "How do you like the show so far?"

He put his lips against my ear. "I'm starting to think this sucker will never end. Which makes me believe it's for more than just entertainment. Plus, you remember the background stuff they made us read so we'd sound like we belonged in this business?"

"Yeah. The practical part of this shouldn't take more than twenty seconds."

"Any tingles in your Sensitive areas?" He wiggled his eyebrows. *Dork.*

"No. How about you?"

"Nope. As far as I can tell it's just a couple of hacks up there doing their version of a third-grade dance recital."

Iona leaned into our powwow. "What are they doing?" she asked.

Cole said, "They're supposed to be carving a breach in the Thin. One just big enough for the ghosts who call this castle home to step through. It's pretty exacting work, but doesn't take that long if you know what you're doing. Except—"

He jerked his head toward me. I'd felt it too. A rumble beneath my feet, like the aftershock of a mild earthquake. A gasp from the back of the room turned my head. Something moved over the heads of the crowd sitting on the opposite side of the aisle.

At first all I could see when I stared at it was a rippling in the air, like heat rising from asphalt in the noonday sun. As soon as the light engineer figured out the score, he directed the lasers to the disturbed air. They rebounded, outlining the figure of a short, squat man. I opened my Spirit Eye as wide as I could manage, straining my extra sense, but I couldn't see into his plane. It wouldn't be long until I'd wish differently.

The crowd did an audio wave, moving their murmur of wonder from one edge of the room to the other in a perfect progression of sound that washed over us, giving Rhona goose bumps. Yeah, I was watching more than the show. But it sure seemed like she and Iona were glued to the sight of more forms, these clearly visible, appearing from inside the walls, dropping from the ceiling, one even emerging from the podium, making the expert who sat closest to her scream.

In the end seven ghosts stood just to the right of the center aisle, including the one who could only be seen in reflected light. They lined up like homecoming court nominees. I wasn't a great judge of costume, and theirs weren't easy to make out, but it looked to me as if they covered almost the whole life of the castle, from the time it had been built in 1630, to the 1960s.

"I'm Seeing something now," I whispered to Cole.

He slipped into the chair Vayl had vacated. "What is it?"

"It's like a noose around every one of their necks, connecting them to the Raisers, but also to the ceiling and the floor. Do you See it?"

"No. They look like apparitions to me. Except now they're floating. Hey"—he smacked me on the thigh with the back of his hand—"I just thought of a new game."

"What's that?"

"Splat the Specter."

"Rules?"

"You can help me make them up. Right now all I know for sure is that it involves water guns filled with grape Kool-Aid and two ferrets named Biff and Chlamydia."

Vayl's voice filled our ears. "Why ferrets?"

"Really?" I asked. "You want to know about his *choice* of pets when he's named one of them after an STD?"

Rhona shushed us, jabbing her finger toward the stage. The ghosts had risen at least three feet into the air, one by one, as if being introduced to the crowd. And the audience was fixated. Especially when it came to the phantom Highlander, who must've towered over his comrades on the battlefield just as he did now, and who'd remembered his claymore so clearly in life that he still carried the sword in death, strapped to his back for those occasions when the dirk at his waist just wouldn't fill the bill. Yup, he impressed every Connie in the joint. Except for Humphrey Haigh. Who hadn't read the program. Or, apparently, been terrified into sleeplessness by his buddies' ghost stories like the rest of us had when we were kids.

He reached forward, his hand hovering within inches of the

Highlander, who'd sunk back down to the floor. Francine Werry, not daring to move from her spot, shook her head at Humphrey. Despite the thickness of his glasses lenses, he didn't see her. Or maybe he just chose to ignore the don't-touch-the-ghost-warrior alarm in her triple-wide eyes.

His fingers spread apart, as if he meant to grab a fold of the Highlander's kilt. Though I could see the stage through it, the green-and-black plaid still spoke of his family's proud heritage. This soul had taken a great deal into the afterlife with him. But not enough to merit a full move. Why had he stranded part of himself in the Thin? Could he, or any of the others, ever escape? Did they even want to?

Humphrey knew what he wanted. And that was to go home at the end of his vacation with the right to brag about how he'd touched an actual phantom. At the last second Lesley tore her eyes from the magnificent ghost and caught her husband's intent. She grabbed his arm and yanked it down, hissing into his ear. He shrugged her off. Since she kept a firm grip on the hand she'd captured, Humphrey reached forward with the other. And shoved it through the Highlander's hip.

Chapter Sixteen

It only takes one dickhead to spoil a party. The amazing thing is that the host keeps inviting the girl who's dating him. Our version had about half a second to slap her asshole upside the head before the ghost he'd defiled roared with outrage.

The nooses I'd Seen flamed bright blue up the entire length of the rope and disappeared as the Raisers' control over their shades snapped. For a moment I thought I Saw each ghost wearing a braided metal torque, its ends tipped with large pear-shaped heads. But before I could be sure, the entire group of them disappeared, joining their laser-lit brother in surreal form.

I stood up, along with the other audience members who'd realized wait-your-turn didn't apply to people trying to beat a potential stampede. As my fellow survivors began to quick-march toward freedom, I murmured, "Vayl, things are about to get interesting in here."

"Viv is still in the bathroom," he replied from his far-too-distant location. "She is feeling some extreme emotion. If I had to choose, I would pick despair."

"*Very* interesting," I insisted.

Sigh. "I will be right there."

The Raisers dumped the choreography and pulled out the blue-collar show. Gerard yanked a handkerchief from his pocket and laid it flat on the floor. Francine dug a pocketknife out of her bra (no, I'm not kidding), unfolded the biggest blade, and quickly slashed her forearm. She let the blood drip onto the cloth. As the splotches hit, soaked, and spread, a bell-bottomed ghost wearing a crown of daisies in her hair came back into focus. She seemed fascinated by the evidence of vitality raining onto the reddening material. The next to join her was a uniformed soldier. He looked to have been a member of the RAF—I guessed a casualty of World War II.

Rhona said, "This is exactly why ghosts need protection! If Humphrey Haigh knew he was facing a hefty fine, or even jail time right now, I'll wager he would have thought twice before he started groping that young man."

"Young man?" said Cole as he tried to keep a woman in the row in front of us from shoving her chair through his stomach. "He probably died before your great-great-grandma's great-grandparents were done crapping their diapers!"

"Is arguing really going to help us right now?" asked Iona as she swiveled her head, keeping her eye on the crowd, frowning at what she saw, as if she feared at any moment it might turn into a mob. The way three or four of the women had begun yelling that they wanted to get the hell out of there, I thought she might be right.

"Iona's got a point," I said. "Let's move to a safer location; then we'll debate just how stupid this whole setup is. Viv's probably worried sick about you by now, Rhona."

But everybody seemed to have the same idea at the same time. People poured past us, clogging the back exits so quickly and severely, if there'd been a fire we'd have roasted within seconds. And Rhona wouldn't budge. "We should take pictures," she announced. "This is just the sort of fiasco I am working to prevent." She began digging in her purse.

"What is happening?" Vayl asked.

So my explanation for Vayl wouldn't sound überbizarre to those around me I said, "Humphrey really made the Highlander angry, Rhona. But he's not going to sue. He's going to take immediate action. And the Raisers may not have enough blood or power between them to lure him or the other ghosts back into passivity."

"What's blood got to do with anything?" she demanded, her hand moving up, down, and around like a mixer beater.

I sighed. "Ghosts are attracted to blood. Raisers use it as a lure. But they have power too, along the lines of a necromancer but not that refined. So they can keep them under control once they've brought them out of the Thin. The reason we need to get out is that the Highlander is pissed. And if he or any of the other ghosts draw blood from Humphrey, or any of the other Connies, the Raisers are going to lose their influence. And then all hell's going to break loose."

"That's never going to happen."

I wanted to strangle her. Especially when she pulled a camera from her purse with a triumphant smile. I said, "Rhona, have you ever been fed on by a ghost? I hear it's . . ."

But she'd stopped listening. Too busy clicking off shots of the milling crowd and the ghosts as they swam back into sight. Just as I'd decided to grab Rhona's camera and smash it against the first wall I could reach, the press of people in the middle aisle eased slightly as more than a dozen Connies realized they could get out via the smaller door and veered off in that direction. That allowed Vayl to shove his way through them and reach my side.

"What happened?" he asked, because the women would expect him to.

"Yogurt-brain over there violated one of the ghosts," I said, pointing to Humphrey, now surrounded by a group of yelling Connies, the biggest of whom seemed primed to punch him.

"We were going to leave, but Rhona's click-happy, the doors are blocked, and the Raisers seem to be getting things back under control now anyway, so . . ." Maybe I wouldn't have to punch Viv's mum in the face after all. I was slightly disappointed until I decided I didn't want to be the one to provide another trauma for the poor girl to live down.

Vayl's sharp blue eyes scanned the group of ghosts now gathered to the left of the stage at the Raisers' feet. "Which one did Humphrey touch?"

"The guy with the terrific knees."

Onstage, the Raisers were starting to sweat. Francine's blood had slowed to a drip and all but two of their puppets had returned to form. But we could still follow the holdouts' movements because the lighting dude had stayed at his post, splitting his spots so that the lasers outlined them. Even out of visible mode the Highlander seemed formidable. The stumpy gent—not so much. His silhouette had begun to remind me of Nathan Lane. And though I was pretty sure this dude's sense of humor had shriveled up and fallen off ages ago, I still couldn't get too worked up over him.

"Another cut!" Gerard demanded.

Francine put the blade to her arm again, but before she could slash it, the two unseen ghosts began to howl. The sound, combining the harsh scream of a heavy-metal chorus and the keening wail of a bereft mother, made my entire body go cold, as if I'd just slid into one of the city morgue's refrigerated corpse decks. *I take it back, Stumpy. You're a badass! No more dissing, I promise!*

Vayl turned to our group. "Everyone out! The wall is splitting!"

"What wall?" asked Rhona as she dropped her camera back into her bag.

"The one that protects us from them." He pointed toward the ghosts, who were rising toward the ceiling as they slammed into each other like a couple of rugby players psyching themselves up for the big game.

"Why do we need protecting?"

"Think of the wall as emotional control. What we might use to keep ourselves from suddenly snapping and killing one another. The Raisers can pull ghosts through it while keeping it intact. When it begins to crumble, they need blood to build it back again, which is why Francine has cut herself. But if the wall falls and a ghost cannot be lured into submission, it becomes more dangerous than a maddened killer. Because all it wants is blood and, ultimately, your company on the other side of the wall."

Suddenly the Highlander spun and dove for Humphrey, who'd ripped himself away from the angry Connies and was stomping toward the door to the right of the stage. The ghost careened through him, making him stop and shiver.

Rhona pointed. "What's the fuss all about? Mr. Haigh wasn't even hurt!"

"Not on the first pass, no," said Vayl. "That was simply an expedition."

"For what?"

Vayl nodded at the Highlander, who'd gained color and solidity in the past few seconds. "Humphrey's humanity. He only needs a bit of it to become . . ."

"Become what?" Rhona demanded.

Vayl pointed as the ghost charged at Humphrey again. The jeweler gaped at the Highlander, began to shake his finger, *tut-tut-tut*. But this time the two collided.

Vayl said, "To become physical."

Humphrey let out a surprised grunt as he hit his back and went rolling into the legs of a group of people who hadn't quite decided whether they should run for the hills or stay and take video.

As an Ann Boleyn lookalike helped Humphrey to his feet,

the Highlander struck again. I could see the disturbance of air as his arm slashed forward, catching the old jeweler across the face and neck.

He staggered backward, shrieking like a little girl as his hand flew to the claw marks already filling with blood. His shoulders finally hit solid wood and he spun, his entire face lifting as he realized he'd made it to the door. He rushed out, slamming it behind him, leaving Lesley stranded on the other side.

Cole gripped Iona by the arm. "Let's go," he said.

She pointed to Rhona, Floraidh, and Dormal. "Not without them."

The rest of the crowd didn't seem to feel the same loyalty. Relatives separated, dates split, people rushed toward the exits like the place was under a bomb threat, yelling at each other, dumping chairs, and shoving the slowpokes aside in their attempt to escape the rising fury behind them.

We'd been able to push everyone to the aisle, and this time escape seemed a real possibility. Until Rhona jumped up on the chair, her purse dangling from her elbow like an enormous tumor. "The ghosts don't mean you real harm!" she yelled, holding her hands out as if she really believed she could stop the tide of humanity rolling toward safety. "This is exactly why they need to be protected! Write your local MPs!"

Suddenly something rose in the room. An unfamiliar power that gave off the psychic scent of a foul burning, like bodies roasting on a pyre. I turned to Vayl so the women couldn't overhear. "I'm feeling vast weirdness," I murmured. "Something *other* is . . ."

I tried to zero in on the source. It could be the ghosts ripping into our world. Or the Raisers pulling off some kind of stunt I hadn't believed them capable of. I concentrated, trying to focus my Spirit Eye on that signal.

"It's Floraidh and Dormal," I whispered. "I think they're conjuring. Maybe it's some sort of ghost-be-gone spell."

Iona gasped loud enough that I swung my head around to check on her. A panic-stricken bald man wearing years of pub visits around his gut steamed toward her. He'd already knocked the two chairs in front of her aside in his bid to pass slower pedestrians, and he clearly intended to mow through her now, since she blocked his path to safety.

"Get out of my way, you!" he snarled.

I moved to deal with him, but stopped when I realized Rhona had pulled a snub-nose .38 out of her bag. She clutched it in both hands, which shook just enough that I feared she'd shoot the guy accidentally before she could even start with her demands.

"You leave my employee alone!" she screamed, her voice high and wild.

As the guy tried desperately to shift into reverse, Vayl spoke in his gentlest, most convincing tone of voice. "Rhona, put down the gun."

She jerked the barrel on a track meant to land on him, yelling, "You men are all alike! Shouting orders! Making demands! Raping innocent young girls! You should all be shot!" Time slowed, as it always does when you realize a deadly weapon is about to swing past you and the person wielding it is out of her gourd.

I started to raise my hands, to say something harmless, but those jittery fingers of Rhona's whoopsed into the trigger before the .38 had quite made it to Vayl. I dove to the floor, but even with the increased speed my donation to Trayton had given me, I couldn't outquick a bullet. I felt it hit my arm and knew immediately the wound was minor. The impact hadn't even made my shoulder twitch, though I could see blood welling through the hole in my jacket. *Goddammit, that was expensive!*

Rhona screamed again, dropping the gun, which thundered out another shot. Thank God it had twirled to face the opposite direction or I'd have been one dead Jaz. Iona moved quickly toward Rhona, holding up her hands, talking so softly I couldn't understand what she was saying. *She's like a Horse Whisperer,* I thought. *Only for nutty old mums. Iona Clough, the Mum Whisperer.*

At the same time Cole let out a surprised whoop. The guy who'd spooked Rhona had tried sidestepping to get beyond her, but his bulk wouldn't allow a clean pass. He'd banged into Cole on the way out, who'd fallen into Iona, who did a domino and knocked Rhona off her chair. Though the Mum Whisperer tried to catch Rhona even as Cole reached out to cushion the ladies' fall, they all crashed to the floor like an amateur circus act gone terribly wrong, pulling chairs with them while bags and bobby pins went flying in every direction.

When Cole sat up Vayl growled, "Dammit, boy, now you have done it! Your forehead is bleeding!"

Cole touched the cut with his fingertips, winced as he realized the truth. But the pain of his injury wasn't enough to wipe out his indignation. "What the hell, *Jeremy?* Aren't you supposed to be a little more concerned about the welfare of your *employees?* Not to mention the nice ladies here?"

Vayl began hauling people upright, starting with me. "Too much blood in one place is going to attract the ghosts," he said. "We must *go!*"

"My dears, are you all *right?*" asked Floraidh. As she helped Rhona up, I glanced toward the front of the room. Vayl had predicted too well. The hippie and the soldier had blinked out of sight again. And the Highlander, along with Stumpy, were flying toward us like a couple of doomsday missiles.

I grabbed Rhona's gun and stuck it in my jacket pocket as Vayl jerked Iona and Cole to their feet. Floraidh was hunting a tissue because blood streamed down Rhona's cheek where she'd caught it on the edge of a chair back, but she looked so dazed she probably didn't even realize she'd been injured. Iona shoved Rhona's purse into her hands as I pushed them both toward the exit. Floraidh put her hands on their shoulders in a show of guidance and comfort. But they only took a few steps before stopping to look back. When their eyes went wider than my poker chips, I glanced behind as well.

We'd wasted our head start. The ghosts had arrived.

Chapter Seventeen

Though the tech guy had flipped on all of the lights in the great room, I had no trouble seeing our attackers. At this proximity, with the wall between our worlds crumbling as Rhona, Cole, and I bled and the ghosts moved toward the smell, I began to pick up their outlines. To catch glimpses of their hideous, grinning skulls. This is what would leap through to tear at our living skin. Not the pretty remnants Gerard and Francine had raised, but true-form ghosts. I'd been right about one aspect of their appearance though. They really were wearing torques, ancient necklaces favored by fierce warriors now long fallen to dust.

"Where's Dormal?" I demanded as we struggled to get everyone into the aisle.

"Right behind me," said Floraidh.

But she wasn't. She'd gotten lost in the crowd, which had swelled in our section of the room as escapees bottlenecked at the main exit doors, forcing us and those around us back toward the main stage. Our path toward the door Vayl had used earlier looked even hairier. A bonfire's worth of thrown chairs blocked our immediate escape, and it looked as if a heart attack victim had caused a backup closer to that exit. The door Humphrey had left through might've worked, if we hadn't been forced to charge through a couple of rampaging shades on the way there. And Rhona couldn't have pulled off that kind of move anyway. In fact, she kept spacing out, ambling forward with such a lack of concern and, more important, speed, that I began to suspect concussion.

"Come on," Floraidh said, pulling at her just as the Highlander hit her. She screamed as the impact sliced into her already cut cheek.

Behind us I heard an enormous crash, almost like a bookcase falling, and someone yelled, "Snakes!"

Shit! It's Bea! Of course, this is the perfect time to—

As I turned to look, I felt the blow, not unexpected, but still sharp and painful, as Stumpy opened an eight-inch gap along the length of my wounded arm. *Cold!* My mind shivered as what passed for his tongue darted out for a taste of the new blood that poured from the cut before the Raisers could rebuild the wall that bound him.

I wanted to run. God yes! Follow the example of my fellow me-firsters, shoulder these slow, struggling women aside and sprint toward the exit. Anything to keep that netherworlder from touching me again. Because in that moment I'd fully Seen.

Fear rested square on my head like a cage full of spiders, making me shiver as I came to my first realization. In the Thin everything is hungry. And I'd leapt in without weapons.

I stood, as ethereal as any ghost, hoping no one would notice yummy little me tucked away in the corner of a big, open room so dark I shouldn't be able to tell it was a dungeon. But I knew.

The phantoms, glowing red with their own inner light, explained their Castle Hoppringhill absence by their presence here. Even now the RAF shade hadn't jumped through the breach because the flower child was feasting on his entrails. I put my hands to my ears, certain his screams had made them bleed. But our worlds hadn't experienced so much a collision as a near miss, so his howls couldn't hurt me any more than he could die from the wounds her fangs inflicted.

I tried to blink. But my Spirit Eye doesn't work like that. It's either on or off. Lately—mostly on. Which was why I couldn't look away when *he* strode in, the force of his personality placing color and form on what would otherwise be the thick inkiness of the Thin. The room he made consisted of rough-hewn stone. An arched doorway grew behind him, the brackets that flanked it containing not torches, but stacks of skulls whose eye sockets blazed with fire.

His boots thumped against the unfolding floor, hard and cold as his obsidian eyes as they caught mine. His dark, braided hair flew out behind his bare back as he moved, giving me a full view of his tattooed chest and arms. The barbed shards and looping whorls that painted his flexing muscles imprinted themselves on my brain. *Remember this,* I thought. *It's like the Phaistos Disk. Don't forget.* Because I knew, just watching that purposeful stride emphasized by rawhide breeches tied at the waist with a leather band, that anything carved into this man's body wasn't just decor. It meant something.

He glared down at the cannibalism taking place at his feet. Leaning over, he grabbed the gorging specter by the hair and yanked backward so hard I heard something snap.

You can do that here? Touch and twist? What the hell kind of rules apply in a place inhabited by the bodiless?

I'd thought what I was seeing was a version of hologram, the restless soul's outpouring of its physical sense. Just like the visuals you get when a ghost materializes in the bedroom where it died. But the hippie girl screamed as her neck cracked. And the flyer, trying desperately to shove his intestines back into his stomach cavity, cried real tears. *What the hell?*

The tattooed man gave the girl a kick that sent her scurrying into a corner, her head listing so badly to one side that she had to support it with one hand. He stepped over the soldier, ignoring his whimpers as he moved toward me.

I swallowed. Well, I tried. My throat was too dry to allow more than one sad attempt. He raised one powerful arm and made a curt, come-to-me gesture.

I shook my head.

He stopped, slapped himself on the chest with both hands.

"Aw, for chrissake, I'm not your poodle," I said. "I'm not even a—" I pointed to the soldier.

"No, you are unique. But what?" His brogue twisted his words hard enough that I didn't understand him at first. His voice, so gruff I'd have sworn he'd spent the last decade lining his windpipe with nicotine if I wasn't sure he'd been dead for millennia, gave me an involuntary shiver. I knew he'd commanded death with that growl. As he was trying to control me.

"I'm just a girl who Sees too much," I said. "And now I gotta go."

"No! Stay!"

"Seriously, guy, you'd better stop with the doggy demands. It really pisses me off."

"Brude."

"Huh?"

"My name is Brude." Even his beard demanded a curtsy.

Ahh. As in King Brude. The guy Floraidh's loeden threatened us with. "Well, *King* Brude, you ghosts are trespassing and it's about to get really ugly. So I suggest you back off—"

"I am no ghost." *And that's final,* his tone pronounced, as if he'd just passed a law.

"Sure you are." *Dumbass. You're in the freaking Thin!*

"You dare to argue with the king?"

"Well, yeah. I mean, it's pretty obvious you're wrong. And if I don't set you straight, I'm fairly sure nobody will. They're all too busy chowing on innocent humans. Or"—I jerked my thumb at the flower child—"each other."

He folded his arms across his chest. "You should be frightened. And you do not quake. You should kneel and beg for mercy, yet you stand. You are certainly wrong about who I am, but in the absence of other proof I see that you will defy me." He nodded slowly. "You are the one I need."

Oh, crap, I do not like the sound of that.

"What is your name?" Brude asked.

"I'm Lucille Robinson. Now, if you'll excuse me, we're in the middle of a crisis down there. And your damn ghosts are the cause of it."

"So your witches share no blame?" He pointed over my shoulder. I looked, and through a gap in the wall I could see the Raisers, panting and sweating. It was like waking up to sunlight after a week of rain. I reached for them with every bit of extra oomph I'd gained since becoming a Sensitive and snapped myself back to real.

We've gotta get outta *here!* I wanted to grab the PA and boom my message across the room until people had managed to crash through the walls and the place was empty as a midnight crematorium. Except for the bloodthirsty phantoms, of course. But, as I recalled, someone had hollered *snakes.* And it was my job to make sure Bea didn't succeed tonight. Of course, they could belong to somebody else. But the way our evening had turned, I truly doubted it.

With Iona and Cole's help, Floraidh had finally gotten Rhona into the throng blocking the center aisle. But the blood rolled down her face, so she continued to suffer the threat of attack, her ripped clothing and scratched skin evidence of the damage that had already been inflicted. I looked over my shoulder. The gap between worlds had closed for now, leaving Brude in his dungeon where he belonged. Instead the face I wanted to see filled my vision. And though Vayl's lips were pressed together so tightly the outline of his fangs showed through his skin, I smiled as he put his arm around my waist.

I said, "You won't believe where I've just been."

"Tell me later." He pushed me forward as Stumpy came at me again, corporeal enough that we could see his black tongue dripping blood as he ran it across his long, pointed teeth. My entire skeleton tensed for another cut, a second ride into the Thin. But the ghost whipped past my left shoulder, the wind from the near miss making my ear ache.

I spun around. "Vayl? Do you—" For a second I couldn't figure out what had happened to him. Under Bergman's sunblock his face had taken on the marble quality of a tomb ornament. His fist clenched and I saw the droplets of blood splatter onto the floor. His shirt tore as Stumpy attacked, leaving a line of red from neck to navel. As Vayl's eyes lost momentary focus, I realized. He'd bitten himself. Drawn the phantom's attack with his own blood.

I grabbed him by the hips, as if I could pull him into a safer reality by sheer will. "No, you—"

"I can survive this," he said between clenched teeth. Another slash, leaving Vayl's left shoulder bare and bloody. "I will get them out. You find out what you can about the snakes. But do not endanger yourself." He pulled me close, so no one could've heard him, not even from an arm's length. "If we should fail this mission, so be it. Your life is of much greater value than Floraidh's."

"But Pete . . . the Oversight Committee . . . our jobs?"

His eyes burned into mine. "I will never let you down."

I nodded curtly, tucking my emotions tightly into my heart as I watched him join Floraidh, Cole, and Iona. He offered Rhona his arm, which she took gratefully. His strength, coupled with his ability to make suggestions most humans found compelling, caused them to make actual progress down the aisle.

Following Rhona's earlier example, I stood on the chair next to the one she'd downed, trying to get a sense of where the threat originated. I noted Dormal, stuck maybe twenty feet in front of Floraidh, craning her neck to see if she could find her leader in the crush. Behind Vayl's group by another twenty feet, the experts had deserted the stage, managing to knock over the podium on their way out. But Gerard and Francine still worked to wrangle the ghosts into submission. Four of them had gathered around again, though they markedly avoided the aisle. It was almost like they were making way for the panicked escapees. But I knew that couldn't be true.

I watched as the RAF boy reappeared at the far left edge of the stage, keeping his distance from the flower child. They'd both managed to repair the damage I'd seen on them before. And then, without any outward signal from the Raisers, the ghosts turned toward the right-hand speaker, all of them giving it a look of revulsion. A snake had slithered to its top edge, reached out with its neck and forked tongue, tasting the air.

"Snake on the stage. I can't tell what it is," I told the guys on my party line. "I'm going forward to look."

"Be careful," said Vayl.

"Are you okay?" I asked, then immediately wished I hadn't. My backbone was going to buckle if I couldn't learn to deal with Vayl in pain.

"The ghost has retreated. Something put it off the moment I moved into the aisle. Perhaps Francine and Gerard have convinced it to behave once more."

"How about you, Cole?" I asked, mainly to cover up the massive relief I felt at Vayl's news.

"I've lost Iona," Cole said.

"Find her quick," I told him. "We don't want anybody snake-bit." *And if you catch her trying to control this reptile, so much the better. This mission sucks and I wanna go home.*

Staying off the floor whenever possible, I stepped from row to row, approaching the stage at a diagonal. Francine hadn't seen the snake, which held its place closest to her. It hesitated, as if undecided what to do next. But when forty of its fellows joined it, I realized what was happening.

"It's going to be a mass assault," I said. Now that I'd made it closer to the stage I added, "And they are Inland Taipans. Bea definitely has an affinity for snakes, but she's not a Medusa." *Which is somewhat of a relief. But not much. Because she must be wielding some major* wham *to be able to transport and control that many wild, venomous creatures.*

Vayl glanced back to the stage, took note of what I'd just described, and said a bad word into our receivers. He never swore. Unless, apparently, the danger was snake related. "Let us get moving, ladies," he urged. I could see him shoving people aside now.

Dormal had stopped in her tracks, allowing traffic to flow around her like a highway median. The group had nearly reached her when Floraidh stumbled. She'd have fallen, and probably been stomped by the people behind her, if her Gatherer hadn't caught her.

The snakes began to move, slithering down the speaker and across the stage like a living carpet. They didn't spread out much or move in random directions. It was as if an unseen hand guided them resolutely in a single direction. Forward, down the edge of the platform, onto the event floor.

The Connies who'd seen them spread the hysteria quickly, so that everyone who hadn't panicked to start with now began screaming and shoving, the people in the back literally crawling on top of those in front of them to avoid the reptiles at their heels.

The last of the crowd had made it halfway down the aisle now. But the snakes were advancing. When the Connies realized they couldn't escape straight ahead, they voted for the side routes and began parting like the waters of the Red Sea.

My group had nearly made it to the door. The cushion between them and the Taipans had flattened alarmingly as the crowd scattered. And yet I could practically feel their freedom, like the cool hard steel of a cell key in my fingers. But they were never going to make it without help. And I had so little to offer.

I could try some spark and sizzle. But I'd probably end up burning the castle down. Plus with my luck, I'd end up ashing out the last corner of sweetness left in my soul. So, despite my misgivings, I kicked in the Mongoose.

At the time Bergman had invented the gizmo, we'd figured on battling a Medusa. So it was geared to hit a human-sized target. Not a huge problem, considering the snakes still hung together, tightly woven as a carpet. The issue, frankly, was Bergman, whose prototypes let me down about ninety percent of the time. Already I was thinking, *What am I going to do when this doesn't work?*

Feeling a doomed sort of resignation, I pulled up my left sleeve, pointed the device at the Inland Taipans, and triggered it. White foam poured out of the spout as if it was a fire extinguisher. Wherever it hit, the snakes began to writhe wildly as smoke rose from their glistening scales. Even better, their neighbors abandoned the Floraidh chase and began to attack them.

It's working! Holy crap, Bergman, you're a genius!

A booming echo rang in my ears as the main doors closed, leaving me and thirty-odd people stuck in the great room with maybe half of Bea's attack snakes still crawling. But the rest of my crew held out, safe, on the other side. Cool. Right?

I moved down the aisle, almost back to the spot where I'd started, and shot the last of the foam at the Taipans. Now I could count the remaining threats on the fingers of one hand. I pulled out Rhona's .38.

As I took aim I felt the familiar scent of pine that told me Vayl had returned. Considering how he felt about snakes, he must be gripping his self-control with white-knuckled fingers.

I squeezed off a shot, sending one of the reptiles flopping as my *sverhamin* slid up behind me.

"Could you use some help?"

Part of me wanted to reach back and hug him. But he wasn't a three-year-old hoping to be rewarded for his brave-boy moves. "I wouldn't mind if you dropped the temperature by a few," I said. "These suckers are quick."

The familiar glacial breeze of his power chilled the snakes' blood, slowing their advance.

Two more shots. Two more dead critters bleeding onto the carpet while the remaining two sank their fangs into the twitching bodies. I was siting in my final target when Vayl yanked me backward, falling with me on top of him, onto the carpet.

"What the hell?" Then I saw the Highlander, swooping just over our heads. I ducked, covering the cut on my arm as I spread myself across Vayl's vulnerable chest wounds. But the warrior wasn't interested in us. He wanted the snakes.

He dove over the chair Rhona had crashed and into the pile of Taipans like a blitzing linebacker, making the corpses shiver as he hit them. The blood on the ones I'd shot splattered onto the remaining, living snake. The Highlander immediately hit it, leaving gashes all along its length. It writhed in agony as the ghost slashed again and again until at last the snake lay still.

"Highlander!" Francine commanded. I peered through the legs of the chairs just in time to see the Raiser lift a newly dripping arm. I thought the phantom would fly straight down the aisle to her. Instead it came back at us. We flattened ourselves one more time as it buzzed us, then rose to the ceiling. It looped around, gaining color and form, and floated sedately to Francine's feet.

"Are you all right?" Vayl asked.

"Uh." I took inward stock. All the imaginary people in my head had huddled together in a closet, as if to escape a tornado. Upon realizing they wouldn't be eaten by a ghost or paralyzed by deadly venom they sent up a single, shuddering shout. *Fuck!* "Yup," I said as I swallowed a hysterical giggle. "I'm fine." Deciding it might be appropriate to give him some space, I tried to climb onto a chair. He wrapped his arms around me.

"A moment please," he murmured, lifting his head so he could breathe in my scent. His eyes closed, a smile lifting one corner of his lips as if he was savoring a rose.

When he dropped his head I asked, "Better?"

He opened his eyes. "Talk to me."

"Okay. Let's discuss suspects." I thought he'd make fun of me, choosing work over, well, you know. We were cuddling like a couple of newlyweds. But public displays kinda freaked me out. And I didn't need any more stress at the moment.

"Do you know what I think?" he asked mildly.

"I doubt it."

"Viv did this."

"But . . . she's so fragile!"

"She was deeply upset just now. I have heard of mages needing that kind of extreme emotion to help them raise the kind of power required to call forty exotic snakes into a room."

"A female mage—isn't that kind of rare?"

He shrugged. "It is not beyond the realm of possibility. Who would you choose as our culprit?"

"Humphrey," I said instantly. "I know. Bea would actually have to be a guy. And it's probably not him anyway, because he irritates the crap out of me and that would be too satisfying. Do you think . . . Rhona?"

Vayl raised his eyes to the ceiling as he considered. "Perhaps. That entire outburst tonight might have been staged. Or the snakes may be an outgrowth of her rage. One she is not even aware of."

We looked at each other for about five seconds before, at the same time, we said, "Rhona is not Bea."

I went on. "I thought about Bea being clueless as to her true identity, at least part of the time. But even she wouldn't be so stupid as to draw a gun in a public place like that." Without really considering the consequences, I ran my fingers through his curls, smiling at the soft silky feeling against my fingertips. Such a contrast to the rest of him. "Don't you think we have to consider who Bea's going up against? This is no ordinary hit, you know. She's got to know what she's getting into, and that if she doesn't play it smart every second of the day she's going to be real dead, real quick."

"Iona certainly has more going on than meets the eye."

"Yeah. Did you see her case the room before the program started? And the way she handled Rhona? That's cop training if I've ever seen it. Which would give her a solid background to go into business for herself."

"Thank you."

"Excuse me?"

"I . . ." He took a deep breath, glanced at the snakes. "I just needed to talk sensibly for a moment. As if those creatures had not just chased me down the carpet like a mass of ravenous multiheaded dragon spawn."

I brought my hand down to his face. Took time I'd never

had before to brush my fingers against the hard planes of his jaw and cheekbones, to wonder how the slant of his dark brows and the shape of his glittering green eyes had managed to sear themselves into my soul. And I knew, if I traveled through eternity or lived a million lives, I would always find him, always know and love him with the kind of fiery passion that scares the hell out of you because, God, it burns. And yet when you've walked out the other side you know you haven't lived until this moment.

"Vayl, I . . ." *No, not here. Not bleeding on the floor. Say something else, not as important, but still meaningful.* "I want to thank *you* for what you did before. Taking those hits for me." I blinked, surprised to find tears welling. "It means a lot to me." More even than I'd realized.

"You are my *avhar.* I would die for you."

I grimaced. "I'd much rather you didn't."

The smile lit his eyes first. "Then I will simply say, you are welcome." He ran his hands lightly up and down my back. Shifted slightly beneath me. "Jasmine?"

"Yeah?"

"When you look at me that way, it is difficult for me to remember I am still in public."

I looked around. The survivors had huddled into small groups of five or six. Nobody had opened the door yet. Maybe they were afraid the snakes would revive. Or they were still pissed they'd been shut out. "Everybody's pretty distracted," I whispered.

"Yet, I would not trust my—"

I silenced him with a kiss, slow and delicious, one to savor the next time we were apart. "Do me a favor?"

"Anything."

"Don't ever die."

He raised his hand, slid it around my neck, his thumb brushing up under my chin as he leaned in to nuzzle my bottom lip. "I shall live forever, if that is your wish."

"It's a start." I plastered myself against him, marveling at how well we fit together, wrapping my arms around him so tight I'd have worried about crushing some ribs if he hadn't been Vampere.

When he opened his lips, I gave him the kiss that had been building in me since the last time. Hot-breathed, lips and tongue, clinging bodies that couldn't wait to move *on,* dammit!

I moaned when Vayl lifted his head. "Don't stop."

"I must," he breathed, his voice husky with desire.

"Why?"

"Because we have company."

CHAPTER EIGHTEEN

When I was sixteen Albert caught me making out on the front porch with Sheldon Anderson. We'd have been okay, except every time he leaned me against the side of the house, my ass hit the doorbell. After about eight rings Albert came to the door, Bud Light in one hand, Louisiana Slugger in the other.

Sheldon kind of disappeared after that. Something I wished I could do now that I found myself surrounded by a group of Connies dressed as the shades of outlaws and serving maids who, once they realized they had our attention, gave us a hearty round of applause.

"Hear, hear!" they yelled. And, "Hi, ho to Lady Snake Killer!"

I felt myself go bright red as I tried to crawl off Vayl and under the nearest chair. Vayl, his chest heaving with suppressed mirth, cooperated very little. Which meant my hair tangled in one of his shirt buttons and I had to yank it free before I could move more than a few inches. Then my leg caught in a fold of his coat, causing me to fall on my butt. "Stop laughing!" I ordered. "We're supposed to be pros, remember? You? Me? World's greatest ghost busters?"

Of course, by that I meant America's finest assassins. But I could hardly say that in front of the dispersing crowd, a few of whom still stood close enough to eavesdrop, as proved by the fact that a tall, lanky man with a fringe of gray hair that started under his nose, curved in both directions down his jaw, and worked its way clear around his head leaned over the row of chairs in front of us to say, "I thought you were more than just ordinary Connies." He stuck out a long-fingered hand decorated with two turquoise rings the size of robin's eggs. "How do you do? My name is Thomas Hoppringhill."

"You'd better shake his hand." I nodded to Vayl. "Mine seems to be stuck to the bottom of this chair. I think somebody spilled a Coke on the seat and didn't clean the underside." As the guys greeted each other, I worked my fingers free and checked out the brown sticky I'd picked up. Ick. *When I retire from this gig I'm going to work somewhere sanitary. I'm even putting that on my résumé. No blood. No guts. No dropped sodas. Maybe I'll buy one of Humphrey's jewelry stores.*

Hang on. Why do I need a Band-Aid? Where did I cut my pinky?

The chair was the one Rhona had fallen from. A tiny white jewel had been cemented just under the seat. The smudge of red next to it proved its guilt. This little diamond had ripped my finger open. The question was, who the hell had put it there in the first place? And why?

I wanted to explore this curious development further, but I could hardly crawl around the wreckage when Thomas was explaining that the castle had been in his family since it was built. Admiration must be paid. And rightly so. Geez. The Parkses owned a few relics, but nothing as major as an entire building. In fact, nobody I knew even wanted their grandparents' old homeplace. I liked his family's commitment. But I hoped they hadn't sacrificed too many of their own dreams to keep the ancient stone giant alive.

"I couldn't help but overhear," said Thomas as he sat down and tossed one tweed-covered leg over the other. "You are in the business of ghost release?" He laid his brown-jacketed arm across the back of the chair next to him and waited patiently as Vayl rose to his feet.

"Indeed," said Vayl. He introduced us and handed Thomas our business card. "We hope to make several new contacts at the convention, which we greatly appreciate you hosting." I regarded my boss with that sense of awe that stole over me at the oddest moments. He could be the most polite gentleman you had ever met one second, and turn around and tear your throat out the next. Of course he only killed bad guys now. But before he'd come to America in the twenties, he hadn't been so picky. I liked a guy who could make that kind of change.

"And what was that stuff you sprayed on the snakes?" Thomas asked me.

"We use it in our business all the time," I said, hoping a great lie would come to me as I stalled for the time my brain needed to switch from sticky diamonds to snakicide. "It's a special pressurized chemical mix Jeremy invented that helps us to—" *Nope. Nothing.* I turned to Vayl. "Well, Jeremy, it's really your baby. Maybe you could explain it better than I could."

"It allows us to detect whether or not a ghost frequents an area so that we can decide where best to set up our recording equipment. We spray the foam on the floor and it picks up spectral footprints."

Cole laughed in our ears. "Spectral footprints? That's the best you could come up with? Dude, they don't even wear real shoes! Oh, there you are, Iona!"

While I was glad he'd finally found our lost groupie, I kinda wanted to box Cole's ears. Mostly because I couldn't pull that stunt on myself for forgetting he could hear our every word. But also because only our backup boy could put that pinched expression on Vayl's face. Neither of us could act, however, while the Laird of the Castle held court.

"How fascinating!" Thomas said. "You know, I can't thank you enough for disposing of those vermin for me. Rather out of your line, but you still dealt with them quite handily. Perhaps I could introduce you to some people who would appreciate your services?"

Vayl and I traded appropriately excited looks. "That would be wonderful," I said.

"But first, I'd like to hire you myself."

"Oh?" *Shit! Run, Vayl, run!*

"As you've seen, the Highlander and the stocky old ghost, whose name in life was Aodh Hoppringhill, are a real danger to our guests. This is the first time they've drawn blood, but I fear it won't be the last. And those snakes. I cannot imagine which one of my ancestors brought them forth, but its shade must be dealt with as well."

We nodded politely, though I had to swallow hard when a giggle tried to let loose. Bad timing, I realize, but I'd just had the thought that, *Damn, when you own a castle you deal with an entirely different class of pests, don't you?* And then I imagined Thomas setting out these Hummer-sized bait traps for the critters that plagued him.

He was saying he'd rather not exorcise his hard hitters. "Many of my visitors would shun me forever if they heard I'd done such a thing. But your card says you lay shades to rest. That would be ideal."

Vayl said, "I am afraid we are in the middle of another investigation, having encountered a mysterious walker at Tearlach—"

"Ah, yes, Floraidh told me about her new ghost. She said it appeared in the kitchen?"

She's a quick worker, isn't she? Haven't seen her talking to Thomas here, which means she must've called him from her car. Or maybe her bedroom before the fake skinny guy even made his entrance.

"Yes, that's where we saw it," I agreed.

"It will be a great boon to the area's tourism industry. Now we can list her bed-and-breakfast on the Haunted Scotland Web site. Of course our registrants will want to include Tearlach on their GhostWalk tours, which should bring Floraidh a nice income for the week. Bless her, she works so hard to keep that old house running, I'm happy something good has happened for her. Are you enjoying your stay there?"

"Oh yes, it's quite a place," I said. "But you talk like this incident won't shut down the convention."

Thomas smiled, revealing a set of teeth as gray as his hair. "Far from it. Despite their initial panic, our attendees will already have turned this moment into legend." He shrugged. "That's how it is with Connies. Now nothing could make them leave the convention before the closing ceremonies."

Wow. Sometimes people are so stupid. "I guess you will have to count us among them," Vayl said, giving him Jeremy's tight-lipped smile. "We would not miss a moment."

"And you're sure I can't talk you into dealing with my issues?"

"Perhaps after our investigation at Tearlach is complete," he said gently. "It should only take a day or two."

A thought hit me. "Actually, I think your real problem is not the Highlander or Aodh Hoppringhill."

Thomas raised his eyebrows expectantly. Crap, now I had to think really fast. Because I hated people knowing about my Sensitivity. And I was pretty sure that was the reason I'd been able to See into the Thin. I held up my hand, let him see Cirilai glittering on my finger. "This is actually a monitoring device

Jeremy invented that picks up incredibly faint spectral readings and sends them to a wire"—I showed him the receiving end of the party line wrapped around my left ear—"that translates phantasmic signals into our language."

"What kind of bullshit are you shoveling out?" asked Cole.

Vayl's raised eyebrows wondered the same, but Thomas was glued. "Through these I was able to overhear a commander shouting out orders. It seems to me your two ghosts are under his thumb. So he's the one you want to get rid of. And I'll tell you right now, just locating him is going to take more equipment than we currently carry. You're going to need a real hard hitter. Find the best in the business and tell him to go after a ghost—*or whatever he is*—named Brude."

"Brude." Thomas thought for a minute. "Of course. There are three or four different kings named Brude in our histories, but the most famous of them ruled over these lands for about thirty years before he was killed in battle. Quite a hard-handed man, but he kept the people safe from marauders." Thomas shook his head. "Well, it's time for him to rest." Thomas rose and stuck out his hand. "Thank you for your help. Now, if I can just find someone to dispose of these creatures." He shook his head at the pile of snakes cluttering his great hall.

I said, "Can I suggest a specialist? Animal control? Somebody like that? Those are venomous snakes, and if someone were to accidentally poke themselves, they might still be poisoned."

"Good idea," Thomas said, motioning to a couple of his employees. They came forward to cordon off the area while two others decided it was high time the Connies who'd escaped to the front hall, and the great room prisoners who hadn't, got reacquainted. They opened the big doors, giving us insiders a chance to trade stares with the fringes of the outside group. They had a hard time meeting our eyes. Many of them dove deeper into the crowd. Since they were the ones who'd physically closed the doors on us, I could see why they didn't feel like a reunion just yet.

"What are you two doing now?" Cole hissed into our ears. "I have six hysterical women with me discussing how badly they want hugs and then giving me pouty lips while Humphrey demands an ice pack and an apology. From who I don't know, since he's the jackoff who started it all. I don't *want* to play nice!"

I did some mental math. "So Viv came out of the bathroom?"

"Yeah, but when she got the full story she started freaking about the possibility of jail time for Rhona. Iona keeps telling her nobody saw, but she's signing so loud she's already hit three different people and we can't just keep apologizing."

"Sure you can. It's the perfect time for people to be hysterical. I'd get Rhona out of the room though. Once folks start calming down a few of them are bound to remember the crazy lady with the gun. They're probably going to want to lynch Humphrey too."

"Jaz, this was not covered in Assassination 101! I'm not cut out for this!"

"And you want *me* to deal with it? You're like the ambassador to Iraq compared to me." I thought a second. "Are you telling me nobody out there seems disappointed that Floraidh's not covered in bite marks?"

"Nope. Dormal actually looked like she was crying there at the end. I saw her wiping off a few tears as we got close to the door."

"They must be pretty tight."

"Seems that way." Impatient sigh. "So what do I do?"

I raised my eyebrows at Vayl, who'd spent the whole conversation wiping the sticky off my hands with his handkerchief. He said, "Cole, stop talking to the ficus, or whatever strange pretense you are pursuing to make it seem as though you are not speaking into a microphone. Suggest to Floraidh that perhaps the Haighs should take Rhona back to Tearlach in her car. And give the rest of the ladies a hug. Beginning with Dormal."

"Dammit!"

Chapter Nineteen

The opening ceremonies had been scheduled to end half an hour after midnight. By 1:15 a.m. the crowd had remixed and decided they were ready to continue with the convention. And they say kids are resilient!

As Floraidh and Dormal helped the jeweler's wife shove Humphrey into the front of the Bentley, Rhona stared resolutely ahead from the backseat. I'd told Lesley not to let her sleep (if she could even manage that) for more than an hour at a time because she'd taken such a solid knock to the head. It would've been best to take her to the hospital, but she'd refused. *Arrogant bitch,* I thought. She'd never apologized for winging me. Probably never would. Still, I couldn't quite despise her. At least she'd pulled that shit out of love.

Floraidh and Dormal had warned us all that Tearlach would be the subject of a series of GhostWalks throughout the night. Nobody seemed to care. Even Rhona barely showed any interest in the subject.

"I'm sure we'll stay clear of the crowds and they won't bother us a bit," Lesley said. With a frown at Humphrey she added, "And you can rest assured we won't be meddling with your ghost should he reappear."

"How about you, Mum?" Viv asked through Iona. "Will you be all right? Why won't you let me come with you?"

"I'm certain I've got no need to be nursed like some invalid. I'll just have a cup of tea and go to bed."

Viv bought the lie, probably because she wanted to. *I* tried to figure out what was on Rhona's mind. Since her brains had been slightly battered and she'd been pushed to relive at least part of her traumatic past, I couldn't quite nail it. Was she going to try to undermine the GhostWalks somehow?

Her hand snuck up to pat her hair back into place and I saw her check her reflection in the rearview. *Holy shit, she's going after Albert while the getting's good! Should I call and warn him? She is kind of a lunatic anyway. And after tonight's episode, God knows what she's capable of.*

Then, out of nowhere, rose the memory of my father marching into my junior English class, where I sat next to gorgeous Mickey Meffort and thought up great names for our future kids. Mallory Meffort. Michael Meffort. Midterm Meffort. Okay, that one needed more work.

Albert carried a green plastic laundry basket full of whites above which loomed his beet-red face. "When you have chores to do I expect them to get *done,* young lady!"

He'd dumped that load of clothes all over my desk and left me there, wishing I could physically melt behind that pile of towels, bras, and boxers. Needless to say Gorgeous Mickey never asked me out, and for the six months I went to San Diego Unified I was known as Jazmaid.

I'm not calling that son of a bitch! Not even if he needs a kidney and I'm the only donor left on Earth who matches him!

I watched Rhona's Bentley pull out of the lot with such a sense of triumph it was an effort not to pump my fist at its taillights. Only Viv's sad wave kept me from letting out a whoop as I imagined Albert's face when he opened his door to find Rhona on the other side, wearing a hideous blue negligee and holding out a bottle of zinfandel like she might clonk him over the head with it if he didn't cooperate.

The Bentley had only been gone a minute or two when another car drove up. Yup, some solid citizen had finally remembered the gun and decided maybe the cops needed to pay us all a visit. Except they displayed such a lack of interest in the whole affair, I kinda wondered how much they would let Thomas Hoppringhill get away with in his own castle before they'd cart *him* off to jail.

A nice young constable with a nose that tended to drip, which meant he kept having to excuse himself to find a tissue, did ask us a couple of questions. But once we showed him our IDs and suggested he direct the rest of his queries to Interpol, he decided maybe he should swim into shallower waters.

Inverness's version of Animal Control arrived shortly afterward, and since they required everyone to clear out of the great room while they worked, we stood in one corner of the front hall, pretending to study the program for the rest of the evening while we watched Floraidh. She and Dormal sat with a couple of black-shirted castle employees at a registration table that had been transformed for GhostWalk signup. Despite everything that had happened, Floraidh seemed extraexcited. Like a senior getting ready for prom, she went all shiny eyes and fluttery hands every time somebody dropped a ten-pound note into the basket and slapped on the Guided Tour sticker.

"What the hell?" I murmured to Vayl. "Surely the money she stands to make from these extra tours won't bring in the amount she needs?"

"I would not think so. Perhaps she has another plan that requires the tours?"

"You mean as a smoke screen?"

He shrugged. "Or a draw."

Either way one of us would have to go along with the first group, try to figure out her angle while the others stayed behind to protect the old bat. One guess who that would be.

A ruckus near the front doors distracted me from my thoughts. Raised voices, indecipherable at first. And then a man spoke in a tone I'd never mistake.

"I'm legally blind, you twit! Why else would I bring a dog into a public place? The diabetes might have finished the job, but it started in the Vietnam War when I was hit in the eye with a piece of grenade shrapnel. You have heard of Vietnam, haven't you? Well, I've fought in that war and every one since. So show some goddamn respect for a veteran and let me in!"

Oh. Shit.

Putting my head down as if I meant to bull my way through the mass of Connies who, like us, were standing around and planning the rest of their evenings, I strode toward the sound of my father's voice. I tried to visualize my anger as the flame of a Bunsen burner, complete with control knob. Not the kind my high school chemistry partner had turned on full blast and then aimed at a billowing burner on the opposite lab table. No, we didn't want to incinerate the science department today. Because then poor Thomas Hoppringhill would never be able to convince anyone to return to his castle, Connie or otherwise. So I kept breathing, remembering Tolly's nuggets of advice. *Nobody can make you angry if you don't let them.* And, *Most of your fury stems from your inability to control events. So stop trying.*

By the time I reached my dad and my dog, I felt moderately sure that the mass of paperwork on the check-in tables wouldn't burst into flame the second I began speaking.

"Albert! What the hell? I told Floraidh you were zonked on Tylenol PM. So can you stop making such a damn *scene?*"

He blinked. Gave me his bland face. But he couldn't hide the red blotching his cheeks and neck, his heaving chest, or the fact that he held Jack's leash like the rope you throw to a drowning man. "Lucille? Is that you?"

I threw a fake smile at the gap-toothed woman who'd voted herself GhostCon's bouncer. "This is my employee, Albert Parks. He's a late arrival, which is why we hadn't had a chance to clear his seeing-eye dog."

"Why isn't the dog wearing a harness?" she demanded, her second chin shaking with ire. "Not to mention a jacket?"

Sudden image of my friendly neighborhood fur ball sporting a tuxedo. Which would give him three tails. Which I suddenly found hilarious. I gulped down a laugh. "Huh?"

"The ones I've seen wear a harness with a bar," she said, jabbing her fat, nail-bitten fingers at Jack's collar. "Also some sort of signage declaring that they are working dogs. Where's his?"

"He has back problems," I said. "The chiropractor trashed his harness and told us if we used it again he'd turn us in."

"Ch-chiropractor?"

"Yup. If you have a problem with it, I suggest you talk to Thomas Hoppringhill. Tell him Lucille Robinson and Jeremy Bhane sent you. I'm sure he'll be very interested to know how much you've insulted the ghost resters he just tried to hire. The ones he called his own doctor out of bed to patch up after we single-handedly killed the snakes some loony let loose. I believe you'll find him in the great room."

"Well!" She raked me over with a scalding look, as if my mere presence was an insult to our gender, before waddling off to intimidate some other Connie. I grabbed Albert's arm and walked him halfway up the stairs, a punishment to him for descending on me unannounced as well as a chance for me to get a better view of the room.

"What are you doing here?" I hissed. I shoved a program into his hand. "Hold this in front of your face. If Floraidh sees you we're toast."

"I just wondered what you were up to," he said, flipping open the program. "So. What's new?"

Breathe. Count to ten. No, make that twenty. "Don't bullshit with me. You were in for the night. I know what a pain in the ass it is to get a shuttle to come pick you up. That's half the reason we drove. So give it to me straight before I dump your butt on a plane for America and to hell with your big investment. Are you okay?"

"I'm fine." He thought for a second. "How are you?"

Oh, God, he's dying. The ghosts are all walking, the Grim Reaper's come along for the exercise, and he's found the perfect victim. I knew this because Albert hadn't even asked about my welfare after I'd broken my ribs (among other things) fighting a nether creature called the Tor-al-Degan. And after I'd cracked my collarbone— not even a call. But now—genuine concern in that rough old voice of his.

I said, "If there's something you need to tell me, you'd better spit it out now. Because if I have to find out from somebody else, I'm going to be spitting pissed."

He stared down at Jack, who'd managed to wiggle most of his head through the banisters so he could pant from fifteen feet up. I hoped the guy standing beneath him moved before something dripped off Jack's tongue onto his bald head. Otherwise I'd have to move into a cave. Forever.

Albert dropped his hand to Jack's furry shoulders and said, "It's back."

Instantly I knew what he meant.

It had started with repeated phone calls. Nobody ever spoke. And when he tried to trace the call to its source, it had none.

The escalation had been fast and violent. A two-vehicle crash involving a minivan and my dad's motorcycle. The driver had since vanished. Albert's recovery still seemed miraculous no matter what angle I viewed it from.

But while he'd been in the hospital, he'd received a visit from Beyond. Eventually he'd managed to shrug the whole thing off as a morphine hallucination, but I'd never bought his shtick. When your ICU nurse suddenly sprouts a grinning skull over his regular face that says, "Do not try to escape her," I figure you should sit up and take notice.

I leaned against the rail, allowing a group of about ten Connies to pass us on their way to one of the programs that was being presented upstairs. I searched the crowd below for Vayl, and wasn't surprised when he met my eyes. Even without Cirilai to message him, he could sense my strongest emotions. Within seconds he stood beside me, having greeted Albert and given Jack a pat that the malamute acknowledged with a short wave of the tail before he stuck his nose back into the lower floor's business.

"What is happening?" Vayl asked.

"The thing I saw in the ICU," Albert said. "It reappeared while Jack and I were watching that movie."

"What did it say?" I asked.

He shook his head. "A lot. I can't even remember it all now."

"Okay, start at the beginning. You were sitting, where, in that rickety white chair by the window?"

"No, I'd moved to the bed. I figured I might as well be comfortable while I was waiting for my snack."

Hell, I'd forgotten I was supposed to bring back food. "So you're watching *Hot Fuzz* . . ."

"And I get to the part where the good cop, Sergeant Angel, meets his new boss for the first time. Angel's got this constipated look on his face because the drunk guy he locked up the night before turns out to be the inspector's son—"

"I know, Dad, I've seen it."

Albert held up his hand, his finger raised in his hold-on-I'm-getting-to-the-good-part gesture. "And then Angel's face just melts off. It makes no sense at all as far as the story goes, so I'm yelling at the TV. 'What the hell kind of idiot move is *that?*' I said, or something like it. 'The guy offers you cake and your face disintegrates?' Then the eyeballs roll around, so loose in their sockets I'm wondering why they haven't bounced to the ground. They stare straight at me and those grinning teeth start clacking. And though the face is a little different, the voice is the same. It's the ghoul."

I wanted to tell Albert it couldn't have been a ghoul. More likely a *loeden.* But I didn't say a word. He'd probably just snap my head off before continuing with his story, which I would never get to hear the end of because my ears would be stuck inside his massive jaws.

"So what did it say?" I asked.

"I can't remember exactly. Something like, 'Time is dying. Run no more.'"

"Are you sure?"

"No, I'm not *sure!* I'm staring down a juicy skull on a TV that won't turn off! What, you think I'm going to be taking notes?"

I stifled the urge to smack him. At some point it would count as elder abuse and I just didn't need that sin on my infinite list. "I think you're more observant than you'd like credit for. Why you want to keep me out of this, I have no idea, but drop it. I'm in."

Vayl spoke up. "Do you think it could have been something the coven conjured? We know Floraidh is planning something expensive. And we think she is going to try something devious during one of the GhostWalks tonight."

"That's kinda what I thought at first," Albert agreed. "I was sitting there supposing one of the Scidairans had set up some kind of hex to give me a heart attack or something. Then it said, 'You must not cut the line nor turn off the road less traveled. That is how the first accident occurred.' Which sounded like a crap-covered threat to me. Plus the longer this skull yapped at me, the more arrogant it got. So I pretty much told it I wasn't the type to take orders from anybody. It said, 'Meet her at Clava Cairns tomorrow at midnight,' and I said, 'Like hell I will! I don't even know who "her" is!'"

Albert put his elbows on his knees, leaning forward as if that were the only way he could hold his own weight up. He glanced at me. "And then it started talking about you."

"What did it say?" Vayl demanded.

"I didn't let it say much besides, 'Your daughter, Jasmine—' before I yelled at it to get out. And then I started changing channels. Jack was barking up a storm too. I think that helped. Anyway, it left."

We stood silent while another line of people passed us, Albert patting Jack as if the dog were the one in need of comfort, while I tried to figure out what the afterworld could possibly want with my old man. Finally he said, "I didn't think it would be able to find me once I left the States. I already spent time with Dave and Evie. So when I called Pete and told him I was coming along on this assignment whether he liked it or not, he gave me terms. They were totally unreasonable, but I took them, figuring I'd be dead in a few days anyway. I thought I'd stay a while with you, then I'd go back to the apartment where the ghoul would find me. And when Shelby came back from his honeymoon he'd see me there, sitting in my La-Z-Boy, looking a little blue and a lot stiff, with a cheesecake in my lap and a beer on the table beside me. Maybe he'd think it was heart failure."

"How the hell did you suppose we were going to pay for your funeral when you blew your savings on this trip!"

Vayl put his hand on my shoulder. "Jasmine, it could be that you are ruining a special moment here."

We both ignored him as Albert shot back, "I imagined you'd toss me in the back of a pickup truck and dump me over some cliff to be eaten by vultures like you threaten to do every time I get sick!"

"I only said that once, and it was because you hadn't checked your blood sugar in, like, a month! If you're going to be an idiot I'm not going to pay for it!"

"Don't you think I know that? That's why when the senators from the Oversight Committee called me right after I got off the phone with Pete, I didn't hang up on them!"

Vayl's grip on my shoulder tightened. This message I got. *Pay attention, Jasmine. This is important.* "The Oversight Committee? For our department? Called you?"

Albert clamped his lips shut, a damn-I-said-too-much grimace lining his face. I inched so close to him our noses practically banged together. "What did they want, Dad?"

"They're going to reimburse all my expenses in return for a report on how you guys operate." He stuck his forefinger in my shoulder and pushed me backward. "I don't know what you're worried about. You're the best."

"Albert, part of the reason we're good is because nobody knows how we work." I glanced up at Vayl. "What do you think?"

He leaned against the wall as if he had all the time in the world to ponder. "I am distinctly unimpressed by this group of imbeciles, but sometimes their type can do the worst damage. We must discover their motives, but later. Albert's issue presses, especially if he feels his death will be a sure result."

I studied my dad, who'd had a helluva a lot more people try to kill him than I'd ever battled. I thought now that he would've preferred that end to the diabetes doing the trick, and either one to a "ghoul" that he had no idea how to fight. I said, "Listen, before you hand over your golden years to some ooglie booglie, maybe you should let me take a stab at it."

Albert shook his head. "This is demonic stuff, Jaz. Something you have no experience with. And the last of the great demon hunters died with—" He stopped. His stony face betrayed a hint of grief as he said, "They're gone."

I just barely prevented myself from laughing in his face.

"Let's just say there's a new game in town."

CHAPTER TWENTY

Before the games could begin, however, Vayl, Cole, Albert, and I had to pick our positions. While Iona and Viv remained on the floor of the front hall with Floraidh and Dormal, trying to decide what to do with the rest of their evening, we held a quick powwow on the stairs.

"One of us must go on the GhostWalk," said Vayl.

"I think the girls are leaning that direction," Cole said. "If they do, I'll tag along."

Something in the way he stared down at Viv as she signed to Iona stopped me. "Cole? You're not developing feelings for them, are you?"

"No!"

"Because one of them could turn out to be the—"

"I know that!" Still, I could see it in his eyes when he dragged them back to mine. Tenderness. Especially for the blah dresser with the funky shoes, who, despite everything, had still found the strength to smile tonight.

Albert began flipping through the pages of his program.

"You know, if you're going to play blind, the least you could do is act the part," I said. "Take Jack for instance." My dog looked up at me, licking his chops as if I'd just offered him a treat. "He's fully into the part of seeing-eye dog. If we were at a busy intersection right now, I bet he wouldn't step into the street until the light turned."

"Yeah, I know what you tell that mutt when I'm not around," Albert huffed. "If I was really blind you'd probably have him lead me right into the path of a semi. Here"—he held up the booklet, showing me the GhostWalk page—"look at this." He pointed out a full-color picture depicting Clava Cairns. It was a day shot, revealing huge beech trees shading three large burial mounds, all of which were surrounded by standing stones, themselves like tall, rectangular grave markers. The cairns had been built as circular hills, with large boulders forming the outer ring and smaller stones making up the remaining construction. Two of them had paths to the inside. The one in the center was a complete ring.

Vayl touched my arm as I felt a coldness steal over me, watching my father's fingers graze the photo of the four-thousand-year-old grave site he'd been ordered to visit the next evening.

"I'm going on this walk," said Albert.

"No." I spoke before I had time to think. The sound he made reminded me he still had too much mental capacity for my orders to hold any weight.

Before Albert could slam me, Vayl said, "I share your daughter's concerns. What if your visitor decides to come early? At the very least, it would throw off our entire mission to have to bury you this week."

Harsh. But a message Albert understood. "All right. One of you is going anyway, you said so yourselves. Just get Cole to convince the girls to come along. Then two of you will be there to protect me."

When we both still hesitated, he said, "Look, Floraidh's not going anywhere. It's not going to take all three of you to keep an eye on her for the next half hour. And if the girls are on the walk they're not going to be here trying to kill her."

Cole nodded and trotted down the stairs to talk to Viv and Iona.

Vayl and I shared a short, silent powwow.

Do you wanna go? I asked.

He is your father.

Why do you keep reminding me?

He glanced at Albert. "When does the first tour leave?"

Albert checked the program. "Five minutes."

"Never enough time," Vayl muttered. "Come," he said to me. "I believe I may have left something in the van you will find helpful if Albert's friend turns out to be an early riser."

He led me out of the castle to the deserted parking lot. When he raised the back door of the Alhambra I expected to find some sort of megaweapon crated up and waiting for me. The storage compartment was empty.

I turned to Vayl. "What—" He motioned for silence as he removed his party line transmitter and motioned for me to do the same. As soon as I'd pocketed mine he took my free hand, turned Cirilai with his fingers, making the rubies reflect the moonlight.

"I can feel events begin to spin out of our control. Soon we will not even have a moment to call our own. That is the way of our lives." His brows drew together. "I should be used to it by now." He glanced at me, his eyes so dark I could feel whole universes sifting, birthing, and dying on the other side. "But I have become greedy of late. I am not sure this is right. I am certain it is dangerous. But I cannot resist."

He yanked me into his arms, pulling me onto my tiptoes. Our mouths met with such force I knew my lips would burn for the rest of the night. The feel of his body, hard against mine, rocked me to the core. I felt like all the paintings I'd never understood, all the stars that had shone cold in the sky above me, every joke that had left me unmoved suddenly shifted into place. Everything I'd ever done made sense because I'd found someone who made me forget to breathe.

Now.

Vayl lifted his head. *Cool, he's panting too!*

Don't wait, Jaz. Don't ever let it be too late again.

I loosened my hold on him. Maybe digging my fingernails into his shoulder blades, while fine for a passionate embrace, wasn't quite appropriate for the next move I had in mind.

"Jasmine?"

"Did I ever tell you I love the way you say my name?"

He shook his head, his face almost completely in shadow. Suddenly I needed to see how he'd react. I squeezed my eyes shut. The contact lenses Bergman had made for me kicked in, bathing the area in see-in-the-dark green. My Sensitivity added more color. Enough that Vayl's face showed clear, if slightly reddish yellow. *You know what? It'll do.*

I said, "The fact that you went back home? That you said goodbye to your boys? Although I know you still have a lot to do, it's enough of a start for me."

Vayl went still, as if the slightest movement might interfere with his hearing. "What are you saying?" he whispered.

I slid my hands across his broad shoulders, down his arms, and in around his waist. Given a choice, I knew I'd never leave his side, never go without this kind of touch again. "I love you, Vayl."

A hitch in his breath, the slightest double take accompanied by a tender, dawning smile. *"Yeeees!"* He picked me up and twirled me around so quickly my feet flew out behind me like they had when I was a kid and Gramps Lew wanted to play Merry-Go-Grandpa.

As soon as he set me down he demanded, "Say it again!"

"I love—"

"Ha, *ha!*" Triumph in his fierce, fangtastic grin as he pulled me in for another kiss. And then a whole bouquet of them, raining down on my face like drought-relieving waters. "Again," he growled.

"I love you, all right? Geez, are you always going to be this insatiable?"

His expression took a wicked turn. "I cannot wait to show you." He took my hand, pulled me away from the van so he could close the hatch. "Let us go tell your father."

Gulp.

"Yeah, sure." *I don't mind dying young. Always thought it would happen this way. Not by Albert, necessarily, but then, the family is usually in on it somehow.* More to stave off execution than because I really needed to hear it I said, "Um, was there anything you wanted to say to me? Now that it's somewhat appropriate?"

We stopped beside one of those sweet little Minis that, if it came to America, would immediately be set upon and eaten by a gang of SUVs. Vayl turned to me, pulling me into his arms once again.

I could get used to this. I want to. Is that a bad thing?

Vayl's lips brushed against my hair, forehead, eyelids. "You know I have been saying this to you, in one way or another, for months?"

"Uh."

Soft laugh, carried away by the warm Scottish breeze. "Jasmine?"

"Yeah?"

"Never have I been so glad to have lived so long. You are the woman my heart has waited for all these centuries. I love you with every—are you laughing?"

"I'm sorry! It's just . . . are you really that mushy?"

Hint of dimple. "Why? Are you sensing the need for galoshes?"

"More like hip boots!"

"How shall I tell you, then? Would you prefer it in writing? A sonnet to my darling's eyes?"

I made a gagging sound.

"All right, then. Perhaps if I leaped in front of a stray bullet?"

"God, no!"

He lifted my hand to his lips, kissed the ring he'd slipped on my hand during our last mission, when I'd finally admitted we needed each other whether I liked it or not. "Will you give me some time to ponder? I may yet come up with the perfect medium for my heartfelt confession."

"Sure, yeah. Ponder away." I looked at my watch. "We should be getting back. The GhostWalk's going to start any minute now."

"That will give us very little time to discuss our relationship with your father. Perhaps we should do it—as you Americans prefer most occasions—over a meal."

"Definitely," I replied, swallowing hard to keep the relief south of my vocal chords. "But not breakfast. I don't really want something this special shared among Scidairans."

"All right, then. Our first free meal after this mission ends will be the one in which we share our news."

"Excellent!" *Maybe I'll get zapped by Bea and spend the next two weeks in the hospital. One can only hope.*

Chapter Twenty-One

Here's how bad I had it. Walking back to the castle, I wanted to hold hands with Vayl. Like teenagers at a football game. Worse, I wanted to walk into the front hall with that strut in my step that let everybody know I'd landed the captain of the team. Everybody but Albert, that is. Oh, and Cole. Except neither one acknowledged me when I joined the GhostWalk group just inside the entrance, my party line firmly back in place. Albert sat at the bottom of the stairs, patting Jack while he stared off into space, doing his "legally blind" act. And Viv, Iona, and Cole were signing so quickly their fingers practically blurred. Then the three of them would dissolve into giggles.

And there you have it, folks. After just a few hours of concerted effort, Cole has charmed the shy girl and the cold-fish lesbian. Give that man a bonus! And while you're at it, give me a new damn coat!

I still wore my leather, just because I needed to cover my shoulder holster. But the bullet hole followed by the ghost slash had ruined it. *Dammit.* I didn't care if Pete had to squeeze the money out of his own ass, he was going to pay for this one.

The buzz at the back of my brain distracted me, signaled that Vayl had clicked in the camouflage. Since he might need a set of wheels, I handed him the keys to the van and he glided from my side, no one in the group even acknowledging his exit. But I noticed. In fact, I felt his absence like the surgical removal of an organ. *Is it gonna be this way every time we have to separate? Because if so . . .* I sighed *. . . I'm just going to have to learn to stop whining and deal with it.*

I glanced up. He'd intercepted the Raisers on their way to their next event. A short conversation laced with his subtle suggestiveness ended with the exchange of business cards. After everything that had happened, he'd still given a thought to Viv. To her possible decision to dispel a murderer's ghost. And it looked to me like he'd just laid the groundwork in case she made that choice.

I caught his eye, mouthed, *I love you.* He touched two fingers to his lips and lowered them to me, as if real kisses should never be blown, just gently released in your sweetheart's direction.

Damn, that's hot! I did a quick personal check to make sure I wasn't slack-jawed, tongue-dropped gawking as I watched him settle into a corner of the second-story hallway, sliding into a high-backed chair like he belonged there. Nobody looked up. And no one walking by glanced his way. It wasn't that he had the ability to become invisible. Just that he put out a strong vibe that caused everyone close to ignore him. Completely.

I pretended to scratch my ear, checked to make sure I'd reset my equipment correctly, and mumbled the first sensible thought that came to mind. "What kind of fool survives a ghost attack only to go trolling through the countryside in the hopes of finding yet more ghosts?"

"I believe you are surrounded by them," murmured Vayl. "Now play nice. If you offend the entire group we may never find out what Floraidh has planned."

I snorted. *So much for romance. I guess I'm supposed to keep that totally separate from work like some damn adult or something. This day just keeps getting better. And it's only been May thirteenth for like*—I checked my watch—*an hour and a half!*

"All right, everyone, gather round, gather round!"

At first all I could see was a ripple of people as the group moved aside for a smaller but more forceful personality who, it turned out, would be our guide. As he mounted the first five steps, the better to be seen and heard by us GhostWalkers, I felt my mouth drop. Cole came up beside me.

"I like his look, don't you?"

"What would you call it?"

Cole pointed his foot in front of him as he crossed his arms and pursed his lips. In the girliest voice he could manage he said, "Do you see how the orange scarf offsets the tiger-striped shirt, which is quite brilliantly tucked into the black spandex pants so we're left in no doubt as to the fact that he's at least two hundred pounds overweight?"

I covered my mouth to hide the smile. "Yeah, I noticed that."

"Brilliant. I know *I* want him."

"I don't think you're his type. Look at you. White button-down Western shirt, blue jeans. The only thing that's not boring about your outfit is your shoes!"

"Let's introduce him to Albert. See if he can resist yanking out a handful of this guy's chest hair. Who told him he should unbutton the top three anyway?"

"Maybe his designer's suffered an identity crisis."

Our guide had held up his hands as if we'd greeted him with deafening applause and must be calmed down.

"My name is Bartolomé Felipe Penilla and I will be your GhostWalk guide for this evening," he said in a tone even more feminine than the one Cole had used. I thought his Spanish accent sounded forced. But something at the back of his words stirred my memory. By the end of the tour I might be able to guess his real birth country. "Now, I'll be wearing this portable microphone"—he pointed to the headpiece threaded through his funky hair, which was spiked on one side and straightened on the other—"so even though we have a group of twenty tonight, you should all be able to hear me."

A hand shot up in the crowd. I nearly moaned out loud. There's always one gabber, isn't there? "Yes, sir?" said Bart.

"Where are we going first?" asked the guy, a dome-headed nose pincher who'd evidently never learned how to follow an itinerary. Because it was all written out for us in the program. Even Floraidh's stop had been penciled in.

Our guide held up a finger. Was that light pink polish on his nails? He'd better not be waving his hands around much tonight. If Albert caught a glimpse he'd tackle the guy and make him cover his hands with dirt. Or worse, Jack droppings.

Bart said, "I think you are going to be quite delighted. This year we have finally gained permission to tour Clava Cairns by night. After that we'll visit Siorruidh, which is the Hoppringhill cemetery. And that will lead us to our surprise stop. A ghost has been sited at Tearlach this very evening!"

As our guide clapped his hands enthusiastically, cheers erupted from the GhostWalkers. I studied the crowd, young and old, well dressed and grungy, all bright-eyed as a bunch of World War II volunteers. Idiots. Bart went on, assuring them the sites were all within a reasonable walking distance of each other, pumping them up till they were practically drooling, but I stopped listening. Albert had decided to join me.

"What the hell is wrong with these people?" he asked, his voice carrying at least as far as Glasgow.

How refreshing that, for once, nobody knew we were related. "Gosh, Albert, I don't know. Maybe they'd rather spend time with the dead than insensitive mooks like you." I know, I know. Nobody can turn me into a hypocrite faster than my dad.

I crouched down to pet Jack. Something told me I was going

to need this moment of peace before setting off on a hike with my half-crippled father and a coworker who acted like he wanted me one second and then flirted like a maniac the next. *Jealous any, Jaz?* I glanced at Cole. *Nope. Just worried he's about to do something really dumb.*

The GhostWalk started off fine. The path to Clava Cairns had been mulched and lit at decent intervals with solar lamps mounted to poles. The group spread out, following Bart in a line that stretched the length of a city block. With Albert moving at cracked-knee pace, we quickly dropped to the back. But the pack began to close again as we neared our first destination, which was lit to an eerie ambience with lanterns hanging from the lowest branches of the spidery-armed beech trees that grew throughout the area.

The picture Albert had shown me of Clava Cairns's burial mounds didn't convey the feel of the place. Sure, everywhere on Earth is ancient. But the places where people bury their dead seem to hold on to that history better than anywhere else.

As we moved toward the mound Bart wanted to show off, a well-dressed woman who'd decided that spiked pumps were the ideal touring shoe tripped over a smaller circle of stones and would've given herself a nasty gash if her companion hadn't caught her on the way down.

Yeah, this place wants us outta here, I thought as I looked around grimly.

The talkers in the group lowered it to a spooked murmur as the atmosphere sunk into their awareness. We all kept checking out the borders, as if we expected a line of mourners to burst through the trees, chanting and wailing, carrying with them a shrouded body on a litter.

Bart led everyone to the northeast cairn, which stood taller than the average man, a testament to the old race's commitment.

Had they loved and missed their dead as we do? Or had they simply feared that if they didn't bury them right, they'd return. Angry and famished. Looking for a little soul to sup on?

"My friends, this huge burial mound is the source of the most activity," Bart began, darting his eyes around the group, oozing suppressed excitement. "We estimate that over two thousand people were cremated and/or interred in this space before it was closed over their bodies." He waved dramatically toward a narrow passageway leading toward the center of the cairn. "Of course, the cairn lost its seal hundreds of years ago and has been open to the elements for all that time."

"I dare you to go in," one young guy with shaved short hair and side mirror ears said to his friend, a tall, skinny dude who walked around with an unlit cigarette dangling from his lips. I was betting he hadn't had a date in, well, ever.

"I will if you will," said Cigarette Lips.

"Fine, I'll go!"

"Do you hear that, ladies and gentlemen?" asked Bart. "We have two volunteers to lead us into the cairn! Since we're such a big crowd, however, we'll have to split up. Ten and ten should do it, I think." He separated us, grouping our crew with Shaved Head and sending us first.

Jack wasn't thrilled with the idea of entering the cairn and resisted at first, jerking his head against Albert's hand a couple of times. But when Cole took Albert's arm to keep up the pretense that he needed to be led and I grabbed Jack's leash, he settled down. Iona signed to Viv, with Cole translating, "Are you scared?"

Viv thought a second. Shrugged. "No, not really." She put her hand on Cole's free arm and smiled up at him. Together we walked into the cairn.

Chapter Twenty-Two

First I noticed the stifling feeling caused by a combination of my mild claustrophobia and someone's overactive sweat glands raising a mild stench where we stood in the center of the stones. The mud floor had been swept clean of debris. The stones, held back at their base only by a small ring of rocks, pressed in on me as I looked around. My vision, limited by the presence of so many others, began to blur and fade.

I blinked and looked up at the sky. *Breathe, Jaz. Inhale and listen to Bart the Spandex Wonder gush about the Clava Cairns ghosts.*

"Maybe if we're very, very quiet," he said. And he closed his eyes.

The last thing I wanted was another ghost encounter. I looked around, trying to decide who would be the least pissed off if I decided to shove my way through the meditators. I'd just about picked my route when Jack distracted me. He was digging.

What are you doing! Good God, defacing public property? That's probably a felony in this country! Stop, you crazy mutt! Sometimes Jack picks up on my unspoken suggestions. Sometimes not. This time he looked up at me and stuck out his tongue.

Don't give me that; I know you're not hot! Now cut it out!

But Jack had found something interesting. Probably a bone

belonging to some poor schmuck who hadn't been so great with the flint.

I took a step back. Pulled Albert and Cole together in front of me like a pair of curtains.

"What is it?" Cole murmured.

"Cover me," I whispered as I knelt behind them. "Stop it!" I hissed, shoving dirt back into the small hole Jack had made. "If this is revenge for the neutering, I'd just like to remind you, that lamp you mistakenly took for a golden retriever cost me a hundred bucks to replace. And I'm still having issues peeing in my own toilet after catching you . . . ugh! It makes me shiver to remember! So if you think this makes us even, think again!"

He dug like a Caterpillar, making it nearly impossible to keep up with him. I finally leaned my shoulder in to him and shoved him far enough aside that I could refill the crater he'd begun. But as I began to push dirt back into the spot he'd chosen, I felt something rubbery move under my fingers.

For a second I reverted to age twelve, when Mom decided Dave and I were old enough to stay home alone and look after Evie while she worked. At night. We'd felt like big shits in a little bowl until we heard the scraping at the back door. Then, just like now, a moment of bone-deep paralysis accompanied by a dam's burst of thoughts. *Did we lock the door? Maybe it's the dog scratching. Nope, he died last winter. Could it be the freak we saw passing by the house this morning? The one who looked like his nose was about to rot off? And why am I sitting here trying to figure stuff out when he could already be in the dining room? With a knife! Mommy, I'm scared!*

That time we *had* locked the door. And a good thing, too. Because it had been our neighbor, Mr. Moore. So drunk he'd confused our house for his. When he couldn't get in, he'd tried the right place, gone inside, and shot his family to death with a .22-caliber rifle.

Now it took me a second to realize I didn't have hold of a body part. After I'd had a moment to shove my heart back into my chest, reinflate my lungs, and feel around the hole, I realized Jack had dug up something leathery and strappy. I pulled him back to the spot and let him finish the job while Bart waxed poetical about all the souls who hadn't been able to move on from this place. In particular a nightly walker they liked to call the Chief.

"The Chief is a tall, commanding figure with long hair and a braided beard," Bart said, his tone taking on the lyrical quality I generally equated with radio preachers. "He usually appears right here, in the center of this cairn, leaning on a tall staff as if he's guarding something. Visitors have also seen him walking among the cairns, but much more rarely."

While he was talking I fished the rest of the leather out of the hole and refilled the spot. The bigger challenge was to convince Jack it wasn't a chew toy. Luckily Albert had brought a spare doggy treat, which he slipped to me like it was a roll of microfilm from his active-duty days. Jack wavered for a second, debating which would be more delish.

"Trade me right now, or I swear we are not going Rollerblading at all next time we're home," I whispered. He dropped the unburied treasure and went for the treat. I'm telling you, this dog of mine is smarter than he looks.

I tucked the leathery whatnot under my armpit, looping it around Grief's holster for extra hold.

"I don't think the Chief is going to show," Cole murmured to Iona.

"Where would he even stand?" she wondered.

"Maybe he'd just hover over everybody and knock heads with his mighty staff," Cole suggested.

"Why would he do that?" she asked.

"How would you feel if a bunch of nosy jerks came in and

started stomping all over your grave? I know I'd be pissed, and I'm not even going to be buried."

"You're not?"

"Nope. I'm debating between being shot into space and having my body stuffed and mounted on a pedestal at the Playboy Mansion." While Iona giggled I slapped my hand to my forehead. Where did he come up with this stuff?

"Do you think we'll see something spooktacular tonight?"

I snapped my head around. It was the key phrase. The one identifying my contact. Who turned out to be the broad with the inappropriate footwear. She'd sidled up beside me, dropping one handle of her enormous bag off her shoulder. As soon as Cole caught her drift he directed the girls' attention to Bart, signing and saying, "Look, I think our guide's about to show us a funeral dance."

As Viv's shoulders shook and Iona laughed aloud at Bart's badly disguised soft-shoe, I rescued the bag-o'-nastiness from its spot in my pocket and slid it into the woman's purse. She slipped her arm through the dropped loop, brushing her hand against my arm so I'd feel the scratch of paper folded in her hand and nab it from her as she turned away.

We filed out of the cairn, nobody seeming that disappointed that the Chief had been a no-show. *Wait a second. The Chief sounds a little like . . . Could he be that Brude guy? Naw, probably some Stone Age tribal leader with a bone through his nose.*

I decided these people took GhostWalks for the stories more than anything else. Although one woman insisted she'd felt a cold hand touch the back of her neck.

"Probably the icy tingle of a psychotic hallucination," Albert growled as we joined him.

I rolled my eyes. "Come on, let's see how many more people you can offend over by that parking lot, shall we?"

We ambled away from our group as the second one joined Bart and Mr. Skinny for a look inside the cairn. "Cole, keep the girls away from us, will ya?" I murmured as Albert, Jack, and I moved toward the gravel lot.

As we reached an actual light pole, four of which lit up the corners of the quarter-acre space, I unfolded the note. It said:

> We think the apparition you described is one seen by several locals who claim he's the original owner of Tearlach. A quiet solicitor named Oengus Meicklejohn who was supposedly poisoned by his wife back in 1867. But they were never able to prove it because the doctor's office where the body was being held burned before an autopsy could be performed. The grave was robbed a week after what was left of Oengus was buried. Funny coincidence. Mrs. Meicklejohn's first name was Floraidh.

I sucked air so fast the sides of my nose nearly touched. Because I didn't believe in coincidences. Floraidh Meicklejohn must be Floraidh Halsey, an incredibly well preserved old crone who'd murdered her husband in the nineteenth century and was now signing people up to gawk at his image for ten pounds a pop. Which made the presence of his actual ghost, lingering at the edge of his property, kinda sad and pathetic.

I wasn't sure why the Scidairans would raise his image in the kitchen, except that you use the ingredients you have on hand when working a last-minute plan, and maybe to make an ethereal figure appear you had to have something of his to start with. *Like his ashes?* Or wait. Hadn't they mentioned his *skull?*

Who knew? By the time the labs came back on the bowl-o'-yuck, this mission folder would be gathering cobwebs in Pete's ugly old file cabinet. And the skull must be well protected.

Albert hawked and spit. "You gonna act like a space cadet all night or are you going to tell me why we're pretending to enjoy the great outdoors?"

I pulled Jack's find from my jacket and untangled it. One piece of leather decorated with studs. I recognized it instantly. "It can't be. No, there have to be thousands and thousands just like the one he had."

"What is it?" asked Albert. The question echoed in my ear. Vayl, still within transmission distance, had caught the concern in my voice. He'd probably also noted my jolt of fear as I'd stretched out the item in my hands.

I said, "While we were in the cairn, Jack dug up a harness that looks just like the one he wore when he was Samos's dog."

Albert reached out to rub some dirt off the buckle as Vayl took time to let the information sink in. "Do you have any way of telling what dog truly wore it?" my boss asked.

"I don't think—well, maybe." I turned the harness inside out, peered at the leather, moving my fingers along its length, trying to feel what I might not be able to see in the poor light. I found what I was looking for under the shoulder strap. A carefully engraved name. Four letters that sent my heartbeat into overdrive. Ziel. The name Jack had answered to when he'd been the pet of Edward "the Raptor" Samos.

Chapter Twenty-Three

Okay, I have maybe five minutes before I need to get back to this ridiculous GhostWalk and pretend all is right with the world. So chime in anytime. Why is the harness we traded to a rental car clerk for information in Ljubljana, Slovenia, on our last mission, dangling from my hands in Scotland tonight?"

"What is significant about that particular item?" asked Vayl. "Let us concentrate on that for a moment, shall we?"

"Jack wore it when he belonged to Samos," I said.

"And you have been seeing visions of Samos," Vayl said.

"Yeah."

"I thought he was dead," said Cole.

"He is." I went over the moment of his passing one more time in my mind. "Yeah. Definitely dead."

"So maybe somebody's trying to raise his ghost," said Albert.

I stared at him. "Why would anyone—" I remembered the slashes on Vayl's chest. Samos could still do damage if Albert was right. But it didn't make sense. Ghosts are tied to places, especially those associated with their deaths. Which meant if Samos was walking, he should've been trotting around the base of a mountain in Patras, Greece. Plus, I'd never heard of a vampire shade. Because in order to leave something behind, you kinda have to have something to start with.

I sighed. "Any other ideas?"

"Maybe someone wants to hurt Jack. Or, more specifically, hurt you by hurting him," said Vayl. "It is no secret that you took possession of him after Samos died."

"Then why not a direct attack?" I asked. "Why bury his old harness in a place they didn't even realize either of us would turn up?"

"Looks like we're moving on," said Cole.

"All right, we will continue this discussion later," said Vayl. "Meanwhile, everyone keep an eye open for suspicious behavior relating to Jack. And, Jasmine, if you see Samos's face again, tell me immediately."

"Okay." I knelt down and rubbed Jack on the head, just where he liked it best. *What's up with you, huh? Who would go to all the trouble of tracking down your old harness? Who would even have the power to—*

Floraidh.

Fucking Scidairan who had given Samos the idea to burn me and mine to death when we battled in Patras, assuring him it would imbue him with awesome powers. Now that I thought about it, that sounded like more than a simple ally. In fact, it kinda sounded like someone who cared. Someone who would, maybe, want to see her honey again. And nothing could move Samos like his beloved pet, Ziel.

Back off this right now, Jaz. You're supposed to be protecting Floraidh, remember? Anything short of that could get you canned.

I looked at the leather straps hanging from my hands. I could fling them off into the trees. Cut them into tiny pieces and scatter them across the Highlands. Or rebury them.

Goddammit. I shoved them back in my jacket, tucking enough of the leather down my sleeve that I was sure the harness wouldn't slip out accidentally. I headed back toward the party, linking my arm loosely through Albert's as Jack sauntered between us.

"We're heading to the Hoppringhill cemetery next, right?" I asked.

Albert checked his itinerary. "Yep. This says we might see the ghosts of a couple of star-crossed lovers who both drank poison there after the girl's parents forbade them to see each other." He looked up from the paper in his hand. "Star-crossed? Don't they mean mentally ill?"

"I don't—"

"Well, come on. What's romantic about pouring bleach down your throat when all you have to do is wait around for a couple of years till you're old enough to tell your folks to shove it?"

I sighed. "Is that what happened with you and Mom?"

He glared at me, like he usually did when I brought up his mostly miserable marriage. "Don't you even have any idea when we got together?"

"No."

"She was already your age." He hesitated. "She'd been married and divorced by the time I met her."

I stopped, nearly toppling him over when I jerked him to a halt beside me. "What?"

"She never told you." He shook his head. "I guess I shouldn't be surprised. Secretive, that one. It was like pulling teeth to get her to tell me how she spent her goddamn day."

He started us walking again, leading me while I stared at the shadowed path, trying to make this new layer settle onto the portrait of my mother that I thought I'd finished the day she died. "Did you ever meet him?" I asked.

"No. He'd left her long before I came on the scene." Albert shook his head. "Your granny May tried to warn me. She thought he took something, I don't know, he took all the softness from her when he went. But you can't really talk to me once I've made my mind up."

"No kidding?"

"Do you want to hear this or not?"

"Yeah."

"Then listen for once." I swallowed my smart-ass reply and let my dad talk. "He wasn't the kind of man Granny May and Gramps Lew wanted for your mom, but what could they do? She was as bullheaded as you. Unfortunately she wasn't nearly as smart. And I don't think, deep down, she understood what she was worth the way you do."

"So . . . she ever get over it?"

He shook his head. "I believe she always loved him. Our biggest fight happened after I found out she'd kept in touch with him, especially when I was out of the country. That's, uh, when she left me. I thought it was forever. She thought it was for the night. Until she found me with her best friend the next day."

I held up my hand. "Okay, you know what? Enough. Parents aren't supposed to have secret spouses. And discuss their messy breakups with their kids."

"Then why did you ask?"

"Because I'm an idiot!"

We walked in fuming silence for about five minutes. Finally I said, "I have to go."

"Where?"

"Away. I've put it off long enough. And I'm just pissed enough not to care what happens while I'm gone. You just hang on to my arm and don't let me fall on my face during my trip, okay?"

"What are you blabbing about?" Albert frowned at me. "Are you on THE drugs?"

Here we go. How many times in my life had he accused me of being on *THE* drugs? Like there was a brand out there made just for me. "No, Dad, I'm as sober as you are." I sighed. "There's a guy I know who can help us both with our problems. But the only way I can visit him is to leave my body. I've never tried it while I was moving, so I'm just asking you to keep me from walking into a tree for the next few minutes. Will you do that for me or not?"

He stared at me for so long *I* had to steer *him* clear of a low-growing limb. "How can you do that?"

"Well, it all started the night I lost my virginity—"

"Never mind. I don't wanna know."

I could've told him the truth. But we were too far from a portable defibrillator for me to feel comfortable breaking the news that I'd died while he was puttering around his apartment, pissing off his former nurse because he wouldn't test his sugar levels more than once a week.

"So will you lead me for a while or not?"

"Fine. Just let me hang on to you, will ya? That way it still looks like I'm the one who needs a guide dog."

We rearranged our arm linkage while Cole stole looks over his shoulder at us. He motioned to me. *You need help for this?*

I shook my head. *Just keep the girls busy.*

He nodded. Gave me thumbs-up, like I was a pilot ready to take my F18 airborne.

It sounds almost that easy. *I'm going to leave my body now.* Like I can just zip down the runway and lift off. Not so much. Especially when the dude I'm headed to meet isn't one I'm thrilled to be seeing.

Before I'd met Raoul "in person" he'd been a thunderous voice in my head, pulling me toward a destiny I couldn't have imagined before he'd reconnected me with this life. His were the words that split the two halves of me, allowing my body to continue as if it were run by remote control while my invisible self bounced around the atmosphere like a weather balloon.

I repeated those words now, whispering them into the night, noting that they provided their own kind of light when I looked at them in just the right way. The parts of me resisted the call to separate, every movement of my body working to keep them united. I concentrated harder, closing my eyes, trusting Albert to keep me walking upright. The words buzzed in the back of my throat, gathering the threads of my traveling self, winding it into a cohesive unit that spilled out of me in a single exhale.

I looked down, watched automatic me walk beside Albert and Jack while Cole, Viv, and Iona carried on an animated conversation about the cemetery lying just ahead of us, a monument-marked clearing among the surrounding trees. Above me, nine golden cords, including my own, shot into the sky like ropes dangling from a celestial helicopter. I knew if I brushed against them they'd sing a tune unique to the person they connected to on the ground. Weird to see two of them actually streaming from my guys as they ambled below. And, hey, what do you know! Another, silver streamer flying up from Jack that was so finely woven it practically disappeared against the black background of wide-open sky.

All the cords seemed to orbit around a tenth one, which contained every color of the rainbow, and a bunch more I'd only begun to see after Vayl had taken my blood. The first time I'd seen this cord I'd thought it belonged to a high-level gatekeeper. Somebody who could whisper the password to heaven in your ear if you truly believed. Now I wasn't so sure. Because Raoul leaned against it like it was a streetlight and he was some hood deciding whether or not to mug me.

I felt my nonstomach clench as I read the expression on his face. Or rather, the lack of it. I'd been around enough guys to know that wasn't a good sign.

I nodded to him, deciding to keep my distance. After all, the hands that could heal your broken neck could resnap it. "Raoul."

"Jasmine."

"What's up?"

"Not much. Just wondering why I'm wasting my energy here when I could be lounging on my sofa, talking to you like a regular person." I wanted to yell, *We're not regular people, you doof!* But I'd decided to play nice. At first.

I said, "I haven't seen any portals since I got to Inverness."

"There's one in the castle!"

"Oh." I cleared my throat. "Raoul?"

"What!"

"I didn't really want to go to your place." I held up my hands, marveled that you could see through them. *Hey, I'm kind of a ghost up here. Weird!* I rushed on. "Not that your penthouse isn't magnificent. And oddly large given the dimensions of the building," I added, recalling a visit I'd made to be outfitted for a demonic battle. The guy's rooms must unfold into a parallel universe or something. Which was cool in itself. Neater still were the contents: weapons and armor I still routinely recalled with a feeling so close to lust you might as well not even split hairs.

Raoul's eyes narrowed. "If nothing's wrong with it, why are we meeting here?"

Because I only have a limited amount of time before I have to go back. Which gives me just the excuse I need if [when] this conversation goes sour.

"Because part of this is about him," I said, pointing to Albert. I filled him in on the visitations. "What does that sound like to you?"

"Nothing good. Does your father have any enemies? I mean ones who would take their anger with them to the grave?"

"Dozens."

Raoul nodded. "I'll check with my scouts and see if there's been any unusual activity that we can connect with his troubles."

"Thanks." Next I told him about finding Jack's old harness and seeing Samos's face. "What do you think?" I asked. "Can vampires rise from the dead?"

Raoul shook his head, though his troubled expression didn't comfort me. "I have never heard of such a thing. The very fact that they are reduced to smoke and cinders at the end belies the idea that anything spiritual might remain."

"Okay." Despite the fact that none of me currently rested in the physical, I expected a certain amount of unwinding to take place, as if I'd been bound with an ever-tightening cord that only Raoul's reassurance could loosen. It didn't happen. I sighed. "Look, I'm totally buying into your argument. I've made it myself. But my gut's telling me something's wrong. While your scout's nosing around anyway, can you ask him to find out what was in that contract Samos signed with the devil? Demon? Whoever? I know he had to give up his most precious possession to get to me. Which was Jack. But maybe there was some fine print. Something that allows him to hijack a poor innocent's face and stick out his tongue at me every twelve hours or so."

Raoul nodded thoughtfully. "I think we can do that. Hell's archives are never well guarded."

"Cool." I began to hope I was going to get out of there without a fight. Then Raoul said, "You're still with Vayl."

"Of course. We're a team."

"I didn't mean that."

I clenched my hands, which wasn't at all satisfying in this form. "Are you spying on me?"

"That's not allowed. I simply observe you from time to time to make sure you're not in need of intervention." His tone, shaded with just enough self-righteousness to make my eyes cross, jerked the calm right out of me.

"What are you saying? That I'm headed down a bad road? Lucky me to have you looking over my shoulder, otherwise I'd be a crack whore by now?"

He jerked upright like I'd yanked him by his dark brown crew cut. "I said nothing of the sort! But you are Eldhayr. That designation brings with it certain responsibilities."

"Well, that's news to me!" Not really. I'd known for a while.

But I'd decided some time ago the only way I could function after everything that had happened to me was to hold tight to the part I liked best. The one that kept shrinking but still yelled the loudest, laughed the hardest, and knew everything there was to know about that gorgeous two-and-a-half mile oval located at 16th and Georgetown in Indianapolis.

While we glared at each other, Raoul closed the distance between us. Fine. If he wanted a nose to nose I'd give him one! "Our business is akin to *holy* war," he said. "There's no room in it for vampires!"

"First of all, if you're going to get all fanatical on me, you can just back the hell off and get another grunt to do your dirty work. And second, I fight my targets, my way, with *my* people. If you don't like my crowd, you can wrap your Eldhayr responsibilities around a Popsicle stick and shove them up your—"

"Raoul! Do we have a problem?" We snapped our chins in the direction of the question, because the command in that voice demanded it. Walking toward us across the—well, I don't know what you'd call the stuff we stood on—dark mist? Really tickly shadows? Anyway, this dude moving at a fast clip wore the uniform of a Civil War colonel. Union side. His black hair had been slicked back, emphasizing the worry lines on his forehead. Just a hint of bottom lip peeked out between his droopy black mustache and precursor goatee.

"No, John, nothing's wrong," Raoul said. "I was just talking to Jasmine about her affinity with the vampire Vayl."

As I watched the colonel approach, I fought the urge to salute. Geez, the guy oozed authority like vice principals emit detention slips! And my reaction so pissed me off. You'd think by now I'd have learned how to stifle that urge to obey that all Marines' daughters are trained to. Realizing my emotional cocktail had made for a potential explosion, I did what any reasonable, level-headed woman of my background would've done. I shook it.

"I'm not dumping Vayl," I snapped. "I don't give two craps about your rules. Hell, I didn't even know they existed until this moment." Ignoring the fact that Colonel John had winced when I swore, I bulldozed on. "I don't appreciate you people cranking out the high-and-mighty on me when I've fought on your side ever since—well, you know. And so has Vayl!"

I stopped. Realized I'd taken a pretty aggressive stance with my hands on my hips and my legs spread. And didn't change it when Colonel John said, "Are you finished?"

I thought a second. "Yup."

"You're fading, you know." I looked down. Shit! Time was running out on me and I wasn't even close to done! He held out his hand. "May I?"

I shrugged. He touched me on the shoulder, sending a tingling warmth through me that tasted of honey and roses. I know, no tongue to do actual sensing, but that's what it felt like. And when I held a hand up, it looked more solid than it ever had in this form. "Cool." Then I remembered I was pissed off and frowned. Which made Colonel John laugh.

"You must forgive Raoul. Though he would never tell you this directly, he cares a great deal for you. He fought passionately for your inclusion among the Eldhayr when the Eminent met to decide whether or not to invite you. And again when your brother's fate hung in the balance."

I glanced at my Spirit Guide, who'd crossed his hands over his chest and glued his gaze to some distant star. "Really."

"And perhaps you could also pardon his feelings about your vampire. He has . . . personal reasons to resent them. The fact that he still struggles, after all these decades, should tell you how deeply their kind hurt him."

I nodded, not daring to look at Raoul at all now. I knew the last thing he wanted was a sympathetic stare from me. "Now." The colonel slapped his hands together and rubbed them. "Did someone call for a Hell Scout?"

We briefed Colonel John on the details of his mission, and I told him everything I could remember or that I'd concluded about Samos. "Excellent," he finally said. "I'll get on it right away."

"But . . . don't you have to, I don't know, hang out at headquarters? Send out orders while somebody else pulls off the dangerous stunts?" I asked.

Colonel John shook his head. "Rank works differently among the Eldhayr, Jasmine. Here, the higher you climb the ladder, the more risky work you're required to do." He nodded to me and then to Raoul. "I'll report in when I have something interesting to discuss."

"Godspeed," said Raoul.

"Yeah, that," I agreed.

Colonel John grinned and marched off into the shadows as quickly as he'd arrived.

"I think I like him," I said after a long, strained silence.

"He grows on you."

"So . . . how are we?"

Raoul refused to meet my eyes. "Fine."

Small spurt of anger, quickly doused when I remembered Colonel John's advice. "Vayl's not that kind of vamp. You know that."

"He's a killer. Closer to pure predator than you realize, Jasmine."

I said, "So am I." Raoul met my eyes then. "That's why you recruited me, right?"

His nod barely moved air.

"I love him." It was the first time I'd ever told anybody. The feeling nearly brought me up on tiptoe. "You, of all people, know what I've been through. What I've lost. I never thought I'd find anything remotely close to that again. And now that I have, I'm telling you, I'm never letting it go. Never."

Acceptance in Raoul's eyes. A hint of a smile at the corners of his lips. "So that would be a not ever?"

"Yes."

"As in, eternity?"

"Pretty much."

Long sigh, followed by an okay-I'll-deal nod. "Do you really think it will last that long? After all, you are an absolute pain in the rear."

"Raoul!"

"Always interrupting me with your demands. Wreathing my head with obscenities. Borrowing my equipment. Bringing it back all bloody and chipped."

"I did not!"

By now he was grinning. "Do you irritate everyone you work with this much?"

I didn't have to stop to think about it. But I hesitated anyway. Finally. Reluctantly. "Yeah."

"Good. That makes me feel much better about what I'm going to do next."

"What—"

He set the heel of his palm against my forehead and said, "Return!"

I rocketed back into my body so fast the entire world blurred. The pain dropped me to my knees, where I stayed, trying not to heave supper all over the tombstone I'd landed in front of. I'd never experienced the bends, but I imagined this was what they felt like, as if all my joints had been stretched to their limit and then compressed by g-forces equivalent to those experienced by astronauts and race car drivers.

Swearing would've relieved some of my pain and a lot of

stress. But Raoul's words still rang in my ears. Plus, as my eyes focused on the words carved into the granite before me, I figured neither Caitir Burns (born—1779, died—1804) nor her family would much appreciate me dropping the F-bomb on the final monument to her memory.

Well, what do you know, my body walked all the way to Siorruidh before it keeled over like an unmanned muppet.

I forced my chin up, let my eyes wander over the Hoppringhill family's old burial grounds. The stones marched along in symmetrical rows, as if a city planner had mapped out the whole place for the first castle laird with ease of mowing in mind. Younger than Clava Cairns by around thirty-five hundred years, the cemetery lacked the pagan hue of its neighbor. Until I felt movement under my fingers. A ripple of the earth, as if something lying far below had turned, disturbed in its rest by all of us clunking around above. I jerked my hands off the grass. But not before the psychic scent hit me. A mix of wood smoke and old blood.

Brude.

"Did you feel that?" I asked.

Albert checked over his shoulder, as if I'd just warned him of a sneak attack. "What?"

I pointed to the ground. "*That.* Just now. Like a mini quake?"

"Nope. Maybe you had gas."

I cocked my head up at him, wishing once again that I could claim to be adopted. "You've gotta be kidding."

He spread out his hands. "Hey, you haven't been around me on chili night lately. Swear to God, some of those farts lift me right off the chair."

Despite the lingering pain, I scrambled to my feet. Albert didn't offer me a hand. Of course. I began to curse him inwardly. Then I stopped. Looked at him. He stared back, waiting for me to pull it together. And I realized this had been his gift to me. Always being a presence in my life. Never more than a phone call away. But holding back his strength. Allowing me to find my own, so that when I fell, I could learn to stand again. I might not agree with his methods, but I suddenly understood his reasoning.

"You ready to move on?" he asked.

"Yeah."

I noticed the bulk of the GhostWalk crowd stood about thirty yards away, surrounding Bart as he narrated the romantic and yet depressing story of Vika Dwyre and Lyall Hoppringhill, whose shades could often be seen holding hands as they strolled through the cemetery. *Wow, kinda like Vayl and me,* I thought as Albert led Jack to a birch tree.

"This looks like a good one," he whispered to the dog. "Go ahead."

As Jack lifted his leg I hissed, "You're not letting him pee on holy ground!"

"Why not? It'll be a story he can tell the other pets when he gets home. I'll bet none of them has ever pissed in a Scottish cemetery."

"Oh my God. Just when I thought—"

Vayl's voice, hushed and urgent in my ear, silenced my rant. "Floraidh is leaving the castle. Dormal is going with her, but two other coven members have arrived to take their places at the GhostWalk table."

"What do you wanna bet they're skipping off to raise the shade of that old-timer who nearly crashed us this afternoon?" said Albert.

"That ought to make this group pretty happy," I said. "All they've gotten for their money so far is a long walk and a couple of pathetic stories."

Cole and the girls joined us as the group moved on, taking a narrow path into the trees, which Bart said connected the cemetery to the southernmost property line of Tearlach. I watched my third slide his hand under Viv's elbow as they came to a part of the trail that wasn't as well lit by the widely spaced lanterns as the previous bit had been. When she looked up at him, the question in her eyes made me wish I could give her a medal. Or, what the hell, bequeath a knighthood. Not because she needed to ask Cole if she could trust him. But because she still managed the hope that anyone deserved it.

I stopped breathing. Crossed my fingers. *Come on, Cole. All those girls were just practice for this one. Don't let her down.*

His smile started in his eyes, and by the time it reached his lips even I wanted to give him a hug. He turned toward her, his shoulder blocking Iona's view, and signed something with his right hand that I could barely see. Viv caught his fingers in hers and pressed them against her cheek. A second later they'd gone back to their silent chatter with Iona, but the change had begun. She stood straighter, with a confidence that matched her shoes much better than it had when she'd slipped them on earlier this evening. And Cole. The way he threw his head back and laughed, I was pretty sure he enjoyed the weight of the superhero cape he'd just earned that was flying straight back from his shoulders.

"Hey, Lucille!" Cole said as Albert and I caught up to them, "we've got a bet on as to whether or not our equipment picks up some ghostly activity at our next stop. What do you think?" he asked.

"I'll put five bucks on our equipment. Which reminds me, is there any part of the house we don't have covered? Because we probably should station someone in the blind spots just in case."

"Well, Floraidh didn't want her or Dormal's bedrooms filmed, or the bathroom. And she thought the guests would be put off by cameras in the lounges and the dining room."

"I guess that makes sense," I said. *The dining room, where everyone would be standing to watch the show from the cutout to the kitchen.* I took out my phone. "I'll tell you what. I'll call Vayl and see if he can meet us there. Maybe he can monitor the dining room with one of our phantasmic detectors while we do the firsthand observations."

I dropped back, letting everyone get ahead of me as Vayl answered the phone. Yeah, we could've used the party line, but this way I could talk out loud without seeming utterly whacked. "Were we right about Floraidh and Dormal?"

"I believe so. They seem to be heading straight back to Tearlach. That was an excellent excuse you gave me for showing up unannounced, as it were."

"Um, Vayl?"

"Yes."

"I really like the way you talk. It's so quaint sometimes I just want to hop into a hoop skirt and learn to waltz. But nobody says 'as it were' anymore."

"The world would be a better place if they did. Do you know what else people should say? Specifically me, now that I have removed my transmitter?"

"No."

His voice dropped into an oh-baby purr. "I have been entertaining the most erotic fantasies involving you, me, and a bathtub full of whipped cream."

My entire body tingled, as if he'd just run his fingertips over every inch of my skin. "Ahhh."

"They are frustrating me somewhat because I have never seen your bare breasts. Therefore I can only try to imagine what they might look like covered with sugary white foam."

"Oh."

"Perhaps we could rectify that omission sometime soon. Yes?"

Nobody says "rectify that omission" anymore either. But since his words had woven an erotic web around my body that would cling to me until his hands descended to pull it off, I gave him the only answer my heart and mouth could agree on. "Oh, yeah."

Chapter Twenty-Four

Tearlach rose from the trees ahead of us like a giant open hand, poised to reach down and slap us if we took one step in the wrong direction as we emerged from the woods. The hike had nearly done Albert in, though he'd never admit what he wanted most was a plush recliner and a cold glass of water. I kept eyeing him peripherally, wondering how much I'd have to pay Shelby to get him and his bride to join us if Albert didn't improve after a good night's rest. The only reason I didn't rush him upstairs and shove some pillows under those knees was his stiff-backed pride. It had gotten him through more firefights and forced marches than he'd care to remember. I figured he still had enough steel left in him to get through this night too.

We walked around to the front door. Floraidh, Dormal, and Vayl had already arrived. They sat in the front lounge, chatting like old friends, when we walked in. I felt the spell immediately, like pepper in the air, making me want to sneeze. While Bart assembled his people in the back lounge so Floraidh could explain the first appearance, Albert sank into the pink chair she'd vacated.

"What do you say, Lucille? You up to grabbing the old man a drink?" he asked. Which was how I knew he was really hurting. The more pain he's in, the more *wah* he gets in his tone. He's not as bad as he used to be, but the old habits still clung.

"Fine, Jack needs one too." I took the malamute's leash and began to lead him toward the kitchen.

My *sverhamin* came after me, saying, "Perhaps I should check the camera one last time. We would not want to miss a single frame of what is to come."

We strode down the hallway and through the kitchen door, which someone had propped open with a cast-iron bean pot. I poured Jack a bowl of water, grabbed a bottle for Albert from the fridge, and huddled with Vayl by the camera he and Cole had set up between the back door and the window that stood next to the stove.

"Magic's in the air already," I murmured. "And it feels different than before. I don't think they're doing the same spell."

"Can you tell at whom it is directed?"

"Can I . . . Do I look like a bird dog to you?"

He touched a button on the camera, which made a red light blink alarmingly. So he touched it again. All better. "Come now, Jasmine, after all this time have you learned nothing from me?"

"You've taught me a ton, but—"

"When spells are directed they stick. Just as vampires, Weres, and witches scent a certain way to you, the victim of the spell will suddenly pique your awareness. Untouched one moment. Enspelled the next."

"So you want me, what, to go back in there and stick my nose behind everybody's ears?"

"If you must. Or . . . if it would help, I could give your extra Sight a boost."

No mistaking the desire in his eyes. It said, *Your blood is like nectar on my tongue. And it has been so very long.*

I was suddenly aware of my father listening in on the party line. "That won't be necessary. Uh, thanks." I pointed to the camera. "Looks like everything's up and running here. I'll just get in there and start sniffing." I backed up. Jack, having finished his water, decided we were about to have fun and followed me. I said, "Maybe I'll make it into a game. I'll tell people I'm trying to get into the Guinness World Records for most perfumes guessed correctly."

Halfway out of the room, still not looking where I was going, I ran into the table, bounced off it, and nearly fell over a chair that hadn't quite been pushed under it.

Dammit! Would you calm down? He's not going to chase you down and sink his fangs into you!

That's not my problem!

No? Well, then, what is?

That I want him to. Right here. Right now. Screw the audience. To hell with Albert. And I don't care what side effects come back to slap me later on.

Whew! You got it bad.

I know. And if I don't do something about it soon, I am so going to embarrass myself.

Somehow Vayl knew. One of the advantages of having lived so long, I guess. With that barely smile that drives me wild he said, "Very well, then. Let me know what you turn up." His eyes took a long stroll down my body and back up again, leaving me breathless when they met my own. My heart practically stopped when he put those blunt, strong fingers to his lips and dropped me a kiss.

Okay, we're quick-marching out the door now. Move those feet. Don't fall over the dog on your way into the lounge. Are you remembering to breathe? No? Could you please recall that passing out will only give him an excuse to do mouth-to-mouth? Stop. Strike that image from your brain immediately. If you don't quit thinking about him that way you are going to melt. Down.

Later I decided the only reason I found the Scidairans' victims was because of my desperate need to reestablish control. The second I left the kitchen I focused so hard on their spell that

I could practically see the weave of it as it drifted over the heads of the GhostWalk group, which had begun to head toward the dining room. If I'd been more familiar with their kind of manipulation I might've been able to put a name to it. As it was, all I could smell was the *wrongness* in the atmosphere, like I'd spent too much time breathing manufactured air.

I wandered over to join the tourists. Bart had lined half of them, including Cole, Iona, and Viv, up at the pass-through. He'd sent the other half to the doorway.

"This is so exciting!" said a busty blonde whose bright eyes had more to do with the silver flask peeking out her half-zipped purse than any real anticipation. Her companion, a big strong dude who obviously had no qualms about the cancer risks related to tanning beds, put both arms around her.

"Just don't grab any ghost tushes tonight," he said. "I don't think I can outrun any more stampedes."

"Hear, hear!" seconded a cheerful, barrel-chested man whose wild white hair made him look like he'd just had an amazing idea that would probably lead to the invention of a tasty microbrew.

While the rest of the window crowd went into some vocal re-enacting, I covered my mouth and made a party line announcement. "I can See the spell. It seems to be working off these people's emotions. I mean, they're keyed up anyway, but every time one of them expresses any feeling beyond neutral, the cloud above them writhes and grows. That must be why they're here. Their emotion is like fuel."

I glanced over at Viv, whose bright pink cheeks and sparkly eyes had transformed her into the girl in the "before" pictures I'd seen online. That someone evil should take advantage of her yet again made my stomach turn. I said, "Cole, do you think you could convince Viv to go upstairs and hang out with her mom?"

"We talked about that already," he said as he wandered over

to the wall to pretend the plates mounted there fascinated him. Not that we knew she could read lips, but the Agency prides itself on taking extra precautions in matters of this nature. "She's desperate to help her mom, but not in the way she wants to help herself. And Rhona's pretty overbearing. I think she's enjoying her time away."

"Dude, this isn't the place—"

"I know. I'll try to keep her calm." Which was when he looked at me and we both admitted we didn't believe that Viv had killed anyone. Ever.

"Cole—"

He winked. "I think she likes me. Are you jealous?"

I sighed. The fledgling romance I'd seen blooming in the woods didn't have a chance if he couldn't let me go. "Dude, you need to find a girl who loves you *and* needs you. I don't think you realize how much you enjoy protecting people. If you did, you'd see there's a woman in this room right now who fits you like a damn Speedo."

"That's pretty tight."

"Uh-huh."

"But you're not referring to yourself."

"No."

He glanced over his shoulder at Viv. When he turned back to me I sighed in relief. He didn't wear the look of a man who's just lost his home to a tornado. More like somebody who's misplaced a library book and knows he has to pay to replace it. "We would've been good, Jaz."

"Maybe. Until you left me. Or I killed you. Whichever came first."

He snorted. "So this spell. Who are they zapping with it?"

"Nobody in your area. Must be one of the people by the door."

"Excellent," said Vayl, the extra bounce in his voice letting me know he fully approved of my break with Cole. "I will meet you there."

I stalked around the corner, grim and focused as half of a hunting pack closing in on its prey. Who were . . . giggling like a bunch of kindergartners. Gawd. Are people always the most oblivious when they're inches away from stone-cold killers?

This group could hardly stand still. If I'd had access to a jug of Ritalin I'd have climbed a ladder and emptied it into their gaping mouths. And no, it wouldn't have been hard to get them to open up. They were all talking at once, none of them shutting up to listen to anyone else for more than ten seconds before they zoomed on with their own stories.

Tall, anorexic girl: "So my mom died really suddenly when I was, like, fifteen, you know? And that's terribly hard on an impressionable teenager."

Attractive bank clerk who'd either live an unremarkable life or commit suicide before his thirtieth birthday: "I didn't even believe in ghosts before I came here. I just thought, why not? I had some vacation time coming and I really hate the beach."

Half-wrecked forty-something holding a ragged handker-chief: "My husband's been haunting me since the day after I buried him, over three months ago. I've seen him standing in our bedroom window as I take my morning walks. But when I run inside, he's always gone. I've got to figure out how to lay him to rest. He's never rested, not even in life."

And the Haighs, having heard the ruckus and decided to make the most of their free vacation despite the fact that Humphrey had nearly caused a riot two hours before. Reassured that nobody in their group recognized him for the rabble-rouser he'd turned out to be, Humphrey had relaxed into the moment: "Don't you think the ghost stories are fascinating, though? So many different reasons why people get stuck in between."

Lesley, twittering on taut nerves that anticipated yet another dumbass move on his part but were trying to make the best of the pleasantness while it lasted: "But so heart wrenching as well. Some of those tales just yank the tears right out of you."

Humphrey, patting her on the back: "Aw, Lesley, you always were such a softie."

As soon as he touched her, the spell coalesced into a pitch-tinted web that wrapped them both. They didn't react, but my Spirit Eye could see the strands of Scidairan magic bind them head to toe until I wondered how they still managed to speak.

Vayl edged through the door-blocking crowd and moved toward me. As he reached my side I coiled my arms around his, smiled up into his eyes, and said, "Jeremy, I hope someday when we've been together for years we're still as happy as *these two* lovebirds."

I nodded at the Haighs, who smiled graciously. I returned the favor, though I squeezed Vayl's bicep so hard he'd probably have bruises to show for it. For a couple of seconds anyway.

The spell reached inside the Haighses' mouths every time they spoke, as if to steal something vital hidden at the backs of their throats. Watching that sinister black blob crawl over their tongues was definitely going to give me nightmares. And I'd just shaken the ones from the last mission, dammit!

Vayl's steely blue eyes marked Lesley as he took her hand. "How nice to see you again. And what a lovely necklace that is. I do not believe you were wearing it the last time we met," he said, pointing out the diamond-encrusted rose around her neck. It hung from a diamond-link chain that sparkled every time she moved.

Putting a self-manicured hand up to her throat, she fluttered her lashes in embarrassed gratitude as she said, "Why, thank you! It's actually one of Humphrey's creations. I didn't even realize he'd brought it, because he usually keeps it in the safe. In fact,

I've never worn it until this very moment. But Floraidh had sent us a coupon for a free dinner at Adair's, and Humphrey knew I'd want to look my best for the occasion."

I looked at my watch. "It's nearly two thirty in the morning. A fancy restaurant like that can't be open this late. Unless they're doing a special service just for you?"

"Oh, no, nothing like that!" She giggled. "Our reservations are for tomorrow night. I just put on the necklace tonight because Floraidh said the diamonds would protect me against angry ghosts."

"Oh." *What, are you casting spells now, Lesley? Because unless you're bowing down to Scidair, I think Floraidh's yanking your chain. The question is, why?*

The jeweler's wife pointed at Cirilai. "I see you have a few diamonds in your ring. But that might not be enough to protect you. Floraidh said I should use as many as I had. The necklace contains a thousand diamonds altogether. Isn't that amazing?"

Yeah. Especially when we all know Humphrey would much rather hook that chain around a rich customer's neck so he can do the miser tuck-and-roll. Wait. What did you just say?

Suddenly I knew. Floraidh and Dormal didn't need a thousand pounds. They needed a thousand diamonds. Whatever they were planning required major protection from exactly the sort of entity that only diamonds would divert. And what I'd overheard Dormal talking about in the hallway was a spell that had coerced Humphrey Haigh into bringing that necklace to Tearlach. Since Floraidh was trying to make it as an upright businesswoman, maybe she'd only meant to manipulate him into giving it to her wholesale. But time had run out on her, and now she had to get it the heinous way.

I looked a question at Vayl. He shook his head slightly. *Let it go.*

You're shitting me.

I think it is the quickest way to understand what she wants. And from her own mouth we know time is of the essence.

I usually appreciated understanding his unspoken communications. In our business, sometimes having that edge can save your life. But now I didn't want to recognize his expression. Because it reminded me, once again, why we were here. Not to prevent the wicked witch from riding her broom. But to keep Dorothy from dumping water all over her.

Just for now, I promised myself. *That's all Vayl's expecting of me. Keep Floraidh alive. Terminate her assassin. Then find out what she's up to. And if it ends up threatening the safety of our nation, or anybody I've grown to like in the past fifteen minutes, to hell with our original mission. She's outta here.*

A squeal from Lesley Haigh brought my attention to the kitchen. Our visitor, who I should probably now refer to as Oengus, had come back to reempty the cabinet. I didn't know why he was so offended by the cookie sheets. Maybe Floraidh had slipped arsenic into his gingersnaps. I stifled the spurt of rage that flared at the thought and made my mind stick to business. Who'd brought the ghost clone this time? Dormal didn't seem to be making any effort as she sat at the dining room table, keeping watch over the awed GhostWalkers. But I could smell the spell cooking, stinking up the atmosphere as it mixed with the pollution they'd already floated up there. Which meant somebody else had taken over her job.

I reached out with my senses, already nearly overwhelmed by the gook flooding the lower level of Tearlach—and found what I was looking for outside. Somewhere behind the house, maybe in the barn, the stench of Scidair flowed toward me like a garbage-filled river. So hard not to charge outside and pound a couple of heads together. At the very least I could get them for fraud. But that wasn't my job. Which, at the moment, was to stand around twiddling my thumbs. Dammit!

Vayl's breath, whispering against my hair, distracted me. He murmured, "I was going to search the bedrooms while everyone enjoyed the show down here. But perhaps, considering the frustration rising off you like lethal radiation, you would prefer that task?"

"Are you kidding? I'd agree to play the pony at a five-year-old's birthday party if it meant we were making some sort of progress on this crap deal."

"Be thorough. Be careful. I have plans for you, after all." Hopefully Cole and Albert would take that as a professional comment. But the soft touch of his tongue tracing the edge of my earlobe let me know exactly what he meant.

"Okay," I said, my voice pitched half an octave higher than usual. I turned, not even needing to channel Lucille to unlock the bright smile I gave Floraidh as I danced toward the stairs. "I think I'll check the rest of our equipment. Lots of times when one manifestation occurs another will be happening at the same time in another part of the house." I paused at the dining room's entrance to shake her doughy hand. "This is so exciting!"

The smug expression on her face let me know she felt sure she'd pulled off a major play with this whole scenario. Great. Now let's see if I could do the same.

I took the steps two at a time, understanding at some level how pathetic it was that one guy sticking his tongue in my ear should make me feel capable of flying. *Don't care,* I thought stubbornly. *It feels good to let go. Even for five seconds.*

Skipping the second floor, I jogged to the third, stopping at Rhona's door long enough to learn that Viv's mother snored like a drunken logger. I hoped that meant she slept like one too, but just to be on the safe side I snapped the wristband of my watch. The hair on my arms tingled as the sound shield rose around me.

My lock pick hung around my neck, a coral and shark's tooth necklace that looked like jewelry any spring breaker could pick up between raves at Miami Beach. Except Bergman had crafted the tooth, which meant when you stuck it in a lock, wiggled and waited, it took the form of the mechanism inside. A couple of seconds later, voilà! Illegal entry.

Having spent way more time with Rhona than I'd have liked, I expected the room to reek of soldierly order. Nuh-uh. More like postriot sprawl. She slept in the full-sized bed, making enough racket to shake the table, the lamp, and the nearly empty bottle of sleeping pills beside her. A green mud pack covered her face and she'd pulled an orange shower cap contraption over her hair. Seriously, if I'd encountered her in the hall and I was drunk, or under the age of twelve, I'd have screamed, "Alien!"

The twin-sized bed looked like entire kindergarten classes had spent recess jumping up and down on it. She'd strewn clothes all over the floor and across the long pine dresser, whose drawers remained empty. Nothing under the beds or in the closet either. The bathroom sink, small as it was, had been packed with the junk you need to make yourself publicly presentable. Toothpaste flecks on the mirror. Hair in the tub. Gee-ross!

Other than that, no sign that she'd taken up murder as a hobby. No weapons besides the one I'd confiscated. No weird potions that would call forty Inland Taipans out of their natural habitat into this one. *Dammit!*

I flipped up pillows. Looked behind the dresser. Slipped my hand under the mattresses. Zip. I moved on to Viv and Iona's room.

Nothing interesting there. At all. Unless you counted Viv's underwear, which Cole would certainly get a kick out of. What is the deal with thongs? I think they were invented by some tow-ering chauvinist who knew the best way to blow a woman's concentration was to make her think she needed to run around all day with a piece of string wedged in her ass crack.

The Haighses' room proved equally disappointing. It was so pristine I'd have thought nobody was staying there except for the suitcases standing at attention beside the dresser. I left the room just as I found it.

"How am I doing?" I asked as I moved to the fourth floor.

"Fine," Vayl murmured. "The ghost is addressing people in the crowd now, mainly warnings about what will happen to them if they do not leave Brude's lands posthaste. He is quite abusive, but they do not seem to mind. It is amazing."

"Okay. I'm going to check out Floraidh's room."

"I expect more talking now. I want to know what you are seeing."

What he really meant was that I should be careful because she might've set some sort of trap that would leave me a shivering glob on the floor.

"I don't see any obvious triggers," I said as I unlocked the door. I held my breath anyway, hoping she hadn't set some sort of poison dart or cloud-o'-death trap. *This is stupid. You're messing with major mojo here, Jaz.* As soon as the door opened I stepped aside. Nothing happened.

Why should it? She's in and out of this room all the time. She's already shielded the whole house. Nobody's in here but the guests she allows.

Granny May looked up from the clothesline. She'd just taken off a pair of Gramps Lew's overalls and was folding them in that I-don't-give-a-crap-if-these-wrinkle way she had with all her laundry. *You should still be careful,* she warned me.

Okay, Granny's right. No sense in making a rookie mistake that'll get me killed here. That would be such a humiliating way to go. I sent a feeler out ahead of me to see if I could smell anything similar to the gunk Floraidh and her gang had pumped into the air downstairs. Yeah. Faint enough that I figured I hadn't triggered anything yet. But then I hadn't crossed the threshold either.

I pushed the door open.

Her room resembled mine. Cheerful fruit-inspired wallpaper. Clean white comforter on the bed. Wooden floor covered by a couple of bright red throw rugs and a sweet old rocker in the corner. Nothing a passerby would blink at if Floraidh happened to open the door to find them wandering around soaking up atmosphere. But she'd hung a white silk curtain on the other side of her bed, as if to give herself a dressing area. I had a claws-on-the-heart feeling that whatever hid on the other side would've made her boarders run screaming for the door.

I scanned the room one last time, frustrated that I couldn't tear it apart, find some damning piece of evidence that would give me leave to gun her down like a thirties-era gangster. The only personal item I could see was a five-by-seven picture in a sterling-silver frame. It sat on a large upended barrel that Floraidh had covered with a doily and turned into a bedside table. I moved to my left so I could get a better look. Yeah, Floraidh was smiling up into the eyes of her grinning companion like a smitten coed. She stood on the deck of a fancy-ass sailboat, leaning into the strong arm of Edward "the Raptor" Samos.

"It is time to get out," said Vayl.

"Okay." I shut the door. Glad to put any sort of barrier between my face and the Raptor's. But as I moved down the hall to "check" the equipment Cole had set up there, I could still see him. Looking so alive.

I paused at Dormal's door. Checked over my shoulder. "Is anybody coming upstairs?"

"No. But they are asking about you."

Just a peek. Then I'll leave. I worked the lock and opened up. As in my room, the door gave you three steps and then offered you a bathroom experience you might want to pass on given Dormal's obvious interest in growing multiple types of mold. She'd masked the view of her living area by hanging a dark blue curtain from the ceiling just before the room opened up. Since I smelled latent magic at work in Dormal's place too, I knew better than to step inside. But, damn, I badly wanted to see what lay beyond that drape.

"Jasmine!"

"Just a second."

"No. Floraidh is off the couch. I cannot tell where she will head next. Get down here!"

Albert's voice next. "Excuse me, Floraidh. I've been wanting to ask since we got here and found such a terrific house waiting for us. Have you owned Tearlach long?"

Floraidh's answer came back as a murmur. But I didn't really care what she said. Just that my dad had saved my ass. The feeling was too weird to relish. Plus I really wanted to see what was behind door number 402.

If only I had Vayl's cane. I glanced around the hall, trying to find something I could use to pull back the curtain with. There, on the wall. A needlepoint hanging depicting an old mill by a stream, its loops neatly threaded onto a black metal rod with fancy pointed ends that reminded me of fire pokers. Just the thing to hook the material back, like so, and reveal . . .

A life-size cutout of Samos taped to a corkboard. A target had been painted on his chest, but his crotch was just riddled with dart holes. The darts, themselves, sporting neon-green flights, stuck out of random parts of his physique at odd angles. Dormal might not be good at the game, but evidently it provided her with great therapeutic relief.

I began to grin as I pulled the curtain back farther. She'd hung a punching bag in the corner and taped a picture of Samos's face to it. "I like the way this woman thinks," I murmured. But maybe somebody should tell her she could relax now, he was dead.

She'd tacked a map of the world over a quarter of one wall, while she'd covered another with a five-foot-by-eight-foot design, painted in lavish reds and blues, that reminded me, oddly, of the tattoos on the ghost guy Brude. Not in substance, necessarily. Just that you could tell the squiggly lines topped by a flaming candle (or was that a stick of dynamite?) surrounded by thirteen pentacles *meant* something. Despite my rush, I decided the pentacles deserved a second look. They resembled the one Tolly wore on an amulet, a five-pointed star contained within a circle. Except this star broke the circle at every point.

I pulled my Monise out of my pocket.

"Jasmine, is your party line dead?" demanded Vayl. "Why have you failed to rejoin us? Floraidh is halfway up the first flight of stairs."

"I found something interesting in Dormal's room. Just taking a picture to send to Tolly."

I clicked off a few shots of the mural, moved the Monise around the room to forever preserve the Samos hate that had rivaled my own.

"Jasmine, get out!"

I pulled Dormal's door shut just as Floraidh's clickety-clacky shoes echoed on the wooden steps just below my floor. Hanging up my temporary tool shouldn't have taken long. But its nail chose that moment to fall out.

Shit! I glanced down the hall. No Scidairan yet. *Okay, don't panic. Breathe. Calm. Smooth. Pick up the nail. Shove it back in the hole. Rehang the needlepoint. Scurry your ass to the end of the hall.*

As Floraidh rounded the corner I made a big show of adjusting the ectoplasm sensor Cole had set on her pretty table. I glanced up as if I'd just heard her. "I think we've got some really good readings here," I told her. "Like I said, activity seems to feed on itself. Would you like to see?"

She shook her head decisively. "I'll just wait for your final report, shall I? I'd hate to spoil it by learning too much ahead of time."

The wall hanging I'd just abused suddenly dropped sideways, the nail I'd reset bouncing onto the light green runner that covered nearly the whole length of hallway.

Floraidh jerked her head toward it. My aw-crap reaction dissolved as soon as I caught her expression. Was that . . . fear in her eyes?

"Oh my gosh, did you see that?" I demanded. I poked a couple of buttons on the sensor and hoped I wasn't turning it off as I did. "Definite spike here. Floraidh, you are in such luck this week! Not one, but two, ghosts to entertain your guests!"

She visibly swallowed, her eyes darting first to the strange diamond-studded inscription on her door, then to the matching one on Dormal's. Only when she'd reassured herself that they were both intact did she seem to thaw slightly. Her chuckle sounded only half hollow as she said, "The Tourism Board will be so pleased." But her fingers shook as she wrapped them around her doorknob.

"Well, I've been gone as long as I can possibly stand it!" I told her brightly. "See you downstairs." I rushed past her, not even glancing back as she entered her room. But as soon as I heard her door close I ran back to get a couple of pictures of the symbol she'd set on her door. Something in my gut told me to find a laptop as soon as possible. The quicker I could send them to Tolly, the sooner she could confirm the new theory stirring its muddy claws in the evolutionary swamp of my brain.

Chapter Twenty-Five

Floraidh and Dormal's guests, both uninvited and bespelled to come, were so keyed up by the entertainment that they stayed up talking for nearly two hours after the last of the GhostWalk crowd had trickled out, and didn't hit the hay until the sun had begun to peek over the horizon. Though I was prepared for the length of days in this part of the world this time of year, I still couldn't get used to them. At five a.m. we'd already experienced over half an hour of daylight. Which meant Vayl had maybe two and a half hours left before he'd be forced to sleep—*dammit, Jaz, can we just say he dies?*—for the day.

The Scidairans had finally stumped off to bed as well. But not before Floraidh had convinced Humphrey to let her stow Lesley's necklace in Tearlach's safe until they needed it for the Adair's outing. "I didn't like the looks of that suntanned buffoon," she told him as the spell sunk into his skin. "He might come back when you and Mrs. Haigh are out shopping or walking, and if I was in the garden and didn't hear, and you lost that lovely piece, I would never forgive myself."

I barely kept myself from snorting as she and Humphrey took the treasure upstairs. When they returned he patted his wife on the shoulder and said, "It's safe as houses now, my dear. Time we got some sleep." Which signaled a mass exodus.

Our crew convened in my room to make plans. Cole stood by the door while Vayl sat on the dressing table bench. I leaned against the table beside him, acutely aware of how easy it would be to reach out and run my fingers through those dark, silky curls. I licked my lips and glued my eyes to Jack, who'd curled up at the base of the bed before I even had a chance to unsnap his leash. Albert sat on one corner of the mattress and worked it free while Cole said, "I'll admit it, I'm wiped out. You wouldn't believe how much energy it takes to be charming all the time."

"And yet you make it seem so effortless," Vayl said. "The mark of a true master." As Cole bowed his head at the compliment and I dared to hope this meant two of my favorite guys might be working out a temporary ceasefire, Vayl went on. "It only makes sense for me to watch Floraidh until I have to rest. I suggest you three get some sleep."

"Works for me. See you in a few." Cole took off, nearly slamming his face into the door until he roused himself in time to open it wide enough to slip his body through.

"You sure you don't need some help?" I asked Vayl. "I could probably go another few hours."

His almost-smile told me he knew better. "You look as sleepy as that dog of yours." His glance sent mine to Jack, who'd already started a twitchy-leg dream. "But if you must, perhaps you and Albert could have a little talk before retiring. I believe you both have left a great deal unsaid between you."

He gave me one of those you-know-what-I-mean eyebrow lifts. And left.

Wait a second! I thought we were waiting to tell my dad until we could hope he choked on a chicken bone!

Granny May chuckled from her seat at the bridge table. Weird. Today she'd chosen to partner with Buddha against General Patton and Elmer Fudd. What the hell was my mind trying to tell me with this setup? Before I could figure it out she said, *Vayl knows when you're stalling, Jazzy.*

Albert and I watched Jack change positions. Now he lay completely prone, his back legs full out behind him, his front ones copying them. "I don't think I'll ever be as comfortable as that mutt," my dad said enviously.

"Depends what your needs are," I replied. "Maybe if all you wanted was food, a couple of toys, and an occasional pat on the head, you'd be content too."

Albert emptied his pockets onto the minuscule space the bedside table provided, piling his phone on top of his wallet to make room for the loose change and his room key. He settled on the bed, shoving the pillows up behind his back just so until, when he leaned back, his lids fluttered happily. "Don't get comfortable," I warned him. "Your place is down the hall, remember?"

"It's haunted."

"But Cole's in there."

"Cole's not the one they want."

No trace of fear in his tone. Just the obstinance of a man who will not be moved.

"O-kay."

He pulled another key from his shirt pocket and tossed it to me. "I already checked with Vayl. You can sleep in his room until it's time for you to relieve him." He crossed one leg over the other and shut his eyes completely.

What a double meaning we have in that statement. Geez, I can't even do video without blushing now that my dad's in the room. Sucker makes me feel like a teenager again. "Fine. If you answer a question."

"Shoot."

"How do you feel about vampires?"

His eyes snapped open. "They suck." He thought about it.

Hooted at his own pathetic joke. Got serious again almost immediately. "Why?"

"We have one in our department. And, um, I don't know. He kind of wants to date me."

Albert yanked off his party line and gestured for me to do the same. I took off my transmitter and pocketed it. "The receiver stays," I said. "He might need backup."

He nodded. "How does he feel about the vampire?"

It took me a minute to figure out what he meant. "Oh, you mean what does *Vayl* think of him?"

His look told me he thought I'd recently inhaled a substance that had killed off the majority of my brain cells. "You do know Vayl's got the hots for you?"

"Dad!"

"What? I'm just saying. He might have something to say about this vamp who, by the way, I can't get any information on."

"You *snooped?*"

He held out his hands and shrugged his shoulders. "What? The guy's a legend in the Agency! Who's not going to dig a little? And I'm damn good at it. But his files are sealed so tight I hear only Pete and the president are allowed to peek. Which means all I know is what you tell me." He waited. "You could start with a name."

Or not! "It's not like I'm going to marry the guy. Just a date or two." *There ya go, the old Albert flush, neck to forehead in just under a second. I knew it would piss him off. Not that I need his approval. It would just be nice if he wasn't yapping in my ear for the next decade.*

"What is it with the women in your family?" he muttered.

"What do you mean by that?"

"Why do you think your mom got divorced the first time?"

"He couldn't stand the way she blew smoke in his face every time he asked her to pass the macaroni and cheese?"

"She couldn't hack being married to a vampire."

I laughed. It just sounded so dumb the way he said it. Like,

"Your mom tried out the new eternity-based calling plan, but she couldn't keep track of the minutes. The fights they had regarding overcharges were phenomenal."

"It isn't funny," growled my father.

"No," I agreed. "Uh, do you know why . . . ?"

"She told me she had a bad-boy complex that he satisfied. I believed her." Albert wiggled his pinky into his ear, checked out the diggings, brushed them down the side of his pants. I had seen people torn to pieces and not gagged the way I wanted to now. Which was when I decided my dad had been alone way too long. He needed a woman to kick his gross habits for. Maybe Shelby knew somebody nice in Chicago. "Jasmine!"

"What?"

"Whatever you're thinking about your mother, it's probably not true."

"She wasn't on my mind at all."

"We were just talking about her!"

"No. You were. I've taught myself to zone out anytime anyone brings her up in conversation. It's a terrific defense mechanism. You should try it. You should also try not defending her. She doesn't deserve it."

"How would you know?"

I didn't see how I could tell him about meeting her in hell without explaining how I'd gotten there in the first place. Which would lead to a description of Raoul. Which would end up with me giving him CPR. *Blech.*

I said, "I just do, okay?"

"No, not okay. The woman's dead, for chrissake. And you're standing there spitting on her grave. She was a good mother to you—"

"No. Not even close." I strode toward the bed, each step fueling my rage. I sat on the edge beside him so the lamplight caught me at the edge of its glow. "You wouldn't know, because you were gone. Always off defending the country when you should've been protecting me." The last came out like I'd shoved it through a grater, shredded and somewhat battered.

Before he could demand to know what I meant, I tore off my jacket, yanked my shirtsleeve up over my shoulder, and revealed the inside of my upper arm. The part that hardly ever shows. Unless you hold up your hand to answer a question in class. I'd learned never to do that.

"What the hell are these?" Albert demanded, brushing his thumb against eight separate raised circles marring the smooth pale skin that comes naturally to us redheads. "Are they scars?"

"Geez, Dad, lemme think. Was I born with these marks? I mean, I know you were gone a lot, but surely you would've noticed this kind of disfigurement on an infant."

He clamped his jaw shut and yanked me toward him. "Who did this to you? Tell me right now. And be honest, or else—"

"Or else what?"

"I might kill the wrong man." Watching the color rush to fill his face once again, I thought, *He didn't know. All these years I thought he had to. How could he not?* But it was like he'd leased his brain to the military and all we got was sloppy seconds. Which is okay for some things. But not so great when Dad's oblivious to festering sores on your arm. And in your family.

"It wasn't a man," I said. "It was your wife. With a cigarette. Anytime one of us caused her to lose it."

Albert's eyes went back to my arm and he began to shake his head. Of course he wouldn't believe me. She'd said he wouldn't. I was ready for a big, fat denial. But all he said was "It sounds to me like you took the punishment for everybody."

I nodded. "Evie only made her that mad once, and though I

was only nine at the time, I knew she wouldn't be able to handle it. A couple of the others are Dave's, but the rest are mine." I watched him worry at those marks, as if he could somehow erase them if he brushed his fingers across them enough times. When he still didn't respond I said, "I guess I could've done what Dave and Evie did. Learn to read her moods. Figure out when to keep my mouth shut."

Still not meeting my eyes he asked, "What did you do?"

I shrugged. "By the time I was twelve I'd grown taller and tougher than her. One day she came after me with that goddamned cigarette and I beat the crap out of her."

I tried to pull my arm from his hand, to wrap it around my stomach as it lurched at that awful memory. The knowledge that I'd done what a daughter never should. Forced into it by a mother who'd broken her trust. The worst part—Evie crying. Screaming really. Begging me not to kill her mommy. It was the first time in my life that I'd understood what I was capable of.

He put his arms around me, patient through my initial resistance. Crushing me to his chest when I finally allowed the embrace. I didn't cry. Those days had passed. But something at the icy core of me flared. Suddenly painfully warm. Even more so when I leaned back to see the single tear running down the old man's face. The only one I'd ever seen crack the hard rock of those green eyes. "Jazzy," he began.

I shook my head. "It's over now."

"Is it?"

The question caught me off guard. Do you ever get past something like that, when the scars slap you across the face every morning in the shower? I realized I couldn't answer him truthfully. "About the vampire guy," I said.

Albert took a deep breath. Tightened his hands on my shoulders. Let them drop. "I wouldn't recommend him. They're only after one thing, you know."

"Dad!"

"That's not what I meant! Well, maybe a little. But I was really talking about the blood. Don't let him fool you. Just because he's had a few lifetimes to school himself in our ways doesn't mean he's like us. He's a predator. A parasite. You strip away his act and he's no better than an undead tick." He nodded wisely. "No. You stick with that Vayl. He'll take care of you."

Ha! If you only knew! "Don't you think he's a little old for me?" He'd been turned at thirty-eight. And while no gray hairs sprinkled the coal blackness of his hair, he'd never pass for a twenty-something.

Albert shook his head. "I don't see you getting comfortable with a young buck now. Seems to me you need somebody who's survived the same kind of crap as you. Looking at Vayl, you can tell. He's been through it."

I thought of the scars I'd seen once, crisscrossing his shoulders and back. Even in his relative ignorance, my dad could still make a valid point. I got up. "It's definitely time to leave when you start making sense." I whistled to Jack. When his ears perked I said, "Come on, boy. We're outta here 'cause Dad's freaking about the Amityville room again."

When I grinned at Albert he growled, "It's not funny! That thing's gonna kill me, you know! And when I'm dead—"

"You're never going to die because the gatekeepers of heaven and hell will never stop arguing about which one wants to keep you out the worst!"

He snorted and slapped me on the leg. "You're all right, you know that?"

"Yeah, I do." I threw my weapons bag across my back and grabbed my trunk.

He looked at me sideways. "Good. I'm glad she didn't take that away from you." I nodded and had turned to leave when his next words stopped me flat. "And I'm sorry."

I put my hand on the wall to steady myself. Not even daring to look over my shoulder, I whispered, "For what?"

"I'm your father. It's my job to protect you. And I failed."

I thought about what he said until Jack came to stand beside me, rubbing his cheek against my thigh like he thought he was a tomcat and needed to mark me. Finally I said, "Apology accepted."

Chapter Twenty-Six

I didn't sleep right away. I lay on my stomach under the covers, still fully dressed because I'd have to go back to work in another few hours. And because if I took one article of clothing off, they'd all go. Just lying in Vayl's bed did that to me. I was beginning to think when we finally did pull off an all-nighter, we might need to arrange a somewhat remote location for the deed. I had a hunch it was going to get noisy.

I dangled my left hand over the edge of the bed, leaving it tangled in the fur of Jack's neck as he lay on the floor beside me. "I'm a sad case, Jack," I whispered. "And the worst part is, I don't even mind anymore."

As soon as I closed my eyes I began dreaming.

I recognized the zooming delight in my heart even before I glanced to my side to smile at my hiking partner. Matt grinned back, his teeth practically glowing against the deep tan of his face. I stopped right there on the trail, threw my arms around him, and gave him a long, luscious kiss.

"What was that for?" he asked as he raised his head.

"Bringing me here. Look at this!" I demanded, my gesture encompassing the whole of the Highlands. We stood on a flat brown trail sided by acres of heather, dotted by small rocks and large boulders. In the background the steep granite slopes of Ben Nevis beckoned. "Have you ever seen anything more beautiful?"

"Yah. That would be you, lass." I spun, jerking my arm out of his grasp. Matt had been replaced. By Brude.

"What are you doing here?" Did my voice have to go all squeaky-breathy like that? *Um, yeah, dumbass. That's what happens when you're freaked.*

Hard not to be with those dark, fathomless eyes boring into you. That massive picture-puzzle chest reminding you a mystery remained unsolved and now you'd be lucky if you woke again to pursue its unanswered questions.

"I came to fetch you," he said in that rich, rolling accent. "The flavor of power sweetens like honey with a good woman beside you to share the spoils." He emphasized his point by banging his staff into the ground.

I shrugged. "Am I supposed to be impressed by that?"

"No. By me."

He tried to pull me into his arms, but I evaded his hands, backing slowly down the path like I'd just encountered a grizzly bear. "Who are you?"

"I told you before, lass. I am King Brude. These are my lands and have been for nigh onto four thousand years. But now they will be more. I have been Satan's Enforcer long enough. It is my time to rise. My armies are ready. The dungeon is complete. You saw how strongly it is made."

He waited long enough that I realized I was supposed to respond. "Oh, yeah. Lovely workmanship. The blocks were, uh, very thick. But it doesn't seem quite practical. I mean you ghosts could just—"

"I am no ghost!" he cried, as offended as if I'd questioned his manhood. "Do I not have dominion over them, and e'en all the unkind spirits who flock to my domain?"

"First of all, I don't know what e'en means. Also, I'm waking up now."

"Wait! You must stay with me!" His raised fist added a threat to the demand. But the voice I paused for was Raoul's.

"Jasmine?" I turned, relieved to find my Spirit Guide striding up the hill behind me. "I've been looking for you. Why have you been so elusive?"

I pointed a finger at Brude, glad to see it wasn't shaking. Much. "The Neanderthal wants to drag me off by the hair." In a lower voice I asked, "People don't do that here, do they? Because I gotta tell you, I have sensitive roots."

Raoul shook his head, smiling past the concern in his eyes. "I've never heard of it. But since you're not yet trained to protect that bundle of curls in the Thin, would you mind stepping behind me for a minute?"

The Thin? You mean . . . I really can't just make this go away by sitting up in bed? In that case, if I had the time I'd build a fort between me and that maniac. I switched positions with Raoul and looked around for a big stick. Or maybe a rock. Surely anything I found here would work as a weapon. And my Guide deserved at least a show of backup, even if I suspected Brude could take us both with one arm strapped to his side.

Raoul bowed, keeping his eyes raised in case the king fought dirty. "We have no quarrel with you. But urgent business requires us to move on," he said.

"I cannot allow that," Brude replied. He pointed to me. "My claim is on her. She must stay and rule at my side."

"You are such a throwback," I informed him. "Your *claim.* Do I look like a gold mine to you?"

Raoul snapped a *shut-up* look over his shoulder. "Let me handle this, please."

I wanted to say something really mature like, "He started it." But maybe this wasn't the time.

Raoul said, "She's Eldhayr. Do you really want that kind of fight? I could bring the whole Eminent screaming down on your head, and when we were done with you not even a spark would remain to prove you had ever existed."

"You could," said Brude, grinning craftily, "if they were at your shoulder. But they must be scattered to the seven winds at the moment. No, I will take her now, while the time is ripe." He looked at me as he savored that last word, his eyes full of the plans he'd made for us.

"You can't make me stay," I told him. I put my hand on Raoul's shoulder. "Can he?"

"He's a Domytr. That gives him the ability to try."

I paged through my mental dictionary. "I've never heard of that."

"You wouldn't have. They're rare. Hand-picked by Lucifer. And exclusive to this side."

The Domytr and the Eldhayr began to circle one another. I shadowed Raoul, still searching for some form of naturally occurring weapon. I saw rocks, but they were all set into the earth so deep, no way would I be able to extricate one before the fight had ended. I clenched my fists, and when the movement didn't even crack my knuckles, I wondered if the Thin had even left me enough strength to heft one.

Brude charged, yelling a battle cry that liquefied all the food in my bowels. *Shit! We should run!*

Ah, the voice of reason. Why is it we never listen to her when the battle is on? It would spare us such a lot of pain. Or in Raoul's case, a blow to the nose that seemed to break it, and a punch that glanced off his eye, but only because his head was already rocking backward.

Holy crap, that guy can swing a staff! Only it's not just the wood talking. I think his tattoos are getting darker when he attacks. Al-

most like they're being reinforced. And look at that. They're coalesc-
ing! Forming some sort of second skin. Except I have a feeling it's a
lot more durable than most armor.

Raoul pulled his sword. A rune-covered steel that shone like
sun on the water, he wielded it with the ease of a master. A
lunge. A slash across Brude's upper chest that bled so freely it
began to look like he'd slipped on a red T-shirt for the occasion.
But as I watched, the tattooed armor folded over the cut and the
bleeding stopped.

"Your metal cannot harm me here," Brude said triumphantly.

Oh, that's reassuring.

Raoul snapped, "Play with someone else's head, Brude. Mine
is bent on your destruction." He jumped forward again, smash-
ing his blade against Brude's staff. Something should have broken. Maybe it was Raoul's pride. He backed away.

"Are you done playing already? Good enough." Brude's
eyes jumped to mine. "I believe it would be better to finish this
quickly, after all. It has been so long." He nodded in decision
and slowly lifted the staff, walking around Raoul as he also
turned. Waiting for him to make a mistake. He leaped forward,
moving so quickly I barely caught the shift in his shoulders that
signaled his intentions.

I bounced away from Raoul, allowing him the room he needed
to adjust. He veered sideways, cracking his sword against Brude's
staff as it passed within a millimeter of his head.

Raoul's heel to the king's ribs should've scored the best shot
he'd made so far. Brude grunted, but only with effort. The
armor had slid forward to intercept Raoul's blow. I'd fought
supernaturally shielded opponents before, so I knew Raoul felt
like he'd just connected with the radiator of a Mack truck.

He reversed the sword in his hand, holding it so the blade
emerged from the back of his fist like you might hold a dagger

in a knife fight. Rushing toward Brude, he battered the king with multiple kicks to the torso and a blow to the temple with the hilt of the sword.

Brude didn't bother to block the blows. The armor did all that so well his head barely jerked, though Raoul had hit him hard enough to snap his neck. He responded with a combination of slashing attacks that forced Raoul to pull back or lose some choice parts.

*Oh goody. How about I just stand here like a helpless Victorian Miss whilst the menfolk battle for my honor? Or I could—*I looked around. Nope. No heroic rescue wrote itself on my brain as I scanned the scene. *Well, this sucks.* I moved completely off the path, avoiding the sweating, heaving fighters on my way to a light-gray boulder. I leaned against it, brushing my hands against the rough crags of the stone. Down by my hips I discovered a stash of small rocks in a recess where either the wind or a bored hand had chipped them off and left them for later. I picked one up. Tossed it up and down in my hand.

And lofted it at Brude.

It hit him. Of course it didn't hurt. His inked-on shell came to his rescue. But I threw another anyway. It became the only way I could find to amuse myself between rounds.

Round One: Raoul busting his ass to no avail.

Medium-sized piece o' granite to the small of the king's back. *Bang—two points!*

Round Two: Brude nearly taking off Raoul's head.

Two small pebbles to the Domytr's left thigh. *Hey, they hit at the same time. I am the Queen of Rock Pelting!*

Round Three: Raoul throwing such an intricate combination of moves I didn't recognize what discipline he'd pulled them from, which meant he was now fighting out of the School of Desperation.

Flat stone, perfect for skipping, bounced right off the ear. *It's no fun when he doesn't even flinch. How are we ever going to get past that goddamned armor?*

Round Four: I zinged another one. At the same time Raoul landed a punch that should've shattered Brude's jaw. But the crack I heard was his hand breaking. To give him credit he didn't cry out. Didn't even delay his next move. Just switched back to his sword, which clanged against Brude's staff at the same time that he threw a front kick into the king's diaphragm.

"Raoul, this is pointless," I said. "Back off, dude. Maybe I can talk some sense into this guy."

Raoul's response was a kick that caught Brude in the ribs. Unfortunately he didn't pull his leg back fast enough. Brude grasped his calf with both hands and twisted. I heard Raoul's knee pop just before he screamed.

Brude tossed Raoul aside like a bag of laundry, sending him flying at least ten feet into the heather. Then he came for me.

Because he expected it, I scurried out of his reach. Ran to Raoul's side. Nope. Forget pulling him to his feet, much less making for less-populated spots. "Are we done for?" I asked.

Raoul shook his head. Not an answer. Just an attempt to clear the woozies. "He's pulling strength from somewhere beyond himself. *Look* at him."

I had been, but only casually. I opened my third eye as wide as I could manage. Brude's lips curled upward as he strode toward me, his arms swinging confidently at his sides. He moved like a true warrior, comfortable in his skin, capable of instant lethality from any position. But his eyes added a disturbing dimension. They said he'd be happy to stab, hack, or impale given any lame excuse and the weaponry to pull it off. *Beautiful,* whispered the part of my brain that recognized how closely that trait must link him to evil here, where the prettier you were, the higher up the nasty ladder you got to climb.

As I watched his tattoos detach from one another, become

just another set of funky body squiggles, I caught another movement. Like a longer length of hair flowing off his shoulders, down his back. A nearly invisible cape that fluttered behind him as he walked. It wasn't like one you'd see on, say, Superman. Where a couple of guys on the ground might look up and say, "Yo! Mr. Hero! Your sheet's stuck between your legs!" right before he plummeted to the earth and put a big hole in some poor woman's kitchen island. This item seemed *muscular.* Almost like a pterodactyl wing, it wrapped around him as he approached us. A shield, or maybe a supernatural steroid pump, it was definitely the item that gave him that extra edge. And I had no idea how to cut it from him.

I leaned into Raoul's ear, whispered the secret to Brude's advantage just as he reached me. He grabbed my arm and yanked me to my feet. "You will be mine."

"I don't see how I can do that," I told him, working hard to force calm into my voice. Could I really get stuck here? *No. Don't even allow the possibility. You're not staying. Because if you do, you'll probably die. Plus Vayl would be so pissed.* I thought of him standing guard over that damned Scidairan when I needed him here. *Now!*

"You will do as I say," Brude said, his hand tightening painfully on my skin. And that's when I knew what I had to do.

"You like getting your way, don't you?"

"Of course."

"Well, you know what?" I stepped up to him, put my free arm around his waist, and shoved my body against his. "So do I." I nuzzled my mouth against his neck. As he moaned I felt the cape slide out from between us. And wrap around me. I was in. With one chance to get this right.

I pictured Vayl. Pretended it was his body pressing against mine. His skin under my canines. And bit. So hard that my teeth nearly met each other inside the bloody tissue of his carotid. Though I tried not to swallow, I felt Brude's blood spurt down my throat.

It's okay, this isn't real, I told myself.

It's not a dream, insisted the librarian in my head, who was already shelving this experience into the vast, unending Horror area of my biography section.

But the blood . . . it's not like I'm really stomaching the stuff that powers him.

Lies. All little fibs to keep my mind off the disaster I was making of his throat. The gurgling screams in my ear. The pounding on my back as he tried to release himself from the clench I'd taken on him.

He tasted of thick, sweet metal. Behind it the heavier flavor of stolen vigor, coming straight from that ghost-cape enveloping us both. As his blood gushed down the sides of my mouth, I had less and less of a problem resisting his onslaught.

Finally he appealed to Raoul. "Get her off of me!"

"And what?"

"I will allow you to cross my lands freely for the next fortnight."

That was good enough for me. I released him, spitting until my mouth cleared, backing until my shoulder blades hit Raoul's chest.

Wait a second. My Spirit Guide couldn't stand. I whipped around.

"Vayl, how did you get here?"

He motioned to Cirilai. "You needed me. You called. I came." When his eyes met mine they were blacker than I'd ever seen them. Angry fountains of red rose and fell from his pupils as he stared at Brude's throat. His words cut into me like a garrote as he said, "Jasmine, what have you done?"

Chapter Twenty-Seven

The accusation in Vayl's tone brought the blood rushing beneath my cheeks. Which was when I realized I probably had quite a bit on top of my skin as well. I pulled out the neck of my shirt and wiped my face with it. Wondered if, when I woke up, I'd still have this taste in my mouth, still want to brush my teeth as badly as I did at this moment.

Neither Vayl nor I felt like looking at each other, so we spent some time watching Brude make a poultice out of dirt, spit, and his own blood. Once he'd packed the entire mess onto his neck, he pointed at me. Kind of satisfying to see that finger trembling.

"Woman, you are a viper," he said.

I shrugged. "Most of my enemies end up thinking something similar."

He shook his head, causing his shining black braids to brush back and forth across his sweating shoulders. "You think us adversaries, but in fact we fall on the same side and always will. So the prophets predicted: *And Brude shall take unto himself a queen of unsurpassed skill, strength, and beauty, whose astonishing wit will find itself outmatched by the sharpness of her tongue.* Mark my words, we will rule this land together, you and I. And all of Lucifer's demons will tremble at our dominion."

"Like hell!"

His smile made me shiver. "Now you begin to understand." He kept his distance, but somehow the intensity in his eyes made me feel as if he'd sidled right up to me. Like his hands had found their way under my clothes, and where they touched my skin burned. "When you need me, call my name and I will come to you. Say it now, my queen. 'I need you, Brude.' Let me hear it once before I leave."

Beside me, Vayl made a noise I'd never heard before. But if I'd caught that sound in the jungle I'd have scampered up the nearest tree. Because I was afraid even touching him would set him off, I just sent calm thoughts in his direction as I gave Brude my coldest stare. "Go away before I shred you like last year's receipts," I said.

"I shall. But only for a time. You will beg for my return. And thank me as well."

"What makes you think I'd ever thank you?"

"Your enemy is mine just as *you* are mine. I never supposed you would hear my calls at Clava Cairns. But your pet has much sharper ears. And an obedient heart."

"You . . . you showed Jack where to dig for that harness? Why? What does my enemy want to do with it? Which enemy are we even talking about?"

With a nod of his head and a smile that let me know he loved the fact he'd filled me with questions, he left. Fading to nothing just like his ghostly subjects.

"Well, shit!"

"So how did he taste?" asked Vayl. "I am guessing earthy with a hint of ass."

I didn't realize my fists were clenched until I raised one to his face. I unwound a finger, saving the middle one for later, and shook my pointer under his nose. "Where do you get off with the snotty attitude? I was saving my life just now! *And* working!"

"You were practically rutting with that oaf!"

I held out my arms. Twirled around. "See this? Get a good look, will ya? Fully clothed, yeah? How the hell—"

He widened his eyes in that you-are-the-ultimate-idiot expression of his that made me want to grab a pair of tweezers and start plucking out all his nose hairs. "How could you possibly *be* more intimate than to take another man's blood? That should have been me!"

What the f—... *Ohhhh.* "Vayl, I was not trying to pleasure the freak. I was trying to kill him. Ask Raoul." I gestured to my Spirit Guide, who was looking properly pathetic over by the edge of the path. Unfortunately he didn't feel making peace between us was his job. Totally ignoring Vayl's questioning expression, he said, "Jasmine, we have to go. Colonel John has located the source of your father's problem. We were supposed to meet him at my penthouse—"

"Goddammit, Raoul, this is important to me!" He winced at my obscenity and sighed as he faced Vayl.

"Obviously I couldn't beat Brude, though I wasted a great deal of effort trying. Jasmine found a way to breach his defenses and used the only weapon that would work for her in this place at this time."

Vayl nodded stiffly, but when he turned back to me I could tell he wasn't satisfied. What the hell? He had all the facts. What else could he need?

Raoul struggled to rise, failed, gave me a frustrated look. "I'm coming," I said, striding past Vayl, avoiding contact I would've sought half an hour before. As I helped Raoul to his feet I asked, "How come you can't just zap your parts back to fine?"

"For the same reason Brude needs to spend the next hour with an excellent needlewoman. We can be injured here. We can even 'die,' though the consequences are somewhat more frightening than those we faced as mortals, considering the power of the beings we fight in these planes."

"Oh." Without a word, Vayl arrived at Raoul's other side and together we walked him down the hill, back the way we'd come. Somehow the greens and purples of the meadow I'd begun this dream-hike through didn't lift my spirits like it had to start with. In fact, if I could get a guarantee that I'd never see this landscape again, I'd be willing to make payments to any of a number of Raoul's favorite charities. For life.

After a couple of minutes I said, "Um. Aren't we kind of in my dream?"

"Technically," said Raoul. "But only in that your dream allowed Brude to pull us into the Thin, where his realm seems to be flourishing like mold on bread."

His frown didn't stop me from asking, "So what're we doing now?" Because I was beginning to seriously worry about my Spirit Guide, who was sweating like a college wrestler in mid workout. The pain must be excruciating.

"We're looking for a door."

"You mean like the one I used to visit your place last time?"

He nodded, biting his lip as his toe accidentally hit the path. "They exist in every plane. Remember I told you there was one in Castle Hoppringhill?"

"Yeah."

"That's the one I'm looking for."

"But it's miles from Tearlach!"

"It's miles from your body. But your mind always keeps one close. Ah, yes, there it is." He pointed across the meadow to a flaming rectangle framing a black portal whose center could lead us any number of places depending on the words we chanted before we walked through it.

"Explain that," I demanded. "Why's the door always close in my mind?"

"I don't know. It's something unique to you. I've never known anyone else who's been able to do it."

Oh great. One more weird spot on the mustard-and-blood-stained T-shirt that was my life.

Raoul murmured the appropriate wordage and the door cleared, automatically widening to admit the three of us at the same time. When we emerged, what hit me was the thought of how starkly my two bosses' workplaces contrasted. Raoul worked out of his home, a penthouse currently overlooking the sparkling skyline of Caracas. Pete's office looked like it had come straight out of a library basement.

Colonel John waited for us by a bank of large windows, his hands clasped behind his back as he observed the city below him. He took one look at Raoul and his mustache seemed to drop an extra inch. "Over there," he ordered.

We lowered Raoul onto the soft white couch Colonel John had directed us to.

Clearing a place on a glass coffee table that Raoul had added to his decor since the last time I'd visited, Colonel John sat opposite him with his knee between Raoul's booted legs. We watched him pull a long, well-maintained knife out of the sheath at his left side and split Raoul's pants from thigh to hem. My Spirit Guide's knee had swollen to three times its regular size. And the noise he made when Colonel John laid his hands on it made me turn away.

I strode to the sleek black bar, where I poured myself something that smelled a lot like whiskey from a glass decanter and stubbornly ignored my reflection in the mirrored wall. "Do you want something?" I asked Vayl as he came up to the other side and sank onto one of the black cushioned bar stools.

When he didn't answer I met his eyes. Same color as before, and not the one I was hoping to see. "Vayl—"

"Why could you not wait?"

"What?"

"Now his blood is in you when mine should have been first."

I clutched my glass so hard I was surprised it didn't shatter in my hands. I wanted to yell at him that I'd had no choice. I considered throwing my booze in his face and screaming that drinking blood was grosser than sucking toes, neither of which could he expect me to do at any time during our relationship. Then I got this image of my big toe, painted bright red, suddenly developing a face and a hot Southern temper to match, screaming, "What the hell is wrong with mah bad self?" And I started to giggle.

His brows lowered so fast they would've crossed if it had been anatomically possible. "Oh, stop," I said. "I'm not laughing at you. I never do. You should consider that. It's not necessarily a good thing." As his jaw began to tighten I went on. "If you'll recall, you *were* first. In Miami. Your fangs? My neck? You seemed to think it was a big yummy moment."

"That is . . . different."

"Bullshit. And I haven't forgotten the night you explained that you make it a point to sample your targets' A-positive whenever possible, just to make sure they taste as guilty as the CIA led you to believe they were to start with. So, using *your* method of judgment, *I* should also be pissed that you're the equivalent of a blood whore."

"A *what?*" His voice went so deep it practically tolled. I wasn't sure when he'd slid off the stool and come around to my side. Usually I noticed things like that. But his eyes had captivated me so completely I'd lost all awareness of my surroundings.

"It's all in how you look at things, isn't it?"

"You are mad."

Once I'd have kicked him right in the teeth. Or done a quick hunt for the looney van. Now I laughed. "You're jealous."

"I am not."

"Now you sound like Cole."

"Are you actively trying to snap my control now, or is this just part of your overall charm?"

I sidled up to him. Whispered, "When I bite you, it'll be because I want to make your toes curl and your hair stand on end. And you won't need stitches afterward. You'll need crutches."

Finally. The black bled out of his eyes, replaced by that emerald green I'd grown to adore. I heard a sharp crack, looked down and realized the edge of the bar had buckled under the pressure of his grip.

"Aw, Vayl, just when Raoul was getting used to you."

"It is your fault. Pushing me to within a hairsbreadth of explosion and then spinning me so quickly into desire it is all I can do to keep myself from taking you right here."

I almost said, *Taking me where?* Like a ditz. Because the second I kicked in my eighteenth-century translator my mind went, *Oh. Ahhhh! Blush. Giggle. Cool!*

Vayl said, "I have never seen that expression on your face before. What does it mean, I wonder?"

"Um, probably something along the lines of, *I can't wait to get you alone.*"

Crack. An entire triangle of the bar's edge came loose in Vayl's hand. He looked down at it like it had just deeply disappointed him. He shook his head and murmured, "Damn." I snorted. He glared at me. "You are not helping."

"I'm sorry, it's just—"

"Aaaah!" Raoul's cry of pain made my shoulder blades ache. And how did Vayl choose to distract him?

"Raoul, I just broke your bar."

Chapter Twenty-Eight

It turned out that Raoul was so relieved for Colonel John to have put his knee back right that he didn't mind much about the bar. "It came with the room," he told us as we sat on the couch that met his at a forty-five-degree angle, staring at the bit Vayl had torn off as it balanced in the middle of the coffee table. "I've been thinking of replacing it."

"With what?" I asked.

He laid his head back. "I can't tell you."

"Why not?"

"You'll lose all respect for me, and then how will I ever get you to believe anything I have to say?"

Before I could even begin to think of begging, Colonel John said, "Come now, Raoul. This hedging is paramount to torture. You must let us in on your secret now."

Raoul raised his head. "I want a train set." He waited. When we didn't laugh he allowed a hint of excitement to enter his eyes as he said, "I could build one all along that wall. Two levels. With a working yard. And at least five engines running at once. I had one when I was"—he glanced at me—"well, you know." Boy, did I. I wondered, had Colonel John brought him back from the dead long ago, to fight as an earthly Eldhayr like I was now? And then, how had he finally ended up here? A blast from some suicide bomber he just couldn't come back from?

"Do it," said Colonel John so decisively it sounded like an order.

"Really?" Raoul eyed the bar like it might attack him if he tried to dismantle it. "I don't know. It seems kind of—"

"You do understand that is what makes us different from them." As Colonel John waited for Raoul's full attention he fished a pipe out of his pocket and began to fill it from a roll of tobacco he pulled from his boot.

"What do you mean?" Raoul finally asked.

"The ability to play. Nothing we fight, be it demon, klor-icht, slyein, or faorzig ever indulges in lighthearted amusement. Every single creature that calls itself our enemy has lost its power to laugh. To joke. To have fun. Which is why we must hold to it as if it were the most treasured part of our souls." He looked at each of us, one by one. "Perhaps it is." He lit the tobacco he'd packed with a match struck on the side of a battered red box.

Raoul jumped up, standing on one leg like a flamingo who thinks the water's a tad too cold for both feet today. As he hopped toward the hall he said, "I have to get some paper. Where's that pencil? It was just here! If I design it in a U-shape I should be able to—no, that won't work. Or will it?"

"Raoul."

He stopped, teetered so precariously I half rose from my seat before he finally caught hold of one of the white chairs that surrounded his dining room table. He turned around. "Yes, Colonel?"

"Are you forgetting something?" Colonel John squinted over the cloud of smoke he'd puffed up, which smelled sharp and yet sweet, an aching reminder of Gramps Lew.

"Oh." Raoul pogoed back to us, only a shade of guilt marring the anticipation on his face. He plopped down on the couch between me and Vayl. "Colonel John couldn't locate Samos's contract, but he has found your father's attacker."

I sat forward on the couch, watching the colonel enjoy his smoke. One bit of me found it amusing to note that even here, so far removed from his time, the man had found it impossible to lose his old habits. But the rest felt like a tabby clawing her way up a curtain, yowling because the dude holding the catnip wouldn't freaking share!

Finally the ancient veteran squinted at me through the haze he'd created and said, "I am sorry to be the bearer of bad news, young Jasmine, but I'm afraid your mother has escaped from hell. She seems to be the one who hit your father with the van. And, ah, the incident with the pineapple cans?"

When I gave him a blank look, he nodded wisely. "I supposed your father had kept you in the dark on that one. No sense in worrying the children unnecessarily. Well, it seems she was trying to gain his attention, and in her frustration at being unable to do so, she knocked over a large wooden pineapple that had been erected by Albert's favorite grocer. If Shelby had not quickly pulled him out of the way, a sea of Del Monte chunks in their own syrup might have crushed the life out of him."

When the colonel first gave me Mom's news I'd shoved my hands in my hair, prepared to yank out handfuls as she'd pushed me to do so many times in my adolescence. I froze, fully aware I was giving myself mini bunny ears, and began to laugh.

Colonel John traded puzzled looks with Raoul. "I fail to see the humor here. The Gatekeeper has unleashed the dogs. And if they catch her before she returns voluntarily, I can foresee no end to her tortures."

I felt the laughter burn to cinders in my throat. Nearly choking on the ashes I said, "According to my count, she's done exactly four nice things for me in the past twenty-five years. You want to tell me why I should give a shit?"

When all three men winced at my four-letter-word choice I jerked myself off the couch and stomped to the window. *What the hell? Is this your idea of a joke? You put me in the most stressful situations you can imagine, where you know I'm going to need to swear, and then you surround me with old-world prudes? Matt never cared what I said. Matt liked me just the way I was.* I was talking to the Big Kahuna, but I addressed the broad expanse of skyscrapers and twinkling lights hiding masses of pissed-off poor people who thought the only way to make life better was to give all the power they didn't realize they had to the biggest dickhead they could find.

Vayl's hands, warm on my shoulders, let me know he cared despite my potty mouth. I looked up, caught my breath as his amber eyes met mine. *Maybe even a little bit because of it?* The heart-crushing longing I'd felt for my dead guy eased as I stared up at my undead one.

"Do you suppose we should do something about your mother before she kills your father?" he asked.

"Fine. Let's call Dave. He likes them both better than I do. He can be the mediator." Colonel John cleared his throat. The apologetic look in his eyes led me to ask, "There's more?"

"I am afraid so," he said. "I was able to intercept a third message from her *loeden*. She wants to meet both your father *and* you at Clava Cairns. It seems to be a repeat of a message your father already received and did not acknowledge. It is here, awaiting your reply." He nodded toward the hallway that led to the biggest part of Raoul's penthouse. A series of locked doors hiding treasures I'd only begun to uncover the last time I'd visited.

I turned around so I could search Vayl's expressions better as we talked. "What do you think she's after?"

He shrugged. "You know her better than I." He lifted the curl that rimmed the right side of my face. The one that had turned white after she'd touched me when we'd met in hell. "Has she changed?"

I wanted to think so. And the fury that rose at that little-girl yearning filled my lungs like glue. I slammed my hand against my chest, reminding myself how to breathe. "Nobody who's done what she did changes," I said.

"What did she do to you, my Jasmine?" His whisper was so soft it could almost have been the doors of my own memory creaking shut, trying to block access.

I glanced past the comforting barrier of his shoulder to the men sitting beyond us. They hadn't heard. In fact, realizing we needed privacy, Colonel John had restarted Raoul's toy train conversation and my Spirit Guide was yapping deliriously about track layouts and the proper turn radius for HO scale.

I moved to the side, so their view of me would be completely blocked by Vayl's broad back. For the second time tonight I shed my jacket and revealed scars I'd kept hidden up to this point. Boy, was I getting all therapied up lately, or what? After one look at my *sverhamin's* face I decided "or what" should probably apply next time. Because if my dad had been furious, Vayl had snapped.

Blood filled his eyes until the only relief from the frightening redness was the hard core of black at their centers. His lips pulled back, revealing his fangs, like a lion's will when he's warning another male off his territory. And his powers spiked, an Arctic gale to my Sensitivity, making me ram into the window so hard I could feel the wood of its frame biting through my shirt.

"Vayl?" I whispered.

"What is happening?" demanded Colonel John. He and

Raoul had risen off the couch. Despite the fact that one supported the other, they still managed to make a threatening duo.

"Back away from her, Vayl!" Raoul shouted. "You are a guest here. Only allowed because I have pronounced it neutral territory for the duration of your stay. If I invoke the holy protections once again you will burn as surely as if you had entered a cathedral!"

I put my hand on Vayl's chest, willing him to be calm. "I know you're pissed. So am I. Every day. But this isn't helping; you see that, don't you? Come on, if you're not going to be the levelheaded one, we're pretty much screwed."

"I want to be there when you confront her," he growled.

"Okay, fine. No problem." Never mind that I'd have agreed to slip into a frilly apron and bake a carrot cake if that would take the vengeance out of his expression. I turned to the other guys and smiled brightly as Vayl's powers began to ebb. "It's all good," I assured them. "I just opened my big mouth one too many times. You know me, F this, F that. He's so sick of me swearing sometimes he could happily throw me off the roof. Not that he'd ever do that," I hastened to add, realizing my babbling was about to get us into worse trouble. Best to finish our business and get out.

I went on. "Tell my mother I'll talk to Dad and, if he's okay with a meet, I'll get back to Raoul with the arrangements. But we won't have time to do anything until after our mission's accomplished. Which means she needs play it cool until then. Okay?"

Still looking somewhat suspicious, Colonel John nodded. Which gave Raoul little choice but to agree.

I let my smile widen. Now my entire face hurt. How did beauty queens do it? "Thanks so much for your help. Can't tell you how much I appreciate it. Big weight off my mind." I took

Vayl's hand, clenched it hard to make sure he followed me as I said, "Don't worry about seeing us out. We know the way. Sorry about the bar again, but it sounds like you've got a great plan in place for the train dealie. Keep me posted on that, will ya?"

And, having reestablished an expression of avid interest on Raoul's face, at least, I led Vayl out the door and back to the real world.

CHAPTER TWENTY-NINE

I opened my eyes and took a deep, whopping breath. The kind you want after you've been stuck inside a gas station bathroom way too long. "We're back."

Vayl stirred. Which was when I realized how Cirilai had found him so easily. He'd come into his room, into his bed, and wrapped himself around me so tightly I felt like I'd crawled into a kid's sleeping bag. "Um, Vayl?"

"Mmm."

"We should get up."

"Why?"

I strained my head to see past his curls to the little round alarm clock on the pretty railed table beside the bed. "I'm assuming you had Cole take your place when you came in here."

"Yes."

"Well, I have to go relieve him. And you're going to be dead to the world [*literally!*] in less than half an hour."

He lifted his chin from where it rested on my shoulder. His warm breath tickled at my cheek as he said, "Then surely another twenty or thirty minutes will not hurt him."

"You're damn straight it will!" Cole cut in, which was when I realized Vayl, at least, hadn't taken off his transmitter. "Get your ass up here, Jaz." Ooh, our third sounded pretty irritable.

"Tell him I'm coming," I said.

"I heard," said Cole. "What are you, sitting on Vayl's lap or something? Never mind, I don't want to know. Just get up here. Strange things are happening and I'm tired of trying to figure out if they're designed to pull me off Floraidh watch or if I really should investigate."

I shoved at Vayl's chest. It worked about as well as poking an elephant with a daisy. "We'll be right there," I said anyway.

Vayl began to nuzzle that sensitive area right behind my earlobe. Which made my eyes roll right up in their sockets. Tough not to make any noise as his hand slipped under my shirt. I wanted it to continue . . . well, was forever too long? But Cole needed us. The mission loomed. Not to mention my crappy mother. And did I really want to lock in the memories of our first time with a Scidairan's spell-drenched B and B?

Not to mention my nap breath. Not as bad as morning breath, but still skanky enough to warrant a brushing. Because underneath it the aftertaste of Brude's blood had lingered. *Impossible,* my mind whispered. *Your body was here the whole time.*

Tell that to my taste buds.

Unbelievable the effort it took to peel my hands off Vayl's ass. Apparently they'd discovered it fit them better than a pair of driving gloves and they didn't appreciate the order to move. Because they kept trying to pull the old cup-and-squeeze, I shoved them under my thighs where they proceeded to pinch me for depriving them of such pleasure after a long, *long* absence. "I have to pee," I said.

The nibbling at my ear stopped. Frustrated scream from my bimbo libido, who'd been chained up so long she resembled a skeleton hanging from Brude's dungeon wall. Which raised a whole slew of new questions I wasn't yet awake enough to deal with. I struggled to sit up. Vayl pulled back slightly. "You do?"

I reached up to kiss him, feather-light, on the chin,

whispered, "Does this feel like the right time to you? The right place?"

"Yes."

I laughed. His chuckle sounded less strangled every time he let it roll. And when he let me up, his smile even looked less murderous than usual. "Shall I wait for you, then?"

"Up to you. I won't be long."

I spent five minutes in the bathroom and came out feeling a lot more like the old Jaz, who would never have dreamed of biting her opponent on the neck. At least I hadn't suffered any bad effects from it. *Yet,* whispered a new voice in my mind, one I'd never heard before and didn't have time now to pinpoint.

At six thirty in the morning Tearlach stopped reflecting the personalities of its owners and guests, and began to show its own individual quirks. A light rain had begun outside, along with a wind that made the house whisper and creak as we walked down the hall toward the stairs. Vayl could see in the dark, and with my contact lenses activated, so could I. The knickknacks and frills that had seemed homey in the light now took on a spook-house freakishness as we passed them.

We crept up the stairs, Vayl moving silently inside his camouflage, me shielded by my Sensitivity and Bergman's watch, Jack just naturally quiet on his padded feet. We reached the fourth-floor landing before I smelled it.

"Vayl. A witch is working a spell here," I whispered.

"Yes, you told me. The Haighs—"

"No, a *witch*. A Wiccan, like Tolly."

Cole met us a few steps into the hallway, his eyes wide and glittering as he swung them from my face to Vayl's. "Look at the doors," he whispered, shining his flashlight on the entrance to Floraidh's room.

At first it looked like any quaint old door that's been painted repeatedly. A dull shine reflected the off-white Floraidh had chosen to color her entryway. She'd hung a basket of silk forget-me-nots under the room number.

"You know what, I don't think the paint on that door was cracked when I opened it earlier this evening," I said.

"Look at Dormal's," he murmured as he swung the light in that direction.

Hers was in even worse shape. Paint had peeled down in strips, as if a clawed hand had scraped it top to bottom. The door creaked, and then the diamond-embedded symbol on its upper-right-hand corner flared, as if it had begun to burn deep within the wood. The jewel itself glittered so brightly I'd have believed the sun was shining straight on it if the window wasn't shaded.

Cole swung his light to Floraidh's door. We watched the same action take place there. And then, as suddenly as I might snap my fingers, the scent of Wicca died.

"It's gone," I said.

"It is?" Cole trained his light all around the hallway as if to catch the culprit who'd tried, and failed, to breach the Scidairans' defenses. "Was it Bea?"

"I don't know. I didn't scent witchery at Castle Hoppringhill when all those snakes appeared. So either she was trying to mask herself there because she was in public . . ."

Vayl flicked Cole's light off. "Or Floraidh has *two* mortal enemies staying under her roof."

After such an exciting start to the day, you'd have thought the action would swing right on into overdrive.

Nope.

Vayl went back to his room to crawl into his specially made blackout bed-tent.

After sleeping until one in the afternoon, Albert accepted the news about Mom and our plan to deal with her remarkably well. He grabbed a bite to eat and took Jack back to my room to watch a *My Family* marathon until we decided we needed them.

Cole and I took turns napping, attending GhostCon events with Albert and Jack like we really gave a crap about the feng shui of a haunted foyer, and watching Floraidh. Since our ward spent most of the day in her room concocting weird Scidair spells while Dormal looked after the B and B, we'd had to improvise our stalker spot, turning the walk-in linen closet beside Dormal's room into a Scidair-hide. I came up with the name. It helped alleviate my minor claustrophobia to imagine I was a *National Geographic* photographer, surrounded by vast expanses of jungle, just waiting for the elusive kangahipposeal to appear, at which time I'd film that sucker like a paparazzi on speed.

We furnished the Scidair-hide with a laptop and folding chair, from which we eyeballed the empty hallway like we thought the walls were about to sprout ninjas. Sure, it would've been a lot more comfortable, not to mention safer, to guard her from one of our rooms. But if Bea tried something during the day, seconds would count. And though I could move a lot faster than I used to, I still wasn't superhuman enough to race up two flights of stairs in time to save her from an assassin standing right at her door.

The first time Cole relieved me he came with good news. "Rhona's driving your dad nuts. She keeps knocking on our door, asking him if he'd like to accompany her to her GAPT seminar tomorrow. I think that blow to her head has lodged an obsession for him deep in her cortex."

"Cool!"

"Plus, while I was fending her off for him—"

"What!"

"He gave me twenty bucks and promised to fart under the covers for the rest of the day." I shrugged. How could you argue with that? "Anyway, it gave me the chance to talk to her about Iona. She came with great references. Which I plugged into the database along with one of the shots our cameras picked up. She's clean. Squeakily so."

Bummer. I spent my break trying to solve the mystery of Bea's true identity while some GhostCon idiot droned on and on about why people who die violently have such a hard time resting in the ever-after. I wanted to jump out of my chair and yell, "Well, I'd be pissed too!" I settled for relieving Cole early. Since I couldn't shuffle my chips for the noise they'd make, I practiced walking one across the tops of my fingers. Amazing how much you can improve at something when that's the only thing you do for two hours straight. Oh yeah, there was that ten minutes when I figured out Dormal's secret.

Before my first nap I'd sent the pictures of her room to Tolly along with a request to let me know what she could make of them. She'd gotten back to me with the results right around the middle of my last watch. The symbols on Dormal's and Floraidh's doorways were charms of protection, ones meant to keep ghostly and magical attacks neutralized. The squigglies on her wall? A massive curse aimed at one Edward Samos. The kind, Tolly said, that a scorned lover chooses, because wound around the curse is the demand for the stolen love to return.

"Meaning what, exactly?" I'd asked Tolly.

"If I had to guess, I'd say Samos broke up her happy home," Tolly replied. "Do you know of anyone she's holding out hopes of reuniting with?"

"Actually, yeah, I do."

Around four Cole came to relieve me. "Anything new?" he asked as I handed him the laptop.

"Not much," I replied. "Oh. Except I found out that Dormal's in love with Floraidh, who's in love with Samos."

"Well, that could be significant."

"I don't know. Samos is dead. Why would Dormal want to kill Floraidh now?"

"Love is, like, the least logical emotion on earth," he said, avoiding my eyes. "Look at us. On paper we're perfect for each other, but in real life . . ." He shrugged.

I crouched down in front of him so I could get a better look at his expression. Hurt. Despite all my efforts, and although he'd pretended otherwise, I'd made his heart bleed. What to say now? Where were the words that would heal him without leaving ice between us?

"What are you looking for, Cole?"

"You!"

I shook my head. "Come on. You knew I wanted Vayl almost from the second we met. And you still came after me. What is it that you think I can give you?"

He closed the laptop lid, spread his fingers out across it and studied them, turned his hands over and watched his palms for a while. If he could've seen his future there, would he have felt any relief? "I want what my parents have. Real love. A whole lifetime of it. I've been looking, God, since I was probably fifteen. Every time I meet a woman I think, *She's amazing. She could be the one.* And then, no. I realize she's somebody else's one and I let her go. Then I found you. And I still keep thinking, *Yeah, this is it.*"

I knew, if I had made a single different decision in my life, he might've been right. No Matt. No dead Helsingers. No life as an assassin and no Vayl might have all added up to a Jasmine Bemont with lots of Cole Jrs running around her suburban split-level. Because I did love him. And part of me wanted to be that woman for him.

I said, "You know I can't do that to you. As much as I might want to, I can't give you that life. You only think I'm the one because you don't really know me. You've never seen the horror I'm capable of."

"Jaz—"

"If only you'd consider somebody better. Like Viv."

"She's a great girl. We may go on a few dates. We may stay together for a month or two. Someday we'll probably be good friends. But I can already tell she's not the one."

I'd put my hands on his knees to make my point. Now I dropped them. "I'm sorry."

When Cole's answer turned out to be a shrug, I shuffled off to his room to try for a last power nap before Vayl rose. I'd been worried about sleeping after my confrontation with Brude, but Raoul and Colonel John had assured me that his promise of safe passage meant I'd be okay for the duration of the mission. Coming back to his territory after his two-week freebie concluded might be a problem, but they were working on a way to protect me from him should I ever need to cross his lands again. And it turned out they were right. Despite the niggling worries about Brude, and Cole, I slept well. No dreams. No interruptions. Until Vayl knocked on my door.

His hair sparkled, still wet from the shower. Wearing a black button-down shirt with pinstripes tucked into faded jeans he looked good enough to eat. I felt like a leftover taco. "Hi."

"I am up for the evening." Really, should it be legal for one man's smile to make your heart skip a beat? *Maybe if he's not a man at all, but a vampire who has finally taught you the meaning of the word "luscious."*

"I need a shower. And some food." I thought a second. "And lessons."

"Oh?"

"I'm pretty sure there's no way I'm going to be able to keep you interested if you continue to catch me when my hair's standing on end and my breath smells like drooly pillow. But maybe if some svelte supermodel could teach me a few tricks—"

The alarm in his eyes made me reach for Grief. Which was currently hanging in its holster on the headboard of the bed. So all I got for my trouble was a handful of armpit. Lovely. Problem was, I couldn't even make farting noises to entertain him. All I could do was stand there and look like a freak show reject.

I think he might've read some of what I was thinking in my eyes, because his lips curled as he ran his fingertips down my arms. *Oooh, shivery good!*

"My sweet *pretera,* do not change for my benefit. I love you just as you are. Evening breath and all."

"What a nice thing to say. I'm not sure I buy it, but I appreciate the sentiment."

"Ah yes, you always did prefer actions to words." He leaned down and kissed the tip of my nose. "Never fear. I am still working on a most amazing proof for the depth of my feelings for you."

"Well, you could start by letting me get freshened up."

"Certainly. Take all the time you need. I am just going to relieve Cole. I understand he and the girls are scheduled to sit in on Rhona's presentation shortly."

"Wow. So cool that I get to miss that."

Unfortunately my shift at GhostCon started right after Cole's ended, so I did have to endure a debate over what shades do when they're taking a break from the haunting biz. Some panelists voted for them falling into a kind of mystical coma state from which they emerged only when disturbed by our presence. Others insisted they functioned in a society of sorts, one much more savage than ours, where atrocity was the earmark of progress and success. After what I'd seen in Brude's dungeon, I tended to agree with them.

The only other interesting occurrence that evening happened when I got back to the B and B in time to meet the Haighs on the way to their fancy supper.

"Wow, don't you guys look ritzy?" I said as I met them on the walk in front of Tearlach. Humphrey wore a shiny black suit, white shirt, and bow tie while Lesley had chosen an ivory dress with matching low-heeled pumps.

"Thank you!" she said, her hand fluttering up to her hair. "I'm so excited. I've never been to Adair's before."

"Where's your necklace?" I asked.

She looked at me blankly. "Excuse me?"

"The diamond rose necklace you had on last night. You said you'd brought it just to wear to this dinner."

She gave me that polite smile people reserve for eccentrics and friendly drunks. "I'm sorry, you must have me confused with someone else. I don't own any necklaces like that."

"Of course, my mistake," I said, stepping aside to let them pass. *Helluva spell, Floraidh. Just wiped their minds clean of those jewels, didn't you? Wonder what else you erased while you were at it?*

I told Vayl about the conversation as I took my linen-closet watch, but he still wanted to wait and see. "The mission is our priority," he said as he handed off the laptop. "We must neutralize Bea."

"Who's taking her own sweet time showing," I muttered as I grabbed the computer and thumped into the chair. "If she doesn't make a move tonight I'm going to smoke her out."

I know, impatient words from a girl who should've been an ace at waiting by now. But I wasn't the only one who was sick of Bea's lack of progress.

Chapter Thirty

idnight. I'd once read this was the witching hour. Then I learned that only counted if the moon was full. As I jerked upright in bed, jarred awake by the shout in my head, I knew three things at once. The moon was only in its first quarter, showing like a halved dime in the sky. I'd overslept my shift change. And the voice I'd heard wasn't my own.

Jack jumped into bed beside me, a forbidden practice that he knew would earn him a scolding. But as soon as he saw I was awake he bounded over me, went straight to the door, and began to scratch. I adjusted the receiver, which had fallen back into my hair while I'd napped. "Did you hear it too?" I asked.

Jack looked back at me and jumped on the door, the thump he made probably loud enough to alert Vayl, who'd retired to his room to see if he could pull up the results of the ash test we'd sent for, and also to help Albert hide from Rhona, who hadn't given up her clumsy attempts at seduction.

The guys met us in the hall.

Before I could ask, Vayl said, "Cole is in trouble. Come."

He led the way to the Scidair-hide. The door was cracked open. Vayl raised his eyebrows at me. As I drew and cocked Grief, I sent my extra senses into the room ahead of me. Shook my head. No scent of *others*. From the look on Vayl's face he couldn't feel any intense human emotions either. And Jack showed no more than mild interest in the entire exercise. With Albert staying in the hall to watch, we entered the room carefully. Vayl led, throwing frost ahead of him so thick I could see my breath before I'd taken a single step.

How, with a laptop feeding him camera shots, had Cole not seen them coming?

Scidair, my mind replied as it noted the upset chair. The quarter-sized spot of blood on the floor next to it. The wad of gum that had fallen out of his mouth at some point during the kidnap.

Or killing?

No. Hell no! I'd have known! I'd have felt him—pass! Right? Geez, where do you go when you can't stand being inside your hysterical head one more second? Some girls find a sympathetic shoulder to cry on. Some shop. I warm my hand on the butt of my gun and sink into my own center. It's not quite the shelter it used to be. Cracks have opened and the floor's developed a big rusty spot, but it still does the job most of the time.

Vayl pointed to himself, jabbed a finger back toward Floraidh's room. Then he gestured for me to take Jack and check out Dormal's place. We met back in the hide less than fifteen seconds later, where Albert had at least had the presence of mind not to touch anything.

"She's not in there," I whispered. "Although I'm pretty sure we tripped whatever magical alarms they've woven over their rooms. I felt them zap as soon as we crossed the thresholds."

Vayl shrugged it off. His expression said now was not the time to be timid. "Floraidh has left as well. She keeps a shrine to Samos behind that screen."

"Okay, that's pathetic."

"I have not even begun. Besides pictures and ticket stubs she also has hair snippets, fingernail clippings, and a used condom."

"Ick!" I watched Jack sniff at the bloodstain. My first instinct was to shove his nose away from the spot. His desire to take in that aspect of Cole's scent grossed me out. Until I gave it a second thought.

He didn't get that I might disapprove of his behavior. He was in dog mode, pointing on odors that stood out because, for one reason or another, they interested him. Maybe that's how I needed to view Floraidh. Not as a woman who'd loved Samos enough to keep souvenirs of their time together. But as a Scidairan who needed bits of him in order to cast a spell that would . . . what? You can't raise a man from the dead when he's got no body to raise.

Unless you steal yourself another one.

Shit!

They must've been planning this for a while. And Cole probably hadn't even been the original target. But Floraidh had been forced to step up her timetable for some reason. Gather diamonds to fend off ghosts who would interfere because, why? Was Samos stuck somewhere in the Thin? And was it the shades' job to make sure he didn't come back? If Brude was Satan's Enforcer, maybe he was sheltering Samos. Or trying to distract us so nobody could keep him from returning. But, then, why the need for the diamonds?

Didn't matter. She'd manipulated Humphrey into handing over the goods. Taken Cole. And if we didn't find them soon Samos would return.

We did a quick check of the hallway. Kinda redundant, since we knew it went nowhere but past the rooms we'd already searched.

"They can't be that far ahead of us," I fumed. "We just heard Cole's voice!"

"You stay here and keep searching," said Vayl. "Albert, go downstairs and keep watch over their car. At least we will know if they try to leave by the lane."

"Should we"—I didn't want to ask. It hurt to consider cutting Cole out of our loop. But if it would help in the end—"Should we tune the party line to a different frequency?"

"We would be assuming Floraidh and Dormal had found his receiver and understood its significance," said Vayl. "Am I stating the situation correctly?"

"I'd say that about sums it up."

He gave it a moment's thought. "No. At worst I believe they will think it another one of our ghost-reaching gadgets. And anything that might help us find him faster is worth the risk."

They took off, leaving me spinning in the hall, trying to decide if the Scidairans had taken Cole to the attic. Was there an attic? If so, would a coven perform wicked rites there while the guests slept two floors below? *I don't think so.*

We'd closed the fourth-floor doors. Now I opened them wide. Went back into the linen closet where Jack lay, looking despondent, by the wrecked chair.

I crouched beside him. "What do you think?" I asked as he looked up at me with his expressive black eyes. "Can you help me find Cole?"

I heard his tail thump against the floor before I saw it wagging out of the corner of my eye. "Okay then." I caught the end of his leash. "Have another sniff." I directed his attention to the blood. Then we spent some time with the chair. When I couldn't stand the delay any longer I said, "Got it?"

A straight-up perk of the ears told me he'd decided the game was on. I led him into the hall. Knelt down beside him. Said, "Where's Cole? Where'd he go? Let's find him, okay? Let's go play with Cole!"

He sniffed around, with me repeating the command long enough that Vayl had rejoined us by the time Jack reached the wall at the hall's end. The one with the cute little table holding our camera. Ducking under the table, Jack began to scratch.

I looked at Vayl. "I should've known better. My dog sucks at trailing. The last time we were home I accidentally dropped a hot dog on the floor while I was cooking supper one night. And despite the fact that he was sitting beside me at the time I still had to show him where it landed."

"At least Albert is in place," Vayl replied. "They cannot drive Cole anywhere without us knowing it."

Jack yelped and jumped back, all four of his paws clearing the ground at the same time as the section of floor that held the table suddenly lifted and slid three feet to the left.

As we watched the cleverly hidden trapdoor reveal a steep set of stairs, Vayl put a hand on my shoulder. "I suppose you know what this means?"

I leaned over and gave Jack a vigorous rubdown. "That my dog is better than a trained bloodhound?"

"No. That you are a terrible cook."

I shot him a dirty look, but it missed. Because he'd already hit the stairs running. "Come on, boy," I told my canine hero. "We'll bide our time on the cook comment. Delayed revenge is always the sweetest."

We followed Vayl down the stairs, taking a dangerous pace considering the lack of light and their narrow, winding path. At one point Jack stopped. Sniffed. Demanded that I sniff too. Or, if I was going to be crass about it, at least bend over and take a good look. More blood. They must've dropped him here.

We moved on, seeing no evidence of another exit by the time we'd reached what we thought should be the first floor.

"These stairs must end in the basement," Vayl said.

"Makes sense," I replied.

As we continued downward Albert's voice broke the rhythm of my heightened breathing. "I hear an engine," he said. "But nothing's moving out front. It sounds like it's coming from the barn."

"Can you check it out without being seen?" asked Vayl.

Insulted huff. "Maybe someday I'll teach you a thing or two about recon, ya baby."

Ha! If only Albert knew how old Vayl really was! Um, never mind.

We finally reached the basement. Typical clutter you'd expect in a B and B storeroom. Broken bed. Shelves packed with paint cans. A freezer full of wrapped meat and frostbitten veggies. A dehumidifier humming away in the middle of the room. Also the guts of the building, which meant we had to bow our heads or be concussed by large pipes that led to the furnace and smaller ones that rushed water from its outer source up to every faucet in the place. Jack found the stairs that led up to a plank door, which stood open, witness to the Scidairans' rush.

Vayl took my hand, not out of a sense of shared adventure or romance, but because he was getting ready to run and didn't want me to slow him down. As we strode toward the exit I asked, "Will Jack be able to keep up with us?" I could run pretty fast now that I'd shared blood with a Were. But Vayl could practically fly.

He glanced down at the malamute panting happily at my heels. "He should. If not, let him go. He will find us."

Vayl trotted up the stairs. They led us into the herb garden. We could hear the engine now. "Sounds like an ATV," I said.

"It's a Honda Big Red," said Albert. "You've seen those? They're like mini Jeeps with two seats up front, a roll bar, and a small bed in back to haul things with."

"I get the picture," I said. "Where are you?"

"I'm by the barn, looking in through a crack in the outer wall. Four women inside that I can see. Dormal and Floraidh on the Big Red, the other two opening the back door for them. You'd better hustle. They're backing out right now."

We ran. "Do you see Cole?" asked Vayl.

"I've got the wrong angle. There's definitely something in the bed of that thing, but it's hard to tell what from here."

As the distance closed between us and the barn, the Scidairans suddenly came into view. They'd turned the Big Red toward the path we'd taken to get to Tearlach during our Ghost-Walk. Hard to tell where they were headed. The cemetery? Clava Cairns? The castle and its plane-hopping doorway? Who cared? We didn't intend to let them get to the tree line.

I realized I needed a hand free to work my weapon, so I dropped Jack's leash, which had become taut enough as we ran that I realized he couldn't keep up with us anyway. I pulled Grief, estimating the first moment I could fire and hope to hit my target. The part of me that hadn't yet folded down into assassin mode noted Cole's legs, clothed in ripped jeans and his favorite red high-tops, dangling over the edge of the vehicle's bed, and realized he would be so pissed if he was conscious. In fact, he'd probably be saying something like, "This is just my luck. I couldn't get nabbed by some high-class level of criminal who wears bling and rides in limos. No. I have to be kidnapped by the cast of *Bewitched*."

Speaking of bling, was that glitter I saw reflecting from Floraidh's neck Humphrey's forgotten creation? I was thinking so. But before I could figure out how to make that vulnerability work for us, I hit a brick wall and landed flat on my ass. At which point Jack trotted up to me and sniffed my forehead as if to say, "See what you get for leaving me behind?"

I looked up. Whatever I'd hit had no visible boundaries. All

I could see, with every one of my senses maxed out, was a slight bend in the horizon, as if I were viewing it from a telescope. And, of course, now that I wasn't zeroed in on Cole I could smell the spell that had flung me down.

Vayl hadn't been dumped, but he had been stunned. He stood a couple of arms' lengths to one side of me, hands on his knees, slowly shaking his head.

I turned back to search for the cause of our blockage. There, at the corner of the barn. The other two women Albert had mentioned. I recognized one as the girl we'd seen manning the Tearlach table at GhostCon. The other was a fiftyish spinster with a forgettable face who must've decided taking care of her mother as she slowly faded from life wasn't quite as fulfilling as she'd anticipated. So why not bow down to an evil sorceress on the side?

They wore long indigo dresses that clung like spiderwebs as they moved their hands through motions that reminded me eerily of the Raisers who'd inadvertently caused me a shitload of trouble already. These motions, however, demanded where the Raisers pleaded. Their fingers jabbed, their fists punched, the sides of their hands sliced through the air as if to cut through the fabric of the planet itself. And the Raisers had steered wide of introducing sacrifice into their act. I couldn't tell what had once animated the lump bleeding on the ground between Floraidh's rear guard, but I suddenly felt like the most irresponsible pet owner ever, bringing Jack into a situation where animals his size ended up lying limp and lifeless so that wicked shitbricks could progress.

He didn't seem too happy about the deal either. His ears laid back as he caught the scent of the carcass. Or maybe it was the Scidairan chant that put him off. It did sound like it had been written by someone who enjoyed the noise of whiny two-year-olds.

I shivered, realizing that the wintry lifting of Vayl's powers was only part of the reason. *I'm over my head this time,* I thought. *These women are going to fry us like moths in a bug zapper and there's not a damn thing we can do to stop them.* Still, I struggled to my feet. *Better to die upright than flat on your tush,* that's what Granny May always used to say. Though why she'd ever had cause to develop that philosophy I had no idea. Too bad she wasn't here to pour more pearls of wisdom into my empty brain. It could've used some bright ideas right about now.

As if he could read my mind Vayl murmured, "These cannot be full coven members. Floraidh will need those for whatever she has planned for Cole. These are novices, Jasmine. We can beat them."

"With what?" I whispered. "How do you battle something whose weapons you can't even see?" We'd never had to kill a Scidairan before, dammit. Pete saved those kinds of hits for our warlock.

He came to stand at my shoulder. "Use what you know. And then improvise."

I took a deep breath. And yelled, "Love those outfits, girls! You look like a couple of litmus test strips. Yo, Vayl, did we bring the acid? Let's turn these bitches red!"

Anybody with even a week of field experience wouldn't have missed a step. But these bimbettes must've come fresh from the Scidair School of World-Ripping. They both hesitated. And in that moment, as it so often does during the most violent times of my life, everything slowed down as everyone moved at once.

Albert stepped out from hiding, swinging some sort of club at the shorter of the two Scidairans.

She fell to her knees as her partner spun to face this new threat. I hoped the shock of Albert's attack would send her into instinctual attack mode. If she just jumped him, he'd be fine. Even at his age he could pound the crap out of men twice his size. Unfortunately she kept her cool. Sweeping her power from the shield that had barred us, she shoved it at my dad, throwing him into the barn's wall. He crumpled to the ground.

Already halfway to them, Grief in one hand, my bolo in the other, I kept one eye on Albert and the other on the girls. The one he'd felled was stirring, moaning. The other had begun to turn back to me. *Thank God!* Albert moved. But it was to clutch one hand to his chest. *Shit!*

Vayl swept past me, grabbing my hand on the way and holding our arms outstretched. We clotheslined that Scidairan whore like a WWE tag team, laying her out like a corpse on an autopsy table. I took aim.

"No," said Vayl. "Remember the mission."

For a second I couldn't. Not even the part about why we had to work it in Scotland. All I wanted was to shoot that black heart full of steel, guarantee that nobody else's dad would ever suffer a heart attack because this twisted bit of snot couldn't see the good in anything. Then Albert belched.

"Ahh, that's better. Did you see that, Jaz? She knocked the breath right out of me!"

As I turned my head, my neck aching with the effort it took to hold up my unbelieving brain, Vayl said, "Albert, can you find some rope? We must not leave them free to roam while we chase after Cole."

I watched Albert struggle to his feet, his knees seeming to be more of a problem than the blows he'd taken from the Scidairan. As soon as he disappeared into the barn I said, "I always suspected he was indestructible. Now I know it."

However, when he didn't immediately return I started to wonder if I'd spoken too soon. "You two might want to come in here," Albert finally said.

Nodding to one another, we each grabbed a girl and shook

them awake. I'd chosen the smaller one, who came to all at once. She sat up, grabbing her head and screeching like a pissed-off parrot.

"Be quiet," I said as I grabbed her wrists and shoved them high enough on her back that she squawked again. "You're just going to give yourself a bigger headache."

Vayl's old gal decided the whole situation was horribly humiliating and began to cry as we walked them into the barn. Or maybe she thought we'd sympathize and let them go. Ha!

Albert stood in the open space between two rows of empty stalls. In one hand he held a tarp. The other motioned to an enormous black-lidded barbecue, the kind you'd expect to see beside a food vendor's tent at a street fair. "I lifted the lid," he said. "People store all kinds of stuff in their grills. I thought, *Why not rope?*" He pointed.

Shoving my charge ahead of me, I moved toward the cooker. And stopped again just before my hip hit the side table.

"Vayl?"

"Yes, Jasmine," he said gravely.

"Is that an eyeball lying in the cinders under the grate?"

"I believe so."

"Jesus." I spun my girl around, but before I could even begin to question her she threw up. The only reason she missed me was that I read the signs correctly and shoved her away before any damage was done. "Tie her up, Albert." For once, he just nodded.

Turning to Vayl's prisoner, I stalked toward her, noting with satisfaction that the closer I got the bigger her eyes grew. "I don't know anything!" she squeaked.

"Sure you do," I said. "Your boss is cooking people in her backyard. That's not something she's going to be able to sneak past the novices. In fact, I'm guessing you probably had to spend time at the grill. Part of your training?" When she caught her breath I knew I'd hit the mark.

I lifted my knife. Pressed the tip against her cheek. "We could add another trophy to the one in that grill real easy." Change of angle, just enough to draw blood. Vayl held her tightly, not allowing her to jump and injure herself further. Giving me complete control. "What are they planning tonight?"

"Floraidh is bringing the Raptor back to the skies."

Raising Samos, just like I thought. Okay, don't panic. "How?"

"We're eaters of the dead. It transforms us, and allows us to live beyond our mortal lives." She sounded like she was reading from a textbook. The same one Tolly had stolen a peek from when she'd dipped her foot into Scidairan magic.

"What does that have to do with my friend?"

She gasped as I twisted the knife, letting her cheek feel its sharp edge. "When we eat the *living* we can make other transformations. With the right words, the right components, we can—" Her eyes widened in horror as they focused on a spot behind me. "She knows I'm talking to you! You must promise to protect me!"

"Of course. Where's she headed?"

"Clava Cairns. She's already buried the items she needs there. She just had to get the diamonds to pro—" The girl gasped. "Floraidh! I'm sorry. I had no—" Both girls began to choke. I pulled the knife away from the talker's face as her body bucked and writhed, struggling for air.

Within a minute Vayl had laid her beside her partner. Though Albert had called an ambulance, it would serve only as a hearse.

I grabbed Vayl's arm. "Let's go. We can still catch up to them if we hurry, right?"

He looked off in the direction they'd gone, cast his eyes back down to me. "Possibly. But I would hate to be drained of my energy at the very point I might need it the most."

"The van, then. I'll drive," I said, digging into my pocket for the keys. "Albert, you stay here with Jack."

"And explain the dead girls how?" he asked. "The way my luck's been running, they'll have stood me in front of a firing squad for murder before you two get here to back up my story!"

The fact that Albert had managed to keep up with us as we hurried around to the front of the house explained better than anything how he felt about being left behind. And I sure as hell didn't have time to argue. "Fine. But you keep your ass parked in the van until we tell you it's okay to come out," I said.

"I might be able to help you," he told me. "I'm pretty handy with a golf club." Which was when I finally got a good look at the weapon that had taken down girl number two. Hard to tell where he'd found the nine iron he was currently using as a walking stick, but at this point I wouldn't have cared if it was a bazooka.

"You're in the vehicle or you're stuck here and I don't give a crap if they dangle you from Castle Hoppringhill's tallest tower."

"I knew you were gonna say that. Fine. But if you need me, yell." Albert hefted himself into the backseat of the Alhambra as Vayl, Jack, and I jumped into the front.

The dog settled between the front seats until Albert said, "Yo, mutt. I've got a goody for you back here." While it wasn't advisable, I glanced behind me. My dad was just pulling a sausage out of his pocket, which Jack reacted to with a bouncing turn that slapped his tail against my jacket as he enjoyed his snack.

"Why are you carrying fresh meat around with you?" I asked as I turned my eyes back to the road.

"I never know when I'm going to want a snack."

"What's in your pants pocket?"

"A Fruit Roll-Up and half a ham sandwich."

"You're joshing."

"I never joke about food."

I wished he'd find something to kid about. My insides were wound up so tight a good guitarist could've played the opening riff to "Smoke on the Water" on my intestines.

"Cole is fine," said Vayl.

"How do you know?" I snapped. "It's not like we have any clue what her plan is. Hell, she might have already started snacking on his fingers. Which means even if we save him he'll never be able to talk to Viv again!"

Albert laughed.

"You are such a dick," I said under my breath.

"What did you say?" my father demanded.

"You're a selfish dick!" I yelled.

"That's better! I knew I taught you not to talk behind people's backs!"

The turn to Clava Cairns appeared on my right a lot sooner than I'd anticipated. I slammed the brakes and spun the wheel, making my dad swear as I slid him into the window. Even Vayl had to clutch the door handle, and I wondered for a second if the vehicle was going to roll as the tires screeched like a pissed-off diva.

As soon as I had the vehicle straightened out again, I killed the lights.

"Is that such a good idea?" asked Albert.

"I can see fine," I replied.

"What kind of approach were you considering?" asked Vayl as we rocketed past the sign that told us we had less than five kilometers to go before we reached one of Scotland's most ancient landmarks.

"Quick and violent," I said.

He considered. "That might be a problem if she has a shield in place like the one that felled us."

"I'm driving a van toward them at seventy miles an hour. That gives you a little more than two minutes to think up a better idea."

His answer was to tighten his seat belt and reach back to get a good grip on Jack's collar.

"Oohrah!" yelled my dad. "This takes me back! Anybody got a weapon I can use?"

"Goddammit, you're staying in the van!"

"What if somebody sneaks in through the back? Or breaks a window? This glass isn't bulletproof, you know."

"I am driving an unfamiliar vehicle down a narrow road I've never seen before. Do you really want to be pissing me off right now?"

Vayl handed Albert his cane. "Just twist the blue crystal on the top," he said. "The sheath shoots off, which many of my opponents have found detrimental to their health to begin with. Inside is a weapon made by an Indian sword smith known the world over for his secret forging techniques. The blade is over seven hundred years old and it has never lost its edge."

I glanced in the rearview in time to see the respect squaring Albert's jaw as he accepted Vayl's sword. The fingers of one hand brushed lightly against the tigers stalking each other from one end of the sheath to the other. "Thanks," he said. "I'll make sure it gets back to you in good shape."

"Brownnoser," I whispered to Vayl as he settled back into his seat.

"Whatever I have to do . . ." He let the sentence hang long enough that I shot a look his direction. His eyes, luminous in my Bergman-enhanced vision, made suggestions that sucked the breath right out of my lungs. I forced my attention back to the road, but didn't try to hide my growing grin. Why was it that when we were about to pull something extreme he managed to wind up my nerves and spin them like a basketball on the tip of his finger? Hard to freak about the possible cannibalization of your friend, or your own imminent doom, with Mr. Right exuding confidence and desire in equal doses at your elbow.

I glanced at him one more time, let him see the smile that showed I understood his message: *Relax. We're going to kick ass like we always do. Because it's us.*

Cirilai sent a shot of warmth up my left arm. It linked Vayl and me in a way that suddenly became clear as we hurtled around another corner and found ourselves careening through the parking lot of Clava Cairns on our way to disaster.

For a second it was hard to see past the glitter, as if hundreds of reflectors had been set in the small cavities of the cairns and around the trunks of the nearest trees. *Seriously? Could those all be diamonds?* I wondered. Then I had no time left to ponder.

Eleven Scidairans, varying in age from eighteen to sixty, danced around a fire whose flames flared in vivid blues and purples. Did I mention most of the ladies were naked? My father, who had once gone for two weeks before realizing I'd gotten my hair cut short, noticed right away.

"Son of a bitch, look at the tits on that brunette!"

"Yeah, Dad, we're all about boobs in the CIA," I snapped. "We have whole courses in how to tell the difference between the real ones and the fake ones."

"Who cares?" my father responded. "As long as they bounce I'm a happy camper. How about you, Vayl?"

Hard to interpret the sound that came from my *sverhamin*'s throat. Either he was dying of asphyxiation or he thought my dad was the funniest man on earth but didn't want me to know it.

Rather than scattering as soon as the headlights of our Alhambra hit them, the coven members huddled together, their long, stringy hair and heavily lined eyes combined with their lily-white skin to make them resemble unearthed corpses. The two who'd retained their clothes hung back, somehow familiar but too hard to place at our current speed.

As one of the coven screamed a phrase I didn't recognize, the rest smashed their hands together. Whatever they threw must've been potent. Because I could smell it before it crashed into the windshield. A spell of such combined ill will that as soon as it hit, it took color and form. A green, hollow-eyed Fury with serpentine hair and fangs the size of my fist.

I turned my head, raising my right arm to protect it against the flying glass. Something screamed, sounding like a tire squealing on pavement, though by now we were bumping over the grassy path that led to the cairns. I felt the bracelet on my wrist shiver, as if I'd grabbed the handle of a working chain saw. When cool air hit my face instead of glass, I dared a look.

The bracelet had released its own form. An image of Tolly, looking miffed. At me. "For this I'm missing Animal Planet?"

I shrugged, my hands still full of speeding van. I aimed it straight for the coven as Tolly frowned. She grabbed the Fury by the throat just as it lunged for Vayl. Opening her mouth as big as she could, which was pretty wide considering her relative size at the moment, she bit its head off.

"I thought you were a vegetarian," I said.

"I am," she replied. "Philosophically speaking."

"Huh." I spun the wheel, sending the Alhambra into a high-speed turn that raised dead leaves, new grass, and dirt as high as the windows. Best of all, the coven members ran like spooked squirrels as we circled around for another go at them.

"Don't I get a thanks?" she demanded.

"We're not through yet," I said.

"Well, I am, doll. I've only got so much juice for one night. And it's used up."

"Well, then, thanks. I owe you one."

"Yes, you do." Still chewing, she disappeared into the leaves of the nearest beech tree.

"I do not see Floraidh or Dormal among the crowd," Vayl reported.

"I think Jack's about to puke," Albert said.

"Why'd you feed him that sausage, then!" I demanded.

"Well, I didn't know you were going to play bumper cars tonight!"

I stood on the brakes, yanking Grief out of its holster as I threw my dad the keys. "Get out!" I said.

"You mean if things start to go south—"

"No, I mean now! I just realized we're in Clava Cairns after midnight, which is right where you shouldn't be." *Because my mom's a bitch who waits for no one.* "So leave!"

I jumped out and rounded the front of the van to join my boss.

The coven had hidden behind trees and bushes. I'd spotted over half of them within the first ten seconds of my search. But they weren't the threats. I was concerned about the ones I couldn't place.

Something came flying at Vayl from the lower branches of a huge old fir tree. He dodged left to miss it, and it landed at my feet, a mutated pinecone that flamed first red, then black as it ate its way into the earth. I took aim, but Vayl beat me to her, leaping into the tree like a panther, his powers leaving a wake of frost behind him. She dropped first, a frozen corpse, touched by the *cantrantia* of a wraith. He followed, landing in a crouch, his fangs bared as he searched for his next victim.

Movement inside the cairn we'd toured earlier caught my enhanced vision. "Come out of there right now or I start shooting!"

"Don't! We're on our way!" A line of three women paraded down the narrow path. The GhostCon lanterns, already lit in anticipation of the tours that would begin in an hour or so, shone on their pale and unrepentant faces.

"Raise your hands!" I yelled. I counted palms, coming up with an uneven number just as the third woman jerked her hidden hand out and pointed at me, as if accusing me of some heinous crime. I hit my knees and rolled behind a standing stone, my hair rising off my scalp as one of the cairn rocks spun to the spot I'd just vacated and exploded. I covered my head until the hail of fragments slackened, then popped cover just long enough to bring her down. She'd probably been a grandmother.

A piercing scream from deeper in the woods brought me to my feet. "Cole," I whispered, though my mind insisted no man could take his voice that high, not even under torture.

I ran in that direction, holding out my free hand for Vayl to grab. Together we raced into the forest, a couple of night creatures prepared to deal death to anyone who blocked our paths.

We stopped just outside a clearing made unnatural by the creatures inhabiting it. I was sure it was only the second time Inland Taipans had ever set foot, er, scale in Scotland.

Floraidh stood with her back to us, trying to get Cole to vacate the spot where Dormal had dumped him, probably during the wreck. She'd rammed the Big Red into a huge spruce, hitting it so hard that the headlights shone into one another. I couldn't see her at all. Maybe she'd been thrown under the low-growing branches of another tree.

A ravine drew a line between us and them. The depth of a grave and just wide enough that even a world-class long jumper couldn't make the leap, it divided the clearing on the diagonal without even a fallen tree to simplify the crossing. Moss covered the ground on both sides, and in places small patches of white wildflowers reflected the moon's light. The place probably made visitors gasp in delight during the day. Right now it made me want to puke. Mainly because Floraidh kept slapping Cole, and his only response was a groggy roll of the head.

Vayl touched my arm, calling my attention to Dormal. She'd just walked out of the trees on the opposite end of the glade, but still on Floraidh's side of the land split. The collision hadn't improved her hair, leaving it ratty and full of pine needles. Her dress, a dark brown sack that might've doubled as a grain tote, had ripped at the hem, but she'd left the shard of material to hang like a lifeless tail. She resembled a homeless woman who's just gotten her fix for the day. Her mouth moved without emitting sounds. Her fingers rubbed together as if she was fantasizing about money. And she scented of burning pitch.

But none of that mattered.

For her it was all about the snakes, at least a hundred of them this time, slowly closing in on Floraidh and her captive. Now I understood why Cole thought he'd seen Dormal crying in the castle. Sweat ran down her cheeks like tears, and her shoulders shook from the effort it took to control the animals as they slithered over one another's bodies, often rising three or four feet like cobras in an effort to intimidate each other. And when that didn't work they struck, trading bites that left both reptiles twitching in the wake of their brethren.

We'd finally found Bea. Now it all clicked into place. Of course I hadn't picked up on Bea's *otherness,* because I was already sensing Dormal's abilities and writing them off to Scidair.

Floraidh looked over her shoulder, the whites of her eyes

practically glowing in the dim light of the glade. "Dormal, you have to understand!" Floraidh cried. "This is the only way to bring Edward back—"

"Fuck Samos!" Dormal cried, temporarily losing track of her spell and the snakes as a result. The mass stopped. Milled. Began to fight. Those on the outskirts glided off to find more reasonable-sized prey. "I *told* you we didn't need him! But would you listen? No, you were smitten the moment he slithered into Tearlach. Just like one of these Damned Ones, he was. Lovely and smooth on the outside. But dripping with venom! I won't lose you to him twice! Better you should die to one of his nature than fall prey to his intrigues again!"

Floraidh gave a mighty heave that ripped Cole's sleeve, exposing most of a lean, tanned shoulder. But she still managed to pull him to his feet just in time to save his toes from a curious Taipan tongue. "Dormal, please! We'll do anything you say! Just don't let us die this way!"

Cole's eyes finally focused. "Did somebody say die?" He looked down. "Shitsuckers! The ground's moving!" He tried to back up, couldn't because of the trees crowding him, and shook Floraidh until her head rocked. "*Do* something!" he yelled.

Floraidh's response was to scamper up the nearest branch, leaving Cole to try to haul himself up after her. It didn't work as well for him since his brain hadn't quite reconnected with his extremities. But then she grabbed his outstretched hand. Moments later they were perched beside each other like a couple of enormous bats, Cole bitching at Floraidh like she hadn't just thrown him in the back of an overgrown golf cart and hauled him into the woods to act as her lab rat.

"Why didn't you throw some kind of counterspell down there?" he demanded. "You're supposed to be the big bad coven leader. Kick some ass already!"

"I can't!" Floraidh cried. "All my powers are tied up in the resurrection."

"I told you not to waste yourself on that brute!" Dormal screamed. "What will you have left when he returns? You'll be nothing but an empty husk!"

"You don't know that!" Floraidh yelled back.

Great, the cats are fighting and the snakes can climb trees, I thought as Dormal began chanting again and the Inland Taipans responded in force. I elbowed Vayl, pointed to a spot where I thought I could get a clear shot without endangering Cole. He blinked, nodded, even smiled a little as if everything was just fine. But he'd bitten his bottom lip as we'd watched the snakes advance. And while blood trickled down his chin, everything below his neck seemed to have frozen in place. *I despise snakes,* his wide eyes told me.

I nodded my understanding. Wished he hadn't lent his cane to Albert. Though his innate powers kept him well armed, he'd have felt better with his sword in hand.

Aha! I reached into my pocket, pulled out my bolo, and offered it to him. A nearly audible pop as he took it and relief loosened all his major muscles.

Using the new skills I'd developed in my funky joinage with Trayton, I slunk to the new location I'd picked. Dammit! She'd moved, pressing her left side against a thick-trunked oak as if she needed the extra support while she conducted the slitherage.

I could keep circling. But I'd seen a couple of snakes move in that direction and I didn't love the idea of surprising one of them. I could retrace my steps and try coming around to the other side of her. But that would take time I didn't have. So I stepped into the clearing.

"Back those snakes off or I splat your brains all over the forest," I told Dormal.

CHAPTER THIRTY-ONE

As soon as Dormal's mouth began to move and my bracelet shook I realized we'd run out of time. I shot her just as she drew back behind the tree. Instead of burying my bullet in her ear and ending the nightmare of Bea and her wiggly pets forever, I only managed to destroy the lower half of her face. She couldn't talk, but she could gesture. And the abrupt shove of her hands resulted in a wave of air spinning me off me feet, sending Grief bouncing into the ravine. *Dammit, Tolly! Why couldn't you have given me two bracelets!* Well, at least the snakes had stopped their progress again. Except some of them had decided to reverse course. Climb down into the ravine and see what they could find on our side.

Vayl's *cantrantia* filled the glade, edging the leaves and our clothes with frost. As in the castle, the snakes shifted into slow motion, their heads reaching left and right, as if scouting for ground that hadn't suddenly frigidized.

Dormal searched for the culprit. Not finding him, she turned her attention back to me. I saw the plan in her raging eyes. Finishing me off would even the odds and give her such sweet revenge.

What she didn't know was that I'd never been the big hitter. As had happened countless times before in my work with Vayl, my job was to cause fear, kill if possible, but mainly distract the target from my boss. Who stepped up behind Dormal, silent as the ice that had begun to form on the tips of her eyelashes, my bolo tucked into his belt like he was some misplaced jungle explorer.

One of his arms slipped through and trapped her elbows, preventing the motion that would lead to my last breath. The other shoved into her hair and yanked her head sideways. His fangs sank into her blood-soaked throat, making her jump. Just a taste. That was all he took before he raised his head and spit, coating the Taipans closest to them in red.

"You are foul through and through, woman," he growled. "Let us have an end to you now."

Despite the fact that she must've weighed twice what he did, he lofted and tossed her like a caber at the Highland Games. She landed among her creations, her screams choked with blood as they swarmed her, the only warm spot in a sea of winter. Her panic did her in, the jerky attempts to slap them away, to roll to her knees and crawl free enraged the torpor right out of them. By twos and threes, and then in groups too large to count, they attacked, many of them striking multiple times before they were satisfied their prey was no longer a threat.

The venom acted almost instantly. One moment Dormal was writhing in panic and pain. The next she was dead. And the second after that, the snakes shriveled into long lines of dust.

"Aaaah!" Cole's yell yanked my head around. Floraidh had sunk her teeth into his shoulder. He tried to punch her, but his angle sucked and his blows weren't hard enough to knock her free.

"Vayl!" I cried as I leaped to my feet.

He'd reached them before I'd finished saying his name, leaping into the tree as if he had wings. His arm was a blur as he brought it around to strike Floraidh, sending her flying. The bed of the Big Red broke her fall and, from the sickening crack when she impacted, her spine.

Vayl helped Cole down and leaned him against the tree trunk. I crossed the ravine to join them, getting a good look at Cole's wound as Vayl pulled him around for a better view. She'd torn a chunk of flesh away and left a gaping, bleeding hole.

"Jesus Christ!" Cole said as he felt the crater with his fingers. I checked him for shock. Yeah, coming on slow but sure.

"Vayl," I said, "I think he's going to need your coat."

"Of course. Let me see if I can stop this bleeding first."

A low laugh from the vicinity of the vehicle made me turn to look. Though Floraidh's legs twisted eerily beneath her, she still managed to raise her head. "It's done!" she said triumphantly. "The way is prepared for my Edward's return now."

"Bullshit," I told her flatly. "We killed two of your women back at the Cairns."

"Their part had already been played," she said. "They had completed the resurrection ceremony before you arrived."

I went on. "Plus, my dog dug up his harness earlier this evening. You didn't have the right components to make your spell work in the first place."

She didn't even flinch. "I never needed that to bring my lover back. And to use it for its real purpose you'd need a spell caster. I happen to know your warlock is off chasing some renegade *mattick* from the Treasury Department who's pissed off the Secretary of Education."

Oh, no, not again. "Which member of our Oversight Committee is on your payroll? Come on, spill. That's the only way you could've—"

Her trickle of delighted laughter cut me off. "As if I'd waste my hard-earned cash on those dolts. It will be such a pleasure watching them tear your—" Her words trailed into a gargle. She grabbed the bed of the Big Red, clutching it as her body, which should never have moved again, began to writhe.

Goddammit! As Vayl wrapped his coat around Cole's shoulders I said, "Cole! Do you feel any different? *Talk* to me!"

"I'm . . . I think—"

Floraidh laughed again, her voice moving deeper down the scale. She threw her head back, her face contorted with pain.

Vayl and I moved toward her together, of one mind without even having to discuss our intentions. Kill Floraidh, kill the spell. Then Samos couldn't take Cole's body. Couldn't return at all. Hey, it had worked with Dormal. It was certainly worth a shot, even if the suits back home raised hell. I pulled my knife from his belt as he called on his *cantrantia.*

A young woman's voice said, "Stop right there!" We kept moving. Neither of us follows orders well. Plus, Cole was close to passing out and Floraidh had begun to seize. If we waited any longer—

"Stop or we kill the old man! *And* the dog!"

Fuck.

Chapter Thirty-Two

For some reason I looked at my watch. It was like a part of me wanted to mark this moment in my life's history: 12:34 a.m. May fourteenth. My inner librarian spoke up. "In precisely thirteen days you will turn twenty-six."

If I live that long.

Exhaustion dropped on me like a chronic disease as I turned to face our newest crisis.

"Drop your weapons!" My knife hit the dirt. Vayl pulled his power back and the air warmed by a couple of degrees.

I said, "Viv! Iona! What the hell?"

I realized they'd been the two dressed women among the coven that I'd seen back at Clava Cairns. Now they stood with the rest of Floraidh's flunkies on the opposite side of the ravine. All of them wore clothes now, shapeless knee-length robes and sandals that brought out the vivid whiteness in their legs. Why, at these moments, did my mind come up with thoughts like *That chick should always wear pants?* Most of them carried flashlights as well, which I found ironic. The scariest monsters out creeping around were afraid of tripping over a tree root in the dark.

I tried to meet Viv's eyes, but she dropped her head, leaving Iona to answer my question. "When Floraidh heard about what happened to Viv all those years ago, she was appalled. She explained how her group has learned a form of self-defense that only ghosts can beat. She invited her out here tonight to learn more about them. Of course, I had to come to translate. And to show her how wonderful life in a coven could be. It's actually pretty neat, Lucille. You should join too."

She'd been signing the whole time, of course. Not easy to see from all the way across a dimly lit clearing, but then I wasn't the intended audience. Her message was for Cole.

"Jaz!"

I turned back, rushing to put my hand into his. He pulled me close. "One last hug before I go," he said. When he'd pressed his lips against my ear he said, "The girls are faking. Iona's actually a witch. A Wiccan. She's been sent by her circle to stop Floraidh."

Ahh. So *she* was the source of the spell I'd sensed earlier. I wasn't sure why I hadn't been able to pick her out as *other* to start with, but she'd probably found a way to guard herself from discovery just like I had. Maybe that funky belt of hers was for more than keeping her crack from showing.

"Iona, Viv, your move I understand," I said, hoping they'd get my double meaning. "Albert, I hope this trip cost you every cent you had." I stared at my dad, currently being held by a petite young blonde who carried a blade almost as long as her leg and a tall, spectacled woman with a professorial demeanor who carried a cleaver like she'd been raised by a butcher. I should've known he wouldn't leave like I'd asked. He'd never listen to me, because in his mind I'd never outrank him.

He didn't say anything, just squared his shoulders and looked straight ahead as the blonde brought her sword closer to his throat. I memorized her face, so that when the time came I could exact just the right amount of revenge on those sweet, even features. Nope, she didn't look evil. You couldn't tell by the appearance of any of the Scidairans what they did in their free time. They all seemed like pleasant women. The kind you'd expect to trade idle gossip with at the grocery store or the bank line. Nine faces at nearly every point on the circle of life. But all of them joined by their shared lust for eternity. The weapons they carried proved it. Blades mostly. Ancient and wicked sharp by the look of them. Strangely, each woman had tied a leather bag to the hilt of her sword, or axe, or dagger.

Maybe it's their lucky charm, I thought.

A couple of the younger women had traded metal for plastic. Naw, not that toy gun crap. This was heavy-duty stuff, so new even Bergman had just mentioned it. The lancers they carried shot a steel bolt into the victim, which pulled electric current without the need for a connecting wire. Don't ask me how, I'm no engineer. But the black marketers couldn't get enough of these fourth-generation tasers, because they killed within the first fifteen seconds of contact. Yeah, talk about your cruel and unusual.

Vayl came back to stand beside me. "Look at Floraidh," he murmured. When froth started to bubble out of her mouth, and I realized the bits of tissue swimming in it must have come from Cole's shoulder, I couldn't watch anymore.

I turned to my friend, put my hand on his arm. "I'm sorry. For everything. If we'd never met in Miami—"

"I wouldn't have lost my business. Gotten the shit kicked out of me. Taken a job with the CIA." He took a breath. Met my eyes. His began to sparkle. "I'd never have saved your life in Corpus Christi. Or fallen for you."

I winced. He took my hand. "It's okay. I know you've chosen Vayl. I love you enough that I just want you to be happy. I've never felt that way for anyone before, Jaz. It's always been about me before this. What I wanted. What felt good. It hurts not to have you. But I'm glad to have felt this way about someone before—" His eyes cut to Floraidh. He took a deep breath. "Before Samos gets me."

Vayl, staring down at him, snorted. "Now I know what they mean when they call people drama queens."

"Vayl!"

"Oh, come now, he is just working on your sympathies so he can—how do you say?—get into your pants. The man is incorrigible!"

He'd used that word before. I was really going to have to look it up. If I survived. Vayl sure thought we were all going to skate through. But it seemed to me like our chances were fading even as Floraidh's increased.

She stopped shaking. Sat straight up, as if she hadn't practically been broken in half minutes before. She swiveled her head, making sure we were all paying attention as she said, "Now, Cole, say your goodbyes. There's not going to be room in that fine young body for the both of us." Her face had hardened, as if her seizures had sanded off all the soft edges while I was looking the other way. Her voice had deepened by a couple of octaves too, and taken on the slight accent I'd recognize even if I lived forever. Finally I couldn't deny the change any longer. "She" had just made too much of a transformation.

"Samos?" I whispered. As in my earlier visions, his face had stretched itself across hers. But when her eyes turned brown and her teeth squared off like she'd just slid in a pair of dentures, I realized this time it was for real.

He said, "My real name is . . . But why should I tell you now? Such a shame you didn't know it when I was still a vampire. You might have killed me for good then. It was certainly a weak point in my contract."

Floraidh emerged again, her pink lips fighting for supremacy over his tanned ones. "Quickly, Edward. To the Cairns before the ghosts—!"

Samos banged the heel of his hand against his forehead. "In *my* time, woman! Do you know how long I have waited to gloat over this bitch's failure?"

Vayl said, "You rush to judgment, Samos. After all, she has killed you once already. Just because you have *raised* the bar, who is to say she will not do it again?"

I caught his emphasis, along with the look he sent Albert. When he met my eyes again I asked him silently, *Are you sure?*

Only someone who loved him like I did could've interpreted the minuscule move of his head as a nod.

"Do you know what I want to do, Jasmine?" Samos asked me.

"Invest in an underwire? I'm sorry, Eddie, but you've got a real case of the droops going on."

Samos stood, stunned by his own intense rage while the younger women in the coven tried to swallow their giggles. He swung a shaking finger at Floraidh's followers. "Kill them all!" he shouted.

One of the older members, a wiry old gal who wore her long gray hair in a braid over one shoulder, cleared her throat as she half raised the dagger in her hand. "Excuse me, Mr. Samos?"

"What is it?"

"I know you're new to the territory, so you probably haven't realized that we're not in Clava Cairns. Where all the diamonds are? We're standing about three minutes east of there. We should probably go back before we spill a lot of blood in Brude's—that is—you know how the ghosts . . ."

Her eyes darted toward us as she trailed off, unwilling to say out loud what Vayl and I already knew. Killing us would attract the ghosts. In fact, completing the resurrection here would probably bring Brude and his nasties running. They needed to do it at Clava Cairns, surrounded by all those glittering diamonds and the power of Scidair.

Samos glared at the woman so fiercely that she put a hand to her throat, as if she could feel him strangling her from a distance. "In another time I would skin you alive for daring to gainsay me. And then I would feed you to my guests, who would've been invited to supper simply to be reminded that it would be in their best interests to continue to cooperate with me. Or they might end up just like you." The soft sibilance in his voice reminded me so strongly of the snakes whose fangs had sunk into Dormal's soft flesh that I shivered.

"You don't have to kill us, you know," said Cole. "In fact, it's kind of a stupid idea." He wasn't talking to Samos, but to the women, who naturally responded to his I–know-you-wanna-hug-me smile. "We're CIA. If you kill three of us, you're going to bring the whole Agency down on your heads. They'll wipe you out faster than you can say genocide."

"That is not, technically, the right term for what they would be doing," Vayl said.

Cole flashed him an irritated glance. "Would you please stop messing with my rhythm?"

"Sorry."

The younger women weren't impressed. I could read the thoughts on those expressive faces. *So what? Big deal if the whole world turns against us. That's what attracted us to this practice in the first place!*

Their elders took more time to raise the rebel flag, but they knew they'd dug themselves in too deep to climb out now. Their eyes, showing lots of white as they darted toward Samos, confirmed that his venom had spread through them all. And with nobody shifting toward mutiny . . .

"Vayl?" I whispered, so softly only his enhanced senses could pick up my words.

"Yes."

"Is it time?"

"Not yet. Albert is still too vulnerable. We must keep talking, seem to be conspiring until—"

"You two!" yelled Samos. "I want you walking on separate ends of the line! Vampire—to the front!"

Casting me a slow wink, Vayl jumped the ravine and strode to the forward edge of the column the Scidairans had begun to form. Not a smart move on our enemy's part, because it put him within reach of Albert and Jack.

I helped Cole to his feet as Samos crowded us into the gully. He didn't carry a weapon that I could see. But we both sensed waves of dark energy emanating from him, power he could focus on us anytime he pleased, and likely would as soon as he had the protection of Clava Cairns's diamonds. For a second, standing at the bottom of that narrow gorge with muddy walls ahead of and behind me, I had a vision of a mass grave. This was just the kind of place soulless pricks like Samos shoved their enemies into before blowing their skulls to pieces. I felt the skin tighten on my scalp. Too easy to imagine an entire row of gunmen standing at the ravine's lip, rifles at their shoulders, ready to make me into another statistic.

No. Not today. I scrambled out of that hole like I'd been goosed by the Midas Man, yanking Cole up after me. Leaving Grief lying there felt like desertion. But I was quickly distracted by the fact that I'd grabbed Cole's mauled arm, and the moan that jerked out of him as he stumbled into the back of the Scidair at the rear of the line was totally my fault. She glared at him with that polite, contained rage he might inspire if he'd poked his finger into the middle of all the cupcakes she'd baked for the PTA meeting. Viv ran to him and put her shoulder under his arm.

"Thanks," he said gratefully. He pulled back. "Wait a second. I don't think I'm supposed to be nice to you."

While she signed something that made him huff I stole a look at Vayl. To anyone else his expression would seem blank. I read his message clearly. *Now is the time to strike, while they are still milling. Before Samos takes complete command of that temporary body of his.*

I lowered my lashes, which he'd interpret as a nod. I slipped my left hand into my pocket. Wrapped my fingers around the ring that sat there like an omen.

"What are you doing?" Samos demanded.

"My head is killing me so I was getting a couple of Advil from my pocket," I moaned. "Are you stirring up some sort of spell?"

"Not yet," he chuckled. "But just wait until you see what I have in store for you, little imp. A headache will seem like bath bubbles compared to the tortures I have been planning these past decades."

"You've only been dead a few weeks."

"Hell runs on different clocks."

"Oh." I squeezed my fingers around the pear-shaped emerald Matt had given me. Cocking the side of my thumb against the setting I jammed it down as hard as I could as I drew it fast across the spiked metal tips that held the jewel in place. Blood welled into the material of my pocket. Not much, but enough. I thought, *Brude. I have a present for you.*

A breeze wafted through the glade, lifting my curls off my shoulders, drying the sweat that had begun to bead on my forehead. When I felt it raise the hem of my shirt, I knew it wasn't a natural phenomenon.

Keep your hands to yourself, you son of a bitch, I silently snarled.
How did you know about my mother?
I had a feeling.
I knew if I waited long enough you would call. His triumphant laugh was the first clue to anyone else that visitors had entered the clearing. It rang like a mallet off a gong, sending shivers up the spine. The Scidairans began to fling their lights back and forth like they needed to direct a plane to the runway. As in the castle, the rays glinted off human-shaped figures. A whole crowd of them, grouped on either side of Samos's line, holding weapons that towered above their heads. Could a ghost spear kill a Scidairan? I sensed I was about to find out.

Dimly at first, as if they were still marching on us from a distance, we heard the stomp of booted feet steadily advancing. As the sound got louder, a white mist rose from the ravine and spread its fingers over the ground.

"Get them out of here!" shouted Samos.

The Scidairans prodded Vayl and Albert. But the women were so busy looking over their shoulders, they barely noticed when my guys took a single step and then stopped again. Because the mist had begun to rise. And as it did, like a slow theater curtain, it revealed the legs, torsos, weapons, faces of Brude and his phantom army.

They were dressed like they'd been when they died. A mishmash of costumes, ages, and sexes. They didn't even line up in formation, but stood where they pleased, poised to move, their expressions fearless and eager. This was no ordinary army. Brude had raised a horde. They'd kill and enjoy it. Aim to maim and laugh when the screams made their ears pop.

Brude stood at the head of the group that had appeared on my left, holding his staff at his side.

"What is your deal?" I had to ask as he surveyed the Scidairans with a mocking smile on his face. "Watch too many hangings as a kid? I mean, Christ, where do you find these creeps? You're like some kind of Dark Age gangsta. And that is seriously not a compliment," I added as he started to pose.

His frown, as quick and unappealing as instant coffee, made the women closest to him back up a step. "Watch your tongue, woman. Or I may reconsider and leave you here to perish."

"You will not." When his eyebrows arched at me I explained, "Whatever Samos has in mind for me doesn't include a trip to your world after I buy it. In fact, I'm pretty sure his contract calls for some eternal tortures only his new boss could arrange for me. You and I both know that, or you wouldn't be here." Light dawned in my overworked brain, making the menagerie that manned it cheer. "In fact, that's why you led Jack to his old harness. Isn't it?"

"I never do anything for a single reason. You should know that if you are to be my queen." Brude turned to Samos. "I cannot allow you to harm my woman."

Vayl's reaction came ringing across the glade like a challenge from one stud bull to another. Brude spun. Raised one muscle-bound arm and pointed at my boss. "You are next, Vampire."

"So glad you have your priorities straight," I snapped. "You did notice these bitches have my dad and my dog at a steep disadvantage, didn't you?"

I jerked my head in their direction. To be honest, they didn't seem to be in much danger at the moment. The sword-wielding blonde looked like she was about to pass out. And the professor who'd been holding Jack's leash dropped it the second Brude's eyes fell on her. Plus Vayl stood ready to kick ass should anyone make a truly threatening move.

Brude raised his hand almost neglectfully. "Now," he said.

Howling in glee, the ghosts attacked. But the Scidairans weren't about to cave without a fight. And though their powers dwindled every time they tried to raise a spell, they still wielded power.

Against phantoms, this came in the form of a red powder that trickled down their blades when they sliced open the pouches tied to the hilts. As soon as it hit the metal it flared, as if they'd stuck the entire weapon into a forge. From that moment on, when they found a way to shove those blades into Brude's army, the men fell as if physically gutted, after which they melted into the ground like ice on a sunny afternoon.

Still the shades fought like berserkers, the smell of blood sending them into a frenzy. And when one of them impaled a member of Floraidh's coven, the entire horde shrieked in delight as the woman screamed, her flesh melting away from the blade like plastic put to the flame.

The blonde guarding Albert hesitated for a second, then decided she needed to off the old man before she defended the coven. But that was all the time he needed. He grabbed her wrist, working hard to keep her from moving her weapon anywhere near his vulnerable parts. As they struggled I saw Vayl speed to my dad's side. The sword went flying as he broke the Scidairan's arm and flung her into a tree, taking her out of the battle. Forever.

"Vayl, watch out!" I yelled as one of the lancer-toting women ran up behind him. Then I lost track of the action on his end of the line, because Cole had shoved me to the ground just in time for a blade-swinging Scidairan to graze my neck.

"Thanks," I breathed, as a coven member dropped beside me, her eyes staring sightlessly into the night. I snatched her blade, which looked to be the bastard child of a scythe/battle-axe affair.

"I need a weapon," Cole whispered. Viv handed him her dagger just as another Scidairan fell near us. He grabbed *her* short sword with his free hand, then switched the weapons when his shoulder informed him it could only lift so much weight tonight and the sword wasn't its choice.

"Jasmine!" Vayl caught my eye, directed me to Iona, who'd gone down under the lancer attack of a tall, skinny Scidairan with lank black hair. I tackled the woman from behind, throwing her down so hard I could hear the air shooting out of her lungs.

The lancer fell out of her hands and we both scrambled for it. She shoved me aside, surprisingly strong for a girl whose arms were no bigger around than string cheese. I responded with a punch that landed just under her chin, snapping her head back.

She rolled aside, giving me room to grab the lancer. Before I could deactivate it she jumped on my back, her bony fingers wrapping around my neck and squeezing until I began to see spots.

I threw an elbow once, twice, three times, but she just kept strangling. So I stood up and fell straight back. Into the ravine. She broke my fall nicely. And, in time, I was sure her ribs would heal. In fact, I hoped they would. Because she'd landed close enough to Grief for me to grab my baby before scrambling back to the bank and shutting the lancer down. "Iona?" I patted her cheeks. "You going to live?"

She shook her head.

"Wrong answer," I said. "Try again."

"All right, I'll live. But don't ever tell anyone that fucking zap gun made me pee myself." I helped her sit upright. Handed her the lancer and took another battle survey.

Brude's force had done a number on Floraidh's coven. But they'd suffered heavy casualties as well. Still, I thought we'd win. Until I spied Samos at the edge of the clearing, holding Viv in front of him, his arm around her neck as if he meant to break it sooner rather than later. Cole stood maybe three yards out, his hands raised, talking so softly I couldn't hear. Why couldn't I hear? We hadn't cut off his audio feed. I tapped at my ear. Realized my party line had fallen off.

"Vayl!" I yelled. "Samos is trying to escape!"

I began to run toward him, realized my *sverhamin* hadn't replied, and peered over my shoulder. Brude's army, having defeated Floraidh's coven, had backed Vayl and Albert to the edge of the ravine. The fact that they'd hadn't touched Vayl and had barely put a slice in my dad said more to me about the two of them than I'd ever understood before.

Albert stood straight as a flagpole, Vayl's sword swinging sure and true in his strong right hand. This was the man who other men had told me they'd willingly die for. Not because he knew pretty speeches. But because he put himself out there first. He understood the cost of battle and the real reason men and women fought; I saw it there in the lines on his forehead and beside his eyes. And his little grin told me he was glad to be back at it. Even though he was grossly outnumbered, the action filled him with the purpose he'd lost when they'd forced him to retire.

Beside him, Vayl wielded another sort of power. It must rise from the same side of the grave as Brude's army, because it was taking a heavy toll. When his blasts of ice and wind hit their shields, they shattered. The ancient warriors flinched and cried out as sleet began to fall from the sky just over their heads, cutting through their armor as effectively as a cleaver through steak.

Nobody could keep up that kind of attack indefinitely, but Vayl would last a lot longer than Albert, whose teeth had begun to chatter despite the fact that sweat ran down his forehead. They needed to win, and fast. Especially since Samos had disappeared into the woods, leaving Viv panting on the ground. Since I couldn't see Cole anywhere, I had to assume they'd made an exchange, Cole's body for Viv's. And now that eternal thorn in my side had what he wanted.

"Brude, call off your men!" I yelled.

He stood on the opposite side of the glade, having found a stump from which to survey his troops. He eyed me like I'd just been led to the sales block. *What a nice piece of horseflesh she is,* said his expression. *So shiny and full of spunk.* "This creature must die as well," he said. "Unless you would like to enter into another agreement with me."

"Jasmine!" Vayl didn't even glance my way. How could he while working with Albert to fend off twelve of the most bulletproof fighters in the multiverse? But his tone made it clear I'd better damn well listen up. "If you make one deal with this scum, you and I are through!"

"What the hell kind of ultimatum is that?" I demanded. Tightening my grip on the hybrid blade I'd borrowed, I mowed into the back of the line, hacking heads and torsos like they were nothing more than jungle overgrowth, blocking my path to the real showdown.

In retrospect, it's probably good that Iona borrowed a Scidairan blade and came along for the ride, because I was so furious I paid no attention to anything or anyone beside me. I did hear her panting, her weapon clanging on the misses and hissing on the hits, so I'm sure she saved my life numerous times. But my mind was on that goddamned vampire.

I swung the blade and beheaded a bald shade dressed like a Nazi, clearing my view so I could see Vayl's pale, frost-rimmed face. I stuck the axe in the spine of my next victim, who went to his knees. When he didn't move out of my way fast enough, I planted my foot in his back, finding myself mildly amazed when I met actual resistance, and pushed. He fell over and I moved forward again, yelling, "Since we hooked up, I've been a stellar girlfriend! Hell, I haven't even had impure thoughts about my neighbor who looks just like Jason Statham. So where do you get off threatening to dump me? Especially when this whole deal was *your* idea!"

By now only a couple of fighters stood between Vayl and me. But the battleground had become no less dangerous, because I'd totally lost my temper and little fireballs had begun to fall from the sky. "*Now* look what you made me do!"

"To me!" Brude called. His remaining forces, some frostbitten, some burning, ran to his side. He glared at me. "This is not over!" he bellowed. "I am not conceding. I only leave the field because I am called by a master I cannot refuse. Do not forget—you owe me a boon!"

"Bullshit!" I yelled. "You killed, like, eight Scidairans. If I know anything about the rules of interplaner battle, and I do, that gives you leave to recruit them. Count that as your payment and get the fuck outta here!"

With a final cry of outrage he snapped out of sight, taking his entourage with him.

Vayl looked into my eyes. "Your language is quite shocking. But I love the way you fight."

"I'm still pissed at you!"

"I know. And I find it incredibly titillating."

I snorted and laughed at the same time. "Vayl, really, you can't say that word and believe people will take you seriously."

Vayl shrugged his indifference to people's opinions as he asked, "Any guesses as to where Brude has run off to?"

"I think he's supposed to be Enforcing for Lucifer, whatever that entails. This other gig"—I gestured to the clearing, now littered with Scidairan corpses—"is just a part-time thing."

"Jasmine?" Albert had dropped Vayl's cane to his side. He was looking around the battlefield, his eyes skating past the bodies to the flaming balls of muck that had dropped in our general area. "Did you really do that?"

"I . . . uh . . ."

"And, Vayl? How is it that you can control the weather? Did Bergman make you some sort of portable snow machine?"

"Yeah," I said. "That's it. Snow. Sleet. Fire. It's all right here." I patted Vayl's breast pocket, which remained agonizingly flat.

Iona stepped up, supporting a weeping Viv. "Samos is probably at Clava Cairns by now," she reminded us. "I've been called by my circle to prevent Floraidh from resurrecting him. And it seems like you're of the same mind. I suspected as much when you cleared our room yesterday, but of course I couldn't reveal myself to you in case I was wrong. So what do you say? Shall we join forces?"

My reaction really pissed Viv off. She began signing like she'd much rather hit me. Iona said, "Viv wants to know how you could possibly smile at a time like this."

"Because Floraidh all but told us we couldn't beat her without a spell caster." I nodded at her. "And now we have one."

Chapter Thirty-Three

My guess is that when confronting your newly risen nemesis who is now trying to cement his remains into a stolen body, your best approach should probably involve some form of stealth. Unfortunately our crew included an untrained civilian, a distracted witch, a rickety old man, and an excited malamute.

Jack hardly ever barked. Strangers remarked on his polite behavior. In the park he refused to woof at bikers, other dogs, or even little kids chasing bright red balls. But now I couldn't get the mutt to shut up!

He sounded a little like a sinus-infected bear as he vocalized. Along the lines of, "Roo-roo, we're coming after you-poo!"

I wiggled his lead. "Jack! What the hell? Where were you when that wild-eyed Bible thumper came to the door trying to save my soul?" He threw a furry grin over his shoulder and launched into a second verse.

I said, "Swear to God, dog, if this doesn't turn out well I'm buying you generic food for the next month!"

We stood at the edge of the woods, staring out at Clava Cairns. The Scidairans' fire had sputtered out, but the GhostCon torches still glowed, making me wonder how soon we'd be running into their first walking tour.

This could get awkward. Although those punishment-gluttons would probably embrace the whole experience. Right up to the point where Floraidh started munching on their juicy bits.

Yet another reason we needed to shut this operation down, like, yesterday.

At least we knew where the body snatchers had set up camp. And considering where we'd found Jack's harness, it made sense that the flicker of their fire reflected off the walls of the inner circle of the northeast cairn.

"What's the plan?" Albert asked.

"There is none," I said.

"You should have a plan," said Albert. He'd resheathed Vayl's sword and was now leaning heavily on the cane.

I didn't tell him I'd tried to put something together during our short trek through the pines. But since I had no idea how you kill a resurrected vampire, I figured winging it would probably work better than developing a play-by-play. Also it would leave me in a more hopeful frame of mind, since if I had to think about it any length of time I was ninety percent sure my conclusions would depress the hell out of me.

I had decided that if I was going to die tonight, I didn't want to do it without making some sort of grand romantic gesture that Vayl would remember forever. Like in the movies. Unfortunately we'd been rushing pretty much headlong through thick undergrowth at the time. So kissing was out. He'd probably view a boob flash as accidental or whorish. *Goddammit, why did I already tell him I loved him? This would've been the perfect moment!*

I tried to calm myself. After all, I'd already dropped a load of flaming coals from the sky and probably ashed out a fraction of my soul in the process. Plus it might be nice if I could think clearly for once. Yup. Time to accept the fact that my mind wouldn't produce a memorable kissy-face moment. It wanted to work. So I'd better damn well survive, because I'd be so pissed if we missed our chance.

I handed Jack's leash to Albert. "You stay here," I said, making it clear I meant both of them. "And this time it would be nice if you didn't let yourself get kidnapped, all right?" I glanced at Iona. "Have you figured out why Jack's harness would be so important to Floraidh yet?" She'd overheard my conversation with the Scidairan and had been trying to decide what it meant ever since we left the clearing.

She said, "I need to know why the dog is so significant that they wanted something that was a part of him for so long."

I filled her in on Jack's background without revealing exactly who I was. But you could tell she was sketching in the missing pieces pretty well all on her own.

She asked, "Would you say Jack was more important to Samos when he was alive than any other creature he knew?"

"Even though he had an *avhar* at one time, I'd say yeah. Without a doubt."

"And now, this is quite important. When you killed Samos, thinking that was his real name, was the dog wearing his harness at the time?"

"Yeah. We didn't get rid of it until we left Greece later that evening."

Iona nodded. "Here's what I believe. Vampires have very little to leave behind. But there is some. Bits and pieces of worldly material. Vapor. Shreds of essence. When Samos left this world, I believe the demon he bargained with caught a bit of his remains. But a portion naturally fell into his pet. This is what happens with those we love. Perhaps all that was left of him settled into the leather of the harness because, as an item formed from the skin of another animal, it still keeps its retentive properties."

Vayl said, "But if Floraidh did not need it to call Samos from wherever he had stored his essence, why did she bury it in the cairn?"

Iona had crouched down to dig up a hunk of moss. "Because it can be used to destroy Samos for good. Having put all her energies into resurrecting him, she wouldn't want him taken away from her again. So she found the one weapon that could be used against him and buried it where she could guard it. Except your dog found it."

With Brude's help. Why would Brude want Samos gone? He'd said he never had one reason. So if not just to help me . . . as revenge against his enemies, the Scidairans? Or in his role as the Devil's Enforcer? At this moment, do I give a crap? Um, no.

Vayl and I shared a moment so intense it could've doubled as a hug, except we didn't even touch.

"Do you know what to do with this information?" I asked her.

"Absolutely." She took off her belt and laid it on the ground. Yup, now I could sense her. *Witchy Woman,* sang the silver-blue flare at the core of my brain. She nodded toward the cairn. "I just need you to distract them while I gather the remaining ingredients. I assume you still have the harness?"

A moment of panic as my mind went blank. *Where the hell did I throw that dirty remnant of Jack's old life after we got back to Floraidh's place? Oh, yeah!* "It's in the van. I threw it in there before the tour group went into Tearlach for its final ghost viewing. I was afraid it was going to fall out of my jacket at the wrong time and then I'd have to come up with some lame explanation nobody would believe."

"I'll get it for you," Albert said.

"You'll stay here!" I ordered. It didn't matter. Viv had already left the shelter of the woods. We watched her creep toward the van, which was standing about ten yards from the middle cairn, its right side toward us, its front tires hub deep in grass and mud. Broken glass glittered in the combined lantern and moonlight, both from the front window and the shattered headlights.

I thought, *I wrecked another vehicle. Shit! Pete's going to kick my ass from here to next Friday. Unless this mission comes out amazingly well.* I crossed my fingers.

Viv froze as a heart-squeezing scream flew out of the cairn. Jack lunged forward, snapping the leash at its swivels. I started to run after him, but Vayl put a hand on my arm. "Not in," he said as he nodded at the rim of the cairn. "Up."

I glanced at Iona. "Go," she whispered. "We can get the rest of what I need." She nodded to Viv, who'd forced herself to move on. "When I'm ready, you'll know."

Leaving Albert holding the broken leash, Vayl and I ran the short distance to the cairn. When we reached the entry Vayl took my hand and together we jumped to the top of the wall that rimmed it. The stones were surprisingly firm underfoot as we followed them along the edge of the passage to where they formed a central pit. We'd started at a crouch, but by the time we reached the inner circle we were crawling, our heads barely clearing the stones before us as we peered into the burial chamber.

The fire Samos danced around didn't look exceptional. Until you realized its source wasn't a pile of kindling, but the contents of the bowl I'd found in Floraidh's oven, with the container itself acting as the fire pit. Jack stood beside Cole, both of them almost underneath our noses. Our third had draped his arm around the malamute in a gesture of protection that went straight to my gut and twisted.

As Samos began to chant, Vayl tapped me on the shoulder and made a few gestures I couldn't mistake. I sent him my *Are you sure?* look. When he nodded, I shrugged. I didn't think it was going to work, but it was worth a try.

I stood. Drew Grief and aimed it at Samos's head.

Boom!

He staggered sideways, the hole just above his ear trickling a line of blood down his jaw. The other side of his head should've blown all over the stones beside him. It didn't. Something protected him, counteracting the force of the bullet, healing the wound almost as soon as it occurred.

I shot him again. Filled his head with steel, and when that was gone switched to bolts. Before I'd finished he'd flattened his chest against the far wall of the cairn, shuddering with every hit. But taking them. Not falling. Definitely not dying.

Vayl had been busy as well. He'd risen to his feet beside me, calling down such a vicious blizzard inside the cairn that Cole and Jack began to disappear under a drift of snow. Thank God Cole had some resistance to Vayl's powers or he'd have been an icicle within minutes. And no way would Jack freeze to death under that pile of fur.

While Samos's lips turned blue, I holstered Grief and moved to my next-best choice, the Scidairan weapon that had saved my hide during the previous battle. I weighed it in my hand, wound up and threw it, burying the axe head in his back. He reared up, screaming in pain as it hit.

Spinning, he pointed to me with fingers that had transformed into Floraidh's pink-nailed claws. *"Ildacante!"* they screamed. The smell of Scidair's rot filled my nostrils as the rocks beneath my feet began to shake. Vayl's arms waved as he, too, fought for balance.

Earthquake? My eyes sought Cole and Jack, hoping they'd had enough sense to take cover. Yup, they were motoring toward the entrance, but Samos blocked their exit. Cole grabbed him. They began to struggle.

Then something imprisoned my ankle. I sucked in a breath. Looked down. A bony hand had reached out of its burial mound, wrapped around my living skin and begun to pull.

"Skeletons, Vayl!" I yelled. "Get out!"

I jerked my leg free, but Samos and Floraidh had animated an entire host of the dead, and at least five of them had clamped their icy fingers on to my other ankle now. It wasn't just that they'd gotten a good grip. The rocks were still moving. Falling out from under my feet. The hands, more and more of them as the seconds ticked by, were pulling me down to join them.

"Vayl!" I looked over at him, horrified to see that he was also knee deep in the cairn. *Oh my God, oh my God, they're burying us alive!*

"Jasmine, do not panic. Take my hand."

"Are you kidding me? We're going to be underneath soon! The rocks will be over our heads! We won't be able to move, or breathe, or—"

"Jasmine." So soothing, that voice. Such calm in the face of certain crushing suffocation. How did he *do* that? "Hold my hand."

Vayl leaned forward. Reached out. I focused on his hand as if it were a lifeline. Which it wasn't. He was going down, down, down too. *Never mind that. Just wrap your fingers around his. It'll be a good thing. Then maybe you won't feel those other fingers, on your thighs now, pulling, bruising, ripping into your skin . . .*

I couldn't quite reach. Part of my mind saw the irony. Like it had always been with him, he remained just out of my grasp. On the edge of an embrace but never anyone I could grip on to.

"You fucker!" I raged, realizing I wasn't yelling just at him. "I'm about to die for good here! Would you just reach out and grab on?"

A huge rumble, like the rocks themselves had split open and the support beneath my feet disappeared. I felt myself fall, the lights of Clava Cairns winking out as the stones rolled over my head. My hand, waving its last goodbye to open air, prepared to follow me down into the crushing weight of the abyss.

And then it was pinned in Vayl's grasp. Cirilai, pressed between my fingers, sliced into them until they bled. And that ignited something within the ring. Some power his ancestors had imbued it with that shot into and through me, making me feel as if I could fly. And I knew Vayl felt the same, because he existed at the other end of Cirilai's line, pulsing with its magic as if it had given him a second heart.

The dead, so eager for us to join them, gave an unearthly scream as they sensed our joining. And they scrabbled away, sliding between the stones, escaping our combined heat. We sent it out in a wave so violent the rocks burst into fragments mere inches from our faces, as if a rain of mortars had fallen on our exact location.

We weren't injured, not even scratched. Cirilai had us covered. Cole and Jack had escaped the worst of the carnage. But Samos lay on the ground, broken, covered in blood. And I suddenly understood the terrible aftermath of a stoning.

Still holding hands, Vayl and I picked our way out of the rubble, all that remained of the wall we'd been buried in. Even Scidair's fire had gone out. But Samos hung on, red bubbles popping out of his mouth as he labored to breathe. His face kept reshaping itself, a weird collage of features that was never quite himself or Floraidh.

"He's like a cockroach," I said.

Vayl nodded. "I understand fruit flies are difficult to kill as well."

"All the creepy crawlies you expect to survive a nuking."

Iona and Viv came in with Albert trudging behind. The Wiccan carried the harness along with the moss. Viv and Albert also toted loads of plants, mostly fungus as far as I could tell, though I might've spied some bark among the toadstools.

"Your timing is excellent," Vayl said.

Iona smiled. "I do know when to step in, don't I?"

She nodded for Albert and Viv to dump the vegetation in a pile and dropped the harness on top. As she knelt over her treasures and closed her eyes, Vayl pulled me aside. I watched Viv run to Cole, help him up while Jack ran around in circles and whumped them with the broad wags of his tail.

"Jasmine?" I pulled my attention back to my *sverhamin*. *Oh goody, time for the big moment!* Vayl leaned down until our eyes were at the same level. "Do you trust me?"

"Sure."

"I need for you to be sure."

Uh-oh. "Yeah, Vayl. I do."

"Then will you help me gather up the diamonds the Scidairans scattered around this cairn?"

"Vayl—"

"It is the right thing to do."

I hesitated. Sighed. Of course, I should've thought of it myself. "Yeah, okay." We went outside to make like little kids on Easter Sunday. Albert helped, and within a surprisingly few minutes we'd picked the cairn clean. It helped immensely that the diamonds glittered in the lamplight, and they'd been set at even intervals around the perimeter.

Back inside, Iona's spell had sprouted. Literally. An empty water bottle stood by her side, making me think she'd poured the contents on the stuff she'd piled at her knees. And while we'd been gone a lush green ivy had grown up through the mound of moss and herbs, twining around the harness so quickly that I could see the stem stretch and twirl, its leaves emerging and growing to full length before my eyes.

The fresh scent of Wiccan magic filled the cairn, blowing away the pollution of Scidair. Samos/Floraidh panted as Iona touched the vine to their foot and it clung, sending out feelers even more quickly now that it had a solid support to wrap around. Within a minute the vine had done a mummy wrap on the shared body. At which point it began to squeeze.

"It can't suffocate him. Her. Can it?" I asked.

"No," said Iona. "That's not the point anyway. It's not squeezing. It's sucking."

Floraidh/Samos bowed so radically I thought she/he might refracture her/his back. Then the vine broke.

Iona whispered words I could barely catch and decided I didn't want to know. As the ivy retreated into the pile, she spat on it. Then she stomped it. Three times she repeated this process as it withdrew into the mound. In the end she scattered all the ingredients, handed me the harness, and pointed to a small brown nut sitting on the dirt floor of the cairn.

"That's all that remains of Samos."

I glanced at Vayl. "Your turn," I said.

He gestured to Cole. "I cede the honor to you. He did mean to steal your body, after all."

Cole nodded his thanks, strode forward, raised his foot, and stomped. The nut split under his heel, the crack surprisingly loud in the stillness of the night. He ground it around until he was sure it could never be reconstituted, then he held out his arms to Viv.

She stood still, signed something, to which he responded, "Of course you're worth the sacrifice. I'd never have offered to trade places with you otherwise."

She ran into his arms and he kissed her hair as Iona beamed at them and Jack did another one of his circle-the-couple runs.

When's he going to do that for me? I wondered grumpily. Which was when Floraidh sat up. Nearly healed. Fully herself. Pissed as a wet cat. Screaming threats so foul I was surprised her teeth didn't melt as the words rolled off her tongue.

Vayl held out his hand. "Albert, I have need of my sword now."

Without a word, my dad passed it over. Vayl unsheathed the blade, causing the Scidairan to clamp her mouth shut tight. She tried to scrabble backward as he advanced on her, but the rocks gave her no escape.

"You wouldn't kill me!" she screeched.

"You are right." He flicked the blade, making a clean cut across her forehead. "But I know someone else who would." He stood up. "Oengus?"

Floraidh laughed. "Do you know how long he's tried to get to me? I'm so well shielded I could . . ." The words jumped off the precipice she suddenly realized she stood upon as Albert and I opened our hands, showing her the piles of diamonds glittering in our palms.

"Vayl's got the rest," I told her. I pocketed the gems. Picked up the bowl and dumped it in her lap. We backed away as an ill wind rose in the cairn. The first slash appeared on Floraidh's neck. Her scream was echoed by an unearthly howl, like the ones we'd heard in Castle Hoppringhill.

"We'll still have our revenge on you!" she cried as a wound appeared across her chest and blood spurted. He'd cut deep this time.

"I don't see how," I said. "Samos is as dead as a throwaway battery and you're about to enter the Thin. Neither of you is coming back, Floraidh."

She began to laugh as both her arms, then her legs, jumped and a score of cuts appeared on each one. Oengus was getting impatient now. He'd waited a long time, after all. Still Floraidh giggled.

"What's so funny?" I demanded.

"Me, for not recognizing you until Samos entered my body. And you," she said. "For believing he wouldn't have some sort of backup plan after having failed to beat you repeatedly in his last life."

"What do you mean?" Vayl asked.

She kept her eyes on me as she said, "Your poor father has been through so much in the past few weeks. These visits from beyond the grave have disturbed him much more than he would ever let on to you. What have they meant? That question has plagued him from the first. So much so that he finally enlisted your help in discovering the true source of his haunting. Isn't that right, Albert?"

"Who are you?" he asked. "What do you want with me?"

"You're just a means to an end, old man. Just a way to let Jasmine know her mommy has escaped from hell with our help. Because she needs a little one-on-one with her baby girl. And Baby Girl is too well protected by"—her eyes rolled upward—"for the direct approach."

"I had to see you, Jazzy." I spun, my grip on Vayl's hand breaking as I recognized my mother's voice. It was coming out of Viv's mouth. Impossible, of course, so I knew it had to be true. Especially when I saw her features settle over Viv's, her honey-colored hair falling over Viv's blond locks like a bad wig. "I knew you wouldn't want to talk to me, so I tried to get to you through Albert. Of course, he's harder to communicate with than a teenager with his iPod blasting." She sent Albert a dirty look, which he returned times twelve.

As Viv stepped forward, tearing herself from Cole's embrace, I backed up. "Why would you want to see me?" I asked. "I thought we'd summed up our relationship already."

She nodded. "I understand why you might think I was the

worst mother on earth. But, having spent the past few years in hell, I can tell you that I may be on the bottom of the barrel, but I'm not scraping it." She glanced at Floraidh, who'd begun to list sideways, her blood turning her sweater a nasty shade of purple. "Not yet."

The Scidairan managed a grin as she said, "Go ahead, Stella. Remember what awaits you if you kill her. No more torture. An end to the pain. Soft pillows and sheets. Daily showers and clean clothing. A chance to rise among the hierarchy and be with your true love again. It's all in Edward's contract. Signed in blood. If only you follow through."

Viv gripped the sword she'd grabbed back at the clearing. I doubted she knew how to wield it. And Mom had no clue. Didn't mean they couldn't kill me out of pure dumb luck.

"Don't hurt her!" Cole yelled to me. "It's not her fault!"

No shit, Sherlock. But then again, I don't want to die tonight. Because if I do—I glanced at Vayl—*I will never forgive myself.* I pulled the bolo out of my pocket.

"Jaz, please!" Cole called. *Shit!*

I backed up some more, hoping Vayl could get a clean shot at her. But she managed to keep clear of him while staying a life-threatening distance from me. She said, "Jasmine, you don't know how it is. Loving someone so much it tears at your heart not to see him every day. Knowing he suffers torments that you could ease."

Despite knowing that she was talking to push me into dropping my guard, I played her game. Too interesting not to. "What are you saying? Your first husband's in hell?" She inclined her head. Feinted an attack. I jumped aside. We both moved back to neutral.

"He can't be. Dad said he was a vampire."

"That was what he told me when we were alive." She shook

her head. "He was afraid I wouldn't love him if I knew he was a faorzig."

Ah. Another blood-sucker. Hell spawn whose bite injected a parasite that drove their victims mad, the majority of whom ended up murdering their families before killing themselves. The police had suspected our neighbor had been bitten by one, though they could never prove it. Now I thought they might've been right.

I said, "He's a demon. What's he enduring tortures for?"

"Me."

How romantic. "And if you kill me he doesn't get tortured anymore?"

"Not as much. Neither do I. We'll both be so much better off. And we'll be together. And really, what does it matter to you? You've died twice already anyway."

"What?" cried Albert.

"I have a lot of reasons to live!" I yelled, ignoring my dad's outburst. "People need me!"

"Who, that vampire you think you're in love with? Vayl is *old,* Jasmine. He'll find someone else within a month. He always has."

"What did she say?" demanded my dad.

"She's in hell," I told him without glancing over. "She's programmed to lie."

"Do this for me, Jazzy," she said in her most persuasive tone. The one she'd used to get me to try out for the swing choir when I was a freshman. Me, the girl who could carry a tune in the shower. And nowhere else.

The sad part was, I actually considered it. This was how deep the woman had sunk her claws into my psyche.

I shook my head. "No." The word, no more than a whisper, couldn't have carried a single foot. But Albert heard it.

"You ungrateful little bitch!" she screamed as she came at me.

I knew right away I was going to get hurt. Impossible to just defend yourself in a fight with blades. Either you go for the win or you get slashed. And sometimes you still end up so bloody you wish you'd brought an endless supply of ammo. Or a less sentimental coworker.

I braced myself for the blow, gauging the angle, pitching my own blade to catch hers at the point where it would be least likely to hack off a major section of my arm. It never came close.

Albert roared, his outrage like a slap on the back of my head, making me sidestep as he let loose. "You're never touching my little girl again, Stella!" He shot Vayl's scabbard at Viv, nailing her in the abdomen. She doubled over with a grunt that provided a strange harmony to another statement. Iona's this time, if my Spirit Eye still focused correctly after all it had Seen tonight. At the same time Brude walked out of the blasted rocks as if they led to a secret cavern only he knew the entrance to. Two enormous black mastiffs flanked him, their eyes flickering orange and yellow with the fires of their homeland. Jack began to growl.

"Grab him," I ordered Cole. Though he badly wanted to stand with Viv, my third knelt beside the dog and took hold of his collar.

"Fool," Brude spat at my mother.

Stella looked up, her face twisting with fear as she realized who had come for her. "Enforcer," she whispered.

"You could have taken my deal. Lived in my lands with your faorzig forever."

"Why would she want to do that?" asked Cole.

"I offer the dead what no other Domytr can. Escape from both paradise and hell." He held his hand out and, like a magician calling his assistant from the disappearing closet, wiggled his fingers until Stella emerged from Viv, her skin pink and healthy, her hair waving in the after breeze of Vayl's blizzard. "Look at what you denied yourself," Brude whispered. "Beautiful, unending chaos."

"The Great Taker will never allow you to continue once he knows your plan." She nodded to me. "This was my best chance. My last chance."

"Just remember what will happen to your lover if you reveal a word of my intentions to anyone."

She nodded.

Vayl stepped forward, began to speak. But not in words I could understand. Soft, deadly syllables only the Vampere shared. As they rolled off his tongue my mother's eyes widened, her mouth opening in a silent shriek. When he turned to me the black had just begun to bleed out of his eyes. Brude nodded. "So it shall be," he said, as if passing judgment.

"What just happened?" I asked.

Vayl stared down at me, his expression so stern I knew he was damming big emotion. His hand came up my arm, fingers brushing scars only he and my dad knew about. "I love you."

Brude jerked a hand toward Stella. "Go." The dogs leaped, taking her to the ground. I looked away as she screamed, surprised to find myself in Albert's arms a few moments later. When I looked back all I saw was her feet, dragging into the ruins as Satan's hunters took her home.

Cole ran to Viv, helping her to sit up, holding her as she looked around in shock. Her eyes finally rested on Brude, who stared at me as if trying to solve a puzzle. He shook his head, his braids slipping off his broad shoulders to reveal matching scars in the shape of scythes. His eyes glittered as they moved to

Floraidh. I glanced her way as well. Couldn't believe her chest still rose and fell. Yup. Cockroaches and fruit flies.

"Oengus!" he snapped. "Leave her be!"

"You're calling off *all* your dogs?" I asked.

"I have my reasons," he said. As he leaned toward me I held up my hand to stop him.

"You promised. Two weeks of safety in your lands."

"You will return to me."

"If I do, it'll be to destroy you."

His laughter lingered long after he'd disappeared, leaving the same way the hell-dogs had gone.

Viv kept making the same sign. "What's she saying?" I asked Cole.

"She wants to know if the monsters are gone."

I nodded. "All but one." I tried to convince myself it was okay that Floraidh had survived. That had been the plan all along. Plus, with most of her coven gone and Samos dead as a dinosaur, she wouldn't be much of a threat until—if—she got out of intensive care.

As I backed out of my dad's arms, listening to him call an ambulance for the second time that night, I watched her struggle for each breath. Then her attention rolled toward the cairn wall behind me. As she looked over my shoulder, her eyes widened in terror. She let out a single, high-pitched scream and froze, her eyes darting back and forth as if unable to tear themselves away from a nightmare. I felt the hair stand up on the back of my neck and turned to look.

Nothing. "What's going on?" I murmured.

Iona said, "I've been casting charms to protect us against whatever has been attacking her."

"It's her first husband," I said. "She murdered him in the 1800s."

"Ah." Iona raised an eyebrow at Floraidh, her pitiless glance taking in the crumpled form of a once-powerful Scidair. "Well, he's taken too much blood from her now. Because she's *other*, he can call her into the Thin anytime he likes. And whenever he does, that's all she'll be able to see. I have a feeling that's all he'll want her to see for a very long time."

Chapter Thirty-Four

The days between Floraidh's "breakdown," Samos's final demise, and my vacation passed with the speed of a fighter plane. So many loose ends to tie up. Cole and Viv had discovered a deep friendship whose brush with death wouldn't allow it to turn into anything else. But he'd still stayed in Scotland to help her find a new interpreter after Iona went back to her circle. And to help her move to a new flat when she finally admitted she didn't want to see ghosts at the bus stop anymore—but maybe her haunter should have to stand there for a couple of hundred more years anyway. And the best way for Rhona to heal was for them learn to live their own lives.

Albert had said his gruff—and brief—goodbyes, the morning after, promising never to mess with my missions again. The Haighs had practically done backflips upon the return of their diamonds and, as a token of their gratitude, had offered us anything in their store. Vayl had taken a look at my ring finger and raised his eyebrows. I'd shaken my head.

"Cirilai is all I need," I'd said. So he'd dropped it.

Then Pete had called us back to Cleveland.

We sat in his bare little office, which looked much more cheerful painted primrose yellow, and waited for him to finish shuffling papers. While he figured out how to get around to the subject, I noticed he'd replaced the dead plant by his closed window blinds with one of those miniature electric fountains. Suddenly I had to pee.

"I see here you wrecked the rental vehicle," Pete said.

"The Scidairans were responsible," Vayl pointed out.

I reminded myself to breathe.

Pete shuffled his stack some more. Cleared his throat. "The Oversight Committee has reviewed this case."

I felt my eyebrows go up. "Already?"

He nodded. Loosened his tie. "They, uh, are not happy that Floraidh has been admitted to a mental institution and her coven has dropped out of the picture."

"Did you explain to them why?" Vayl asked.

Pete nodded. "They don't seem to understand all the shadings and parameters of the situation." He sighed. "They see this as a failed mission. And they've strongly suggested that I suspend Jaz, pending further review."

Suddenly all I could hear was this high-pitched whine. Like the old class-is-over signal at my high school, only farther up the scale. *"What?"*

He nodded. Ran his fingers over the two hairs left on his shiny head. "I'm sorry, Jaz. I don't see how I can deny them. They're threatening to cut my funding if I don't—"

I hadn't realized I'd begun to reach for Grief until Vayl's hand slid over mine. I looked at him, blinking rapidly to keep the tears from forming. I'd never seen him so forbidding. He turned back to Pete. "I smell ulterior motives. First they refused my request for a warlock. Then they sent Albert to spy on us. And now they want to fire their best assassin, despite the fact that she saved Floraidh from Bea? And do not give me that, 'But she is practically a vegetable,' excuse. That is not Jasmine's fault. What message do all these actions convey to you?"

Pete's entire forehead crinkled as he considered the options. "They could be looking to reshape the department."

Vayl nodded sharply. "Or eliminate it completely. They put us in a situation most of your employees would not have survived. And you, slave that you are to the bottom line, allowed it."

I flattened my hand against my chest because I honestly thought that was the only way I could prevent my heart from leaping out of it. Suddenly I understood Albert's point of view. This wasn't how I wanted to die. Flopping on the floor of my boss's office, wishing to God I'd chosen a career where other people didn't have so much control over my future. Then I nearly croaked again when Pete didn't fire Vayl. Or even snap his head off. But sat back in his chair, folding his hands across his stomach thoughtfully.

Vayl said, "Jasmine is due some vacation time, is she not?"

"Uh—" Pete turned to his PC, clicked away at his keyboard for half a minute. "Yes. Looks to me like she's got a month built up."

"Then grant it to her, and mine to me. Do not call either of us in that time. Avoid the Oversight Committee members as well, no matter how often they try to contact you, all right? They cannot touch your budget for several weeks anyway, correct?"

"Right."

"By then I will have everything taken care of."

We both looked at him. Pete said, "Vayl? What are you planning?"

He gave Pete a look as grim as a funeral. "It is better that you do not know."

Apparently Vayl intended to keep me in the dark as well. He'd whisked me off to my apartment, ordered me to pack for a long getaway, and left. When he returned I was sitting just where he'd left me, having done nothing.

"Jasmine." He sat down on the bed beside me. "You have not even opened your trunk."

I stared down at my hands, clasped between my knees, and swallowed the lump that had risen in my throat the minute Pete had dropped the hammer. "He's going to fire me," I said. "You've been around forever. You know how to do different things. But this is all I have, Vayl. This job means everything to me."

He slid his hand over both of mine just in time to catch the tear that had escaped from my eye. "I know," he said softly. "I promised you before that I would not let those cretins harm you. I have never broken a vow and I never will. You have not been fired, nor even suspended. You are on vacation. During which time the Oversight Committee will come to see the error of its ways."

I glanced up in time to see a satisfied little smile play across his face. "What are you going to do?"

"What I should have done the moment I heard they had managed to get themselves appointed." He met my eyes, his own softening to amber as he said, "You will let me do this thing for you?"

"I don't even know what it is!"

"Are you sure you want to?"

I nodded. He leaned over and whispered in my ear, as if he thought my drab little bedroom might be bugged or something. I started to laugh. "Are you serious?"

"I rarely know how to be otherwise."

"You know, that just might satisfy my undying need for revenge on Pete and his goddamn bosses for siccing Albert on us in the first place. Can I help?"

"It would be better if you did not."

I thought about it. "Oh. Of course. Well, then, you have my blessing. And, you know what, this is it!"

"This is what?"

"That thing you said you'd try to find that would prove how much you love me. This is definitely the one."

"Are you sure? Because I had something else in mind." His eyes began to dance as his hand slid up my arm.

I let my eyes go round. Played innocent as I asked, "What do you mean?"

He swung one leg over my hips and pulled me farther up onto the bed. When my trunk blocked our progress he shoved it onto the floor. The crash delighted me. Gave me hope that most of our bedroom meetings would be loud and surprising. As if he could read my mind he asked, "Are these walls soundproof?"

"I don't know," I replied, giggling as he found the ticklish spot under my ear and gently nipped it.

His lips moved to mine and for quite some time I thought our conversation had ended. Finally he raised his head just enough to lock my eyes with his, which had brightened to emerald. I could hardly think now, not with his hands roaming freely and our clothes flying through the air like confetti, but I did think I heard him whisper, "Then you will have to ask your neighbors in the morning."

Acknowledgments

Mountains of thanks to Mike Calder, owner of Transreal Fiction in Edinburgh, for answering my endless questions regarding his lovely country. I'll always appreciate your kindness, Mike! And if I'm ever in Scotland, I won't buy a single book until I get to your place! Thanks also to Gareth at *Falcata Times* for enjoying Albert so much that he wished aloud to see the old coot in a bigger role. I must acknowledge Devin for inspiring the name of one of the ferrets, and thank Darrin Turpin at Orbit for helping me with some language issues. Of course, my deepest gratitude goes to all of those wonderful souls whose feedback and support I've come to rely on: my agent, Laurie McLean; my editor, Devi Pillai; also Alex Lencicki, Katherine Molina, and Penina Lopez. How about that Art Department at Orbit, eh? These covers just kick it through the roof! A big bless ya to my readers, Hope Dennis and Katie Rardin. And I must thank my family for putting up with my crap, loving me through everything, and making the joyful times so much sweeter. I couldn't do it without you. As for you, my reader, my friend, thanks for following Vayl and Jaz through their adventures so far. It's not over, not by a long shot. And what comes next should test their mettle and their love. I can't wait. How about you?

extras

orbit

meet the author

Cindy Pringle

JENNIFER RARDIN began writing at the age of twelve, mostly poems to amuse her classmates and short stories featuring her best friends as the heroines. She lives in an old farmhouse in Illinois with her husband and two children. Find out more about the author at www.JenniferRardin.com.

introducing

If you enjoyed **ONE MORE BITE,**
look out for

BITE MARKS

Book 6 of the Jaz Parks series

by Jennifer Rardin

My ass felt like a slab of dead flesh, too nerveless to even quiver as the butcher slaps it onto his cutting table. Twelve hours of flying from Manila to Sydney with another sixty-minute hop after that is hell on the hindquarters, even when they've been cushioned by the most expensive seats available.

I stifled the urge to massage my butt cheeks as I descended the stairs of Vayl's chartered jet onto the tarmac of Canberra International Airport. After all, my crew would be waiting for me, and I hadn't seen Bergman and Cassandra in over two months. In other words, I didn't want our reunion to remind them we'd begun a shithole of an assignment that, if botched, could severely cripple the U.S. space program, not to mention vital parts of our anatomies. Plus, with Cole as my third greeter, I figured our hey-how-are-yous probably shouldn't start with a lot of ass-grabbing.

While I didn't sense that Cole itched to get his hands on me as he stood at the bottom of the stairs, his ear-to-ear grin, framed by the usual mop of sun-bleached hair, warned me that flexibility might be required on my part. Because Something Was Cooking. Then the music began.

"What have you done now?" I asked as my foot hit the fourth step and I realized he'd rented himself a black tuxedo, though he'd traded the bridal shop's shoes for his own red high-tops.

My question drowned in a sudden wail of funereal blues. Which made me double-check the landscape. Nope, not even close to New Orleans. In fact the airport, surrounded by the brownish green grasses of Australia's autumn, reminded me a lot of the farmlands of Illinois. Except today was May 22, so back in the Midwest everything would be shooting out of the ground, green as a tree frog and bursting into bloom. Here, winter had crept to the country's edge, and I could feel it sinking its claws into my neck along with the chill breeze that swept down the hills into Canberra's valley.

I flipped up the collar of my new leather jacket, the mournful tone of the music reminding me of the bullet wound that had killed my last one. Below me, keeping time to my slow descent, two trumpeters, a trombonist, and a sax man wearing black suits and matching shades belted out a song fit for a head of state. If he'd just been assassinated, that is.

I turned back and whistled. Jack had been cooped up so long I couldn't believe he still stood at the cabin door, sniffing the air as if he didn't approve of this sudden change of season. He stared at me with his expressive brown eyes, his ears twitching as if to ask, *Where did the tropics go?*

"We're here," I told him.

He nodded (no, I'm not kidding; the dog's, like, one step away from hosting his own talk show) and bounded down the steps, racing toward the plane's landing gear so he could make sure everybody realized it stood in his territory.

Cassandra laughed. She stood opposite Cole, her hand on the rail as if waiting to help me down. But we both knew I wouldn't be touching her if I could help it. I preferred a little mystery in my future, and our psychic had a way of spoiling the fun.

As our eyes met, she gave me her regal smile and flipped her heavy black braids over her shoulder, revealing a tangerine stole that she'd thrown over a navy blue turtleneck and white, rhinestone-studded jeans. An enormous bag made from the same orange furball as her wrap hung over one elbow, its various bulges suggesting that perhaps it had been a marsupial on its home planet before Space Commandos had trapped it, shaved it, and shipped the clippings to her favorite retail outlet. No doubt about it, only the former oracle of a North African god could've pulled off that ensemble.

I jerked my head toward the band and raised my eyebrows.

"It wasn't me," she mouthed, her six pairs of earrings waving a double negative as she shook her head and rolled her eyes toward Bergman.

He stood at her shoulder, hands stuffed deep in his pockets, taking such serious note of the rip in the knee of his jeans you'd have thought he'd just been mugged and was trying to decide if his insurance would cover the replacement cost. His beige sweater with its thin red stripes hung limply from shoulders that were bowed under the weight of an army-green backpack. Its bulk helped provide balance for his head, which seemed extra large today, maybe because he wore a brown ball cap fronting the Atlanta Falcons logo. His lack of glasses might've encouraged the look too. I'd forgotten that he'd had corrective surgery and didn't need them anymore.

Genius that he was, Bergman caught my gaze, flipped his own

to Cassandra, and figured out in milliseconds what I was think-ing. "Oh no," he yelled over the dirge. "It was all his idea!" He pointed a bony finger in Cole's direction.

Before I could snap my former recruit's head off, he clasped his hands over his heart and sank to one knee. "We are all so sorry for your loss!" Cole cried. Then he threw a dramatic gesture toward the hold of the plane, where six sober-faced pallbearers were tak-ing the casket from the hands of the jet's flight crew. But it wasn't just any old death box. Some company with a sense of style but no restraint whatsoever had built this sucker to resemble a golf bag. An umbrella, a black towel, and even a couple of irons had been tacked to the side, while the heads of the rest of the clubs jutted from the coffin's end.

I glared down at Cole, so pissed I wouldn't have been sur-prised if smoke poofed from my nostrils. *Control your temper, Jaz,* I told myself. *You know what happens when you lose it.*

"Cole," *you little shit,* "you *shouldn't* have."

He rose to his feet and dusted off his pants. The moment I reached his side he laid a gentle arm around my shoulders. "We all know how difficult this must be for you. As your *former* boyfriend—"

"We were never—!"

"—I realized it was on me to make sure your *dead* boyfriend arrived in Australia in the style to which he has—uh, had—become accustomed."

Cole pulled me toward the casket with Bergman, Cassandra, and the sad band following as he crooked his finger at the hearse I'd asked him to order. Except I hadn't told him to request a white Mercedes stretch with enough room for an NBA player and all his devastated relatives.

It pulled up beside us, its driver stepping out and promptly disappearing. At first I thought he'd taken a tumble. Jack sure seemed interested in his welfare. When my malamute didn't return from his scouting mission right away, I leaned over to get a better view and learned the real story.

I grabbed Cole's arm and squeezed. "If that is a gnome whose crotch Jack is sniffing, I'm going to tie your hair up in a bun and sell you to the pirates that operate off this coast. I hear they're always looking for fresh, young girlfriends."

Cole rolled his eyes in a perfect imitation of irritated adolescence. "Geez, Mom, can't you tell the difference between a gnome and a waiggin?"

I curled my free hand into a fist, then made a conscious effort to relax it before it hauled off and punched somebody without my permission. "Waiggins are at least seven feet tall. And *green!*"

"Oh. I keep forgetting you majored in Supernatural Criminology." Cole sighed. "Okay, Ruvin's a half-gnome. But he's trying to blend, just like Vayl. And he doesn't worship Ufran."

"How do you know?"

"I asked."

Only Cole would have the nuts to talk religion with a perfect stranger. "Still—"

He leaned his chin on my shoulder. "I checked him out. He's fine. And he's over three-and-a-half feet tall, so he could pass for a *seinji*. In fact, he regularly does. Maybe he could help with our . . . project. You never know."

I narrowed my eyes at him. "So Pete's briefed you?"

He nodded.

Good. The less we discussed the son of a bitch who'd agreed to smuggle gnome larvae into the Canberra Deep Space Communication Complex the better. Every time I thought of the kind of scumbag who'd willingly put his own life, not to mention the innocents who worked at the Complex, at risk just so the gnomes could scoop out NASA's third space-gazing eye and stomp it into jelly, my concentration went to hell. But it wasn't just our target.

Despite all evidence to the contrary, I knew my department's Oversight Committee had backed off on suspending me with major reservations. If I screwed up even a little, I could kiss my career goodbye. Which meant we needed to get under cover before the worst happened. I checked my watch. Three thirty p.m. We might just have time. If we *hurried*.

"Let's get him loaded," I said.

Cole squeezed my shoulder. "But then you'll miss the best part."

I snaked my arm around his waist so I could jerk him close enough to whisper in his ear. "You're about to lose *your* best part."

"Hey, this event is costing somebody a lot of money. You might as well enjoy it." He grinned down at me, his bright blue eyes daring me to loosen up and have some fun.

"This is so unnecessary."

"Wrong again, Petunia. Picking up a casket-rider and the woman you're about to fall out of love with is boring. Arranging a funeral procession with a displaced band from the French Quarter and a quartet of professional mourners is one for the diary. You do keep a diary, don't you, Jaz?"

"No! And don't call me that. I'm here as Lucille Robinson, remember?"

Cole frowned. "But if you're Lucille, who am I?"

"Hell if I know. As I recall, your last text said you didn't like the name they'd picked for you and had demanded a new one."

"Damn straight! The CIA has no imagination, you know."

I'd have told him to pipe down, but between the band's latest number and the wails of the four women who'd emerged from the backseat of the hearse to drape themselves and a blanket of flowers over the casket's tee-time accessories, I could barely hear his whispers.

"Sure," I agreed, mainly because I thought I'd seen the coffin wobble. Had one of the pallbearers stumbled, or . . . I checked my watch again. Holy crap, we were cutting this close!

"Do you want to know my new name?" Cole asked as we led Cassandra and Bergman toward the country club casket. Would Tiger Woods be caught dead in one of those? I thought not.

I sighed and said, "Since we're going to be working together for the next few days, a clue to your fake ID might help."

"Thor Longfellow."

I stopped and stared, not even turning when I heard Cassandra stumble to a halt behind me. "No."

His hair bounced cheerfully as he nodded. I asked, "How did you get away with that?"

He shrugged. "The girl who assigns identities really likes Thai food, and I know this place on the East Side—"

"Say no more." I should've guessed he'd charmed that ridiculous cover out of a woman.

VISIT THE ORBIT BLOG AT

www.orbitbooks.net

FEATURING

BREAKING NEWS
FORTHCOMING RELEASES
LINKS TO AUTHOR SITES
EXCLUSIVE INTERVIEWS
EARLY EXTRACTS
AND COMMENTARY FROM OUR EDITORS

WITH REGULAR UPDATES FROM OUR TEAM,
ORBITBOOKS.NET IS YOUR SOURCE
FOR ALL THINGS ORBITAL.

WHILE YOU'RE THERE, JOIN OUR EMAIL LIST
TO RECEIVE INFORMATION ON SPECIAL OFFERS,
GIVEAWAYS, AND MORE.

imagine. explore. engage.